She didn't know how she survived the next few minutes. Standing like a specter as he came toward her in his evening blacks, looking for all the world like a refined English gentleman just home from abroad. As he took her hand and bowed to give it a gallant kiss. As a thrill swept through her, burning her toes in their velvet shoes. As the breath froze like Galway frost in her lungs.

Johnny! How she'd forgotten the effect of him. Those stunning green eyes that pierced her like swords, making a private mockery of his deportment. Was there ever anything so green in all the world? And the black hair that swept back off his wide forehead in fashionable submission . . . She'd forgotten the charm of those wild locks falling into his eyes when the young hooligan had refused to cut his hair. A rush of memories warmed her, as if the room around her disappeared, and she was once again standing by the banks of the river Liffey, her lips burning, her breath like fire, staring up at him in a haze of wonder and amazement.

Oh, how difficult it was not to throw herself into his arms! Or to give his head a good cuff. The nerve of him, testing her reflexes in so public a way!

But her flash of temper was short-lived. This was Johnny!

Bride
of Danger

Katherine O'Neal

Bantam Books
New York Toronto London Sydney Auckland

BRIDE OF DANGER
A Bantam Book / September 1997

All rights reserved.

ISBN: 0-553-57379-9

Published simultaneously in the United States and Canada

Bantam Books are published by Bantam Books, a division of Bantam Dou-
bleday Dell Publishing Group, Inc. Its trademark, consisting of the words
"Bantam Books" and the portrayal of a rooster, is Registered in U.S. Patent
and Trademark Office and in other countries. Marca Registrada. Bantam
Books, 1540 Broadway, New York, New York 10036.

PRINTED IN THE UNITED STATES OF AMERICA

WCD   10 9 8 7 6 5 4 3 2 1

For Bill:

for his help,
for his support,
but mostly for understanding
what really makes me happy . . .

with all my love

Prologue

DUBLIN, IRELAND
1870

No sense of danger warned the guards at the docks. The sun was setting and a soft pink hue tinged the heavy covering of clouds. The tang of imminent rain was sharp in the air, which wasn't unusual for Dublin in the spring—or any other season, for that matter. Working briskly, casting periodic glances at the sky, the English seamen unloaded their cargo of foodstuffs, hustling before the perpetual mist could ruin the sacks of grain.

Along the quay, a motley group of Irish peasants, dressed in rags that hung from their bones, paused to stare at the sides of beef being carted from the ship. Drool was more like it, the captain of the English militia thought sourly. Their sunken eyes greedily caressing the precious provisions, they looked as if they were contemplating an impromptu uprising to snatch a bit of bread from the piled-high stores.

"Might we be troublin' ye fer jest a bite, Captain, sir?" one old man asked, his voice weak with hunger.

Disgusted, the captain raised his rifle and gave a yell, scattering the startled townsfolk, who took to heel and scampered off into the narrow streets beyond.

"Bloody Irish rabble," he cursed to his sergeant. "There's no end of them, sniveling like brats for our food. If I didn't personally watch them every minute, they'd steal the ruddy mess from under our very noses."

The sergeant eyed the retreating supplicants with more sympathy than his superior. "The latest famine's reduced them to eating potato skins to keep from starving, sir. I imagine this shipment looks like treasure to those so poor."

"Well, it's not my problem, is it? My job is to see this food goes to the gentry who pay the proper coin. Look lively, now. I've no intention of being embarrassed again by these miscreants pilfering my charge. By God, but I'd give a lot to be quit of this filthy country."

He would have indulged in more complaints, but the crunch of wheels distracted him. Turning, he saw a large, elegant coach drawn by a matched pair of blooded horses pull up at the dock. It was driven by a dark young man wearing the bright red uniform of a lieutenant in the governor's personal guard, with his hat pulled low over his eyes. Beside him, dressed in homespun work clothes, was an Irish servant with a deep cleft in his chin. As the carriage drew to a halt, the servant jumped down and opened the gleaming door. A moment later, a lady stepped out.

She was dressed in fresh pink finery with a bonnet of flowers completely covering her hair. A short pink veil hid her face, but as she came forth with the young man, she walked with the grace and assurance of a member of the nobility, directly toward the captain. His eyes narrowed as he noted the absence of gloves on her hands—a formidable omission for a lady of quality. Belatedly the girl thrust her hands behind her back, cursing herself for her error.

"What's this now?" the captain grumbled under his breath. It was his job to be suspicious of any break in the routine. But he strode forth to meet them, answering the lieutenant's smart salute.

"Good evening, Captain," the young lieutenant said in a cultured English voice. "May I introduce the governor's daughter, Miss Vanguard. We've come with a commission from her father. I have a requisition for some of the food you're unloading."

The captain's gaze fixed on the girl. "The governor's household has already received its ration for the month."

"These are special orders, sir."

The young woman spoke in a soft, whispery, aristocratic voice. "It's my sixteenth birthday, Captain. We're having a party. All the landed lords will be there. Naturally, we must have the finest food available. To celebrate. You see, Captain, I shall be a woman in a week's time."

The captain blanched at this forward bit of banter. Taking the proffered orders, he looked them over with a practiced eye. They were, indeed, signed by Governor Vanguard himself. Still reluctant, he cast another glance at the governor's daughter. She was reported to be a beauty, though he'd never before seen her up close. It was difficult to tell, with the veil hiding her face. But he detected a delighted smile beneath the veil. Ah, the enthusiasm of youth, he thought, feeling suddenly very old.

"Perhaps you'd care to join us, Captain. I'm sure my

father would be most happy to extend an invitation, were I to ask."

It was highly irregular, but the captain wasn't averse to being invited to the governor's house. Perhaps he could put in a plea for transfer back to England. Still, he hesitated. The governor had never before issued such an unusual request.

He took another moment to study the lieutenant, who was watching him closely. The man was tall and dark, with vivid green eyes that must have set many a maiden's heart to fluttering. But there was something about that youthful face . . .

"You're awfully young to be an officer," he noted.

The lieutenant snapped to attention. "Sandhurst, sir. Class of '69."

"I see. Very good, Lieutenant. We have to be careful. These Irish are always about with their long faces and tragic airs. They'd happily slit our throats for a mouthful of Yorkshire cheese."

The lieutenant's glowing eyes narrowed in an aristocratic sneer. "Let them eat rats, for all I care. The governor wants this food for his daughter's ball, and by God he'll have it."

At this, the servant at his side shuffled, then muttered, "Ye could feed the whole of the starvin' city on what the governor's about squanderin' on his guests."

With a swiftness that startled the captain and made the girl start, the lieutenant smacked the servant's head a vicious blow. "Insolent peasant!" Glancing apologetically at the captain, he added, "What do you expect from these hayseed ruffians? You may rest assured, sir, that this man will be dismissed for his insubordination. God knows there are enough surly scamps to take his place."

Giving a look of grudging admiration, the captain

relented at last. "You, men, load the requested food-stuffs in the governor's coach. And be quick about it."

At once, the food that had been on its way to the warehouse was hauled instead into the vast interior of the coach.

When the coach was loaded, the lieutenant saluted and expressed his thanks. "We'll be certain to tell the governor of your cooperation."

Preening, the captain held out his hand to the girl. After the briefest hesitation, she took it. "There will be an invitation for you directly," she promised in her whispery voice.

Suddenly, the captain froze. Gripping her hand tightly, he turned it over. There, on her palm, were rough calluses. Hardly the hand of a lady.

His eyes shot up and met those of the lieutenant. "Bloody curs. Who are you?"

At once, the lieutenant grabbed the captain's rifle and rammed the butt into the captain's head. "Some of those Irish rabble you so despise," he boasted, "come to make fools of the cursed English crown."

As the captain staggered, the servant sprang to life. He slugged the officer full in the face, knocking him cold, before turning on the sergeant and kicking him in the gut. The sailors, alerted to trouble, came running, and a lively ruckus ensued. The counterfeit servant and lieutenant fought them with the brutal force they'd learned on the back streets, felling each of the sailors in turn as the girl ran with all speed for the coach. She'd just climbed aboard and picked up the reins when the last of the sailors was knocked to his knees. The "lieu-tenant" knocked him over the head with the rifle, then he and his partner raced for the carriage. It was already moving when they leapt aboard. Whipping the horses into a frenzy with the reins, the girl sent them clattering up the quay and into the street beyond.

The sky was darkening and the awaited rain began to fall lightly as they galloped through narrow alleyways, knocking aside passersby along the way. When they were a safe distance from the docks, the man who'd played the lieutenant took the reins and the girl snatched the flowered bonnet from her head, laughing gleefully as she tossed it aside. A wealth of flame-red curls tumbled to her shoulders and was whipped back by the wind.

"Saints preserve us," she cried in her native Irish brogue. "We'll eat like kings for a week!"

They were laughing as they headed through the Georgian streets with their imposing row houses. The impostor lieutenant pulled the coach to a halt in a deserted alley and took the hated military hat from his head, raking long fingers through his midnight-black hair.

"My, but weren't you grand, then." He raised his voice, mimicking her earlier tone. " 'I'm to be a woman in a week's time.' Wanton lass. How the man must have been droolin' in his cups. And you little more than a suckling babe."

"Suckling, indeed!" she cried heatedly. "I'd like to see a suckling put on a show the likes of me own. If not for these cursed hands, we'd have fooled the bastard right to the end."

"Never mind your hands. 'Tis proud you've made me this day."

She looked up at Johnny, feeling warmed by his praise. The three of them—Johnny, Daggett, and Mylene—had grown up in the same orphanage and they'd been thick as thieves for most of their lives. Mylene was just fifteen to the boys' seventeen, but she could hold her own with them, as she'd proved on many an occasion.

Beside her, Daggett—the "servant"—was rubbing his head. "Did ye have to knock me so hard, then, Johnny? 'Tis a right bump ye've given me, and no denying."

"Oh, poor Daggett," Mylene crooned sarcastically. "Ye've a softer head than ye've led us to believe, I'm thinking. And himself bragging to all who'll hear how he can best any man with his fists."

"And so I can!"

"Now, now," Johnny admonished. "We'll have none of that. 'Twas a fine job we did, and the orphanage will sup for our efforts. There need be no bickering amongst the likes of us."

Daggett clamped an appreciative hand on Johnny's shoulder.

"Johnny's right, so he is," Mylene said. "And 'tis sorry I am for me own lack of sympathy. There, now, Daggett, if I rub yer head for ye, will ye favor me with a smile?"

She reached over to smooth his sandy hair and was rewarded with a playful cuff to her own riotous curls.

The night was black as they headed toward the Liberties and the orphanage. This was the worst part of town, the filthy streets crumbling with desperate poverty, where the city's poor—starving, diseased, and degenerate alike—scratched and clawed what meager existence they could.

Daggett reached back into the coach and pried forth a loaf of bread, tearing hunks from it and passing them along. They dug in, mercilessly teasing one another between bites, pointing out faults in the job they'd pulled and making suggestions for how to better their technique next time around. It was done in jest, but the suggestions were secretly taken to heart. One small slip could mean the difference between life and death.

They were chuckling when they turned the corner and came upon a crowd outside one of the haphazard night shelters that served as temporary bedding for the poor. The people gathered there were holding tallows, speaking in hushed tones.

Johnny halted the coach. "What goes on here, man?" he asked one of the onlookers.

"The O'Brien child is dyin'. Starvin' to death, and not a crust to feed the poor lad."

Mylene scrambled down and pushed her way inside. There, on a squalid pallet on the ground, a three-year-old boy lay dying in decay. His family of nine was gathered about him, weeping helplessly. None of them looked far from the grave. The small shelter reeked of death. The child's mouth was black, his eyes rolled back in his head.

When Mylene looked up to find Johnny by her side, there were tears of pity in her eyes. "Oh, Johnny," she whispered. "Couldn't we give them some of what we've just taken? Just enough to—"

Harshly, Johnny interrupted. "Would you be feeding the whole of Dublin then, and see our own starving children perish like this one for our neglect?"

She knew he was right, but it broke her heart just the same. Just then, she spied the bulge in Daggett's jacket, where he'd thrust the bread. In a gesture of defiance, she snatched the remainder of the loaf and offered it to Mrs. O'Brien. The woman took it and blessed her. But Mylene read the unspoken message in her eyes: *It's too late.*

"Come," Johnny urged gently. "They'll be looking for us."

Outside, Mylene felt the old terror clutch her heart. "I'll be hating this poverty till the day I die," she swore. Then, looking back, she added in a desolate tone, "But at least they've a family to console them. Which is more than can be said for the lot of us."

She felt hands of iron grip her shoulders and wheel her around. Startled, she looked up and met the fierce passion blazing in Johnny's eyes. "*We're* your family," he growled. "Don't be forgetting it."

Family. These two orphan boys, these ruffians of the streets, were the only family she'd ever known. They were her brothers, her confidants, the best friends anyone could hope for in this world. In a rush of emotion, she grabbed them both and clutched them to her. "Aye," she said, her tears mingling with the raindrops to wet their close-held heads. "How could I forget?"

St. Columba's Orphanage was housed in an old abandoned warehouse on the banks of the river Liffey in the worst section of Dublin. The main room had been partitioned into two barrackslike wards—one for the girls, the other for the boys. A small kitchen and office had been pieced together, paid for by funds raised in the church next door, the domain of Father Quentin, priest and patron of St. Columba. What little heat there was came from three tiny, rusted stoves, fueled by coal in the odd occasion when it could be begged or "borrowed," and peat from the surrounding countryside when it could not. It was a shabby, barren place, kept clean by the nuns who ruled by threats of damnation and long birch branches that could cut the orphans' flesh with strategic whacks.

The three adventurers were met by a rush of noisy

children who'd been peering out the single window, awaiting their return. As Johnny and Daggett carried in the pilfered parcels, the young ones descended on them, crying out their excitement at such unaccustomed riches. They ranged in age from three to twelve, clean youngsters dressed in rough brown uniforms fashioned from the discarded robes of neighboring monks. In spite of their clean state, they nonetheless sported the same hollow-eyed look of all the children of the ravaged city. Their noses ran—a condition of the perpetual cold—and some coughed raggedly from consumption. But nothing could dim their enthusiasm as they fingered the bags of provisions, tearing them open even as they were heaped upon the kitchen table.

As the young men brought in the food, Mylene squatted down, describing the feast they'd have to the group of wide-eyed children, who hung on every word. In the midst of drawing a colorful picture of the pudding she'd make for them, she glanced up to find Father Quentin standing in the doorway.

"We've done it, Father," she announced proudly. "And a grand haul it was."

Father Quentin, dressed in the black robes and collar of his station, was an elderly man with thick white hair and a ruddy face. He was an anomaly among the priests of Ireland, who used their illustrious status and the fear they inspired to subdue any hint of the rebellious spirit they felt might eventually rob them of their power. In contrast, Father Q, as he was affectionately called, was a rampant Irish nationalist who worked quietly and secretly to bring about the freedom from England he felt was the only hope of his beloved land. To this end, he'd defied the church and his own bishop by educating his orphans in Irish history, covertly breaking the law by teaching them the old language and making sure they knew how to read and write.

It was he who'd found Johnny, Daggett, and Mylene on the mean streets and taken them in. Discovering early that they were exceptional, he'd trained them carefully over the years. He'd taught them the speech of their captors, instructing them to assume various roles that could aid his cause. Through their efforts, they'd supported the orphanage by whatever means were available. If those means sometimes flew in the face of the law, Father Q discreetly looked the other way. What were English laws, when he had so many mouths to feed?

But tonight he was unusually quiet, even grave. Alerted, Daggett dropped a sack of meal, and together the three of them faced the priest.

"What is it, then, Father?" Johnny asked.

Mylene added, "Are you not pleased?"

The priest ignored the query and looked at them each in turn with serious blue eyes. "I'll have a word with you in my office. Sister, see to the food."

Exchanging nervous glances, the three followed him into his office. It was meagerly furnished with a desk and a chair and a potbellied stove, which glowed invitingly with a peat fire. Mylene, sensing his mood, resisted the impulse to go to the stove and warm her hands.

They waited in silence. Father Q's gaze wandered behind them, and as it did, the office door closed. Turning, they saw a man standing in the shadowed corner of the room.

He was as arresting a specimen as they'd ever seen. Not tall, he nevertheless gave the impression that he was a large man, a man whose presence filled the room. He was of middle age, darkly magnetic in a rough-hewn way, with a hooked nose and pockmarked face. His eyes, intent and unflinching, had dark circles under them, making him look as if he never slept. He carried about him an air of fatalism that was tragic and captivating all at the same time.

Father Q spoke in a voice filled with respect. "I'd be presenting Shamus Flynn."

It was as if the breath of life had been sucked from the room. God in heaven, Shamus Flynn! The notorious leader of the seditious Fenians. A legendary character who'd been chased underground by the fearsome price on his head. He was a decidedly dangerous man, a rebel in the raw, the most wanted man in the English books. They'd heard of him all their lives. His exploits were whispered in every pub and on every street corner of Dublin. But no one had ever seen him. Even they, who knew the back streets of the city like no one else, had never laid eyes on the man. Nor were they certain he existed. They'd come to believe he was a figment of heroic imagination, perpetuated to give a crushed populace hope.

"Jesus, Mary, and Joseph," Daggett whistled beneath his breath.

Even Johnny—who feared and admired nothing and no one—was staring at this phantom as if the Blessed Virgin had just made an appearance.

"These are the three I was speaking of," Father Q said. "Johnny, the thinker and planner with the golden tongue. Daggett, our warrior. There's not a better lad at military strategy—excepting yourself, of course. And Mylene. She's our chameleon. She can become anything that's required of her, and can charm the secrets from the soul of the tightest-lipped man on earth. I don't have to tell you, Mr. Flynn has come at considerable danger to himself."

"What are your back names?" Flynn asked with the economy of speech of a hunted man.

Mylene flushed with shame. "We haven't any. We're orphans, now, aren't we?"

"She's a tongue on her," Flynn noted with suspicion.

"They assume last names as needed," Father Q said. "I've told them time and again they're welcome to my own."

Flynn looked them over in silence. What he saw was a striking dark-haired young man with an air of keen intelligence and a face devoid of the florid peasant features that marked so many of his countrymen. The other, the sandy-haired youth with the devil's thumbprint in his chin, looked more like a Roman warrior than an Irish orphan. In spite of his awe, he returned Flynn's stare with a surly, stubborn pride. The girl was too thin to be dubbed a beauty, though she had clear blue eyes and a pouty mouth that held promise. With some food to coax the proper curves, she might make a fetching piece at that. None of them flinched beneath his autocratic stare. A promising sign.

"I've been told about your escapade this day. You've told me truly, Father. They're as good as your boasts."

"They're the best. I've never seen the like."

"And why is it," Johnny asked, "that we've been brought on the carpet to be inspected like country wares?"

Flynn narrowed his tired eyes. "A great honor is being done you this day. You've been chosen—the three of you—to use your talents to serve Ireland on a larger scale."

"You're old enough now to leave the orphanage,"

the priest added, "though how we'll manage without you is beyond me."

"Leave?" Mylene whispered.

"Although you don't know it, you've been trained for a specific purpose. Now that purpose is moving to a new stage."

"What purpose would that be?" Johnny asked.

Flynn took the floor. "Together with us Fenians, your Father Q has been working on a grand plot to free Ireland. 'Tis time you took your proper places in that plan. We'll not force you. If you do this, it's of your own free will. But if you accept, there are no questions I'll be answering. You obey us with blind devotion or you're of no use to us at all. Have I made myself clear?"

Again it was Johnny who spoke. "What will you be requiring of us?"

"That I'll not be telling you. I'll say only it will require the three of you to split up, to be trained with care, to be sent to England, and to be placed in vital positions, the functions of which you'll learn as you go along. Mind, it will take years of your lives. At least five—mayhap as many as ten—before you're ready to carry out your ultimate missions. But when you're ready, my fine patriots, you'll be instrumental in freeing our homeland from the cursed yoke of English tyranny."

His speech had roused them. They could hear the voice of the leader in his quiet, urgent tones.

"You're the most important element of this plot," the priest added. "Because of you, we'll have hope of a new day."

"What say you?" Flynn demanded.

The three friends looked at one another, trepidation mingling with the excitement pumping through their veins. The picture of the O'Brien child was still vivid in their minds. Too many O'Briens. And so little hope.

Johnny read their acceptance. Mylene would risk her life to feed a starving child. And Daggett, though less compassionate, worshiped Johnny and would stand by his decision.

"We love our country, Mr. Flynn," Johnny answered for them. "We'd see our countrymen work and eat like men instead of rats. And taste the dignity of freedom on their tongues. When do we start, then?"

"At once. Mylene is leaving on a ship for England tonight."

"Tonight?" they cried as one.

Mylene stared into the resolute depths of Shamus Flynn's eyes. Tonight. To be ripped from the only home she'd ever known. To be sent to enemy territory, alone and unprepared. She felt the fear of it clutch her throat like a fist.

"But it's too soon! I'm not ready."

"You'll be ready by the time you land. Our man will brief you along the way."

Along the way to what? In a panic, she looked at Johnny and read the same shock on his face.

Flynn's gaze was hard, uncompromising. "You'll wear what you have on. Leave whatever possessions you have. You'll not be needing them where you're going. As for good-byes, have done with them. My man will be by in a quarter hour. See that you're ready."

With that, he slipped out and, like the phantom he was, vanished into the night.

The three of them went out to the banks of the Liffey, unmindful of the rain. There they stood, staring numbly out at the rushing river, their stunned silence speaking volumes.

"A quarter hour to say good-bye to ye," Mylene lamented. "Yer me brothers. How can I do without ye? How can I find the strength?"

Daggett took the treasured knife he kept hidden in his waistband and handed it to her. "Keep this under yer skirts, girl. 'Twill give you all the strength you need."

Typical of Daggett, the warrior.

She turned to her other companion.

"Can I do this, Johnny? Truly?"

His eyes bore into hers. Quietly, he said, "I've every faith that ye can."

Just then, they heard a footfall. Father Q was at their backs. Mylene fought the panic that threatened to choke her. Pride came to the fore. She mustn't let them see how terrified she was. They must remember her as brave and strong.

She turned to Daggett, a lump of tears in her throat. "Take care, then," she said, hugging him.

Then she was facing Johnny. Her confidant in times of despair. How could she say good-bye? Reluctantly, she stood on tiptoes to give his cheek a sisterly kiss. But his arms came hard about her back. Held close, she could almost feel the pumping of his heart. She became aware of the smell of him, of the bristle of his jaw, of the way his hard chest crushed her tender breasts. Something vital, like a shock, jolted her senses. She turned her face and looked into his eyes. What she saw stole her breath. He was staring at her with the same longing she felt inside.

But how could it be? This was *Johnny*!

Her gaze dropped to his mouth. For the first time

she noticed how full and sensual were his lips. How they beckoned like a flame she couldn't resist.

She didn't know how those lips came crashing down on hers. She only knew that nothing had so shattered her like the taste of his mouth on hers. Breathless, crushed beneath his punishing grip, she opened her mouth and moaned with startled desire, losing herself in the drowning sensation of a kiss meant to claim her mouth as his own.

When he released her, slowly, they stood breathing hard, staring with wonder into each other's eyes. She couldn't think where she was, or what she was supposed to do. Her head spun as if she'd drunk an entire bottle of medicinal Irish. All she could see were Johnny's fierce dark eyes boring into her soul.

A hand at her back broke the spell. She glanced about to see Father Q at her side. And Daggett, glaring at her as if she'd just taken his own knife and stabbed him in the heart.

Chapter 1

*M*ylene crept through the dark streets of White-chapel, hot on the heels of her prey. It was a miserable neighborhood. The haunt of prostitutes and their procurers, of hardened men who hid by day and lurked in the dead of night, accosting unsuspecting victims at the point of a knife for the coins in their purse and a watch fob to pawn. She knew the area well by now. It teemed with brothels and doxy houses, with opium dens and dank gambling halls where the aristocracy came to slum and lose their pocket change. The stench of filth and urine accosted her as she limped along past small congregations of dangerous characters, clinging to the shadows in her ragged dress. She was clothed in the timeworn costume of a whore, the faded blue satin torn and reeking, barely concealing the swell of her breasts. She'd broken a heel of her dilapidated slippers, which she now carried in her hand. A small nail dug painfully into the sole of her foot.

Two prostitutes in heavy paint stood beneath a lamppost in front of a public house. They were chatting quietly when they spotted her. "You'll never catch a man in that rag, dearie," one of them called. They cackled like fish hags. Mylene hurried past them, ignoring their jibes. The last thing she needed was to call undue attention to herself.

The man she trailed was a block ahead. She could hear his fine kid boots hitting the cobblestones, see the shimmer of his elegant evening clothes as he passed beneath a gaslight that sizzled and spurted. Sensing her presence, he paused and cast a glance behind. Like a shot, Mylene ducked into an alley and held her breath. He was a cagey one. She'd followed him on five different occasions and had lost him every time. Once a week, this distinguished member of the House of Lords sneaked off to this squalid section of London's impoverished East End, taking a different route each time. His caution piqued her curiosity. Wherever he was going, he was making damn sure he wasn't followed. But to where did he disappear? And what unspeakable act was he committing that should warrant such care?

She had her suspicions. The smell of opium drifted on the breeze, filling the alleyway with its choking fumes. If it was opium he was after, he'd come to the right place. And his caution be damned, she'd discover his dirty little secret if it proved the last thing she ever did!

His footfalls sounded again. Carefully peering out from her vantage point, she saw him turn a corner. Stealthily, favoring her sore foot, she followed in his wake. But he passed the succession of Chinese joy houses and headed for a row of flats instead.

In the middle of the street, he stopped and looked about. The street was all but empty, with one lone hawker carrying his wares in a basket. Mylene instantly flattened herself against the corner of the building, becoming one with the shadows. Watching, she saw the young aristocrat eye the hawker, then straighten his dinner jacket with haughty precision and walk purposefully in the front door.

The building was in shabby disrepair. Only three lights illuminated the aura of vacant isolation. Quietly, she made her way up the street and stood staring at the glowing windows. One was on the top floor, the other two on the third. Which one? And how could she get inside without being seen?

Just then a light went on in the far corner of the building, on the second floor. That must be it! But she couldn't just walk in and knock on the door. She had to think of another way.

"Care fer some flowers, luv?"

She turned to the hawker, who was coming her way. She could smell his flowers as he approached. He held out a bunch of violets with a toothless grin.

"Who lives in that building?" she asked.

"Wot, that one? Families, mostly."

It was mystifying. What could Lord Cadwell want with some poor family? An illegitimate child stashed away, perhaps? But would he keep it in such a disreputable place? Hardly likely.

"That gent in the fine clothes," she pursued in a Cockney accent. "You see 'im afore, gov'na?"

"Wot, 'im? Right enough. 'E comes once a week, regular, like clockwork, 'e does. 'E a customer, wot?" he added, taking note of her clothes.

" 'E owes me five quid, the rut. Scamped off wi'out payin', 'e did. An' me wi' a sorry lot o' mouths to feed."

"Wot can ye do wi' the gents, I ask. They've the run o' the place. Pay when they want, is wot they do. But if it's sport yer after . . ."

She eyed him keenly. He was a hefty fellow. "I'll give you ten bob to 'elp me see what 'e's about," she offered.

" 'Elp you, 'ow?"

"Come along, then."

She went to the far corner, beneath the newly lighted window, with him following reluctantly behind. "Give me a lift, gov'na, so's I can see inside."

He stared at her suspiciously. "It's me 'ead if I'm caught."

Reaching into her bodice, Mylene pulled out the ten-bob coin and handed it to him. He weighed it in his palm and set aside his qualms.

Cupping his hands, he waited for her to put her foot on top, then hefted her up. She could just see in over the windowsill. Grasping it in her hands, she raised herself up and looked inside.

It was a small sitting room with minimal furniture, all of it tattered. Inside, Lord Cadwell spoke with an older man and woman. To the side was a young girl, no more than thirteen, their daughter, from the resemblance. Lord Cadwell offered the man a coin, which was pocketed with a nod. Then the father left the room.

Cadwell spoke with the older woman, who nodded her understanding. She turned her back. And as she did, the distinguished MP turned and put his hand on the young girl's cheek. There was nothing fatherly in the gesture. Mylene felt her own cheeks flame. The girl, blushing, gave a shy yet beckoning smile. Then

Cadwell put his arm about her and led her to a closed door. This he opened, and with a last glance at the obliging mother, he stepped inside with the girl.

Rage filled Mylene's heart as she stared. "Saints in heaven," she muttered. "A child doxy!"

"Well, sure," the hawker groaned beneath her weight. "Were you expectin' a tea party, per'aps?"

In spite of her outrage, a surge of triumph filled Mylene. She had the goods on Cadwell at last. And what goods they were! Far more scandalous than anything her imagination had dared conjure. And she'd caught him in the act!

Lowered to the sidewalk once more, she brushed her skirts with a satisfied air.

"Now that I've 'elped you, wot about that bit o' sport? I could do wi' a bit of a break, so I could."

She looked down her nose at the insolent hawker who sought to take advantage of her goodwill. "Wot, wi' you? Go on, now, gov'na. You couldn't afford the likes o' me."

"I've got ten bob." He grinned, showing his gums.

She turned from him with a swish of her cheap skirts. "Cheeky pup. Ten bob wouldn't pay fer a pat on the cheek!"

At the corner of Lemon and White Horse Streets, a handsome coach stood out like Cinderella's glass slipper in the midst of housemaids' boots. As Mylene approached, the driver tipped his hat. "Success?" he asked.

"A smashing success. Better than I'd hoped."

"I knew you'd do it. There's nary a prey that escapes you, once you set your sights."

She ducked into the coach and at once it lurched

away. Sitting back in the safety of the padded Moroccan leather, she allowed herself a calming breath. In spite of her achievement, and the pride of having bested the young lord, she felt the old fear and horror tug at her racing heart. Her anger was directed as much at the parents of the child as at Cadwell. How could they make their daughter a party to such depravity?

But she knew how. She knew what poverty did to people's souls. It was never far away. The awful knowledge that, if not for Father Q, she might have gone the way of that ill-used child. Her hands shook. She gripped them together to still the tremors. It unsettled her that the old memories, in spite of the turn her life had taken, still had the power to threaten her. That they were always there, reminding her of a destiny she'd so narrowly escaped.

But there wasn't time to brood. She must turn her mind to the matter of covering her tracks. Beside her, on the seat, were an emerald-green evening gown and her best cloak. A box on the floor contained the shoes, stockings, petticoats, and gloves to complete the attire. She stirred herself to action. As the coach drove through the dark streets, Mylene hurriedly stripped off the frayed costume and donned the evening finery. The quarters were cramped, but she'd grown accustomed to such quick changes over the years. By the time they'd traversed the city and crossed into Mayfair, she'd fastened the emerald necklace about her throat, clamped on the earbobs, and was hastily winding her flowing hair into a wealth of fastened curls atop her head. The coach pulled up. A swift glance in the hand mirror told her she was ready. The discarded costume was tucked inside the box for James, the driver, to hide in the stables.

"Welcome home, my lady," greeted the footman. "Lord Stanley awaits inside with Lord Helmsley."

"Thank you, Douglas," she said in the English that was second nature now.

"I trust you had a pleasant evening?"

"Most pleasant, yes."

Douglas helped her up the curving, shallow stairs of the mansion in Portman Square. It was a five-story town house, built by Robert Adam in the last century. Inside, she was greeted by warmth and light, by rich dark woods and opulent tapestries. A maid in a crisp black-and-white uniform bobbed a curtsy and took her cloak and gloves.

"The gentlemen are in the drawing room, miss."

"Thank you, Emma."

Emma bobbed another curtsy and left.

Mylene crossed the grand hall and opened the sliding mahogany doors. Inside, in a cavernous room, a fire glowed invitingly in a twelve-foot grate. The room was luxuriously paneled, decidedly masculine, yet cozy in spite of its proportions. Paintings by English masters covered the walls. The furnishings, in maroon Moroccan leather, looked as immaculate as if they were new. The smell of lemon oil gave the room a pleasant aroma.

As she entered, two men stood, setting aside their brandies. The elder, Lord Stanley, came forth with a smile to take her in his arms, giving the top of her head a paternal kiss. "So you've come at last," he greeted her warmly. "We'd despaired of your company. This old house isn't the same when you're away."

Mylene returned the embrace and kissed the earl's cheek. As always, she felt a rush of affection for her adoptive father, this senior member of the House of Lords who'd taken her in and heaped on her luxuries she'd never known existed. But it was his love for her that caused the fondness she felt as she looked at him—at the proud, patrician features, the thinning white hair, the air of elegance and distinction. He never let a day go by without expressing his appreciation for her company. That she was so grateful for his small kindnesses made him coddle her all the more.

It had seemed too good to be true at first. Lord Stanley, newly widowed, had lost a child to brain fever several years before. A daughter he'd cherished, so the loss of her had left him a broken man. When his wife finally perished from grief, he'd let it be known that he sought to adopt a daughter to fill his loss. It was something he'd tried to talk his wife into for years. Shamus Flynn, unbeknownst to the grieving Englishman, had supplied the perfect candidate. A girl with red hair, like his beloved Candice, who was the very age his daughter would have been had she lived.

On the boat to England, Mylene had learned her role. She was to play an English orphan who'd lost her parents in an Irish uprising and, for want of any relations, had been shipped home to an English orphanage. The story would explain Mylene's knowledge of Dublin. But more, it was calculated to stir the embers of Lord Stanley's heart. He was the staunchest opponent in Parliament to Irish Home Rule. That Mylene's parents had been killed by Irish rabble-rousers garnered his instant sympathy. He'd taken her in at first glance, and formally adopted her within the year.

In the beginning, Mylene had been flabbergasted by her surroundings. She wasn't certain she could perform such an extended role without giving herself away. The luxurious lifestyle, the formalities and graces, proved matters of extreme discomfort. To be awakened in the warmth of her plush canopied bed with a cup of steaming cocoa embarrassed her as much as being waited on hand and foot. But soon enough, James—the driver who secretly worked for their cause—had passed along her assignment. She was to use her position to discover the scandalous secrets of Lord Stanley's friends and associates. Buoyed by the sense of purpose, she'd thrown herself into her task with relish, becoming accomplished at subterfuge in no time.

What she hadn't counted on was growing to love Lord Stanley. Ireland, and her old life, began to seem like the dream.

"How fares the countess?" he asked, thinking she'd gone to visit a friend.

"Well enough, I think, for all that her confinement makes her edgy."

"Well, it's all to a good purpose, as she'll see when the baby comes. But tell me, my dear, did her happy state have its effect? I shouldn't mind a grandchild of my own before too much time."

"The very thing we were discussing when you came in," announced his companion.

Mylene turned and looked at Roger Helmsley. He was a dashing gentleman of twenty-four years, tall with dark brown hair and a fetching pencil-thin mustache. He wore his evening clothes with negligent ease, secure in his wealth and position. He was Lord Stanley's compatriot in Parliament, the driving force behind the Irish opposition.

"Lord Helmsley has been pressing his suit," explained her father. "He informs me, with the most dejected of countenances, that he's asked for your hand on three separate occasions. Yet he says you stall him with pretty smiles."

"She's a coy one, my lord," said Roger, coming to take both her hands in his. "I daresay some of your own impeccable diplomacy has rubbed off on your daughter."

"Is this a conspiracy?" She laughed. "Is a girl not to be allowed her say?"

"If you'd say anything at all, I might bear up. But this blasted silence on the subject . . . Come, my sweet. What must an old bachelor like myself do to entice the heart of such a fair maiden?"

Roger was looking at her with a glow of appreciation that made her flush with wonder. At twenty-two, Mylene had blossomed under the earl's care. The rich food from his table had transformed the scrawny street urchin into a woman with enticing curves. Her breasts were full, her hips ripe and rounded, her legs nicely lean and defined from hours in the saddle and long walks through Hyde Park. Her skin, once so sallow, glowed with rosy health. Even her riotous curls glistened with rich abundance. Her pouty mouth was legendary among the swells of Marlboro House. Her clothes were fashioned by the best dressmakers in London, giving her a regal, polished air—if one didn't look too closely at the impish scattering of freckles across her nose. But when she looked in the mirror, she always gave a start of surprise. She thought of herself still as the ill-nourished orphan without so much as a last name.

It was partly this quest for a family of her own that had her considering Roger's proposal. He was an affable and decent man who, on their outings, had displayed a freewheeling sense of the absurd that had brought an element of fun to her sadly serious life. His wealth, good looks, and charm were the talk of mothers with marriageable daughters. And if his politics appalled her, she'd learned long ago from Lord Stanley that a man could hold differing, even dangerous, political views and still be the kindest of men. Admittedly, the challenge intrigued her. As his wife, she could perhaps influence him to take a more liberal stance.

"You see how she avoids me," Roger complained in a melodramatic tone.

There was a knock on the door before the panels were slid open by Jensen, the all-too-proper major-domo who'd been in the service of Lord Stanley's grandfather. "Excuse the intrusion, my lord, but a gentleman caller awaits your pleasure without."

"A caller?" asked Lord Stanley. "At this hour?"

"His card, my lord."

Lord Stanley took the card. "Good gracious. Lord Whitney. Send him in, Jensen, by all means."

When Jensen left with a stiff bow, Roger asked, "A jest perhaps? A visit from the grave?"

"No, no, my good man. Not old Lord Whitney. It's his son. I'd heard on his father's death that he was on his way. Been in India with his mother since he was a lad. As you know, the climate agreed with her, and she refused to return when her husband's service was at an end. Kept the boy with her. We haven't seen the scamp since he was but a babe."

"Well, well, this *is* news! It's our duty, then, to set him straight right from the start. Curry his favor, so to speak. We shouldn't want the influence he's inherited to go the wrong way."

"He's his father's son. He'll see our way of things, I'll warrant."

Mylene knew what this meant. Old Lord Whitney, while ill and with one foot in the grave, had nevertheless roused himself to Parliament in his wheelchair to lambaste, in his raspy voice, the MPs who favored Ireland's pleas. Lord Stanley, she knew, was counting on the son to take up the cause. It meant another evening of feeling her hackles rise as the gentlemen discussed new ways to squelch the Irish rebellion.

She kept her lashes lowered, cautioning herself to silence, as the gentleman stepped into the room and the doors were closed behind him.

Lord Stanley greeted him. "Lord Whitney, what a pleasant surprise. I'd planned to call on you myself, as soon as I'd heard you'd arrived. May I express my condolences for your father's passing. He was a distinguished gentleman and a true friend. I assure you, he shall be missed by all."

Mylene sensed the gentleman give a gracious bow.

"Allow me to present my good friend, Lord Helmsley. You'll be seeing a great deal of each other, I don't doubt."

The men shook hands.

"And this, sir, is my daughter, Mylene. Lord Whitney, from India."

Mylene set her face in courteous lines. But when she glanced up, the smile of welcome froze on her face.

It was Johnny!

She didn't know how she survived the next few minutes. Standing like a specter as he came toward her in his evening blacks, looking for all the world like a refined English gentleman just home from abroad. As he took her hand and bowed to give it a gallant kiss. As a thrill swept through her, burning her toes in their velvet shoes. As the breath froze like Galway frost in her lungs.

Johnny! How she'd forgotten the effect of him.

Those stunning green eyes that pierced her like swords, making a private mockery of his deportment. Was there ever anything so green in all the world? And the black hair that swept back off his wide forehead in fashionable submission. She'd forgotten the charm of those wild locks falling into his eyes when the young hooligan had refused to cut his hair. A rush of memories warmed her like mother's milk. It was as if the room around her disappeared, and she was once again standing by the banks of the river Liffey, her lips burning, her breath like fire, staring up at him in a haze of wonder and amazement.

But how he'd changed! He was older, more serene and cultured, more devastatingly handsome than any man had a right to be. Gone was any trace of the ruffian who'd roamed the streets of Dublin in bare feet and beaten a band of five boys single-handedly for a crust of bread.

But those lips were the same. Full, sensual, defined in a way that drew her eyes, made her remember all too vividly the feel of them on her own. Oh, how difficult it was not to throw herself into his arms!

Or to give his head a good cuff. The nerve of him, testing her reflexes in so public a way!

But her flash of temper was short-lived. This was Johnny! She glanced at Roger Helmsley, who suddenly seemed a pale imitation of masculinity, a faded painting without character or life.

The conversation flowed over her like a river. She was drowning in sensation, so the words she heard seemed like echoes of some other world. She was aware of Lord Stanley prompting his visitor. "It's my fond desire that you shall be a credit to your father's views. We've need of new blood in the battle we wage."

And Johnny, so charming, so smooth and polished

in his gallantry, bowing at just the proper angle. "I should be delighted to discuss the subject further, my lord. At your convenience, of course."

But nothing registered. All she could think was, *Johnny's here at last!* After all these years . . . After so many years that finally, late at night, she could no longer recall the exact features of his face. So many years that his voice, his very essence, had become as vague and hard to hold as mist on the bogs. Her heart drummed in her ears, hushing the ebb and flow of words.

Too soon, he was leaving. He took her hand. She started as she felt the crisp folds of paper in her palm. Instinct impelled her to clasp the note and hide it in her skirt. But as the men walked the visitor to the door, she found she couldn't wait. She turned her back and hastily read the scrawled words. "Meet me in the mews when all is quiet."

She paced the floor of her room, waiting impatiently for the sounds of nighttime activity to finally cease. It seemed an eternity, as the servants roamed the floors with hushed gravity, dousing gaslamps, banking fires, checking the locks on the doors. Just when she thought all had settled, she opened her bedroom door to see Emma carrying a tray with a glass of hot milk and brandy into Lord Stanley's room. She ticked off the minutes in her mind. Fifteen minutes for him to drink the concoction while he read Dickens in bed. Another ten for his eyelids to feel heavy and for him to put the book aside. Another quarter hour for him to settle back in the starched pillows and fall asleep.

She couldn't bear it. Abandoning her plan to sneak out the back door, she instead went to her side window and raised it high. The spring night was chill, but she barely noticed. Hooking her leg over the sill as she had many times before, she climbed down the lattice she'd had installed for that very purpose.

She was at the side of the house. She would have run to the mews, but a footfall gave her pause. Ahead, in the square, a constable walked his beat, swinging his lantern as he began to whistle a vague tune. He bent to brush a bit of dirt from his boot. Mylene backed against the wall. The lamplight was angled her way. One glance in her direction and she'd be discovered.

The policeman stood and straightened his jacket. Then, with a glance about that caused Mylene's breath to catch in her throat, he twirled his nightstick and continued on his way.

As soon as he was gone, she flew on silent feet to the mews behind the house. This was an alleyway where deliveries were made and the horses were stabled.

Away from the gaslamps, there wasn't enough light to see her hand in front of her face. She stepped forth hesitantly, then stopped short. Was he there? Was he waiting? Or had he given up and gone?

"Johnny?" she whispered.

She took two more hesitant steps, feeling disconcerted in the eerie blackness. Completely blind, she had to rely on her sense of hearing to give her bearings. Nothing, not a sound. She had no warning when a hand gripped her arm. Then a savage jerk wheeled her around, bringing her up to collide against something solid and unyielding. The gasp she uttered was muffled by the pressure of a warm hand on her mouth.

In an instant of unbearable joy, she recognized the scent of that hand. She had lost the memory of the scent, but now, when it was hot in her nostrils, she knew he smelled like nothing and no one on earth. And then the hand in the dark moved. Where a moment before it had sought to imprison her lips, it now cupped her cheek in a rough, possessive caress. It circled her neck, and she felt herself pulled close, felt the wandering hand replaced by lips that were hard and full. They captured her own lips as surely as his hand ever had, crushing them, bruising them, moving with relentless hunger, as if seeking to claim dominion while coercing from her mouth the taste of her very soul.

She felt herself melting into him. She was distantly aware that her legs had gone weak, so she had to grasp his shoulders to keep upright. His arms went about her, anchoring her even as they lifted her off her feet, pressing her breasts into the rugged contours of his chest until he crushed the very breath from her lungs. He flung her back against a wall and drove her into it, so she felt the swelling heat of his desire against one thigh beneath her skirt. And all the while his lips demanded more, pressing and tasting with the desperation of a man too long denied, searching with his tongue the honeyed crevices of her mouth as if seeking answers to questions he was too afraid to ask.

She forgot everything as she pressed her shivering body into his. She forgot to think, to breathe. She only knew she was floating in sensation too marvelous to be real. His tongue stole her nectar, while his body made her ache inside. A man's body now, with its potent virility weakening defenses she didn't know she had, making her feel small and pliable and oh, so very female against the force of his brute strength. The shock of his kiss, his hands, his rock-hard erection, jolted her alive. As if she'd been sleeping all this time, awaiting his kiss to awaken her.

Then his mouth was at her neck, tasting her skin as he breathed in her scent. "Oh, Johnny," she whispered, her voice sounding hoarse and low in her throat. "You've come to me at last."

"Aye," he growled against her fevered flesh. "At *long* last."

"But tell me all. How's Father Q? And the children? Have you seen them? And Daggett? Oh, Johnny, I didn't know until this moment how I'd missed you all! But why is it you're impersonating Lord Whitney's son? You nearly scared the life out of me when I looked up and saw you there."

He'd been nuzzling her neck as she spoke. But when she finished, he lifted himself from her and cast a glance about, like a man who'd lost his head in a rash moment and was only now remembering where he was.

"Stow yer questions, darlin'," he said. Out there, alone, she could hear the Dublin inflection the Fenians had trained out of him. His voice sounded deeper, more melodious, than it had in the drawing room. "It's possible I'm being watched. I can't be too careful. For now, I've come with new orders. Just listen, and do all I tell you."

"Of course." She tried to assume a professional attitude, but it was difficult with him swollen against her thigh.

"I'm to take the information you've been gathering and use it to blackmail votes for Home Rule."

"I guessed it was something of the sort. I've been keeping a secret journal of all I've found out. Shall I get it for you?"

"In due time. There's more. Lord Stanley is to be discredited."

Her earlier joy slipped through her fingers like spilled wine. "Discredited? What do you mean?"

"They want him ruined. So no one will listen to him ever again. You're to be the instrument of his public scandal."

She felt her heart shrivel inside. "Me?"

"Aye. You're to let it be known the reason Lord Stanley has been so adamant against Irish Home Rule is to hide the fact that he's been secretly working as an Irish spy. We've forged papers to prove it, which you're to leak to the proper channels. A grand bit of irony, wouldn't you say?"

She was too shocked to speak. He couldn't mean it!

But before she could even utter a stunned query, she heard footsteps coming along the side of the house. The golden glow of a lantern spilled into the mews. And just as the constable stepped into the pool of light, Johnny shot away from her and disappeared.

"What goes on here?" called the constable, raising his lantern high. Mylene froze in its beam, feeling the panic of her eyes flash in the glare. "Oh, beg pardon, miss. Is anything awry?"

It took every ounce of courage she possessed to answer in an even tone. "Not at all, Constable. I merely couldn't sleep and came out for a breath of air."

"Poor idea for a young lady to be out alone at night. I'd go in, was I you, miss. You never know who might be lurking about."

"I'll do that, Constable."

"Well, I'll be about. Might just check back, make sure you made it in safely. Wouldn't want anything undue to happen on my beat, you know."

"Thank you, Constable. We shall all rest easier, knowing you're about."

When the policeman had ambled off, Johnny came

round the side wall of the stables. "We can't talk here," he whispered in her ear. "Meet me Thursday at Tyburn. Dawn. Tell me how you'll arrange it then."

With a last kiss, he was gone, as swiftly and mysteriously as Shamus Flynn himself.

Chapter 2

Mylene couldn't sleep. She'd been so elated at seeing Johnny. She hadn't thought much about their first kiss in the last couple of years. When she'd thought about it at all, it was with the same fuzzy recollection that dulled the sharp edges of experience. It was as if she'd dreamt it, so it meant little more to her than a vision she'd had before drifting off to sleep. But she'd forgotten more than she'd realized. Because nothing in all her life had electrified her the way his kisses in the mews just had.

In that moment, in his arms, she'd felt that everything was right. That it all made sense. That every moment of her life had been leading to the instant when he'd come to claim her as his. But then he'd told her the awful thing she'd have to do. The price she'd have to pay.

She tossed and turned until the sun filtered through

her curtains, then she abandoned all hope of sleep. Dressing wearily, she went downstairs, ignoring the surprised greetings of the servants. On the main floor, she knocked on the door of Lord Stanley's study and awaited his invitation to enter. As always, he sat in his chair by the fire, sipping his tea while he perused the *Times*. When he glanced over the paper and saw her, he put it down with a welcoming smile.

"Well, this *is* a happy surprise. I don't often see you up much before ten. To what do I owe this fortunate occasion?"

"I thought I'd take tea with you," she said, looking down at him with pained eyes that stung from lack of sleep.

"Delightful! I can't think of anything I'd enjoy more."

When her tea had been poured and she still sat staring at him, he gave her a keen look, then leaned across the table and took her hand in his. "Come, now. Wouldn't you feel better if you told me what was on your mind?"

She considered him a moment, feeling sick inside, her orders running gratingly through her head. *Treason.* She flinched at the ugly word. How could she do it? To publicly accuse him of something so diabolically opposed to all he stood for ... so *untrue* ... It would ruin him, certainly. Nothing could destroy his credibility more thoroughly. But worse, if they charged him with treason ... if she provided the proof ... it would surely mean his death.

Guilt was the Irish curse. Guilt and melancholy. And Johnny had brought them back to her full force.

"Lord Stanley—"

"Now, my dear. Couldn't you honor my request and

call me Father? It would make an old man very happy, you know."

She lowered her eyes, ashamed to look him in the face. She'd never felt so conflicted over her fondness for this man who'd protected and loved her all these years. How could everything have changed so swiftly? How could it all have come tumbling down on her head?

"What," she asked softly, "would you think if I had to leave you?"

"Leave me?" His surprised countenance relaxed into a comprehending smile. "Ah, to marry Roger, you mean. Why, I hadn't considered that you'd leave me. I'd rather hoped Roger might be persuaded to move in here. His parents are young enough. He won't come into his property for some time."

Mylene looked about at the wood-paneled walls, at the leather furnishings, the priceless paintings. She, an orphan, had come to think of this palace as home. Seeing her wistful look, Lord Stanley took her hand again. "This will all be yours someday, my dear. It comforts me to think of you living on here, loving it as I do, once I'm gone."

She wanted to cry. Looking up into his kind eyes, she wondered again how she could possibly betray him.

"Would it make you happy if I married Roger?" she asked to hide her desperation.

He sat back and answered softly, thoughtfully, "Yes, it would. Oh, I know it's the fashion to marry for wealth and position. And Lord knows, Roger has enough of each coming his way. But I want more for my daughter. I want you to be happy. I want for you the love I never had with my own wife, Elaine. She was a good and dutiful mate, but she didn't love me, you see. Roger loves you, Mylene. And I feel you can give something to him that these flighty society girls can't. You have a serious and caring heart that most girls don't possess. Somehow, I rather have the feeling that you were sent to Roger to help him in some way. To lead him in a direction he might not otherwise seek. That sounds fanciful, I suppose, to one as sensible as yourself."

"Fanciful? No." It was, indeed, what she'd come to feel. Only Lord Stanley couldn't guess the direction she'd planned to steer him toward.

But that had been before Johnny had come bursting back into her life like a cyclone. Before he'd turned her world upside down with his awful words.

She looked up into Lord Stanley's eyes. "I want you to know that I love you deeply," she told him sincerely. "I never dreamt that I could find the sort of love and acceptance you've given me. Whatever happens, I want you to know that I shall always be grateful to you. And . . . even if you have cause to doubt it, know that I shall always love you."

"But my dearest girl, you've never given me the slightest reason to doubt your love. Not for a moment!"

Her heart breaking with the burden of her guilt, she excused herself, leaving the untouched tea behind.

The next morning, in the predawn hush, she went to meet Johnny. Throwing a black velvet cape over her dress, she crept out into Portman Square. The only one about was the gas man, turning down the lamps. She avoided him, crossing the square on the west side, heading south, then west, all but running toward Tyburn Lane. There, she stopped. Across the lane was the high wall that protected Hyde Park. Behind it, at the corner of Edgeware and Tyburn, was the gruesome reminder of London's violent past: the site of Tyburn Gallows. There'd been no executions there since 1783, but it took several years after that for fashionable people to be convinced to move nearby. The charming Regency houses along Tyburn Lane faced away from the park, as if turning their backs on Tyburn's notorious past.

It was an odd choice for a meeting place, she reflected, the place where criminals had once been hanged. But then, Johnny had always been one for grand gestures.

She entered the park through the Cumberland Gate, still not certain what she'd say to Johnny when she saw him. What was she going to do? She'd agonized over the question the whole day before, and still no solution had come to her. Her mind felt numb. She wanted nothing more than to sleep for a week and forget she'd ever seen Johnny again.

Dawn was long in coming. The morning was chill, causing her to pull her cloak about her. The dark outlines of trees spooked her, reminded her of the ghosts that surely lingered on the hill. She paced the dewy grass beneath Marble Arch, feeling the wet seep into her kidskin shoes, too restless to find a perch.

Where was he? she wondered. Why didn't he come?

The eastern sky turned midnight blue, then grey, then pink. The sky above her was dark. Then, just as she thought the sunrise would never come, the sky burst into color, filled with light. And as it did, she heard a rustle she knew was not the wind. Turning, she saw Johnny fling back his cloak and step, like a magus, from behind the grand arch.

He looked entirely different from the man who'd stood in her drawing room two nights before. He wore nothing beneath his rakishly open cloak but plain black breeches and a rumpled white shirt. His hair was wild from the wind, the locks tumbling in disarray upon his forehead. A black stubble peppered his strong jaw. He looked rugged and male, dashing and romantic, like the fictional hero of some minstrel's fancy.

His eyes found hers and held. All she could see was a flash of green so vivid it seemed to reflect the emerald of Eire. She felt pulled and drawn. Yet when he stepped toward her, intent on taking her in his arms, she wrenched her gaze from his and turned away.

She could feel him standing there, alone and abandoned, staring at her heaving back. She felt for him. He wouldn't have expected this rude rebuff. But she felt for Lord Stanley, too.

"What's this, then?" he asked softly. There was a timbre in his voice that she'd never heard before. The prideful sound of a man masking his pain.

"It isn't fair that you should ask me to choose," she told him, her back still turned.

"Fair?" He sounded as if he couldn't comprehend the word. She heard the swish of his cape, then his hand gripped her arm and turned her around to face incredulous eyes. "What ails you?"

"If you think for a minute, Johnny Come Lately, that I'll stand by and see me own father so viciously maligned—"

She stopped abruptly. She didn't realize, in her fury, that she'd lapsed into her old Irish brogue. But what startled her was the force of her feelings. They cracked her indecision like a chisel, bringing her face-to-face with a truth from which she could no longer run.

"He's not yer father," he said softly, but with a dangerous undertone of wrath.

"No father could have treated me so dear. Shall I tell you the kindnesses he's heaped on me, then?"

"Bought you, is what he's done."

She stared at him as if he'd slapped her face. "How dare you! What do you know of it?"

"I know you've spent valuable time pussyfooting around aristocratic drawing rooms, having a grand time being the belle of the ball, while yer own countrymen are starvin'."

Stricken, she cried, "That's not fair. I was told to mingle with the aristocracy. It's a vital part of me mission."

"Spy on them, yes, My. But who told you to take to them the way ye have? Who told you to *like* them? Not bleedin' Shamus Flynn. And not I."

If he'd meant to shame her, he would be disappointed. She took in his accusatory words, taking the time to set her thoughts to rights. Finally, dropping her brogue along with her anger, she said quietly, "It's true. I've spent time with the royal family and their friends. I've come to like them. I like this life. And why not?" she added with a flash of spice. "It's better than combing the streets for every meal. Being so cold and hungry and fearful sometimes, you lie in the dark praying for death. Yes, I like being Lord Stanley's daughter far more than I liked being a filthy orphan from the streets. What's wrong with that? I've done my job, and done it well, as you'll find out soon enough. Up till now, I've seen no conflict whatsoever. I've found a way to live among them, to enjoy it, and still to work for my cause. I'd planned to go on doing so, if you want to know." She looked up and met the fire of his eyes. "But I'd give up everything I have, everything Lord Stanley has given me, to save him from this disgrace. Don't you realize he could *die?* Serving Ireland and maliciously ruining Lord Stanley are two different things altogether. He's been good to me, Johnny. I love him like a father. I can't betray the love he's given me."

"You love him and lie to him," he spat out. "Tell me how it's possible to love someone and betray him with every breath you take."

She looked away. His words stirred her guilt.

"You've gone soft," he accused.

"Soft!"

"Soft with yer money and yer fine clothes." He snatched a hand and turned it to look accusingly at her palm. "Even yer hands are soft. Idle hands. You always were the dramatic lass, playin' yer role well. But you've mixed up yer role and yer reality." When she snatched her hand away, he strode forth and grabbed her arm, pinching the flesh with fingers of iron. She could feel the full force of his fury in his grip. "You're not that person. The one who wakes up to a warm bed while her countrymen scour the streets for a cold corner to lay their heads. Have you forgotten what that's like, then? Remember who you are, girl, and what you're about. You're an outlaw in this soft land you love. Your fine, kind Lord Stanley would as soon string you up by the neck if he found out who you really are. Don't you see? He doesn't love you, Mylene. He loves who you *pretend* to be."

His words wounded her deeply, and so did the cold tone with which he spoke.

"You're wrong. I've learned that people can disagree with you but still be good people. He's taught me that, Johnny. He's changed me."

"And how have you changed him, all these years? Has he backed off from his mission one small bit?"

"His position is based on ignorance. He was brought up to think that way. But he can learn. Just as I learned."

"What has he learned in the last seven years?"

She jutted her chin out at him. "To love an Irish peasant."

"It isn't the peasant he loves. But shall we put it to a test? Shall I tell him just what it is his precious 'daughter' has been up to all these years, beneath his own nose?"

She was so stunned, all she could do for a moment was stare at him. "What's happened to you? What have they done to you? They've given you a heart of stone. Do you not care who you hurt, as long as you get what you want?"

He grasped her to him in exasperation. "And what of those who've put their faith and trust in ye? We've spent seven years of our lives on this plan and suddenly you tell me you don't want to do it."

She shrugged him off. "And how dare you be so insensitive as to think I could live for seven years with this man, who treated me better than I have a right to expect, and suddenly you tell me this and I'm supposed to fall in line! I won't do it, I tell you. You'll have to convince them that there's another way. I'll work on him. Convince him to change his vote—"

"The plan's in motion."

"I don't care. You do it, Johnny. Because I swear to you, I'll not do this awful thing."

After a long pause, in which he never took his eyes from her face, he asked, "Have you turned yer back on us, then?"

She slumped, feeling as if the last ounce of strength was draining from her. "Of course I'm with you. I've proved it, haven't I? I've done everything that's been asked of me. But one thing I won't do. I won't ruin this kind man."

"And what of us?"

The word hung in the air.

"Us?"

"Aye—us. What do you think I thought of every night these last seven years? When I was grilled and trained and taught and tested till I thought I'd go mad. Until I couldn't find Johnny beneath all the training that was making me into Lord Whitney's son. Seven years I trained to play a role. And all I could think of when I was so tired I couldn't remember me own name was you." He took her arm and pulled her close. "The feel of your lips on mine." With the back of his knuckles, he caressed her parted lips. "The way you felt in me arms that last night in Dublin, like a bird that might break in me hand. How your eyes told me you belonged to me and no one else."

She could feel herself melting into him once again, transfixed by the lulling rhythm of his words.

"It was dreams of you that kept me sane. Night after night, I'd tell myself how I'd come find you. How we'd finish up our mission, then go back to Ireland together."

His words stopped her cold. She'd been so close to surrender. No man had ever made her feel that way. She'd felt as if nothing and no one mattered, only drowning in Johnny's arms. But she knew now how wrong she was. His words pounded in her brain like a cruel jeer from the past. *Go back to Ireland . . . to Ireland . . .*

Something hardened in her as she felt the cold grip of a fear she hadn't known existed. "Never," she told him, pushing him away. "Never again will I go back to the life I left in Ireland. I'll help the cause here, but I won't go back. I can't."

She saw the defeat in his eyes. "In all those years, in all those dreams, one thing I never expected. That you, of all people, would live to betray your own."

"I haven't betrayed you. But there are ways of doing things. Without violence. And without hurting others. I'm going to see to it."

"And how would you be doing that?"

She didn't know she'd say it until the words escaped her lips. Until the flash of mortification turned to bitter incredulity in his eyes. Until he was staring at her as if she couldn't say anything to betray him more.

"I'm going to marry Roger Helmsley."

"She what!"

The tavern girl placed a bottle of Bushmills on the table with five glasses, forcing silence. She waited a moment, expecting payment, but was summarily ignored. The five men glowered at one another with what seemed to her to be murderous intent. She suppressed a shudder. Working on the Rotherhithe docks as she did, she was accustomed to rough men. But there was something raw about these strangers, some sense of urgency and covert danger that she detected soon after the last bloke had joined them. He was dressed in Bond Street finery but was disheveled and unshaved, swaying drunkenly on his feet. He grabbed the bottle, sloshed the whiskey into a glass, and downed it with the despondency of a man driven by dark demons. He was a handsome man, with fierce green eyes that seemed to see more than he'd likely admit. She might have fancied him, might even have flirted with him in the hope of an extra quid for her pocket or a quick tumble in the sheets. But something about the way he seized the bottle and drained another drink frightened her. This man was itching for a fight. He looked ready to take on the whole tavern of rowdy dockers and still lust for more blood to spill.

"Be off with you," one of the men snarled at her, giving her a glare. Tangling her fists in her splotched apron, she hurried off in search of more amenable patrons.

"You heard me," Johnny answered, slurring his words. "She's after marrying that rotter Helmsley."

Daggett, who'd been watching his old friend with alarm, put his hand on Johnny's as he reached for the bottle again, warning him to caution. But Johnny angrily shrugged him off and gulped down yet another drink.

Keenan O'Flaherty, with his two henchmen by his side, glared at Johnny with the same impatient sneer he'd given the waitress. He was a broad man with titian hair and the flat features of peasant stock— Shamus Flynn's right hand, the eyes and ears of a hunted man. He'd watched for years as Flynn himself had trained this rugged orphan in the secret arts of espionage, watched Johnny become more elusive, more dangerous, more driven than Shamus Flynn himself. He didn't trust Johnny. Word among the Fenians was that O'Flaherty was jealous of Flynn's patronage of this new star, of Flynn's increasing obsession with and affection for the man he'd come to view as his successor. A position O'Flaherty had taken for granted— until Johnny had come along.

Johnny knew this, but he treated O'Flaherty with the dismissive supremacy of a man who knew he'd surpassed the might and wisdom of his senior advisers.

Until tonight. Tonight there was something sinister in Johnny's the-hell-with-you-all attitude that made the hair on the back of O'Flaherty's neck rise.

He covered his discomfiture with a bark of authority. "Then she's to be stopped."

Johnny, raising his glass, halted in mid-motion. "Stopped?"

"Eliminated," spat out O'Flaherty, as if speaking to a tiresome inferior. "She's out of control. I'll not be havin' the plan jeopardized because a silly bitch takes it into her head—"

He never finished the sentence. In one fierce bound, Johnny lunged across the table to strangle O'Flaherty's neck. "You fecking bastard!" he cried as he shook the offender, his thumbs pressing O'Flaherty's throat until O'Flaherty's face flushed scarlet and he choked for air.

His henchmen jerked to their feet, knocking the table aside as they lurched toward Johnny. But Daggett, his instincts already alerted, beat them to it. He wrestled Johnny back, forcing him into the cage of his arms, holding fast as Johnny fought the captive hold.

"Easy, man," Daggett whispered in his ear. "We can't be affording a scene."

O'Flaherty was sputtering, his eyes shooting fire as he, too, struggled against the protective grip of his men. "That's it, bucko. I'd like nothing better than to beat some sense into yer high-toned head." But as the innkeeper came charging round the bar, his men cautioned him and held up their hands to reassure the innkeeper that all was well before righting the table and resuming their seats.

O'Flaherty remained standing. "You do that again," he muttered, "and I'll—"

"I'll not have her harmed," Johnny ground out through clenched teeth, shaking off Daggett's grasp.

"You know the rules, Johnny. Loyalty first. She's betrayed us. And she's betrayed the plan."

Johnny made another impulsive charge, but Daggett held his arm. Breathing like a furnace, feeling the eyes of all on him, Johnny won the battle to lower his voice. He spoke in a soft growl, slowly and deliberately, as if speaking to someone so daft, he could only understand the most rudimentary of explanations.

"The plan was to kidnap Whitney's son and have me take his place. So I could use the information *Mylene* gave me to blackmail votes for the cause. She's an integral part of that plan. Without her information, there *is* no plan. Am I making meself clear?"

"What's clear," O'Flaherty shot back, "is that this lass yer so fond of canna be trusted. She's thumbed her nose in our faces. That makes her a danger to us all, yerself included. What if she takes it into her head to tell that husband of hers what we're about? We canna afford such a liability at this late stage. You know that as well as I."

"I know nothing of the sort. You've no understanding of her. She was picked because she can make the hardest and most furtive of men melt and reveal their very soul. And why is that? Because she has a soft heart. She makes a man feel that he can come to her with any secret and she'll understand. That—in case it's escaped yer limited thinking—is what makes her *invaluable*."

"Not when her soft heart, as you put it, is extended to our sworn enemies. Not when she becomes one of them and casts her compatriots aside."

"She's cast nothing aside. She thinks she can win them over peaceably, from the inside."

O'Flaherty leaned forward and whispered harshly, "And when has an Englishman ever been won over by talk?"

"And isn't that what we're good at, we Irish? We talk and talk until—"

"Until we finally wake up and see that force is the only way."

"I'll convince her, I tell you. She'll listen to me. But you'll not harm a hair on her head or by Christ, I'll—"

"You'll what?" O'Flaherty challenged.

"I need time," Johnny said. "And I'll have it or, by the saints, I'll wring yer sorry neck for good."

O'Flaherty stood looking at his adversary with all his naked loathing glistening in his eyes. "Ye have until the wedding. But mark me words, Johnny. If she so much as sets foot on that altar, she'll not live to see her honeymoon."

Johnny flinched at the last word. Daggett saw it and took his arm, coaxing him away. Stooping to pick up the half-empty bottle on the floor, he said, "Ye've no need to worry, then. Johnny will see to it, so he will."

"Will he now?" O'Flaherty taunted.

Johnny turned and stared into his eyes. "She'll marry that bastard over my dead body," he swore, before Daggett dragged him away.

Outside, it was dark. A few lights illuminated the Surrey dock along the south bank of the Thames. As Daggett led his friend from the Angel Inn, he could see London Bridge in the distance, looming over the river like a symbol of England's ascendancy. It reminded him all too vividly of what was at stake.

They walked along the river in silence. The smell of the water was sharp and distinct. Up the way, a group of brawling dockhands laughed and jeered among themselves, then passed into the tavern as a group. When it was quiet, with only the lapping of the water to lull their senses, Daggett said, "My, but it's grand to see ye again, Johnny. What's it been, then, two years?"

Johnny looked at him blankly, as if he couldn't see him through the angry mist in his head. Daggett remembered happier reunions through the years, when they'd see each other after months apart and run to grasp each other in a manly embrace, ruffling the hair of the other with jests and criticisms they knew were meant as a hearty welcome. But tonight, after two long years, Johnny had other things on his mind. It was as if Daggett weren't there.

To cover the awkward silence, he said, "These are exciting times, Johnny. In the years since I saw you last I've become a new man. I've found me calling. Keenan's been trainin' me in what he grandly calls the military arts. I could blow up the Bank of England, so I could, and leave nary a trace."

A killer was what they'd trained him to be. Highly skilled in the art of destruction. He knew things Johnny didn't about the grand plan, things he'd sworn not to reveal. The impulse was strong upon him to boast his knowledge to his old friend. But loyalty had been drummed into him along with his other preparation. Loyalty to the cause, above all else.

Johnny stood looking at him as if he hadn't heard a word. "You shouldn't have stopped me," he said at last, in the voice of one in a fog.

Daggett sighed. There'd be no happy reminiscing this night. "Ye can't antagonize the man. There's too much at stake."

He handed forth the bottle with wordless invitation, then watched with a frown as Johnny drained half the content before wiping his mouth on his sleeve.

"Ah, but 'tisn't O'Flaherty that has ye licked, is it now? Ye've changed, Johnny. I've never seen the likes of ye. Yer not by nature a drinking man. A clear head at all times, isn't that what ye told me, now?"

Johnny glanced at him, then, defeated, handed back the bottle. "Christ," he swore, rubbing his head. "She's got me tied up in knots."

"I can see that, so I can."

Johnny peered at him closely. "And you, old brother. Yer not feeling the same, I suppose?"

"And what would ye be meaning by that?"

Johnny leaned forward, swaying slightly. "I know, Daggett. I know the truth of it, man."

The breath caught in Daggett's throat. Cautious now, he asked, "The truth of what, then?"

"I know you love her, too."

Daggett's eyes never left Johnny's face. He stood suspended, staring at him as if loath to speak. As if he'd do anything to keep his friend from uttering the words.

But the whiskey had taken hold of Johnny. He'd stayed drunk for most of the day. He'd drunk more in the last twenty-four hours than he had in the last few months. The spirits loosened his tongue, so he couldn't stop now if he'd wanted to.

"I know it, man. I've known it since we were fourteen. Ye'd been beaten near death's door by those shytes from East Dublin. Mylene was cleaning yer wounds. And she touched yer face with that gentle way she has. You remember? To soothe yer brow. And you gave her a look I'll not soon be forgetting."

"What look was that?"

If Johnny noticed the stilted tone, he gave no indication. " 'Twas a look of horror at first. But then you stared at her like ye'd just realized something ye'd never known before. And I knew it then. I knew you loved her, deep in yer heart. She knew it, too, I think. Why you'd been so shy with her. She asked me once why you were different when the two of you were alone. Why you couldn't seem to meet her eyes. I know ye, Daggett, like no one else. We all know it's true."

Daggett shifted his gaze, rubbing the deep cleft in his chin. "That was a long time ago. I've had experiences since then that have changed me. Ye wouldn't believe the experiences I've had."

"I don't know about yer *experiences*. But I know one thing. You can roust with a hundred and one women and ye'll not be forgetting Mylene. Once a man loves her, he loves her for life. Especially you and me."

"And how do ye know that?"

"Because she's in our blood," Johnny cried, passionate now. "She formed in us the image of all a woman is. She's our mother, our sister, our image of all that's courageous, intelligent and wonderful in women. How could you not love the lass? How could *I* not?"

Daggett turned away.

But Johnny grabbed his arm and wheeled him around. "Help me save her, man. Don't let that bastard O'Flaherty take from us the one good and decent thing we've had in our sorry lives. Christ, man, if I lose her—"

The silence hung between them. Presently, Daggett shook himself to life. But he said, in a dead voice, "I knew ye cared for her. But I didn't know it had gone this far."

Johnny dragged a shaking hand through his black hair, looking up into the night as he heaved a sigh.

"It's worse than that. Without her, I'm but half a man."

"And what of us, Johnny? Would ye fight me for Mylene? Fight me like yer willing to fight O'Flaherty?"

After a brief pause, Johnny said softly, "I love you like a brother. You know that."

"But ye love Mylene more."

Their eyes locked. Johnny, tortured, half mad with drink and despair, gave his friend a last look, then turned and reeled away.

Daggett watched him go. Slowly, thoughtfully, he put the bottle to his mouth and drank deeply.

The night grew quiet as Johnny's footsteps receded and he disappeared. Daggett stood where he was, feeling more alone than he'd ever felt in his life. Presently, his gaze was drawn to the bridge in the distance. He stared at it for some time, letting the memories flood his mind. Absently, between sips of whiskey, he began to sing in a soft tone, "London Bridge is falling down, my fair lady . . ."

Chapter 3

The party was in full swing by the time Johnny arrived. He stood at the top of the stairs leading down to the Helmsley ballroom, calmly surveying the sea of faces until his gaze found its mark.

Mylene felt the jolt of that gaze like a rifle shot. Speaking to Roger's parents, she stumbled on her words, forgetting in the stark focus of Johnny's face what she'd been saying.

Fortunately, the majordomo's announcement sent a murmur through the room that covered her blunder. London was abuzz over the recent arrival of the handsome and dashing and deliciously mysterious Lord Whitney. He'd spent the few weeks of his homecoming meeting MPs at their clubs and acquainting himself with the current political climate. As a consequence, scant few of the ladies had yet to lay their curious eyes upon the chap. At the sound of his name, the women swiveled their coifed heads as one and strained their necks to see. Taking stock, mothers with marriageable daughters crooked the corners of their mouths in a satisfied yet competitively eager smile.

"Oh, my dear, I simply *must* meet this fellow everyone is talking about," cried Roger's mother, a woman in her early forties whose bloom seemed far from fading. Her dark, seasoned beauty and her vivacious grace made her as popular among the gentlemen of society as she'd been in her prime.

William, Marquess Helmsley, beamed at his comely wife with the pride of one who knew he'd chosen well. He was eight years older, but she managed to keep him young at heart and interested in her. "I shall introduce you, then. I met him at White's just the other day. A charming enough chap. Although very quiet, what, and peers at a fellow with the most intense look I've ever seen. Listening, I suppose, but demmed unsettling at times. A gentleman should know when to look and when to discreetly look away. That's what I say."

"Now, William," scolded his wife gently, "don't go stodgy on me at this late date. My, but he's a robust swain, isn't he? Do fetch him over, dear. I want to be the first at the ball to meet the illustrious Lord Whitney. I am, after all, the mother of the groom tomorrow. I should be afforded special privileges, don't you agree?"

The marquess raised a properly gloved hand and beckoned to the newcomer with a slight crook of his middle fingers. Catching the gesture, Lord Whitney gave a short bow and began to descend the stairs toward them.

Katharine Helmsley giggled and squeezed Mylene's arm. "Isn't this fun?" she whispered with the girlish enthusiasm that had endeared her to Mylene at once. The Helmsley family as a whole was a merry lot, enjoying life as if it were a banquet to be feasted upon at will. Mylene envied them their easy hearts.

"He's coming at once," said the marquess. "I daresay, my dear Kate, that he can't resist the most beautiful woman in the room."

The marchioness flushed and said, "Oh, William." But as the dark visage of Lord Whitney approached, his gaze was firmly fixed on the pale face of the bride-to-be.

As the marquess made introductions, Johnny's eyes flicked to the marchioness's face before snapping back to Mylene. He mouthed the formalities, but it was clear to all by the intensity of his stare that his interest was absorbed by the guest of honor. His eyes raked over her, taking in the green poult de soie ball gown with its pleated underskirt of white tulle, and the garland of pink camellias that graced the neckline and the gathers of the overskirt at the sides. She wore a necklace of pink sapphires fashioned in a floral motif—the inspiration for the dress. She knew she looked pretty, like a meadow of spring flowers at sunset, but Johnny's contempt was so potent, she could almost hear his thoughts drifting with the waltz: *You're ridiculously overdressed. I liked you better the way you were.*

Noting his pointed attention, William nudged his wife and raised a brow.

"Excuse me," Mylene murmured. "I should see to the other guests."

She left them, but even as she stepped across the ballroom, she could sense Johnny stalking her like a panther closing in on its prey. She wasn't surprised when his hand gripped her arm. But she was startled by the current that sizzled through her at his touch. She'd never once experienced that surge of desire when Roger tenderly and solicitously took her hand.

With Johnny, she was always caught up in the center of some raw and furious storm. Every time he invaded the circle of privacy she'd erected around herself, he tore asunder all her carefully orchestrated plans. Now, even as she was conscious of the civility of their surroundings, of the cultivated eyes that watched their every move, the look of prideful pleading in his eyes was battering her heart.

Frantically, she cast a look about and spotted Roger across the room, deep in discourse with some lords of the realm. "Don't look at me so," she whispered sharply to Johnny. "They're watching. Do you want them all to guess?"

"To guess what?" he asked, boring the flint of his eyes into hers. "That you're in love with me? That your eyes cry it to the winds even as you prepare to take your foul vows?"

She felt damp beneath the heavy ball gown. She had to fight the impulse to dab her lacy kerchief to her brow. "No. That you aren't who you say you are. Do you want them to question how you know me so well that you look at me with ownership in your eyes, even though we met but weeks ago?"

He stepped forward and took her into his arms, swiftly hurling her into the rhythm of the waltz. His arm at her back cut off her breath. His hand on hers gripped so tightly her fingers went numb. "Do you think I care what they think?" he growled. "Do you think I'll care ever again about anything once you've committed this perfidy?"

"Yes," she spat out. "I think you'll go on serving your cause, doing what must be done, no matter what havoc it wreaks to people's lives. You'll think no more of me than of a cake in a window when you're hungry. When that hunger's satisfied by the lust for violence, you'll forget me soon enough."

He grabbed her to him so her breath left her in one forced sigh. "You've been ducking me for weeks now. A fine job you've done, too."

She flashed a confident grin. "I can hide from Shamus Flynn himself, if I want to."

"And what are you running from, then? Because you know you'll never feel for that milksop Helmsley what you feel for me? Are you so afraid of your feelings, now, that you'd flee at the sight of me to keep from facing the truth?"

"And what if I am?" she challenged with a stubborn jut of her chin.

He lowered his head, and as he spoke, his breath mingled with her own. "Don't do this, girl. We belong to each other, you and me, as surely as the stars belong to the night sky. Our souls are one. You can't destroy that, not with marriage to another man."

She was drowning in his words. He was so right. Roger had never made her feel this way. As if her heart was about to take flight from her breast. As if no arms would ever fit the curve of her body the way Johnny's did. As if she'd found the home she'd always wanted by looking into his eyes. Damn his hide, he was right in everything he said. Angrily, she squirmed in his arms, determined not to let him see his effect on her. "Don't hold me so tight, you boor. This is a dance, not a bloody wrestling match."

She saw the flicker of pain in his eyes. "Can you go through with it, then? Can you face the consequences? Because I can't."

"What consequences? Will they expose me? No, because that'll endanger their plan, whatever the plan is. And I'll vow, Johnny, whatever you think you know, it isn't the half of it. They'll spring a surprise or two on you before they're through. But I'm betting they'll do nothing about my marriage. They're bluffing to keep me in line."

"Bluffing? They're after killing you! They've told me solemnly that if you step foot on that altar tomorrow, they'll exterminate you. Bluffing, is it? You'll realize the truth of it when you feel the bullet through the back of your head."

"Then you go tell them I've written down everything I know, to be read on my death. I've named names. I've left a copy of all I've uncovered on the swells. I've told everything I know just in case. They may kill me, but they'll lose everything they've gained in the process."

He was studying her, trying to assess if *she* was bluffing now. "Named names, did you? And what of mine? Did you expose me, as well, in your poisoned paper?"

Her lashes lowered, hiding her eyes. "No," she admitted softly.

"And why is that, Mylene?"

There was something hushed and vibrant in his voice that caused her to miss a step. She looked up at him, looked into the hope suddenly blazing light through the frustration in his eyes, and cried, "Very well. You want me to say it? I love you, Johnny. I love you as I can love no other man. You were right when you said we're one. But what does that matter? I could marry you and have true love. But what else would I have? I could go along with a plan I only know pieces of, a plan that will wound and destroy a good man. But under those circumstances, how long would love last? I'd be the same orphan I always was, with not even a last name to tell the priest. And you, Johnny. You'd never understand what it would do to me to hurt Lord Stanley. It would eat away at us. It would destroy us. Because you're married to Eire, and all of us come a distant second. That's grand. It's as it should be. But don't ask me to play whore to you on the side."

"It wouldn't be like that," he cried, ignoring the curious looks of the dancers that swirled by.

"Oh, wouldn't it? Do you remember what I told you, and you alone? How I was so starved and sick and beaten down on the streets of Dublin that, even young as I was, I came that close to selling my body for a bit of bread. I went to the man, Johnny, and held out my hand. I felt him touch me. He offered up a coin. It gleamed bright in his palm, like a magic lamp. But something inside me couldn't do it. I broke free and ran. But that night, as I was crying myself to sleep, feeling the awful gnawing in my gut, I decided I had to try again. I'd have done it, Johnny, if Father Q hadn't found me that next day. I'd have been a child doxy, like so many other poor souls. That's what I remember of Ireland. And I don't ever want to go back."

He appeared stricken. "And that's what you see when you look at me, is it?"

"Yes. I love you, Johnny, there's no denying it. But when I look at you, I see that man holding out his palm with that ha'penny gleaming bright. A ha'penny for my soul, Johnny. That's what I see."

He backed away, holding her limply at arm's length. "And by marrying Helmsley?"

"I may not have true love, the way I might with you. But I'd have acceptance and comfort and stability. A home to raise my children in peace."

"And what of happiness?"

Happiness. It sounded bitter on his tongue, suddenly

elusive as she saw it for what it was. Contentment and safety with Roger, perhaps. But happiness? She didn't dare think of it. It hurt too much to realize all she was losing to serve their cause in her own way. But happiness was something the Irish couldn't afford. Pleasure was the stuff of fairies and rainbows. Food and shelter and a patch of land to call their own—those were the longings of the Irish heart. "I'd have a real family, Johnny. Don't you see?"

"Aye," he said woodenly. "I see."

"Then wish me well, Johnny. It would mean the world to me."

His bleak eyes stared at her as if he'd never seen her before. Then, reeling away, he left the ballroom as the gaze of the guests followed and the scandal of it sprang to their lips.

They descended upon Mylene en masse, eagerly asking what the brash young fellow had been about. As she struggled for an answer that would satisfy them, yet cloak the real confrontation, Mylene looked after Johnny. She'd done the right thing. But she couldn't help feeling she'd just lost her best friend. And, as he'd so painfully reminded her, the only chance at true happiness she'd ever have.

Mylene stood at the back of All Souls Church with her skirts of white lace flowing behind her, clutching the elaborate bouquet in trembling hands. She'd been determined to go through with this, to accept her decision and make a life for herself. But suddenly, looking ahead at all those English lords and ladies, she felt a sense of doom. She'd been raised by nuns and educated by a priest. What was she doing marrying in a Protestant church? And the Church of England, at that. The imagined frowns of the nuns crowded her mind, warning that this was a sacrilege in the sight of God. If she went through with it—getting married outside her church to a man she didn't love—would she ever feel truly married?

She tried to imagine the ceremony over, the reception but a memory. When, late at night, she'd lie in her new husband's arms and allow him liberties she'd allowed no other man. A shiver chilled her. She looked about. There was a presence in this church that she didn't understand. But she could feel it. It was as if spirits had come to play havoc with this wedding they knew to be a sham.

We belong to each other. . . . You can't destroy that, not with marriage to another man. . . . And what of happiness?

The music of Bach filled the church. There was a collective rustle as guests shifted, looking over their shoulders to catch sight of the bride. She lowered her veil, waited for her bridesmaids to glide up the aisle, then stepped onto the carpet that led to the altar and her husband-to-be. In an hour's time, she'd be an English countess. Mylene, the orphan, defender of the Irish cause, would join the ranks of the English aristocracy she'd grown up hating. Panic seized her. Was she out of her mind?

Faces swarmed by as if in a fog. Dumb, smiling faces that began to look the same, like some grotesque characterization. She wasn't aware of breathing. Her wedding day should be the happiest of her life. Yet, as she looked ahead and saw Roger beaming his pride, the enormity of what she was doing hit her full in the face. She was Catholic, whether her husband-to-be knew it or not. She would marry for life. Twenty, thirty . . . how many years?

She averted her gaze as she continued the long walk. Everyone was here. The Prince of Wales was even in attendance. The very cream of fashionable society. She would be their peer. They'd bow to her and call her "my lady."

She couldn't meet their faces. It seemed suddenly the most dishonest of all the things she'd done—to stand up in church and vow before God to love, honor, and cherish a man she hardly knew. Not the way she knew Johnny. . . .

Her eyes came to rest on a marble carving fronting a tomb encased in the inner wall. The carving depicted a woman dressed in flowing Grecian robes kneeling in front of a large urn. Her head lay upon the top of the urn; her arms wrapped about the urn so that one hand came round and covered her eyes in a gesture of raw grief. It struck Mylene that this picture was a perfect reflection of her soul. She saw again the pain and grief in Johnny's eyes from the night before. She was certain she'd never forget.

Finally, the long walk was at an end. Roger, smiling broadly, held out his hand. She took it, trying to disguise the tremor of her fingers. He looked back over her head and smiled. She turned and saw his parents sitting in the front row, Katharine weeping joyfully, William nearly popping his vest buttons in pride. Across the aisle, Lord Stanley sat alone, struggling with his own tears. She was grateful for his calming presence, for the reminder of why she was doing this. But the empty pew beside him was a cruel reminder of the family she'd never known. The family that couldn't be there because they had no idea where she was. But even if they knew, they wouldn't care.

But that was over. She'd have a family now. People

who cared. People who would sit on the bride's side of the church when *her* daughter married.

Hers and Roger's. Not hers and Johnny's.

She was so lost in thought that it was a moment before she realized the ceremony had begun. She heard the voice of the bishop and, glancing up at him, she felt another warning go off in her head. Was she doing the right thing? She glanced at Roger and saw the love in his eyes. But it was gentle love. Predictable love. Not the wild, turbulent passion she saw in Johnny's eyes. Not the you-belong-to-me-and-no-one-else kind of fierce possession that overwhelmed her every time Johnny's hand clutched her arm. Not the kind of love that made a woman feel weak and trembly, yet strangely empowered in the knowledge of her effect on her man. Not like Johnny at all . . .

Johnny . . .

All at once, Mylene's gaze flew back to the bishop's face. And she knew what had alerted her on first sight of him. The change was so accomplished, she might not have noticed it. The hair was dark, the features expertly altered. The bishop's robes were perfectly arranged. But her eyes fixed like magnets on the one feature he hadn't bothered to disguise: the deep devil's thumbprint in the center of his chin.

Daggett!

There wasn't time for panic. Almost the instant she recognized him, she heard a commotion and turned. High above, standing on the wooden rail of the second floor, was a figure dressed all in black, with a black hood masking his face. Before she could take a breath, he jumped into the air and landed fleetly on the floor at her side.

The ceremony came to an abrupt halt. Daggett swung the gold cross he'd been holding and landed a blow to Roger's head. Roger stumbled back, but another blow sent him crashing into a heap on the floor. As powerful arms grabbed Mylene, the best man suffered a similar fate.

Mylene struggled, but the arms that pinned her to a granite chest held her like a vise. Her bouquet fell to the floor, to be crushed by the intruder's boot. The guests were on their feet by now, and Mylene could hear their cries of protest. As Daggett fought those who had enough wits to rush him, Mylene was dragged through the back of the church, through cool dark rooms and hallways, until at last her kidnapper kicked open a door and the misty twilight spilled in like rays from the hand of God.

Her fierce struggles were in vain. She was thrown onto the back of one of the two horses that stood at the ready, only seconds before the masked man leapt up behind. The restive horse, sensing danger, began to dance in a circle as the reins were gathered up in black-gloved hands. Her attacker reined in the steed, looking impatiently back over his shoulder.

He hadn't long to wait. Seconds later, Daggett came bursting through the door, his red bishop's robes flying as he jumped onto his horse. Without a word, they took off, clattering through the streets of town, knocking pedestrians out of their path.

Along the way, Daggett divested himself of his clerical garb, tossing one piece then the other to the winds so they fell in brightly colored heaps along the road. The whole time, Mylene hurled curses at their heads, reverting to the Irish she'd grown up with in her fury and outrage at such brash duplicity. But they ignored her, urging their horses on to greater speed until the sky darkened and they came to the outskirts of town.

As soon as the horse pulled to a halt along the

London Road, Mylene turned in her saddle to see her kidnapper snatch the hood from his head. Johnny's black hair stood out, then settled in wild disarray about his head.

"You vile, despicable beast!" she cried. "How dare you snatch me like this! As if ye had the right! Do ye think Roger will sit still for this? You'll return me at once, or I swear to you, Johnny—"

Without warning, with her hardly detecting the movement, his hand came round to clamp down on her mouth, crushing it and biting off her words.

"We'd best hurry," Daggett warned. "They'll be hot on our heels."

"The plan has changed," Johnny told him, struggling with Mylene, who squirmed in an effort to beat his hand from her mouth.

Daggett grew still as he looked at Johnny in the last light before nightfall. "Changed?"

"Aye. I'll take Mylene. You report back to O'Flaherty that she's been snatched safe."

"And I'm to meet ye at the hideout after that, is it?"

Johnny hesitated just long enough to alert his old friend.

"Yer not taking her where we planned, are ye, Johnny?"

"No," Johnny said quietly.

"And why is that?"

Johnny didn't answer. He focused all his efforts on keeping Mylene still.

"It couldn't be, could it, Johnny, that ye want her for yerself? That ye want her with ye, where no one else can intrude?"

The seething anger was barely concealed in his tone. Johnny looked up and saw the stark stare of a jealous man. "And if I do?"

"Then God damn you, Johnny," Daggett snarled. "I've a mission to deliver Mylene to Keenan O'Flaherty. I'll see that mission complete, no matter what ye say."

He reached across the horses and grabbed Mylene's arm, intent on ripping her from Johnny's grasp. But before he could make the final jerk that would spring her from the saddle, Johnny took Daggett's shirt in one gloved fist and hauled him to his feet in the stirrups, so he was leaning precariously between the nervous horses. Johnny held him there with a death grip, glaring into Daggett's eyes.

"Don't make me do something I'll regret, man. You know as well as I that they'll not let this go. They'll kill her as soon as they get their hands on her. I'll not see that happen. I'll take her somewhere where no one can find her, until I have a guarantee I can trust. Until Shamus Flynn himself tells me not a hair on her head will be harmed. I mean it, Daggett. Don't try to follow me. You'll not find me."

With that dire warning, he let him go with a rough shove, so Daggett fell back into his saddle with a thud. The eyes of the two men met and clashed.

"Say what ye like, Johnny. I know well enough why yer cartin' her away. Well, have her then, and be damned."

The viciousness of his tone gave Johnny pause. As his hand loosened on her mouth, Mylene wrenched it free and swore, "He'll have me over my dead body!"

Daggett's eyes flicked to Mylene's face. She saw in them a pathetic hope and realized for the first time what Johnny already knew. That Daggett had feelings he'd kept concealed for years.

But there wasn't time to think. Johnny's hand came back to clasp her mouth and pull her once more into his arms. With a swift kick, he sent the horse flying with all speed down the road.

Straining her neck against Johnny's grip, Mylene looked back and saw the solitary figure of her old friend, a forlorn and dejected man sitting his horse like a defeated soldier on a lonely country road.

Chapter 4

They rode for hours through the dense night, traversing vast expanses of forest and countryside, over hills and deep into valleys, with the April mist chasing them along the way. Sometime during the breakneck ride, as Mylene shivered resentfully in Johnny's arms, he reached back into his heavy saddlebags and retrieved a cloak. This he wrapped around her before once again pinning her with his arm. She sank into the cloak's warmth with grudging gratitude. Only part of her quivering was caused by the chill, rainy air. Mostly, it was due to the anger seething through her veins.

She could tell from the stars that they were heading south. Clouds drifted over them, obscuring them from view as the mist dampened her face and left her blinking droplets from her lashes. But when the clouds shifted and she caught sight of the heavens, she realized Johnny was backtracking expertly, heading south, then west, using evasive maneuvers to disguise his trail while stealthily pursuing a westerly course.

The first few hours, she fought and spat curses on Johnny's head with a fury that did justice to her fiery hair. Several times, he had to rein to an abrupt halt to keep them from toppling over the horse's side. "If you don't quit that, now," he warned, "I'll throw you over me knee and whip the hide off you, like the brat you are."

"I'd like to see you try! You and a hundred Fenians couldn't whip the hide off *me*!"

"Don't tempt me, girl," he cautioned. But he rode on until the next time her struggles made it impossible for him to navigate his mount.

Healthy as she was, she wasn't strong enough to fight him. Eventually, her body wore down from the efforts of resisting his punishing grip. Physically exhausted, she resorted to using her tongue to hurt him. "You're a grand patriot, Johnny. Pulling such a stunt in view of the whole of England, with the Prince of Wales himself in attendance. You're a wanted man now by both sides. Hardly the inconspicuous impersonation you had in mind, now, was it? The Fenians will be after us. And Roger and his family will hunt you down like a rabid dog."

"You forget. They don't know who I am, now, do they?"

"And do you think they'll miss the fact that the newly arrived Lord Whitney just happens to disappear the day the fair lady is yanked from her own wedding? Not likely, I'd say."

"I've taken care of that."

"And how have you done that, might I ask?"

"No. You may not."

Every effort to discover the finer intricacies of his plan failed. He'd been trained by the same experts as she ... trained, in fact, by Shamus Flynn himself in the fine art of subterfuge. She'd have to think fast to stay on her toes with Johnny. She had no doubt she could do it. She knew his weaknesses and would use them to escape. Not that she thought he'd harm her. But he could. ...

Daggett's words came back to her. *It couldn't be, could it Johnny, that ye want her for yerself? That ye want her with ye, where no one else can intrude?* She shuddered. She didn't want to think what he could do to her once he had her safely tucked away.

Ah, but she'd escape if it took the last breath in her body. He'd not high-hand her this way and get away with it. He'd not dictate to her what she would or would not do with her own life. Who did he think he was, anyway? Oh, she'd escape, all right. You could bet the saints on that. Until then, though, she must keep him distracted, keep him from detecting the inner workings of her mind. Second nature by now, but she'd never come up against an adversary like Johnny before.

Turn her over his knee, would he? She'd like to see him try!

So skillful were his machinations through the long hours that she lost track of where they were headed. The drizzle abated after hours in the saddle, and periodically the moon began to appear beyond the edges of the clouds. Once, Mylene caught sight of a huge glowing white sphere of mystical light, suspended ghostlike in the raven sky. A full moon. The ancient religions said it was a time of the fulfillment of things, the ripening of the harvest, the blossoming of womanhood, the richness of all that had been strived for and was ready to enjoy at last. A time of feasting and celebration. Yet present, too, was an erratic vitality, a sense of untamed passions, of spirits running wild and seizing chances they might otherwise pass by. Anything could happen on the night of the full moon. *Anything*.

Hadn't Johnny snatched her from the church like bloody Genghis Khan?

Still more hours passed as they rode like phantoms on the wind. They'd come to chalky hills and valleys, and forsaken countryside as far as the eye could see. The moonlight cast eerie silvery pathways in front of the horse's hooves, as if leading them, through some supernatural power, to a destination that had been portended since the dawn of time. Leading them where they were supposed to go, even if they didn't know it yet.

Mylene grew quiet as she watched the fields, watched to see where they were being led. The vista felt haunted, isolated. Ever sensitive to clandestine forces, to the underlying influences around her, Mylene felt again the presence of spirits hiding in the shadows of the moonlit path.

And then she saw them. Monoliths of stone rising above the barren landscape to meet the moon and the stars. Looming before them and summoning them like some ancient temple of the gods.

Johnny reined to a halt, sitting the saddle as still as she, as if he, too, felt the marvel of the stones, felt that they'd been lured here by some miraculous design.

"Oh, Johnny," Mylene breathed, forgetting for a moment the conflict of their day, forgetting all but the sense of union at such a wondrous sight.

Johnny was quiet, as tranquil as the landscape stretching out before them. Educated as they were in Celtic history, they knew what this was. Stonehenge—

the "hanging stones." Reputed to be the largest of the
Druid ruins that dotted the British Isles. They'd seen
drawings in books of the large upright pillars with their
lintels lying across the tops, some of them scattered on
the ground where they'd fallen thousands of years ago.
No one knew who had built them. Few ventured this
way. Some were superstitious, believing it to be a
pagan place of worship, perhaps even a shrine to the
devil. Others had thought to use the stones for other
purposes, but they'd proved too heavy to move. So
here they sat, in the midst of the stark Salisbury plain,
abandoned, neglected, overgrown with the grasses of
centuries.

That's the story the history books told. But Johnny
and Mylene knew the history beyond history. Father
Q, imparting to them the mythic chronicles of their
land, had shared with them things the Christian
Church deemed it heresy to know. The ancient Druid
learnings, unwritten, passed down secretly through the
ages so that they would not be lost in time. These two
insurgents knew the stones had not been built by the
Druids, as common folk believed, but by the ancient
ones, the fairy folk of the lost western continents, the
deer-hunting Tribes. Ruled by the Goddess, believing
all gods and goddesses to be one, they'd fashioned great
stone temples in which to worship and to track the
journey of the heavens. The Druids, who came after,
disdained the thought of worshiping immortal gods in
temples made by human hands. They would not go
near the ring of stones, but worshiped instead in sacred
groves of trees. But those who were sensitive to the
powers of the earth could feel their magic still.

The Land of Truth, they called it . . .

Truth . . .

Johnny nudged the tired horse into a walk. They

approached slowly, one step at a time, silent as the ghostly plateau, with due reverence and respect. Soon, they stopped in the shadows of the great stones, feeling small and trifling amid the grandeur.

Johnny slid from the horse's back and stepped into the vast, ravaged circle. In a trance, Mylene followed, looking up at the giant obelisks that now surrounded and embraced her on all sides. She felt part of it all, linked with the primitive mystery of the place's pagan past. The wild grasses parted before her as she walked, her heavy wedding gown leaving a trail of flattened meadow behind. She was only vaguely conscious of the steed munching away outside the protective splendor of timeworn columns.

I've been here before, she thought. *And not alone. With a man destined to be mine from the beginning of time. . . .*

Unbidden, as if drawn by some force greater than herself, her eyes lit on Johnny, standing like a young god in the midst of unhewn stones. Johnny . . . Her heart, her soul, recognized his form, as if she'd known it many times, in many lives. Johnny had stood with her in this temple before . . . how many times in how many lifetimes? As if they'd been brought back again and again, acting out some mysterious scenario that always went awry, being pulled back yet again to give it one more try. *To get it right.* To fulfill the destiny that was portended for them, here in this most mystical of lands.

Strangely compelled, feeling drugged by the sorcery of the night, she stepped into the light of the moon. Johnny turned and saw her. His lean body tensed as if arrested by the sight, by the anticipation. He looked at her with the awe and wonder of one gazing upon a goddess. But there was something more. A look of longing so intense that it caused her palms to sweat. *He feels it, too*, she realized. *That we've been here before.* And on the heels of his desire came the hard glare of resolution, as if deciding the time had come to claim her for his own.

Shaking herself from her trance, she took a step back, out of the moonlight that had bathed her in its brilliance. She saw a flicker of contempt spark like green fire in his eyes. *Do you think that will stop me?* he seemed to say.

Aloud, he said only, "We'll spend the night here." For all the command of his tone, his voice sounded oddly hushed. As if it had taken on the quality of the breeze, of the moon, of the magic and mystery that was a part of this hallowed land.

Mylene backed up once again—from his despotic announcement with its unspoken threat—nearly tripping over the knee-high grass and the bulk of her train. Abruptly, she felt the impact of a solid wall at her back. She glanced up to see one of the boulders looming above. Blocking her way. A symbol of her captivity. An impediment to escape.

He left to dig in the saddlebags as she leaned back, her hands flat against the cold, smooth stone. Her breath was erratic, coming hard and fast, so that she had to gasp for air. *I'll not let him do this*, she vowed, resisting the feeling of destiny and the drowsy compulsion to follow where it led. *I'll fight him with all my heart and soul. He'll not take me like some trophy of war.*

He was in front of her suddenly. He'd come so quietly, she hadn't heard his footfalls in the silent night. But then, her pulse was pounding so loudly in her ears, she wondered if she'd hear a cannon blast.

He was holding something looped in his fists. "Give me your hands," he said softly.

Then she knew what it was. A rope. To keep her tethered to his side.

She lunged at him, shoving him with her shoulder in her attempt to break past. But he grabbed her roughly, fighting her struggles with a strength that was both brutal and paralyzing, numbing her arms. He yanked her around so her back was to him and, pinning her arms together with one hand, began to coil the rope about her wrists. She fought like a heathen, kicking back beneath her cumbersome skirts, desperately scrambling to repulse his fiendish task until she collapsed with an outraged cry.

"You brute!" Her voice echoed off the cavity of stones. "You beast. You bloody bastard from hell. I'll hate you, Johnny, till the day I die!"

He lifted her by the cord that now bound her trembling arms. Turning her, he put hands on her shoulders and looked deeply in her eyes. "No, you won't," he told her.

He sounded so certain, her rage exploded like an inferno in her chest. She tried again to run, but he'd left the rope dangling and a swift jerk brought her back to collide against him. He looked wild and savage, as much a pagan as those who'd come here to worship centuries before. His black hair tumbled across his forehead. His eyes glinted strangely, seeming to unmask her soul, to strip bare all her reproaches and set to flame her laments. He was glaring at her with a mad, sardonic pleasure she'd never before seen in his eyes. With unbridled conviction that all he desired was now his for the taking . . . her protests be damned.

The rope cut into her wrists, chafing them whenever she moved. She glanced back over her shoulder at the horse eating a path across the nearby plain. She could still ride. She'd hold the reins in her teeth if she had to. She'd leave Johnny here, miles from nowhere, to suffer the same frustration he was causing her. If she could only reach that blessed horse . . .

She turned back to him and saw the knowledge of her plan in his eyes. He stepped closer, so she stumbled back against the pillar, then closer still so his hard body pinned her like a prison. "You'll not escape me," he vowed.

"Oh, won't I, now?"

"No, Mylene," he said softly. "You won't."

A sinister pitch underscored the effortless assertion.

"This is my wedding day," she breathed over the lump in her throat.

"*Was* your wedding day. The twenty-second of April is no longer the date of your marriage. It's the day when you come to understand, for once and for all, where you belong."

"You're taking what isn't yours to take."

"Taking from the English what wasn't theirs in the first place. What they've stolen, like they stole everything else that was ours."

"Is that what this is about?" she cried. "Some misguided blow for Ireland?"

He leaned over so the muscles in his chest flattened her breasts beneath her gown. In the growl of a feral beast, he said, "Do you think I'd let another man have you? Any man? You're mine, Mylene. You were mine since the day Father Q brought you to St. Columba. You'll be mine until the day you die."

"You're wrong, Johnny. I belong to Roger now."

A flare of contempt and challenge sparked in his eyes. "Do you, now? We'll see if he wants you after I'm through with you."

She knew he meant it. Desperately, she cast about

for some argument that would turn the tide. "This isn't you talking. You don't want to hurt me."

"Hurting you is the last thing on my mind. But tell me, then. Is it an Englishman you want? Polite caresses?" He touched her cheek as gently as a feather's swoop. "Tepid kisses?" He leaned over and pecked her lips coolly with his own. "Or is it a wild Irishman you really long for in yer bed?" His hands came up to cup her head, to push it back so she was looking up at him, before his mouth crashed down on hers. She felt an alarming jolt that left her weak in his arms as he conquered her body with a forceful embrace.

"An Irishman," he added, his lips moving against hers, "who'd give his life to set you free?"

"You call this free?"

"Aye, girl. Free to love as you were born to love. Free to be the woman you are, not the one you pretend to be. Free to enjoy the fruits of true and lasting devotion, without the foul imprisonment of marriage to a man you'll never love or know."

He kissed her again. A hot, searing kiss that stole her breath as he was trying to steal her soul. She had to fight to push him off—fight because his possession of her was so overpowering; fight because her traitorous body had begun to sing its own song at his assault.

Wresting her mouth free, she gasped, "You're not vile or despicable enough to rape another man's bride."

His lips, still tasting her own, curled at the foul word. But he captured her gaze and said with quiet resolution, "I'm vile and despicable enough to take back what's rightfully mine. All that remains of that farce of a wedding is this ridiculous rag."

He eyed the lace of the wedding gown that dipped into a squared scoop above her breasts. And as he did, she knew that he would rip it away. And with it, all the safety and propriety of her carefully structured life.

His hand moved to her throat. She thought, in one mad moment, that he'd choke her. But the hand went to her collarbone, where it turned. With the back of his knuckles, he stroked the satin skin, idly exploring, marveling at its softness. One finger drifted lower. She could hardly catch her breath. Yet as she watched, entranced, it seemed that her breath followed the trail of his finger, dancing in fluttering spirals as he caressed the yielding cleavage above her gown.

"How," she breathed, "can you defile me so?"

When he spoke, it was with a voice she'd never heard. Gone was the accent of the Irish rebel. Instead he spoke in a voice as timeless as the wind, as if he'd assumed, in the magic of the night, the sum total of all the lifetimes they'd shared.

"You think I defile you. You suppose that I seek what I have no right to take. That I lust for you so that I would take you like a wild thing, against your will. And so I shall, if you give me cause. Because I've waited too long. But I have no need of force where you're concerned. You know as well as I that this night was ordained, as the stars in the heavens plan all things. You know that we've stood here before, you and I, here in the Land of Truth, where none can hide their faces from the gods. You've turned me away before. You know it—I can see it in your eyes. I can feel it in the beat of your heart. But we were brought here to fulfill a promise made long before our time. I don't know how I know. Some sorcery, perhaps. But we've stood here as man and woman, on the brink of giving ourselves to one another, as only we belong. I had no thought to bring you here. I know not how it came to be. But here we are, to do what must be done—what's been called of us since time eternal. You feel it, I know, as you feel all things. Because you're a fairy at heart. It's why you can wrest from men the secrets of their souls. You cast a spell on them and they're yours. But I tell you now, that spell was meant for me."

"I know nothing of the sort," she said in protest, though her voice sounded flimsy and unconvincing to her ears.

He took her hair in his hand and pulled back her head, pinning her fast. Then, leaning, he licked first one cheek, then the other, with his tongue. It was a primal, savage gesture, blatantly possessive, as if marking territory in some primitive rite. His hair brushed her bare shoulder and she shivered.

"Don't you?" he asked, his tongue claiming her face. "Then know this. I love you as I've loved nothing and no one on this earth. You think I want to possess you, and so I do. You think I hunger for the taste of your flesh, and you'd be right. But I want more of you than that. I want your soul joined with mine. You're the other half of me, Mylene. Without you, I'm not complete. I've tried, God knows. I've tried to forget you in the arms of other women, more comely and more willing than you."

She felt a surge of some unaccustomed feeling, and recognized it, with a sense of shock, as jealousy. Images of other women flashed through her mind. Kissing Johnny . . . touching him with soft, inviting hands. Touching the body she'd never known. Her Johnny . . . *hers*!

"But never," he continued, "could I dislodge you from my mind. You were always there, in my thoughts, in my dreams. Every woman I kissed had your face. Every strand of hair I touched was yours. Every caress, every gift of pleasure I sought to impart, was given to you."

"Stop!" she cried, because she could bear it no longer.

He straightened and looked her in the eyes. "I stole you like a Viking filching a bride because they would harm you if you went through with such a farce. But this was no part of their plan. If they had never objected, if they'd rejoiced at the news, I'd have stolen you still. Not for you, the suffering I endured. Not for you, to endure the embraces of another man, wishing all the while it was me in your bed. I'd have killed to have you with me. That, and more."

She was weakening. Dear God, she could feel the walls crumbling inside. He loved her . . . he wanted her for herself alone. He'd defied even Ireland and his sacred cause to have her at his side. The spell of his words, his unearthly voice, was melting her. Her breasts, of their own accord, were thrusting against his hand, seeking the pressure he withheld with his leisurely touch.

"They don't know what we know. That we're part of each other. That our blood, our breath, are one. Do you think it was an accident that Father Q found you that day? The day you'd made the choice to give yourself so cheaply to one who didn't have the right? Try as they might, no man can come between us. Because the bond we share is beyond space and time. You belong to me, Mylene, and me alone. And come what may, I'll have you for my own."

His hand moved up to tilt her chin, so she was forced to look into his eyes. "Say you love me," he commanded.

With the last of her resolve, she sought to jerk her chin away. But he jerked her back to recapture her gaze. "Say it."

He was too powerful to refuse. Her heart, beating wildly, burst with all the stifled love and longing she'd felt for him in the secret shadows no one else could share. She parted her lips to speak, but the words of protest caught in her throat.

Silently, he mouthed the words. *Say it!*

And when she did, it came out in a strangled gasp. "I love you," she cried. "I love you, Johnny. God help me, I do."

In a swift motion that startled her, he clasped both hands on the neckline of her gown. He yanked the lace away with a rending tear and she felt her breasts fall free. Just as she was now free of the memory of that other man, standing at the altar with a look of shocked realization in his eyes. Free of his brand, which she'd so nearly worn in the form of a band of gold, and of any claim he might have had. Free to be captured in her lover's rough palms before he buried his face in the pliant mounds of flesh.

She felt his mouth at her nipple, warming where the cool breeze had briefly sighed. And she felt the last traces of rational thought dissolve in a mist of love and longing such as she'd never known. She felt herself become one with his warm and roving tongue, felt her soul meld with his in a union more blissful for the frustrated passion of years gone by. Gone was any trace of fear. She forgot that she was a virgin, untouched by any man. Beneath his delectable mouth, she felt the opening of herself, the woman in her blossoming like a flower in the sun. She felt sweet and tranquil, as if this was, indeed, just where she belonged, yet wildly alive, as if she'd never lived before.

She was only vaguely aware of his moving hands, shoving aside the yards of lace that shrouded her from his view. And then she felt the sleeves catch on her bound arms. She'd forgotten the ropes, too, in the spell he wove. As he ripped the sleeves from her trembling arms, she whispered, "Free my hands, Johnny. I want to touch you so." But his mouth closed on hers, rending her speechless in the exquisite agony of his kiss.

She was floating with desire. She wanted to run her hands through his flowing black hair. But when she tried, the ropes cut her wrists, reminding her that she was helpless to his desire. That she couldn't move as she willed heightened her sensitivity to his touch. Every attempt to break free made her feel small and powerless, more helpless than she'd ever felt. Made his mouth all the sweeter because she couldn't guide it where she willed.

Naked now, she felt herself hauled up into powerful arms. Carried easily to be laid on the long grass. He stood above her, shedding his clothes, and she caught flashes of his body in the moonlight, the hard, tempered body of a deity. And then he was on her, as naked as she, his flesh taut against her softly yielding skin. His mouth moved over her, caressing her, tasting her, in shocking, secret places. She was completely at his mercy, yet strangely, as he feasted on her with the appreciation of a starving man, with moans of pleasure low and guttural in his throat, she felt exhilarated by the female power she felt rising in her blood. She'd made him want her so much that he'd risk everything to have her. Even his own soul.

She was drowning in delight. The moonlight shifted and fell upon them, lighting them with its sterling glow. She was all feeling, all woman, giving herself now with all the impassioned emotions she'd bottled up inside. She felt a swirl of her senses that was sweeter than any wine. She was making sounds that seemed to come from someone else, small gasps and cries that mingled with the slurping of his tongue. And just when she felt the pleasure was so intense that there could be no more, she felt herself spinning out of control. The shock of it made her gasp, made her struggle against her bonds, made her thrust herself upon him as wave after wave of intoxicated bliss sent her beyond herself, to become a part of all that was.

He fell atop her again, scorching, heavy, his limbs and sinews damp with sweat. He kissed her with so much love that she was immersed in delight. And, his breath but a whisper in her ear, he rasped, "Mylene, my beloved. You're mine now. You belong to me, body and soul."

And he plunged inside her so that all the delicious melting seized up in an agonized cry that echoed through the otherworldly night. His mouth covered hers, taking her breath and her cry. He lay still upon her, kissing her tenderly, her cheeks, her temples, her mouth, caressing her hair with gentle hands until at last he felt warm and welcome inside. And he began to move, slowly at first, so she could feel him large and hard within, gentling her until her hips began to rise to his thrusts with a will and instinct as old as the land. Only then, when he was sure of her acquiescence, did he take her as he'd always wanted, when the pain was but a memory and her sighs were hot in his mouth. Beneath the great stone pillars that stood like sentinels in the night.

And through it all, she felt the resurgence of pleasure and mad desire, of love and longing so deep they seemed to fill a void inside. She felt herself elevated to more than a mere woman, felt the breath of the goddess sigh over her. She felt that she, too, was a goddess, melding at last with the god of her dreams. That she'd lost herself, then found herself once again, renewed, reborn, as their very souls swirled and twined and became one.

And then the stars and the moon that had bathed them in their luminous glow seemed to live within her, as if she and Johnny had become part of the night sky, sparking a joy she couldn't long endure. Was it possible, she wondered, to feel so close to another human being? To feel so much a part of him that you didn't know where you began or ended?

Johnny waited, pacing himself, until her head began to spin and she was crying his name into his mouth. And then he took her, and himself, to a world of his own making, a world where nothing mattered but the wondrous union that had made them whole.

Chapter 5

Mylene awoke to the sun rising between the vast stone obelisks, shining in her eyes. She became aware of the chill of the morning and of something warm enclosing her in its embrace. Johnny's arms. They were wrapped around her like a protective cage, lending his heat to the cool of the dewy grass beneath her skin.

Then, with slowly dawning consciousness, she realized she lay naked in his arms, as naked as he. They'd slept like this, children of the universe, beneath the stars, wrapped together through the short hours until dawn.

She pushed herself up to look at him, sleeping peacefully beside her. And as she did, she realized that her hands were free of the rope. She didn't remember him untying her. Perhaps he'd waited until she slept. Now, unbidden, her hand went to his shaggy hair, running gentle fingers through the silky locks as she'd so longed to do the night before. Such luxury, to caress him freely, with no restraint.

She didn't feel him move. But when she glanced at his face, she saw eyes of brilliant green gazing tranquilly upon her face. He smiled, the smile of the boy she'd known in Ireland, a self-satisfied grin that tugged the corners of her mouth into an answering beam. She felt immersed in his eyes for a moment, as if they were a verdant meadow she'd wandered into, losing her way. He reached up to cup the back of her head in one hand, then pulled her down so the copper curtain of her hair covered them like a veil. Then he kissed her madly, drowning in her mouth the way she'd become engulfed in the drowsy languor of his eyes.

" 'Tis a sight I've hungered for these many years," he said, rolling her back so his body came atop her, crushing her with its weight. "To wake up to your face smiling down upon me." He kissed her again, and she felt him stir against her thigh. She blushed, remembering the night before—the closeness, the passion, the bliss.

"I'm a sorry sight, no doubt, after the trials of the night."

"Nay," he denied with a shake of his head. "Yer a rare sight, indeed."

He looked up at the world around them, fresh with dew and bathed in sunny splendor. "Ah, but 'tis as if the world was new," he said, sitting up slowly as she followed his gaze with her own. The chill lent the morning a bracing aura of rebirth. Sunlight glinted off the stone temple. They were atop a hill, encompassed by fields of long, golden grass swaying lazily in the early breeze. It was as if this world was untouched by the ravages of man and that she had been born again—

baptized in a night of fire and the sweet mercy of delight.

Conscious thought seemed too paltry for such a morning. It was a time to feel, to breathe deeply of the crisp air, to feel the breeze on her face and in the curves and hollows of her body. Her nakedness, rather than shaming her, made her feel playful, free. She had an impulse to run through the tall grass in her bare feet, like the fairy he'd called her.

She jumped to her feet and, laughing, scampered away. She heard him call after her, asking where she was bound, and she tossed back gaily, "To the river." From the top of the tor, she'd seen the river beckoning some two miles distant, curving through the hills like a serpent. Wild with joy, she ran like the wind, laughing for no reason but that she was gloriously in love, so filled with love that she could hardly contain it.

Everything would be all right now. It would be so much more than all right!

She felt him come up behind her, felt his strong arms scoop up her body so he was swinging her round and round in great circles that left her dizzy and breathless, and gasping for air between her laughter and her squeals of delight. She felt a girl again, running the Wicklow hills with Johnny, playing knights and fair maidens as he rescued her from the dreaded dragons of the underworld.

"My hero!" she cried, as she'd done so often in the past.

His eyes filled with memory, as if she'd sparked something he'd long put from his mind. Then, grinning, he hugged her close before throwing her over his shoulder, as he'd done a hundred times, and racing for the river. Once there, he splashed into the water at a dead run. Before she could warn him not to dare, he plunged in with her in his arms.

The frigid shock of it strangled a scream in her throat. But then they were tumbling, one over the other, through the icy water, tussling like urchins, each bent on dunking the other before being dunked. They came up from beneath the water laughing, wiping water from their eyes. And then their eyes locked, and in that look was an awareness that they were children no longer. They were man and woman. And they'd pledged themselves to one another just the night before.

Without a word, they stepped closer and fell into a passionate embrace. He kissed her as he carried her again, this time to the bank of the river, to lay her in the grass. To taste of her with more leisure than the night before. To hold her to him as if he couldn't bear to let her go. To plunge inside and love her as surely no woman had ever been loved.

They lay spent in each other's arms, becoming aware, slowly, of the cold of their shivering limbs. The horse had followed them, of its own volition, down the hill, and was drinking deeply of the fresh river water. Johnny kissed Mylene's temple, then hoisted himself to his feet, striding toward the horse and fishing about in the saddlebags. As he came back, she could see he had clothes clutched in one hand. But she had no eyes for such practicalities. She was looking at him, at the nakedness of his manly body as he strode her way. He wasn't bulky or conspicuous in his strength. Rather, he sported the sleek form she preferred, lean yet rugged, scarred from countless battles on the sinister streets of Dublin. She watched him approach with a pride that caused her heart to swell. The well-defined shoulders, the sinewy chest above a narrow waist. The stalwart arms, sleekly defined yet hard as iron, so the biceps coiled as he moved. Veined forearms, contouring like marble to powerful wrists. Tough, lanky legs with the wet dark hair plastered flat against his thighs in a way that caused a ripple of lust to flutter through her. And finally, bidding her eyes to look as she never had before, the symbol of his manhood, half erect even now. It looked commanding to her wondrous eyes, richly veined and full of a character all its own. As if all the somnolent power of his body were nothing more than a frame for this magnificent column—the real symbol of the man.

He caught her feasting on the sight of him and grinned, tossing her a dress. It was dark blue and plain. When she slipped into it, she found it was too long, yet the bodice was tight, crushing her breasts.

"My, but it's grand to have you once again where you belong. You've but to make me a promise, and it's back to London for us."

She looked up from the ill-fitting gown. "Promise?"

"Aye. A promise is sacred between us, is it not? I'd not disavow any pledge I made to you, nor you to me."

She stood with her hands still tugging at her neckline, trying to accommodate her breasts. "What promise would that be, then, love?"

"Why, that you'll make the announcement as soon as we return."

She went completely still. "Announcement?"

Patiently, as if speaking to a child, he spelled it out as he donned his riding clothes. "You'll return to Lord Stanley and say you escaped your captor's hands. Say you've changed your mind about the marriage. Then we'll find a way to make the announcement."

"*What* announcement?"

"About Lord Stanley. What else?"

It was as if the sun had slipped behind the moon, leaving the world eclipsed in darkness. "But I've told you, I can't do that."

She saw the flicker of surprise as he glanced up at her. Then she knew. She'd assumed, without conscious thought, that he would abandon his insistence on the Fenian plan. But he'd done something similar. He'd assumed that because she'd made love to him she'd forget all her plans—her principles—and concede to the awful scheme.

"Is that why you seduced me with tender words and loving hands?" she asked, her words so quiet they seemed to disappear in the breeze. "Why you greeted the new day with a smile on your face? Not for the love we shared. But because you supposed, in your arrogance, that once you'd bedded me I'd be so besotted I couldn't turn you down? So that's it, is it? Last night wasn't about wanting me for myself. You thought to bribe me to your will."

He was watching her with intent eyes. "I told you what last night was about. But I've a mission nevertheless. You're part of that mission. You made a pledge you're called to honor now. If it's difficult, so be it. Nothing comes easily in war."

"*Difficult?*" Memories from her childhood flowed through her. Lord Stanley taking the seasoned sixteen-year-old to her first county fair, where she'd stuffed herself on spun sugar like a brat of four. Lord Stanley beaming as he presented her a fine, blooded mare, chuckling tenderly as she threw her arms around him in delight. Lord Stanley hearing her weeping from the hall that first night, when she'd missed Johnny and Daggett so—coming into her room and sitting awkwardly on the bed, taking her hand in his and saying timidly, "Please don't cry, my dear. I hope you shall be my daughter now. We need neither of us be lonely again, so long as we have one another."

Lord Stanley ... the man who'd cherished her better than any father could ... the man they wanted her to destroy.

"Difficult?" she repeated with more fire. "It's abominable! What if someone turned *us* in as spies? How can I possibly do it? How can you ask it of me?"

"You don't know what you're saying," he said softly.

"I know my own mind perfectly well."

"Whose mind? The girl who vowed to sacrifice what she must so that the children of her country—the children she'd have died for at one time—might grow strong and free? Or the woman who's become bewitched by her enemies?"

"Bewitched!" she cried.

He stepped to her and took her chin in a gentle hand. "Aye, Mylene. Bewitched. They've turned yer brain soft. I blame you not, girl. It's not uncommon to become bewitched by yer circumstances. People often are. Many times they come to sympathize with the views of their kidnappers."

"*You're* my kidnapper," she snarled.

He just grinned. An insolent grin that spoke of no regrets.

"You arrogant oaf! Do you think to barter my soul by playing patty-fingers with the likes of me?"

"More than patty-fingers, as I recall."

Her face flushed hot and red. Damn him and his ruddy male confidence! Damn his betraying hide!

She became aware of the sticky residue of his seed on her inner thighs. In a rage, she flung the blue skirts up over her waist and charged into the river, washing herself so forcefully she splashed the dress. "I'm sorry for you, then. You've wasted your precious time."

"Time I have," he said, unconcerned, falling back onto the grass and lounging on one elbow as he watched her with mild amusement. Sticking a long piece of golden grass into his mouth, he continued steadily. "If you'll not concede, I'll keep you with me until you do. It will be no hardship, believe me. And just as you were bewitched by the influence of your grand English friends, so will you succumb to mine."

"You think so, do you?" she asked, stepping from the river and flinging the bulk of her wet skirts to the ground.

"I know so. The longer yer kept from Londontown, the more you'll come to see the right of things. You'll forget yer foolishness and remember why you pledged yourself in the first place. If I have to remind you of every child you ever nursed through fever, every babe who died in yer arms, I'll see to it that you do."

"That's vile, Johnny. But I don't care what you say. You'll not convince me to betray a man I revere. Not with a million stories or a million memories bent to tug at my heart. And you know why, Johnny? It's something the likes of you don't understand. Because if once I soil my hands with your foul designs, what hope is there for me? For my heart? For my soul? What hope of heaven, Johnny?"

He pitched the grass from his teeth and stood in a single lunge. "What hope of heaven while Ireland yet rots beneath her yoke? While the children you professed to love eat grass while you dine on pheasant and tarts?"

His voice throbbed with anger, but it only enraged her still more. "I tell you I've not abandoned your cause. I tell you there must be another way. But you won't listen, you Fenians, who are so bent on violence you can taste the blood in your mouths. I won't have it, I tell you. I'll find another way to help bring peace to Ireland. And when I do, you'll bloody well thank me for my vision. *If* you're not all dead."

So impassioned was her speech that he looked at her as if he'd never seen her before. Finally, as she stood seething before him, he dropped his shoulders and said easily again, "Then it's off to Bristol."

"Why Bristol?"

"Because it's but a ferry's ride from Cardiff."

She knew then what he had in mind. Cardiff, across the Severn in Wales, was a stronghold of Irish sympathizers. He meant to hold her there, among the Fenians, until she relented at last. It sent a chill up her spine. With Johnny, she had weapons she could use. She didn't doubt he loved her, however misguided his love might be. He would be kind. But what of the Fenians, who had no such sentimental attachment? They would do what they must to see to it that she didn't betray their well-laid plans. They had methods of persuasion that could turn the stoutest of men to jelly in their hands.

But Johnny had said the Fenians wanted her dead. He'd told Daggett he wouldn't let them near her. Not until Shamus Flynn himself gave his word. . . .

She froze. It was as if everything in her ground to a halt as she stared into Johnny's eyes. "And what's in Cardiff, then?" she asked cautiously, dreading the reply.

"Shamus Flynn."

Her blood turned to ice in her veins. Defying Johnny was one thing. Defying the faceless Fenians . . . but Shamus Flynn! It was like facing Christ himself on Judgment Day. She couldn't let it happen. Once in Wales, she'd be lost. All her strength and determination couldn't stand against the wrath of Shamus Flynn.

She had to bluff. Make him think she didn't care. If he knew how terrified she was at the prospect, he'd have a weapon he could wield like a cleaver.

She gave a short, derisive laugh. "You think I fear Shamus Flynn when my soul is at stake? And what have you planned should Shamus fail to move me, as he surely will?"

He dropped his gaze. She thought she saw shame tinge his face. "Then it's off to Ireland and Father Q."

It was the lowest blow of all. Even if she could stare down Shamus Flynn's dark persuasions, she knew—and Johnny knew—it was nothing compared to the shame of having to face Father Q with what she'd done. She felt a moment of panic and doubt. If Father Q sanctioned the Fenians' plan, could it be wrong? Was *she* wrong? Was the ruin of Lord Stanley such a high price to pay for the sake of thousands of lives?

She thought of the children of St. Columba, red-haired and ruddy-cheeked, smiling up at her with the faith of the innocent shining in their eyes. Counting on her to see to it they were fed and warm. How could she face them? How could she possibly explain to hungry children that there were other things in this world as important as their hope of a brighter future? Things like honor. Repaying kindness with kindness. Not betraying those who've trusted you.

But hadn't the Fenians trusted her? Hadn't Father Q bragged that she'd do them all proud?

No, this was just what Johnny was aiming for. To plant doubts in her mind. To confuse her so she couldn't think.

"Even you couldn't be so low as that."

There was no use pretending. He knew it would kill her to have to face Father Q.

He hadn't moved. He just stood there looking at

her. But there was a flicker of determination in his eyes. "I've told you, girl. I'll do what I must."

It all came back to her. What she'd seen that morning at the old Tyburn Hill. The hard resolve, the dispassion the Fenians had bred into Johnny for their cause. She understood it now, as she never had. He would stop at nothing. Even if he had to destroy her, use her.

Fool! she cried to herself. *Fool to believe his pretty speeches and fall like some wanton into his arms. Fool to believe I could touch his stone heart and find again the lad I knew and loved.*

She remembered that long-ago day in Dublin when she'd come from the deathbed of the O'Brien child. *At least they have a family,* she'd lamented. And Johnny, grabbing her fiercely, forcing her to look in his eyes. *We're your family!*

Had he forgotten all that? Did he care so much for an ideal that he could coldly trick her this way? Seduce her, so she thought he loved and wanted her, as a means of gaining his own objective? Then to toss her aside, to Shamus Flynn or to Father Q. To the wolves, for that matter. How could he do this? This man who claimed to love her, how could he use her this way?

The bitterness of it choked her so she couldn't speak. She felt tears of frustration prick her eyes, and she turned angrily away.

"I can't allow that," she said at last, when she'd mastered her voice. "You'll have to kill me to get me to Cardiff, let alone Ireland."

"I think not. I think you'll come of your own free will."

"And what makes you think so?" she asked dispiritedly, not even bothering to summon a show of temper.

He came up behind her and put his hands on her shoulders. "Because I know you."

She flinched away from his touch, turning on him. "If you think I'll allow this travesty, you don't know me as well as you claim."

"We'll see about that. In the meantime, since you're so unwilling, you'll remain my prisoner. I'd hoped it wouldn't be necessary, but you give me no choice."

He went to the saddlebags and retrieved the rope he'd used to tie her hands the night before.

She backed away, her wrists still chafed. "No, Johnny. You'll have no need of those. I'll go."

He gave her a stern look. "Can you promise me you'll try no escape? Remember before you speak, girl. A pledge between us is sacred. Think well before you vow to me what you can't give."

Angry and betrayed as she felt, she couldn't bring herself to lie to him. *Fool*, she cried again, and held out her hands.

"Ah, then," he said, beginning to wrap the rope. "My dearest girl. It pains me to treat you so. But mark me well. I'll do what must be done."

She looked up bitterly into his eyes. "If I didn't know that yesterday, I know it now."

His gaze held a flicker of pain. But she knew he'd follow the dictates of his heart, come what may.

But so, by God, would she.

Chapter 6

Salisbury. The walled medieval city that had grown up at the junction of the Avon and Wiley Rivers. An early Iron Age fort seized by the Romans and later by the Saxons, the cultural and religious seat of the Salisbury plains. It still bore the name New Sarum from the old days. The Normans had built the castle on the hill, and later the cathedral—with the largest spire in all of England—had been built and rebuilt in the valley below. The city was laid out in gridiron fashion, with many of the ancient buildings still standing. It was old and seasoned and teeming with life after the vast, chalky plains.

And it was one step closer to Shamus Flynn.

They arrived when the sun was high in the sky. Mylene had used the journey to formulate a plan of escape. It wasn't easy. She had no idea exactly what Johnny had in mind. But she knew him well, had spent hours with him in Dublin formulating daring plans that might reap some sustenance for the orphanage. She tried to think ahead, to plan contingencies based on what she guessed he might do. He planned to board the afternoon train for Bristol—and she had no intention of being at his side.

Sensing her designs, Johnny kept her hands bound, throwing his cloak over her to hide the evidence of her imprisonment. They walked the horse over the stone streets, Johnny alert and cautious at her back. The markets were in full swing, vendors holding forth their fruits and vegetables, fabrics and yarns, ribbons and silks, needles and threads, pots, cutlery, all manner of wares to be inspected by women with baskets on their arms. Children played in the streets as their mothers shopped, hitting rocks with sticks, pitching marbles against stone walls, kicking balls and squealing when one team scored a winning point. A number of clergymen ambled through the throng, pausing to pass the time of day with mothers who struggled to keep their youngsters underfoot. The blacksmith halted in the act of hammering a shoe, wiping his brow on his sleeve and calling a greeting to a friend passing by.

It was a normal spring day. But Salisbury was an isolated city, linked to others primarily by rail. As the two strangers rode into town on their weary horse, people suspended their activities and turned to stare.

And then Mylene heard Johnny swear beneath his breath. A small boy, carrying a stack of newspapers in his hands, was crying out the headline written on the page:

"BRIDE ABDUCTED AT ALTAR.
SOCIETY IN DISARRAY.

PRINCE VOWS MYSTERIOUS CULPRIT WILL BE
BROUGHT TO JUSTICE AT ALL HASTE."

His singsong voice carried all around the square.

And there, on the front page, was a fair enough likeness of Mylene that any of these spectators could recognize her and sound an alarm.

Johnny clutched her head and bent it low over the saddle. "Keep yer head down," he growled. "If you let anyone see . . ."

He left the threat hanging. But as he reined in and paid the boy for the paper, she surreptitiously turned her face. The boy looked up at her. A leap of hope sent her heart racing. But he just smiled and thanked Johnny for the coin, moving on to continue his cry:

"BRIDE ABDUCTED AT ALTAR.
SOCIETY IN DISARRAY. . . ."

As Johnny yanked the horse around, Mylene felt her hope die in embers. The boy sold the papers but hadn't bothered to look at the picture that could have saved her from her fate. As they trotted out of town, she mourned the loss of such an opportunity and silently cursed the sorry lad.

Outside the city walls, Johnny kicked the horse into a gallop and headed out across the valley. When they came to a small clump of trees, he halted abruptly and sat still, scanning the article in the paper he still clutched in his hand.

"They're searching all trains," he said distantly, as if speaking to himself. "The prince has vowed to capture the culprit with all speed. Your *intended* is threatening every barbarous form of punishment such as only an English dog can devise. Sputtering fool. We'll have to be more careful. I hadn't expected the news to travel so fast." He read on to himself, then mouthed the phrase "copper-haired beauty" and let it die.

"What did you expect? That Roger, with all his influence, would sit about nursing his wounded pride? I know him. He'll turn this country upside down until he finds me."

Disgustedly, Johnny tossed the paper and slid off the horse's back.

"Get down," he ordered, all efficiency now. As she dismounted awkwardly with her tied hands, he fished in the saddlebags and drew out what she recognized as the clothes of a boy. So he'd come prepared. It wasn't surprising. On many outings in Dublin, they'd dressed Mylene as a boy to avoid undue suspicion. Johnny withdrew a slouch hat, then untied her wrists with swift tugs. "Get out of that dress."

She would have argued, but she sensed her chance was upon her. He couldn't keep her hands tied when they went to board the train. She must do as he said, lulling him into a false sense of security, keeping her eyes open for the perfect opportunity.

She shrugged the dress off so it fell to the ground at her feet. Since he hadn't thought to bring underclothes, she was naked underneath. His eyes narrowed as he inspected her, and she felt the heat spark in her loins. Flushing, she denounced herself for a fool. But he was looking at her body only as it pertained to his plan. Then he picked up the discarded dress and, with a savage tug, ripped a long strip from the bottom.

He grabbed her shoulder and wheeled her around so her back was to him. "You weren't so voluptuous when we did this last," he muttered. He reached around her and covered her breasts with the strip of cloth, tying it behind so it flattened her breasts.

She squirmed in discomfort, but when he bade her, she quickly donned the worn lad's clothes. He came toward her with the hat, handing it forth.

"Now. You can tuck yer hair under this cap, or I can cut it off. The choice is yours."

Seething at his supercilious tone, she took the hat and stuffed the copper locks underneath. He made some adjustments with dispassionate fingers, gathering stray strands and hiding them beneath the hat so none would show.

That done, they mounted again and retraced their steps toward town. Just on the outskirts, Johnny stopped and dismounted, lifted her down, and, taking the bulging saddlebags and tossing them over his shoulders, gave the horse's rump a swat so it cantered off.

"Someone will find him later and count himself fortunate," he said. But his voice was distracted. All his energies were on the task ahead.

As they walked through the town's gates, Mylene felt a rush of anticipation. Just a few more minutes and she'd find a way to break free. In the crowd at the station, she could easily slip away and lose herself, to find a constable and seek refuge. Johnny couldn't afford to make a scene. He'd have to play it cool, allow her escape, and figure out what to do once she was safely escorted onto a train to London.

The train was already at the station, the steam churning onto the platform so ladies boarding the coaches distastefully pulled aside their skirts. Johnny paused well away from the crowd, expertly surveying the scene. His gaze lit on the constable walking the platform with a paper in hand, perusing the faces of the boarding passengers. But even as Mylene's hope grew, Johnny turned to her with shrewd eyes.

"Not a word from you," he warned between his teeth. "I'll buy the tickets and we'll board the train as quietly as possible. Keep yer eyes on the ground."

Despite her resolve for secrecy, she flashed him a look that spoke of her defiance, that challenged him to stop her if he dared. Abruptly, he took her arm in a fist of steel, hurting her beneath the thick layer of the boy's coat.

"Be warned, my sweet. If you sound the alarm, if you seek in any way to escape—"

Her fury made her bold. "You'll what?" she taunted rebelliously.

He studied her for a tense moment. Then, in a voice like ground glass, he told her, "I'll turn myself in. I'll tell them I'm the one who snatched the *abducted bride*. And you know what they'll do, Mylene?"

She felt the hope dwindle in the unrelenting glare of his eyes.

"They'll kill me. They'll hang me as sure as the sun sets in the west. And then, my little rebel, Shamus Flynn will come after you like the furies from hell, with no protector to spare you his wrath."

"You're bluffing," she spat out. "You wouldn't willingly walk into the noose."

"Wouldn't I?" His hand tightened on her already throbbing arm. "And what will my life be worth, I ask you, when Shamus Flynn learns I've failed at my task?"

Her blood chilled, and she shivered as if the brutal winter wind was battering her naked skin. She hadn't considered what the Fenians would do to Johnny. Surely he was too valuable to waste. . . .

"Mark me well," he warned again. "If once you attempt to escape me by word or deed, by the saints and all that's holy, you do so with my death on yer hands."

She knew then that he meant it. This wasn't a game. This was deadly business, and Johnny was as much at risk as she. He would call her bluff, and once in the authorities' hands, there would be no hope for him. Together, Roger and Lord Stanley would see to it he hanged.

And then she felt a rage such as she'd never felt before. Damn him! He knew she wouldn't put his life at risk. It was one thing to defy him. To vilify him and escape his grasp. But to stand by and watch him hang from the gallows as all of London jeered . . .

She loved him. That was the travesty of it all. If only she didn't. If only she could love Roger as she did Johnny. She could be rid of her captor and let the cards fall where they may. But he knew her feelings—she'd stupidly fallen into his trap. Having confessed her love for him, she'd given him the most powerful weapon of them all.

She tried to imagine being married to Roger, knowing every day *for the rest of her life* that she'd caused the death of the one man most dear to her heart. Weapon, yes. A cruel weapon, indeed. That he would use it against her—use her tender feelings and her unbearable desire for him to bend her to his will—seemed the greatest betrayal of all.

She hated him in that moment. But looking at his face, remembering how he'd looked in the moonlight beneath the shadows of the great stones . . . recalling the love and ferocious longing shining in his clear green eyes . . . she knew that she couldn't bring him harm.

"Damn you, Johnny," she muttered between tightly clenched teeth. "Damn your soul to hell."

"Think you not," he whispered fiercely, "that I'm already damned? Damned that the woman I love turns her face to another? Damned that I'm forced into a hateful position because she's forsworn her loyalty to all I hold dear? Damned because, in spite of it all, I cherish her still and can't bear to see her harmed?"

"But you *are* harming me, Johnny. Can't you see? You wound me as no other has."

She couldn't bear to see the pain in his eyes—a reflection of the anguish in her own heart. Masking it with a flash of pride, he turned and left her. He took his place at the counter and bought the tickets with gruff authority, his body held stiff, as if endeavoring to control an emotion so strong it threatened his very mission. While Mylene waited, the constable changed his course, coming her way. He glanced at her in her rugged workboy's clothes. One word, one gesture, and she'd be free. But even as her lips parted, she knew with a sinking shudder of defeat that she couldn't utter a sound.

When Johnny returned to her side, ramrod straight and seething with an anger tightly reined, she cast a subdued gaze to the ground and boarded the train at his side.

The train chugged westward, closer to Bristol with each turn of the wheels. Mylene sat in her seat beside Johnny, feeling agitated and restless, wishing she could get up and pace the aisle. The rhythm of the wheels seemed to cement in her mind the dreaded destination. *Bristol . . . Bristol . . . a ferry ride from Cardiff . . .*

And waiting for her in Cardiff, Shamus Flynn. A confrontation she would cut her arm off to avoid. What was she to do? She couldn't escape Johnny on English soil. She believed him when he said he'd turn himself in, a sacrifice to the purpose of a free Ireland. It was part of the Fenian training. You must be willing to die for the sacred cause. One dead martyr was worth a thousand soldiers. Johnny, hanged by the English tyrants, could inspire a loyalty and obsessive devotion such as the Fenians had not yet known. *He was willing to die for us*, they'd say. *What about you? Will you sacrifice yourself for Ireland as the sainted Johnny did?*

Even Shamus Flynn would be eclipsed.

No, she couldn't make her move this side of the Severn. But in Cardiff . . . what would Welsh authorities care? There was enough sympathy in Wales for Ireland's plight that they'd likely turn a deaf ear. Yes, it had to be Cardiff, then. She'd suffer the train and the ferry ride and escape him in Cardiff. She'd be free and Johnny would be safe.

The train was small, with no first-class compartments, so they were forced to sit in the public seats. The compartment was half full, mostly with traveling merchants returning home, their heads buried in newspapers. All up the aisle, Mylene could see her picture on the raised pages.

But one, a man with a bushy mustache sitting across the aisle, cast curious glances at the handsome man in riding clothes with saddlebags across his knee and the raggedly dressed boy at his side. An odd sight, no doubt.

"Fine day, what? Sunny for April, all's the luck."

Johnny nodded curtly and shook open the paper, pretending to read.

The man leaned across the aisle. "See here, old chap. Don't mean to be impudent, not at all. But couldn't that servant of yours do with a more proper fitting-up?"

Johnny paused in his mock reading to give the man a withering glare.

The intruder held up a conciliatory hand. "No offense, my good man. I only mention it because mercantile is my business. I've a shop in Bristol, don't you know. Be most gratified if you'd allow me to fit up your lad. Spruce him up for half the price you'd pay in town. My guarantee."

He held out his hand. Instead of shaking it, Johnny looked down his nose in a proper gentleman's sneer. "Are you in the habit, my dear fellow," he said in perfect Bond Street English, "of soliciting trade from a gentleman without a proper introduction?"

The mustached man blushed to the roots of his hair. " 'Course not, my lord. My mistake. It's just that . . . well, with those riding clothes, one is hard-pressed to know a gent when he sees one. No offense intended, I'm sure."

Johnny went back to reading his paper, pulling it up to hide the side of his face. But Mylene noticed the man casting an occasional curious glance across the aisle. No doubt regretting the loss of a sale. She had to admit, the Fenians had trained Johnny well. No MP of twelve generations could have pulled off an aristocratic put-down any better than he.

But Mylene had other matters on her mind. It wouldn't be easy to escape Johnny's presence. She must affect a compliance she didn't feel. Make him think her so afraid of his threat that she'd accompany him to an audience with Shamus Flynn. And when he was least expecting it . . . when he was convinced of her resignation . . . only then would she make her move.

Still, it was a risky proposition. Once free of Johnny, she'd have to find a way to return to England. If Shamus Flynn was in Cardiff, he wasn't alone. A hunted man who couldn't show his face must always have henchmen to be his eyes and ears. The seaport was likely to be crawling with Fenians. Once they discovered her perfidy, they'd hunt her down. And if they caught her . . . she didn't even care to think what they might do. Once she'd made her break from Johnny, she'd have forfeited his protection. They'd likely be as angry with him as they were with her. No, she couldn't count on Johnny to intervene. Once she made her break, she was on her own.

But break she must. For if the Fenians ever got hold of her, she'd never have another chance.

A sudden shiver of fear seized her. She took a swipe at her flushed face, pushing the stifling hat back off her forehead. She was so hot in the stuffy coach, she felt she couldn't breathe.

She glanced around. She must waylay these thoughts, anchor herself in the moment. She knew what she had to do. Dwelling on the ramifications would only hinder her by making her afraid. Fear was something she couldn't afford. She had to stay calm and do what she must, come what may. She must be every bit as willing to use Johnny for her own means as he was to use her.

By chance, she caught the eye of the mustached mercantilian across the aisle. It seemed to her that he was giving her a strange stare. She must be imagining things. Another symptom of her rampant thoughts.

In an effort to gain control, she looked out the window at the farmland passing by. In the west, she could see the faint glow of the setting sun. They were nearly to Bristol. It wouldn't be long now.

The salesman rose from his seat and headed toward the back of the coach, no doubt to use the facilities before reaching their destination. Mylene thought wistfully to do the same, so she could dunk her head in some cold water. Her face was damp with perspiration and her head sweltered in the trapped heat of her hat. She reached up to wipe her face and felt the stray lock of hair that must have fallen free when she'd earlier pushed the hat from her brow.

She stared at it a moment. Then the words came back to her: "copper-haired beauty."

There wasn't time to think. With a halting screech, the train roared to a stop, casting passengers into the seats in front of them. She heard the back door of the compartment open, heard the sounds of running feet. Glancing back, she saw the mustached tradesman leading the conductor and three other men up the aisle at a run.

They'd been discovered!

Instantly, Johnny was on his feet. Grabbing Mylene's hand, he yanked her into the aisle, racing for the front of the car. Once there, he kicked the door open and with a mighty shove sent Mylene flying. She landed in the field by the rails. An instant later he was at her side, pulling her up and running with her as the shouts of the men followed close behind.

Chapter 7

They'd stopped alongside a farm. Hundreds of feet ahead, they saw the workers in the field finishing up for the day. An overseer sat his horse. But when the train had screeched to a halt, all work ceased as well. The farmhands paused to stare, and the overseer, alarmed, rode toward them to see what was amiss.

Mylene, pulled by Johnny to a ruinous pace, panted as she ran, her feet hitting the field so hard each step sent jolts of pain to her knees. She didn't have to look back to know their pursuers were hot on their trail. She could hear them, dangerously close behind, pounding down on them, shouting for the overseer to head them off. She felt she couldn't run any faster, that her feet would trip beneath her and send her facedown into the field. But Johnny's grip propelled her faster and faster, so she was pulled along in his wake.

A hundred feet to go. Mylene sensed Johnny's

intentions and fixed her eyes on the overseer, coming their way. Her lungs felt blistered by the attempt to breathe. Panic pumped like a river through her veins.

Fifty feet. Their pursuers were gaining ground. They couldn't be twenty feet behind them now, their strides made long and fast by their sense of duty and outrage.

Closer . . . closer . . .

The overseer pulled rein. Mylene saw his mouth move, asking what the fuss was about. Ten more feet. Then Johnny loosed her hand and rounded the horse, ignoring the overseer's demands. With a mighty lunge, he leapt onto the horse from behind, cracked the overseer on the head and sent him flying, unconscious, to the ground. The startled horse darted as Johnny stretched for the reins. He jerked the steed about in a half rear and, looking down at Mylene, called, "Get on."

She stood paralyzed. The sounds of running feet came closer still, the shouts loud in her ears. She glanced behind and saw the group of running men descend upon her. Her mind froze. But instinct rose to the fore. All she had to do was stand where she was and these men would pull her back from Johnny's clutches. She'd be free. And he'd have to make a run for it, leaving her behind.

She looked at the men. Then she turned and glanced at Johnny and belatedly realized her mistake. His eyes were fierce, fixed on her face in unquestioned command. The desperate eyes of the man she loved. And she read in them the threat he'd earlier hurled at her head.

"I'll turn myself in . . .

He wouldn't run away. He was prepared to give himself over to these men. And in that moment of truth, she knew she couldn't do it. She couldn't take that chance.

In a rush, Mylene gathered herself and, as Johnny veered the horse, ran and jumped up behind, barely escaping the stretched-out hands of her rescuers. No sooner had she made contact with the horse than Johnny kicked it hard, sending it flying at a gallop across the field, with Mylene grabbing on to him to keep from falling off.

They rode like the devil, crushing crops in their wake, as the shouts receded. Johnny didn't stop. He galloped at a frantic pace through the countryside, passing farm after farm, putting distance between them and any attempt at pursuit. As the sky grew black, the lights of farmhouses passed by in a haze, looking warm and welcoming but offering no succor to those on the run.

Mylene had no idea how long they rode. The stars began to twinkle and the moon rose, full and bright. The farms began to dwindle until they rode through open country with no haven in sight.

But finally they spotted a silhouette, dark and foreboding in the night, up ahead. Johnny slowed the horse and approached with caution through the overgrown field. When they were upon it, they could see the ruins of an old barn, long since abandoned, beside the crumbling vestige of an ancient farmhouse.

Johnny slid down from the horse, approaching the shelter cautiously. He stepped inside, then came out again, brushing his hands.

"It's safe," he told her.

Mylene slid her aching body off the horse and reflected on the word. *Safe*. Safe from what? She'd had her chance at safety and had let it pass. Because of a threat aimed at the soft core of her heart.

Inside, Johnny found a rusted lantern and, after several attempts, succeeded in lighting it. The flame spilled a warm glow over the austerity of their surroundings. The barn was cluttered with rusted tools, with boards tumbled in here and there so the starry sky was visible through cracks in the roof. As Johnny stabled the horse and fed it what hay there was, Mylene collapsed upon a clump of straw, utterly exhausted.

Once the horse was bedded down, Johnny tossed his saddlebags to the ground near her and dropped down wearily at her side. From the bags he brought forth hard bread and a bottle of wine, opening it quickly and passing it to her. She drank deeply, feeling the liquid warm her chest and bring a measure of comfort to her burning muscles.

For a time they ate in silence, hardly knowing what to say. Mylene was acutely aware of him close beside her, of his manly scent, of every move of his long-fingered hands as they broke the bread and fed bits into his mouth. The barn, so far from nowhere, seemed hushed and intimate in the lonely night. And as her tension eased in the sweet comfort of the wine, her eyes wandered to the straw beneath her, the straw that would no doubt form their bedding for the night.

Once again, they'd spend the night together, far away from the world.

"You did well," he said at last. "I thought for a moment you might—"

"Let you die?"

He didn't answer, but she thought she saw a flush of shame darken his face.

Uncomfortable in the pulsing silence, she shrugged out of her boy's coat and laid it aside. Then she took the hated hat from her head. Her hair spilled over her shoulders, glowing gold and copper in the lantern's light. She ran her fingers through it, massaging her heated head, letting out a sigh of relief at feeling unencumbered once again. As she did, she caught Johnny's gaze, arrested on her wrists.

He reached forth and took her hands in his, gently rubbing the red welts marring the tender flesh where the rope had cut the night before. "Ah, Mylene," he moaned, "why does it have to be so?"

His voice throbbed with regret. She looked up and met his eyes and saw in them a look of suffering and desire that melted her heart. She could see in his eyes that he'd do anything to spare her. It was as hard on him as it was on her. Neither of them would have chosen opposing sides.

"Oh, Johnny."

He reached for her, pulling her to him, kissing her desperately as his hands found their way to clutch her hair. His fingers took over where hers had left off, massaging her scalp so that all the tension flowed away, to be replaced by a surge of pleasure and passion. She relaxed beneath the pressure, her body going limp, her lips parting beneath his kiss because she had no will to keep them closed.

She was woman enough to want him. But she was shrewd enough to see her chance. If she could convince him that this fated love they shared was more intense, more powerful than all his plans . . .

She took his face in her hands. Gently, she stroked the lean cheeks with her thumbs, holding his gaze.

"Johnny, my love. It's all for naught, this bitterness between us. You crave a happy union as much as I. We can do this, Johnny. You and I. Together. We can find a way."

"How," he rasped, pulling her to him, "when we're so far from where we began?"

"You must listen to me, Johnny. For once, my love, hear what I say."

His arms tightened about her and he held her pinned against him, so close she could feel the beating of his heart, feel his chest rise and fall against her bound breasts as he drew erratic breaths. But he didn't deny her, so she softly, whispering persuasively in his ear, pressed her case.

"You brand me traitor because you think I've been seduced by English ways. And in a way, you're right. I've lived among them and I've learned from them in ways I never expected. Once I hated them as much as you. I hate still their refusal to set our homeland free. But Johnny, we can learn from them in ways that will make us strong. Look what they've done. During Victoria's reign, this country has changed from an agricultural backwater to the greatest industrial force the world has ever known. They've moved from the farms to the cities. They've increased their population twofold. It's a country of youth, full of energy and the drive to get things done. With the changes came problems. Poverty, overcrowded cities, filth and disease. But unlike us, who complain in our beer, they've seen what must be done. The reforms they've adopted have been no less than miraculous. They've regulated factories so cities might be clean and healthy. When a problem arises, the reformers analyze what must be done and force the issue to ensure changes for the better. They've built railroads that are the envy of the world. All in a short time. And out of chaos they've found a system of order.

"I admire their energy, their industry, their ability to get things done. You know well my frustrations in Ireland. How it seemed we were the only ones, a handful of us, trying to change things for the better while the rest either left or brooded over their lot. Think, Johnny, what such industry and order might do for Ireland. We weep and walk about with the dead look of a doomed race, and curse the fates, letting others address the problems that may destroy us all. The English, for all their faults, are conquering their problems with an energy and determination and view to the common good that we'd do well to adopt. Not with violence, but with their intellect and their willingness for hard work."

He was kissing her neck, sending shivers up her spine.

"And you, Johnny, have an opportunity none before you has had. With all your talent and training, you could work a miracle for our land. You've seen both worlds. You can really help Ireland, not by using violence, but by using your position and influence as Lord Whitney to be a politician. You have the experience. You know the streets of Ireland, you know what we need. And you've come to know the salons of London. You could wield your power to bring Ireland and England peaceably together."

His hands were in her hair again, massaging, kneading, so she had to struggle to think. Magic hands. They were weaving their sorcery, distracting her from her goal, coaxing her to let go of all thought and simply feel. She took a breath and gathered her thoughts for a final argument before she knew she was lost.

"We must talk to Lord Stanley. I've thought about this, Johnny. I think if we confide in him, he'll understand. He's a good man. He wants to be fair. But he's a product of old thinking. If we explain to him how our people feel, how they think, how they're different from the English and have different needs, I know we can convince him. And with the aid of so powerful a man—"

"You smell so sweet," he murmured in her hair. "No other woman has your scent."

Was he capitulating? She couldn't tell. But his hands on her made her weak and trembly. She felt the last of her will evaporate as the words melted before the flame of his desire. It was all she could do to draw breath. The sound of his own breath, deep and heavy in the silence, seemed to fill the room.

"Johnny, please . . . for Ireland . . . for us . . ."

She didn't know how it happened. But she was lying beneath him, her clothes disappearing as if by magic beneath his skilled, insistent hands. She felt a soar of hope as he came to her, and she felt his clothes against her naked flesh. Surely he'd been moved by her plea. Surely his mouth, kissing her, was telling her he was willing to try.

And then all thoughts of policies faded from her mind. She was a woman again, in the arms of the man she loved. Nothing else mattered.

And suddenly he changed. His mood of despair was replaced like a bolt of lightning with a determination she caught in the flash of his eyes. Pulling her to him, he captured the back of her head in his hand and kissed her brutally, a kiss that stole her breath with a startled gasp. She'd intended to seduce him—she knew that now—to control him with her power to make him want her above all else. Yet with her senses reeling, she felt that it was *she* who was rushing out of control. His kiss was like none she'd ever experienced. It was the kiss of a conqueror. It was warm, drowning, electric, not begging permission but demanding a response, stealing her will and curling her toes even as she felt a jolt of raw desire spark her loins. Beneath the onslaught of his masterfully roving mouth, of his hot, searing tongue, she felt that it was she who was being seduced, mastered, by a power stronger than her own. She felt herself melting into him, her mouth greedily savoring the taste of him, a moan of helpless surrender escaping her throat.

This was what she'd intended. To seduce him, to soften him, to woo him over to her side. Yet why did she feel suddenly that *she* was the one under attack?

When he lifted his head, she felt dizzy, keeping her eyes closed a moment longer to try to clear her head and regain her equilibrium. But he put his hands on either side of her face and lifted it so she could feel him staring at her hard. She opened her eyes slowly and saw the green eyes burning into her, seeing every-thing—her confusion, her struggle for control, and the excitement that shattered it. His lips curled into a knowing smile, offering her a challenge, as if he sensed her designs.

It was like the games they'd played as children. Who can best the other and win the prize? But the stakes were so much higher than they'd ever been before.

She rose to the taunting challenge in his eyes. Raising her hands to his shirt, she yanked it open with an aggressive confidence that made a mockery of her fluttery sighs. The sight of his bared chest stirred her madly. The thick hair was dark as dusk, outlining a torso that was like armor. Reaching forth, she touched it with unsteady fingers. Then she brought her mouth to his nipple as he had with her the night before, taking it to her lips, sucking it until she heard his startled gasp, then the low, pleasurable moan from the depths of his soul, as if she'd surprised and thrilled him every bit as much as he'd earlier done to her. With her fingers, she caressed the other nipple, feeling it harden beneath her caress.

"*Good God,*" he said with a ragged breath.

Her hand moved to the lock of his belt. Yanking it aside, she unbuttoned his pants and, using both hands now, slid down the dark breeches so he was bared to her eyes.

He seemed immense, yet it wasn't merely his size that was so impressive. Before her, proudly jutting in its enormity, was a beautifully veined column of power and pleasure. She'd never dreamt that anything of such beauty and grace could exist, so refined and chiseled, a work of art carved from flesh.

She felt immobilized by his power, by the hold he suddenly had over her. She wanted him so much that it shook the foundation of her being. Slowly, shyly, feeling her way, she took him in her mouth.

He was so large, he filled her completely, cutting off her breath. She felt him swelling and thrusting within the moist cavern of her mouth. She felt exalted by the unfamiliar act of taking him in this most intimate communion. She'd never done such a thing, yet she'd been overcome by some primal urge. She'd known she had to have him in her mouth or die.

She was carried away to some place she'd never been. Time stood still. The act of taking all of him in her mouth was so fulfilling that she could easily have continued sucking him through the long hours of the night. And as she felt him harden and throb, she felt again her own power coming to the fore.

He felt it, too. The danger of surrender beneath her mouth. He pulled away, denying her grasping tongue, and pushed her back into the prickly straw, lowering himself atop her to reclaim his dominion.

With his knee, he shoved her legs apart, then fed

himself into her like a long sword. He thrust into her, not gently as he had the night before, but with the right of one who's been given all the permission he needs. He took her like a prize, like something he'd earned and won. To show her that in this contest of wills she had a formidable foe. He kissed her with ferocious domination, grinding his mouth into hers, robbing her of the last remnants of command. But he hadn't counted on how marvelous it would feel, fitting inside her as if they'd been made for one another. As he plunged into her, his head dropped back with a will of its own, the agony too sweet. "My beloved," he rasped, like a painful cry.

And with those desperate words, despite his mastery, she felt the power returning to her. With every frantic thrust, she felt him coming closer to surrender. With his hands in her hair, tearing at it as if trying to grasp elusive moonbeams, knowing his surrender, his extinction, was inevitable, yet unable to resist, he slammed into her with the force of a captor who knows he's the one being lured into the chains.

She laughed then, a laugh that sounded joyous and free, a laugh that mocked all the pretense of conquest when they were both so obviously seduced. He answered it in kind, with a brutal possession that brooked no apology and defied the game. She felt herself soaring. Her hands gripped the straw above her head to anchor her senses. Her teeth were bared in a fierce snarl of pleasure, like a lioness being roughly taken with full consent. She felt again that her body had bloomed to its full potential, as if the womanly taunts she'd used to her advantage had rendered her body, beneath Johnny's onslaught of passion, to become nothing more than a tribute to him. That she gloried in his possession made him take her all the harder. He'd never known a woman more capable of such aggressive surrender, of flaunting her submission like a tool that made her stronger in the act of giving herself to him.

He thrust into her, forcing himself as deeply as he could before drawing back and thrusting even deeper still. As his climax neared, he plunged even harder, faster, breaking his own rhythm as his blood, burning his veins, drove him. As she felt him swell and throb inside, Mylene, too, was swept away, losing all sense of herself and her earlier designs.

Soon they lay collapsed in each other's arms, damp with sweat and breathing raggedly. As she came back to the world, Mylene had to wonder what had happened. She'd become, in Johnny's arms, something she hadn't known she was, a woman of passion and fire, capable of giving herself openly and freely without thought or guilt. An ancient soul who saw the travesty of recriminations when the power of nature was asserting itself in its glorious pulse of life.

She hugged him close, feeling the heat of his body sear into hers. "Oh, Johnny," she whispered in the afterglow of passion sweetly spent. "Isn't it better this way?"

He lifted himself from her slowly, looking down at her with hooded eyes. His lip curled in the slightest trace of a cynical smile.

"Better? To have you my willing seducer? Better, indeed."

"No, I mean to have an understanding between us."

"The only understanding that's between us is we both know you tried to seduce me over to yer side." He shrugged. "There's no shame in trying. I tried it myself. Now we're even, by all counts."

She sat up, thrusting him from her. "You mean to tell me you didn't listen to a word I said?"

"Listen, aye. But it's just words, love. Since when have words solved our troubles? Yer right when you say we Irish have had a pintful of words. The time has come for action. You know it as well as I. There's no way I'm after confiding in your sainted Lord Stanley, to swing from a rope for my pains. The only way Ireland will be free is with blood."

She was staring at him, stunned. "You took what I offered when you had no intention—"

"I'll gladly take what you offer any time. I'm a man, after all, and I love you, right enough. It would take a stronger man than I to turn down such a gift. But if you think to coax me with pretty smiles and—"

He didn't finish his sentence. She lunged at him, punching him hard, so he doubled over, winded. "You lying bastard!" she cried.

"When did I lie to you, then?" he demanded, rubbing his aching chest. "No more than you when you took the love I offered last night with no intention of capitulation. I don't hold it against you. You have yer views and I have mine. But since I can't convince you in me own right, it's off to Shamus Flynn, as planned."

"And what if you're wrong?" she challenged.

He looked at her seriously, the mocking cynicism gone. "It's gone on too long. It's no longer a matter of right or wrong. It's a matter of what works."

And she knew in that moment how great was the gulf that separated them. Right·or wrong—these were just words to Johnny now. He wanted only to win. It was what the Fenians had taught him, to take his rights by whatever means were at hand. But it mattered to her. Softhearted she might be, as he'd often accused. But she knew in her heart that what Shamus

Flynn had planned was wrong. And worse, some sixth sense told her, it was dangerous. Dangerous for her, surely. But dangerous to Johnny as well. Dangerous to anyone who got in the way of the Great Plan.

She must fight them with everything at her command. Because there was more at stake than she'd ever realized. She'd become a warrior as surely as any Fenian alive. But it was no longer Ireland for which she fought and was willing to die. It was more important than any country or ideal or way of life.

She was fighting for Johnny's soul.

Chapter 8

M ylene awoke the next morning to the sounds of someone shuffling about in the barn. Alarmed, she shot up, thinking their pursuers had tracked them down. But it was just Johnny, tossing aside rusted tools to uncover something underneath.

"What are you doing?" she cried, her voice made sharp by her sudden fear.

He stopped and turned to her. He was dressed again in the suit of a gentleman, with a derby set rakishly atop his head, looking dashing and handsome in the sunlight streaming through the cracks in the roof.

"We need a disguise," he said, all business. "They'll be looking for us. It's possible they've guessed we'll try for the ferry. While they don't know who I am or what my motives are, they'll still likely watch every avenue of escape. We'll have to hide you. They'll be looking for the boy's clothes. Yet you can't wear the dress."

"Perhaps we should wait, then, until they tire of the search."

He gave her a sardonic grin. "Or until I change my mind?"

His tone told her there was no chance of that.

She shrugged, affecting nonchalance. "It was just an idea."

She dressed quickly in the clothes that were strewn along the straw. As she did, Johnny bent over and tugged something free. "This might just do, at that."

As she ran her fingers through her tangled hair, Mylene watched as Johnny lifted the corner of what looked to be an old rug. Dust flew everywhere, causing him to cough. But he dragged the rug outside, into the open air.

When Mylene joined him, he was using an old hoe to beat the dust out of the rug. It looked ancient, its colors faded to a dull grey, worn away completely in spots. She wondered what he had in mind, then, as realization dawned, she froze. "Oh, no," she said.

He looked up from his task, amusement glinting in his eyes. "It was good enough for Cleopatra, going to Caesar. It's good enough for you."

She bent to put her nose to the offensive carpet, then jerked away. "It's old and it smells. If you think I'll stand for being rolled up in that atrocity—"

"You have a better idea?"

She opened her mouth to refuse. But her resolution of the night before came back to her in a rush. She had to be careful. She couldn't afford to arouse his suspicions. She had a plan now, and she must allow for no mistakes. She would face Shamus Flynn if she must and make him believe he had won her over to his will gradually, reluctantly. And then, when she'd convinced him, when she was free . . .

She must play this with the utmost caution. Easy capitulation would seem as suspicious as undue resistance. She must, at all times, keep her goal in mind.

"There must be something else," she argued. "In the house, perhaps."

"I checked. It's bare. We're shorthanded of options, so the rug will have to do. Think of it as your magic carpet."

"What if I cough in there and give myself away?"

"I've thought of that. I'll place you with yer head as close to the opening as possible, so you can breathe. I doubt not that a woman of your *talents and training*"— he smirked, parroting her words to him the night before—"can suppress a cough or two—given what's at stake."

The look he gave her was sharp and penetrating, as if he was endeavoring to read her thoughts. "Can I trust you, now?"

She met his gaze. "You know well enough I'll not endanger you. Haven't I proved it, then?"

"Aye. You've done that," he admitted softly. Then, his tone brusque again, he continued. "We've just enough time to make the ferry. It's but a short hop across. You'll be out before you know it. The difficulty will be riding on that horse with you draped over its—"

"You don't mean to keep me wrapped up the whole ride into town!"

"And chance them spotting me rolling you up inside?"

She sighed, accepting her fate. It was little enough price to pay to assure the success of her plan.

It was all she could do to force herself to lie upon the rug at one end, fitting her head just below the edge. But as Johnny began to roll the carpet around her, she felt a momentary panic, a clutch of claustrophobia. She had a sudden impulse to cry out that she'd changed her mind, that they must find another way. But there was no other way. So she took a last long breath of clean air and gritted her teeth, reminding herself yet again to keep her objective in mind.

Finally she was wound up like a mummy, with her arms at her sides so she couldn't move. She heard him traipsing about, heard the nicker of protest as he saddled the horse. Then she felt herself hauled onto the horse's back so the pommel of the saddle cut through the thickness of the rug and pressed against her ribs. Johnny mounted behind and reached over the rug to take up the reins. As he started the horse at a walk, she felt herself slip with the rug, about to fall. But he anchored it and they plodded along, retracing their steps toward town.

It seemed an age that they rode through the fields. It was stifling hot in her prison. She began to perspire. The wool trapped the heat, and she imagined the steam of her body drifting out into the open air. She trained her thoughts in other directions. The warm soapy bath she'd receive as reward. The chill of the river just down the hill from Stonehenge. Anything but the oppressive stench of the rug and the heat of her own breath.

Finally, when he had the hang of balancing her weight, Johnny kicked the horse into a slow trot. She'd hoped for a speedier pace, but now she found the bouncing intolerable, as the jolt of the saddle pinched her ribs with every pounce. *I'll be black and blue*, she thought. But it would be worth it in the end. She'd have her day, Shamus Flynn be damned. She just had to remember that through the long hours of this ordeal.

After what seemed forever, Johnny stopped the horse. "We're approaching town," he said. "Not a sound, now."

She craned her neck so her nose was pointed toward the opening, but even as she took a deep, cleansing breath, she steeled herself for danger. There were no guarantees. Even in his gentleman's clothes and hat, Johnny could be recognized. And it would all be over in a moment.

She heard the horse's hooves resounding off the streets of town. She heard the activity of the streets, the chatter, the laughter, the crunch of wagon wheels. Hawkers crying out the glories of their wares. Then they stopped again and she felt Johnny shift behind her as he dismounted. The carpet tipped precariously before he caught it. Mylene slipped ever so slightly toward the opening, her face rubbing raw against the rough wool. She could see more light and wondered if she was visible. But pinned as she was, there was nothing she could do.

"We'll walk from here," he said.

Then she felt herself lifted and hoisted over Johnny's shoulder as he groaned beneath her weight. The carpet was stiff, so it didn't bend. She was parallel to the ground, jutting out in front of Johnny, anchored at the waist by his restraining arm, bouncing with every step he took.

"We're near the ferry," he told her softly. "Take care. The police are there, and that cursed man from the train. We'll walk right past, if our luck holds. But be warned. I'll take flight if needs be."

She was scared. She couldn't imagine how Johnny could escape them, running with her over his shoulder. If they aroused suspicions, they'd surely be caught.

He started forward with a confident stride. She

braced herself for the inevitable questions, for the possible request to search the rug, for the sounds of alarm. This was too dangerous. They should wait for another time—

Suddenly Johnny stopped. He stood stock-still, and she could feel him hold his breath. She waited for the questions, but none came. Then she heard his low, vicious curse.

"What is it?" she whispered.

He didn't answer. But something had gone wrong. She could sense it. She had to know. Slowly, painfully, she arched her aching neck and strained to see out. The ferry dock was no more than twenty feet ahead. To the right, she spotted the group of police and the mustached man from the train. They were talking among themselves, glancing at those who boarded the ferry as if they didn't much expect to spot their prey. Nothing unusual there. Nothing to cause such a foul curse.

She craned her neck to the side. And then she knew. To the left of the ferry dock, she spied another group of men, dressed inconspicuously in the worn work clothes of the docks. Two of the faces she recognized at once. Keenan O'Flaherty, Shamus Flynn's right hand. And beside him, a figure she'd known most of her life. A tall sandy-haired man with the devil's thumbprint in his chin. *Daggett!*

"Oh, Johnny," she whispered.

"Hush now," he snapped. "If O'Flaherty gets to you, you're as good as dead."

"But surely Daggett—"

He shook her roughly. She could feel his tension through the heavy folds of the rug. Even Daggett couldn't stop O'Flaherty once he had an action in mind. And O'Flaherty spared no love for Johnny. That was common knowledge.

"Let's leave," she hissed.

"Too late," he ground out. "Daggett's spied us."

She strained again to see. Daggett was staring straight at them, a look of frozen recognition on his face. He took a step toward them and she felt Johnny's arm tighten protectively about her.

"Run!" she urged.

But it was too late. Daggett was coming their way. They'd never make it. She cast a desperate glance from Daggett on one side to the police on the other. Trapped! There was nowhere to go.

She could feel the weight of Johnny's dilemma. Hand her over to the Fenians and risk her life, or give himself to the police and endanger his own.

Suddenly, as Daggett increased his stride, she felt the carpet lunge and she could no longer see. Johnny was walking at a furious pace. But where? She couldn't swear to it, but she thought he was headed toward the ferry. Did he plan to board with Daggett and O'Flaherty at his heels?

Then he stopped as suddenly as he'd started. She was hauled from his shoulder so she hit the ground hard. Then she felt a violent tug and she was spinning round and round. The sunlight pierced her eyes and she felt a rush of cool air. She realized, through the dizziness of her head, that she was lying atop the unrolled rug.

Dazed, she looked up from her prone position to see the startled faces of the police staring down at her.

Johnny, standing with the rug still in hand, raised a crisp, authoritative voice for all to hear. "I'm Lord Whitney, Officers. And I've just rescued the abducted bride."

• • •

As the train pulled into Victoria Station, Mylene cast a nervous glance at Johnny. She'd been outraged over his high-handedness at claiming to be her rescuer. But that had long since been replaced by dread. Constable Bishop, of the Bristol police, had wired ahead to Scotland Yard, informing them that he was bringing Mylene in on the next train. After the dire proclamation that things didn't quite add up, he'd taken the seat behind Johnny and Mylene and sat in silence, his arms crossed over his chest, for the remainder of the trip to London. It was clear he was keeping a careful watch. If Mylene turned to speak to Johnny, the constable leaned forward in his seat and listened with the air of one with the right to intrude.

Consequently, there had been no opportunity to ask Johnny what tricks he might have up his sleeve. She knew too well the precariousness of their situation. Johnny's claim as her rescuer, the product of quick thinking forced by circumstances, couldn't possibly hold up in the light of the questions Scotland Yard would no doubt hurl at his head. There were too many incongruities. How, for instance, had Lord Whitney found her? Why had he not captured, or killed, her supposed kidnappers? And most damning of all, why had he run with her from the Bristol train? The mustached mercantilian had recognized Johnny at once as the man who'd forced her off the train and out of the conductor's grasp. And equally perplexing, why was she hidden in a carpet on their way to boarding a ferry to Cardiff? Why, if he'd rescued her as he asserted, were they not heading with all speed for London?

Mylene's head ached as the questions pounded

through her brain. She knew that she, too, would be questioned. Who were her kidnappers? Where had they taken her? How many were there? What did they look like? So many details to explain a deception she'd been forced into in the first place. Furious with Johnny for putting her in such an untenable situation, she nonetheless would have given anything to confer with him before facing the ordeal. If only to get their stories straight.

But that was impossible. Clearly, the constable was suspicious. Mylene couldn't ask Johnny the time without the wretched man answering for him. So as the train slowed at the platform, Mylene wiped her damp palms on her trousers and cast another surreptitious glance at Johnny. This could be the most dangerous test they'd ever faced. It would require all their skills at subterfuge to make the story stick.

The train stopped. Passengers rose, took valises in hand and, casting curious glances at the woman dressed in ragged boy's clothes, moved up the aisle and off the train. Constable Bishop rose and stretched, groaning audibly. "Now to find the inspector."

He waited for them to proceed to the door, walking closely behind, then motioning them toward the steps. As they stepped down, Johnny whispered, "I'll do the talking." She should have felt relieved. But even Johnny would be hard-pressed to explain away the discrepancies.

They were barely off the train before Katharine Helmsley rushed up and scooped Mylene into her arms. "Our darling girl," she cried, crushing Mylene in a perfumed embrace. Before Mylene could gather her wits, she was surrounded by Lord Stanley, Lord Helmsley, and Roger, all vying for a place at her side as they expressed their relief. Roger came last, taking her hands in his as befitted such a public reunion, his relief and fear written plainly on his face. Mylene couldn't look him in the eye. Unbidden, she cast a guilty glance at Johnny, remembering all too vividly his words at Stonehenge: *Let's see if he wants you when I'm through with you.*

Roger caught the look. As his hands spasmed on hers, he cast a look to Johnny and back again to Mylene. In that instant, Mylene heard a crescendo of raised voices. Tearing her gaze from Roger's stricken face, she saw a horde of men descending on them, all shouting her name, jostling the small group in their eagerness so Mylene's hands were torn from Roger's grasp. Suddenly, they were accosted by a group of bustling newshounds barking questions and shoving past one another in their efforts to get as close to the abducted bride as the narrow platform would allow.

Their questions rankled like the baying of wild wolves.

"Who did it, miss?"

"Where did they keep you?"

"Did you see their faces?"

"Are they in custody?"

"Is it true Lord Whitney rescued you at great peril to his own life?"

All bellowed together to create an uproar that was causing quite a scene.

They tore at her with the lust of rabid beasts until she was pushed toward the train, nearly losing her footing at the edge of the platform. The Helmsleys and Lord Stanley were struggling in the mob, their pleas drowned out by the noise. Katharine was jolted and spun so her spring hat fell askew upon her face. Roger was lost somewhere in the crowd. Mylene was shoved again and her foot slipped over the edge.

Paralyzed by panic, Mylene's mind froze. She looked down to see herself slipping again, saw the tracks beneath the train loom up toward her. A scream struck in her throat.

Just then, a force moved through the crowd like a tornado, hurling the reporters back like twigs flung in the wind. And there was Johnny, fighting his way through the throng, picking her up in strong arms and carrying her to safety through the turbulent melee.

"Enough!" he roared so his voice sounded like thunder above the clamor. Then, looking down at the shaken woman in his arms, he added, "It seems I must rescue you yet again."

This silenced everyone. Holding her protectively in his arms, he carried her through the swarm that parted before him, hushed, awed, completely caught off guard. "Then it's true," one man breathed. "You *did* rescue the lady."

Johnny turned toward the voice with an arched brow. "What English gentleman could sit back and see one of our delicate flowers put to peril? Would not every one of you risk his life that this fair maid might be safe?"

This shamed the crowd momentarily. His meaning was clear. The poor woman had only just tasted the luxury of safety before being thrust into this maelstrom. But it was irresistible, the sight of her rescuer dashing through the crowd, carrying her to safety yet again. Even as they paved a path, the newsmen drew pads from their pockets and began to scribble the beginnings of a story they knew would capture and dazzle the public's romantic imagination.

"Tell me, miss," cried one bold soul. "Did you fall in love with your champion, then?"

Mylene stilled in Johnny's arms. Johnny came to a

halt, turning slowly to face the impertinent man. She held her breath, expecting a biting retort. But instead, Johnny flashed the reporter an enigmatic grin. "Alas, my friend, she belongs to another. Your bride, Lord Helmsley. I'm only grateful I was able to return her to you before her . . . *honor* was compromised."

He eased Mylene to her feet, and she found herself standing before her red-faced fiancé. Roger, keenly aware of the eyes of the reporters, swallowed his humiliation and said stiffly, "It's I who is grateful, my lord."

"Think nothing of it. I'm certain you'd have done the same."

The slight wasn't lost on the newsmen, who began to wonder, for the first time, why Lord Whitney and not the bride's intended had rescued her from the clutches of her captors.

"Why, you're a hero, sir," said one of them.

Johnny gave a gracious bow. "I repeat, sir. Wouldn't any upstanding Englishman have done the same?"

It was a stroke of genius. Not only did he appear modestly unassuming, he'd subtly and with utmost finesse hammered home his point. Roger, good Englishman that he was, had sat home brooding while someone else had risked his life to recover his bride.

Mylene glared at Johnny, incensed by his cool aplomb in the face of such calamity. But then she felt, like a magnet, the silent pull of Roger's gaze. She looked at him and saw in his eyes the wounded pride of a shamed man. Her heart went out to him. Let Johnny bait him all he wanted. She'd show him.

She reached for Roger's hand but he gruffly turned aside. "The inspector's waiting," he announced, and led the way.

Stunned, Mylene felt a hand at her elbow. She looked up to see Lord Stanley's kind blue eyes. He put an arm about her shoulders and walked with her up the platform behind Roger's rigid back. The reporters followed, their chagrin forgotten, calling questions now to Johnny, begging details of his heroic deed.

Mylene stayed close to Lord Stanley, feeling the paternal comfort of his arm. "Can't we do this later?" she asked. "I must speak with you at once."

He patted her shoulder consolingly. "I know you've been through an ordeal, my dear, but I'm afraid the inspector insists. But don't worry. We'll bustle you home immediately the formalities are over."

"But it's important that I—"

Just then Johnny stepped to her side. He was watching her intently. Did he guess what she had in mind? It didn't matter. Once she had Lord Stanley alone, she'd confess the whole sordid story. There was nothing Johnny could do about it once Lord Stanley knew the truth.

She felt Johnny's steely grip on her arm. "Shall we face the lions?" he asked smoothly. But she read the warning in his eyes.

They followed Roger through the throng of passengers, past the ticket counters, to an office at the side. There, the reporters were left behind as the constable joined the family group inside.

"You must be Inspector Worthington," he greeted a pale mustached man with a reddish cast to his hair.

The man, in a rumpled brown suit, extended his credentials. "Scotland Yard," he announced with self-important distinction. "I'd like a word with you, Constable, if I might."

The two men stepped aside, and Mylene watched nervously as Constable Bishop spoke to the inspector in hushed tones. The inspector cast a shrewd glance at Johnny, then nodded his understanding.

As he turned back toward them, Mylene pressed her hands together to quell their trembling. She reminded herself of Johnny's admonition to keep quiet. But she sensed the inspector wouldn't swallow excuses easily. He had a determined, even cruel, look in his eyes that warned her to stay on her toes. There wasn't an Irishman alive who didn't mistrust authority—particularly English authority—and Mylene, with so many secrets to keep, was no exception.

"Inspector, really," Katharine said with an aristocrat's impatience with that same authority. "Our poor girl's had a trying enough time, what with the kidnapping and those beastly reporters. Surely this can wait for a later date."

Worthington, accustomed to being castigated by members of the peerage, hardened his tone to assert his autonomy. "It cannot. You're free to leave if you wish, my lady, if the process wearies you."

"And leave our beloved daughter-in-law to this inquisition? I should say not!"

The inspector bristled inwardly but, by force of habit, turned his attention to the business at hand.

"Now, miss, we've a few questions that need answering. This is a sticky affair, but the more help you can give us, the sooner we can bring the perpetrators to justice. Constable Bishop has informed me of the ... irregularities of the case. Perhaps you could enlighten us on some of the more questionable aspects."

Before Mylene could so much as blink, she heard Johnny's voice. "I'm afraid, Inspector, the lady will be of little use to your investigation. She was kept blindfolded the entire time, and so can offer few details."

"Is that true?" the inspector asked, piercing her with his gaze.

"Yes. I was blindfolded. And tied up for the most part." At least *that* was true!

"Then you know nothing of where the kidnappers stashed you?"

"I'm afraid not, Inspector," she said meekly, as befitted a lady who'd been through such an ordeal.

"But surely you heard noises? Their voices? Anything that could help us identify—"

"I think, Inspector, we could save a great deal of time if I tell you what I know."

All eyes turned to Johnny. Mylene felt her stomach curl. What could he possibly say?

"Very well, my lord. Perhaps you could explain to us how it is you knew where to find the young lady?"

Johnny sat on the edge of the desk with an easy air. "A simple case of deduction, Inspector. I surmised that the kidnappers might be East End thugs bent on selling the lady to the Irish."

Worthington gave a thoughtful frown. "It's been known to happen. Those rabble-rousers often use East Enders to do their dirty work."

"Precisely. I asked myself, to whom would the lady be of use? Lord Stanley is well known for his views. If the kidnappers required merely a ransom, why snatch her in so public a place? That could be done at any time. No, they wanted everyone to know she'd been kidnapped. If not money, then what? The Irish have good cause to use such a hostage to force Lord Stanley's hand."

"I hadn't thought of that," Lord Stanley lamented. "My dear, if I was responsible, I'm so terribly sorry."

But Mylene was too busy staring at Johnny to give her father a glance. What a cool customer he was, giving enough of the truth to make his story plausible without directly implicating the Fenians.

"Proceed, my lord."

"That decided, I asked myself where they might take her. Ireland, obviously. The easiest and safest route would be through Cardiff, which is well known as a stronghold for Irish sympathizers. But as the trains from London would likely be watched, I took a chance that the kidnappers would take her by horse until they were safely out of town. The obvious route was to head south and west, making their way toward Bristol, where they could catch a ferry to Cardiff. Do you follow, sir?"

"Go on," the inspector snapped, clearly annoyed that he'd failed to make the same assumptions.

"I guessed again that they might head for Salisbury. The train to Bristol is small and not likely to be watched. So I took the train in the hopes of beating them there. Then I stood watch, looking for anything that struck me as suspicious."

"That brings us to your escape with the lady from the Salisbury-Bristol train."

This, Mylene knew, was one of the stickiest questions Johnny faced. She listened intently, convinced by now of his ability, yet dying to know how he planned to get out of this one.

"I'm getting to that, Inspector. As I said, I kept a close watch. Soon, my efforts were rewarded. A coach pulled up and from out of it stepped two men. They helped a woman down and walked with her between them, each holding one of her arms. The woman was dressed in mourning, with a heavy black veil over her face. By the awkwardness of her gait, it was apparent she was having trouble seeing. I thought it likely she might be blindfolded beneath the veil. A glance at the coach told me there were other men inside, although from the distance, I couldn't determine how many. But I knew I must proceed with caution. I was taking a tremendous risk that I'd guessed wrong and the woman was nothing more than what she appeared—a grieving woman being assisted by her sons, or some such thing. I knew, too, that if I was correct in my assumption, I must time the operation perfectly. One small slip would risk the lady's life."

"But, Lord Whitney, how brave of you!" Katharine cried.

He ignored her and continued. "So I waited until the train was about to leave, then rushed forth, grabbed the woman, and knocked down her companions. Carrying her along, I ran with all speed for the train, boarding as it was just pulling out. A quick glance beneath the veil revealed the blindfold, and I knew I'd guessed correctly."

"But the lady was dressed in boy's clothes, as she is now, when you were spotted—"

"Naturally, I'd anticipated the necessity of hiding the lady's identity and had brought what I deemed the perfect disguise. The thugs would be looking for a woman, not a rough boy. As I glanced back, I saw men running toward the departing train. I had no way of knowing if they might have succeeded in boarding, so I bade the lady change in the washroom with all haste, just in case. That accomplished, we took our seats."

"That was most prescient of you, I must say," said the inspector with wry skepticism.

"What I had no way of knowing, as I've stated, is how many ruffians there were, or how many might have succeeded in boarding the train. Nor what disguises they might be using. When the merchant began to question me about the lad's clothes, I naturally grew suspicious that he might be part of the gang. I tried my best to use the paper I carried to hide myself and the lady, but when he came charging through the compartment with a group of men, what was I to think? That the thugs had discovered us, of course. I could trust no one. I could hardly risk the lady's life by waiting to find out. So I did the only thing I could think of. Ran with the lady to safety, to seek another avenue of escape. Had they identified themselves, I might have saved myself a great deal of hardship."

By now, the inspector was glaring at Johnny as if he couldn't believe his ears. "And how, sir, do you explain the fact that you were boarding the ferry for Cardiff with the lady rolled up in an old rug?"

"Ah, that was a particularly intriguing challenge," Johnny said, crossing his boot over his other knee. "Acting on my assumption—which I now know to be false—that we were being pursued by members of the gang, I had to think of a foolproof plan. I didn't know how many men there were or what they looked like. Anyone could be part of the plot. I had to get away with the lady. The thugs, I supposed, would assume I'd take the first train to London, so that avenue of escape was out. What was I to do? I'd rescued her. We were being pursued. I had to get her to safety. The only way out was to take the ferry to Cardiff. They likely wouldn't head there without her. They certainly wouldn't expect *me* to go there with her. So it seemed the jolly best thing to do. Once in Wales, I could take a more circuitous route back to London and return the lady safely to her family."

He finished with a nod of satisfaction that implied anyone would do the same.

"But the rug—"

"Well, naturally, I had to assume they might have

compatriots waiting for them in Bristol. A kidnapping of such magnitude could hardly be perpetrated without a retinue of accomplices, now, could it? As a precaution, realizing their compatriots would likely recognize the lady, I rolled her in a carpet to hide her. They had, after all, seen her boy's clothes, and how could I be certain they wouldn't be on the lookout?"

"Is this true, ma'am?"

Stunned by Johnny's inventiveness at having covered all the bases, Mylene could only nod.

"But why, sir, did you not attempt to bring in the kidnappers?"

"My good Inspector, I'm only one man. I deemed it my patriotic duty to return the lady. But after all, I must leave *some* work for you fellows at Scotland Yard."

"You could have notified us of your intentions."

"And what would you have done, had I done so, Inspector? Insisted on sending along some of your men? A notion that could only have jeopardized the lady's safety, at best. No, Inspector, I deemed it fitting that I should get in and out as inconspicuously as possible."

No matter how many questions the inspector asked, Johnny had a ready answer for every one. Oh, he was smooth, all right. In one bold stroke, he'd succeeded in making fools of Roger *and* Scotland Yard. And by pointing up Scotland Yard's deficiencies, he effectively deflected blame from himself. As the inspector flushed redder at each thrust, Mylene felt a grudging respect.

Finally it was over. They were free to go, back into the main hall, with the reporters renewing their efforts to gather details. As the newsmen pushed and shoved, making it all but impossible for the small group to head toward the waiting carriages, Johnny stepped to Katharine Helmsley and said, "I fear for your daughter-in-law, my lady. Not merely her safety, but for the strain of having to deal with these reporters. Is there not some place we might stash her for a time? Until the uproar dies down?"

Katharine's face lit up. "I have the very thing! We'll go to our estate in the country for the week's end. And you, Lord Whitney, must come, of course. We must celebrate your heroism in grand style."

As Johnny bowed his acceptance, he gave Mylene a sly glare. She realized then that he'd manipulated the invitation so he could keep a watchful eye on her.

As they were leaving the station with the reporters following behind, she took him aside. "I know what you're up to," she declared. "But you won't get away with it."

He raised a challenging brow. "Won't I?"

Roger stepped to her side to help her into the carriage. As he did, she could see the quiet look of pain in his eyes.

Chapter 9

"A toast to the hero of the hour!"

Mylene seethed inside as the Prince of Wales rose to his feet, wineglass in hand. All around the banquet table at the Helmsley country estate the distinguished guests followed suit, raising their glasses and exclaiming "Lord Whitney!" with the same awestruck simpering that had turned Mylene's stomach since their return. The fine crystal clinked melodiously as Johnny gave a gracious and humble bow. Sipping her champagne, Mylene felt the last thing she wanted was to give credence to this ridiculous farce. She'd like to spit the imported Perrier-Jouët in Johnny's grinning face. But how could she, with the prince himself offering the toast?

"I've always been proud of the derring-do of our fine Englishmen," the prince continued. "But no one has yet exemplified this grand tradition like Lord Whitney."

All up and down the grand dining hall, the faces of the guests—the fashionable aristocracy and country squires from neighboring Sussex estates—were flushed with pride and pleasure. These same luminaries had witnessed Roger's humiliation at the hands of the villain who'd snatched his bride from the church beneath their outraged eyes. To a man, these lords who dictated the rules of the land had felt the theft of the Helmsleys' intended daughter-in-law as a personal affront. They looked upon Lord Whitney now with a mixture of male envy and deference while their wives and daughters blushed and favored the hero with secret, longing smiles.

All but Roger, who'd remained stiff and formal throughout the festivities.

Mylene stole a glance at him and realized he was enjoying this no more than she. Beneath the facade of courtesy that had been bred into him from birth lurked the watchful, jealous gaze of a man who'd been shown up in a public scandal. When he wasn't covertly glaring at Johnny as if he'd like to kill him, he was peering at Mylene with a questioning tilt to his brow. Clearly, he was suspicious—of what, Mylene was afraid to surmise.

Now he sipped his champagne as if he thought it might poison him. Then, as the murmurs died, he spoke in the stilted tone of one addressing another he couldn't openly admit was his adversary. "Indeed, Lord Whitney, I must add my personal appreciation for the return of my bride."

Johnny lounged back in his chair with negligent ease. "Nonsense, my lord. I'm certain you'd have rescued her yourself, had you not been tied up in London at the time."

Despite his training, Roger flushed at the further implication that he'd been sitting on his hands, attending to more pressing matters, while the illustrious Lord Whitney had been scouring the countryside, searching for his bride.

Oh, to crawl under the table and hide! Mylene felt the tension in the catch of the guests' breath, in the prickle of her hair at the back of her neck. Her shoulders throbbed under the strain of sitting erect through this travesty, and she felt her face burn hot and red. But Johnny's smile was amiable, disguising the barb as a compliment to the good man's intentions, and the guests, in their stupor of admiration, chose to view it as such.

"We're so terribly grateful to you, Lord Whitney," Katharine Helmsley gushed. "You can't possibly know how terrified we were for our poor girl."

"So right," cried William as the servant refilled his glass. "We're in your debt, my good man. We'd despaired of ever seeing our dear girl again. The horrors that crossed our minds, you'll never know."

"I think I have some idea," Johnny said in a deceptively silky tone.

Again, Mylene felt Roger's razor gaze bore into her. Damn Johnny's soul! Did he have to look at her with those hooded eyes that spoke of secrets he was loath to disclose?

"And how fortunate we are that you found her before those awful men could besmirch her honor," Katharine added.

This last was particularly galling. Just that morning, Mylene's mortification had been complete when she'd seen the headline on the front page of the *Times*.

HERO FOILS CAPTORS
BRIDE RETURNED UNSPOILED
ABDUCTORS TOO OCCUPIED WITH
ELUDING AUTHORITIES' GRASP

Unspoiled, indeed! The arrogance of Johnny's assertion infuriated her as much as his playing the role of hero when he'd kidnapped her in the first place. The nerve of the swine, to allow this fawning sham, all the while laughing up his sleeve.

At the look he gave her, some of the women twittered behind their fans. Their meaning was clear. Any one of them would have welcomed the opportunity to be "spoiled" at the gallant Lord Whitney's hands. All eyes turned to her as they wondered yet again if she hadn't secretly succumbed to his all-too-obvious dashing charm. There wasn't a woman in the room who could imagine herself possessing the pious fortitude such a sacrifice would require.

Their sly looks compounded the horror of the weekend. It hadn't been enough that Katharine had invited Johnny to Greenwood with the family. She'd had to solicit the company of her curious friends as well, so they could gawk and ask Mylene the very questions she was trying to avoid. She'd thought their companionship just the thing to take Mylene's mind from her tribulations. One last weekend fling before they all moved into town for the season and the opening of Parliament the next week. So she'd filled the house with gaiety and chatter, planning festivities like a general executing military maneuvers.

God help me, Mylene thought. *Will this ever end?*

The prince was speaking, looking directly at Mylene, so she had to blink to bring her mind back to the present.

"—anything we can do for you, you've only to let us know. The Queen, though in seclusion, has expressed her horror at the outrage that has been perpetuated on your person. She asks that you visit her at your convenience so she might express to you personally her concern and gratification at your safe return."

"Her Majesty is most kind," Mylene murmured.

"She's developed a fondness for you on the occasions of your visits. She's often remarked on what a good-hearted girl you are. 'Would that all my subjects were as kind and thoughtful of their queen,' she's often said. Her invitation is most heartfelt, I assure you."

Again, Mylene felt a stirring of guilt. Both Victoria and her son, affectionately known as Bertie, had been kind and solicitous to her during her stay in London. While Bertie was a known womanizer, he preferred married women, and had treated her as a benevolent older brother might. And his wife, Alix, often lonely in her adopted home, had sought out Mylene's friendship on numerous occasions.

"Please relay my appreciation to the Queen, and assure her that I'll make a point of visiting her."

"Is this the beginning of an outbreak of radicalism, then, do you think?" asked Johnny as Mylene shot a glance at him in surprise.

"Good gracious, I hope not!" said Lord Avery, a junior member of Parliament whose sole mission was to impress Lord Stanley. "What a cowardly act this was, to prey on a defenseless woman. Isn't that just like those bloody micks?"

"Are none of us safe?" Johnny asked dryly.

"It's clear," said Lord Stanley, "that we have to take firmer measures against these animals."

"Here, here!" cried several of the men.

"And to think," said Johnny, "there are actually members in Parliament who think they deserve Home Rule."

Mylene eyed him suspiciously. Clearly, he was egging them on. But to what end?

"Can you imagine if those savages were allowed to run free?"

"Balderdash. It's unthinkable, that's what it is. There'd be insurrection from all fronts."

"What they need," said Lord Avery with a smirk, "is a good dose of English steel up their arses."

Lord Stanley squirmed in his seat. "Please, my lord. There are women present."

"Quite so. My apologies. I tend to become heated over this issue."

"Everyone knows the Irish are an inferior race. The buggers mate with their own family members, you know. The priests actually encourage it."

Mylene sat up in her chair, outraged by such a bald-faced lie. But when her eyes sought Johnny's, she found him looking at her with a slightly arched brow.

"Oh, surely not, Lord Dawson," Katharine cried.

"I have it on the best authority. With their own siblings!"

"Definitely an inferior race. Definitely."

"Well, if they think they're going to influence my position on Home Rule by abducting my daughter, they're sadly mistaken," Lord Stanley declared.

"There's a rumor in India," Johnny said, draping his arm over the back of his chair, "that in the days when we English were nothing more than savages, the Irish were a sophisticated race, with a culture and literature to rival any on the Continent. That, they say, is why we English are so bent on keeping the Irish in bondage. That we, from a sense of inferiority, must wipe away such memories by keeping them enslaved."

There was a deathly pause while every person at the table digested this bit of treason.

"Well," said Lord Avery at last. "What do you expect from Indians? They're no better than the Irish. Without us to govern them, they'd most surely fall to pieces."

"Have you read Professor Siffredi's theories?" asked Lady Avery, a woman noted for her peculiar tastes in literature. "He contends the Irish have a diminished brain capacity. While the craniums of the rest of the human species have grown larger through the years, those of the inbred Irish have in fact grown smaller."

Mylene felt her anger churn inside. The nerve of the woman to talk about inbreeding when the aristocracy were so inbred! Wouldn't she like to tell the witch how the two Irishmen under their very noses had made fools of them all! But she felt Johnny's stare and realized, belatedly, that this was what he'd planned all along. To show her the sort of small-minded prejudice and hatred with which they were dealing. Angry with them all, she took a sip of wine to try to calm herself.

"Enough of this talk of the Irish," Katharine admonished. "Poor Mylene, you see how upset she is. Hasn't our poor darling had enough sorrow at the hands of those hooligans?"

"Why I'd forgotten," cooed Lady Avery. "Your parents were killed by the Irish, weren't they?"

Mylene drank her glass dry to keep from saying something she might regret.

"Do forgive us. It was most unseemly of us to broach the subject in your presence."

But they hadn't broached it. Johnny had.

Katharine suggested they adjourn to the parlor. As the guests crowded out into the hall, Mylene hung back. She noted that Johnny did the same. When everyone was gone, she whirled on him in a fury.

"You did that on purpose!"

Johnny shrugged. "To show you what you're up against, if you feel compelled to confession. *That's* the kind of man you're dealing with. Don't forget it."

"I'll concede that this isn't the right time or place. The atmosphere isn't conducive, thanks to you getting them fighting mad at the Irish. But I *will* find the right time and place. And Lord Stanley *will* understand."

He crossed the distance between them and glared down at her. "Understand, will he? You'll be knowing what he understands by that conversation."

Just then, Roger appeared in the doorway. "We're waiting," he said stiltedly.

"Yes, we're just coming," Mylene told him.

He stood there a moment, then gave a formal bow and left.

Mylene turned to Johnny quickly and hissed, "You've been baiting Roger since we returned."

"It's more than talk he'll be getting if he steps a foot closer to you."

"If you think to sway me with your theatrics, you're daft. I'm going through with the wedding as soon as we're back in London. I'll elope with Roger, if I have to. You can't stop me."

"We'll see about that."

"There's nothing you can do about it. You've run out of tricks, Johnny. I'm after marrying Roger. And I'm going to tell Lord Stanley the truth. I trust him. I know I can convince him. He, in turn, will help me convince Roger. And you and Shamus Flynn can rot for all I care."

She was about to leave, but he caught her arm and held her with his fingers biting into the flesh. "You'll tell Stanley over my dead body," he growled. "Or his."

It wasn't long before Mylene realized her mistake in confessing her plans to Johnny.

Long ago, in the orphanage, he'd been her only confessor. They'd shared secrets they'd told no one else. It had become a habit, discussing everything with him. And now, when they were at odds, she couldn't seem to keep herself from blurting things out to him that she should have kept inside. Perhaps, she thought, it stemmed from the years of secrecy in England, having no one to talk to who knew who she really was or what she was doing there. It had been wonderful, she realized now, to speak openly to Johnny, without watching what she said. But she was soon to learn, once again, how Johnny had changed. The boy who'd kept her disclosures to himself had become a man fully capable of using her secrets against her.

It began the next morning. The servants were up at dawn, preparing the house for the day's activities. Many of the guests were up as early as eight o'clock, the men freshly dressed in country tweeds, the women in pastel morning dresses, less formal than those worn in town, to take advantage of the first blush of spring. When Mylene joined them, the smell of bacon and newly brewed tea wafted through the corridors of the ancient mansion that had been the country dwelling of Helmsleys for eight generations. The guests greeted her from the table, inquiring after her health, waving to the sideboard, piled high with eggs, bacon, kippers, and an abundance of country strawberries and cream. But as she headed for the pot of tea, resting beneath a colorful tea cozy, Johnny rose from the table and cut her off.

"You must be tired," he said with gentlemanly solicitation. "Allow me to serve you."

She couldn't very well refuse. But as he brought her a cup of steaming tea and a plate heaped with offerings, he paused to give her a warmly secretive smile.

"How chivalrous of you, Lord Whitney," said Katharine, aglow in her role of hostess. "You play the gallant well. No doubt they train gentlemen better in India than we do on our own shores. I daresay our own husbands could take notes."

The women nodded, envying Mylene, and Lady Avery chimed in. "You must open a school, my lord. Lord Whitney's Academy for the Gallant Arts. I, for one, shall enroll Lord Avery *forthwith*."

The women laughed, making equally cheerful suggestions, while the gentlemen humphed and hawed and protested their own gallantry in an atmosphere of merry goodwill. Everyone was in high spirits this morning, with a weekend of fun to look forward to. Everyone, that is, except Roger, who hid his displeasure at Lord Whitney's so-called gallantry by paying particular attention to his kippers.

Mylene ate sparingly, wondering what Johnny was up to, making so public a point of aligning himself with her. She didn't like it. She sensed Roger's anger. If Johnny kept this up, he might well push Roger too far. And then what?

But it seemed that was Johnny's intention all along.

As they settled in, talk turned to the fox hunt planned for the next day. Fox hunting, Mylene had discovered, was the particular passion of the English gentleman. In fact, no Englishman would dare consider himself a gentleman if not gifted for the hunt. It seemed that political appointments were increasingly given not to those best qualified, but to those men with expertise at fox hunting and entertaining, which invariably went hand in hand.

"I can already feel the blood pumping through my veins," cried Lord Avery, rubbing his hands together in anticipation. "Nothing like a good hunt to make a fellow feel alive."

"Couldn't we go today?" asked another eager sport.

"My dear sir," cried Katharine, "would you spoil my meticulous planning? No, the hunt is set for tomorrow, and tomorrow it shall be."

"But if you're eager for sport," Lord Helmsley offered, "we'll go for a ride this morning. Shoot some pheasant for dinner, what? I don't suppose that will upset my wife's plans too dearly."

"I should love pheasant for dinner. What a charming idea."

Avid horsemen all, they bolted their breakfast and went to make preparations for the ride. Some of the women decided to go along. Mylene, seeing that Lord Stanley intended going, decided to do the same. Perhaps she could coax him off to a private glade and speak to him then.

But Johnny obviously guessed her intentions. When she came out to the drive, the grooms had brought the saddled horses and the guests were already mounting. Before she could choose a mount, Johnny led over a sleek bay mare and, with a glint of amusement in his eyes, helped her up. And as they rode out into the fresh country morning, he remained steadfastly at her side, commenting idly on the miles of wooded pasture that made up the Greenwood estate. If she tried to duck him to join Lord Stanley, he headed her off and made some innocuous comment that forced her to be civil, often leaning over to whisper something to her in an intimate fashion. And all the while, Roger watched and stewed.

As the men shot pheasant, the women stayed back and watched. Johnny, too, declined the hunt, claiming he was saving his energies for the following day. But Mylene knew better.

As the dogs, excited at the outing, ran to point out the fallen birds, Mylene took the opportunity to whirl on Johnny. "Just what do you think you're doing?"

"I thought that was obvious," he said, without the flippant gentleman's tone he'd been using all morning. "I'm going to dog your every step. I'm going to watch every move you make."

Her anger made her want to lash out at him. But instead she gave him a coy smile. "And what do you intend doing tomorrow at the hunt, may I ask?"

His eyes shot to her, then narrowed dangerously. She knew his feelings about the English obsession with hunting for the sake of sport. Johnny had always had a soft spot in his heart for innocent animals slaughtered for the pleasure of foolish men. Once, when he was twelve, he'd beaten an older boy near to death for mistreating a mangy dog. She and Daggett had been forced to drag him off before he killed the bloodied boy. When he'd calmed down, he'd adopted the stray, lavishing affection on the lame mongrel until its death, years later.

"I'll deal with that when the time comes," he said shortly.

But it seemed all the guests at Greenwood could talk about was the hunt. All the way back to the house, they discussed every detail, anticipating the weather, scouting terrain. All through afternoon tea, they planned strategy. When the ladies rose for a game of croquet on the lawn, the gentlemen joined them, though merely as spectators, for they were still discussing the subject like little boys too long deprived of a holiday. Even the Prince of Wales seemed atwitter at the prospect.

Mylene, who had learned croquet out of necessity but wasn't proficient, watched as Johnny grew quieter and quieter throughout the afternoon. Then, as she was awaiting her turn, she heard William Helmsley say, "As our guest of honor, Lord Whitney, I feel it only proper that you should lead the hunt tomorrow. Normally, we'd offer such a prize to the prince, but he's agreed that, to reward your heroism, you should be given the highest honor."

"Quite so," said the prince. "As a tribute to your patriotism, sir."

Mylene watched Johnny closely. Perfectly composed, he gave a bow and thanked them. But as she took her place for her turn, she looked up to find him crossing the lawn with determined strides.

When he was upon her, he stood behind her and wrapped his arms around her, grasping her hands on the mallet as if showing her the proper swing. But she could feel the anger surging through him. "It's just like those arrogant popinjays. To get such joy from hunting down and killing an innocent fox that they make it the focus of their whole bloody weekend. To prove their manhood by killing creatures for the fun of it. We're like that fox, all the peoples they condescend to govern. Hunted down and hounded until they steal from us the very will to live. And they call themselves civilized!"

Mylene realized that her instincts of the morning had been correct. At last she had a weapon she could use to taunt Johnny, the way he was taunting her.

"Poor Johnny," she cooed. "What a dilemma. To expose or not to expose, that's the question. Do you stick with your ideals and spare the fox, giving yourself away? Or do you do as they wish to protect your identity as an English lord, and become one of these men you profess to hate so much?"

His hands gripped hers so hard they hurt.

"How does it feel, Johnny? To have to become one of them for the sake of your cause? Sitting in Ireland, it's easy to cast judgment on me. But I should like to see what you decide. Kill the fox and save your hide, or save the fox and kill your masquerade?"

He was about to speak, but suddenly stopped. His voice changed, and he began to swing the mallet. "I think you'll find if you hold it so—"

Mylene glanced up to see Roger coming their way. "Perhaps I could be of assistance?" he asked. His tone was polite, but it was clear he was annoyed. She'd been so consumed by her conversation with Johnny, she hadn't realized how his helping her would look.

Johnny stepped aside with a bow. "If you think you can be more useful to her, by all means, my lord, give it your best try."

As Johnny left, Roger searched Mylene's face. "I can't say I like the way that chap looks at you."

"Pay no attention to him. He carries his role too far."

"It's difficult to belay acting the champion, all things considered. Still . . . is there something you'd care to tell me, Mylene? I assure you, you may speak truthfully to me, and I shall endeavor to understand."

This, Mylene realized, was what Johnny was after. Having told him she intended to go through with the wedding, he was using every opportunity to shatter Roger's confidence in her affections. Shooting an angry glance at Johnny's retreating back, she said, "You mustn't imagine things, Roger. I assure you—"

"I happened upon a conversation just this morning. Three of the women guests, not knowing I was around, were saying they couldn't for the life of them see how you'd kept from falling in love with your champion. Had it been them, they vowed, they would have—"

"Roger, please, you mustn't listen to idle gossip. I don't care what they say. If you must know, I'm beginning to loath that man. I wish he'd keep away from me."

She felt her face flush hot beneath the passion of her words. Roger stared at her for a moment. Then, very quietly, he asked, "Are you certain it's loathing you feel?"

Before she could deny his implication, he'd walked away.

Chapter 10

That evening, after she'd dressed for dinner, Mylene ran into Johnny in the hall. She grabbed his arm and turned him to face her with an angry jerk. "I want you to leave Roger alone."

Johnny looked down at her with an insolent sneer. "I wonder, now, what manner of man it is that sits back and takes what I've dished out?"

"That's none of your business. I'll not have you hurting the man."

His teeth flashed white with his grin. "I'll not be spoiling me knuckles on him."

"And who gave you leave to be waiting on the likes of me? What's he going to think, with you pouring my tea and following me about like a love-starved puppy?"

"Exactly what I want him to think."

"I mean it, Johnny. I won't let him think there's something going on between us."

"Is that what he thinks?"

"You know damn well he does. You've done everything in your power to convince him of—"

"The truth? Or is your memory as faulty as your croquet? If he thinks there's something going on between us, it's only because there is. I have fond recollections of those nights of passion—"

"Hush now! Do you want them all to hear?"

The grin slipped from his face. "It seems you've forgotten something else. But let me remind you. I'll let no man have you but me. Helmsley's not for the likes of you, my girl. Do what you will, you'll never marry the man. Not if I have to kill him."

His ruthless tone turned her blood to ice.

"You wouldn't dare."

"Wouldn't I? Try me, then, and see."

Her hand that had been clutching his sleeve balled into a fist. "You do and so help me, Johnny, you'll have no bit of me!"

"Oh, won't I?"

Just then, a door opened up the hall. Mylene dropped her hand from Johnny's arm, but in an instant, he pulled her to him. Stunned, she felt herself propelled against him, felt his arms crush her back, felt his mouth crash down on hers. She tried to fight him off, but he held her so closely she couldn't move. He kissed her deeply, bending her back, grinding his mouth into hers.

Another door opened. Gathering her strength, Mylene shoved at Johnny hard and broke his grasp. Wheeling, she saw Roger standing before one door and his mother, Katharine, at another. Both stared with the same stunned look on their faces.

Mylene's hand flew to her mouth, where Johnny's

kiss still burned. "Roger—" she cried, grasping frantically for an explanation.

Johnny had seen him standing there before he'd kissed her. Now as he faced the livid countenance of her fiancé, he straightened his dinner jacket and said, with the flawless understatement of an English lord, "Well, this *is* awkward."

"How could you, Lord Whitney?" Katharine cried. "You're a guest in my home!"

"I confess my feelings got the better of me. If I were the gentleman you think me, I'd apologize. Unfortunately, I can't quite bring myself to feel sorry. I suppose, sir," he added, turning to Roger, "the only thing left to do is fight a duel for the lady's hand. Archaic, perhaps, but it would settle matters neatly."

Mylene gasped in horror. He'd really meant it when he'd said he'd kill Roger. And he'd just lured him into the trap.

Roger stood stock-still, the blood draining from his face. Mylene could feel him ready to explode. He was no coward. He'd surely accept. But, skilled with the pistol as he was, he was no match for Johnny, who'd trained with Shamus Flynn. Roger would die, and it would be her fault.

"Roger, don't, I beg of you."

"Nonsense, girl," snapped Katharine. "Roger's honor is at stake. Of course he must fight."

But when Roger spoke, he surprised them all. "That won't be necessary," he said through gritted teeth, scuttling his anger in a cold show of dignity. "Under the circumstances, the only thing to do is to yield to the better ... showman. I therefore relinquish my claim. And I wish you both great happiness."

He turned to leave, but Mylene raced past

Katharine and caught Roger going down the stairs. "Roger, I swear to you—"

He cut her off. "My dear, if you seek to tell me you were no part of this, please spare yourself. I know you well enough, I think, to believe you'd do nothing to betray me. If I thought the fellow was forcing his attentions on you, I'd be the first to complain."

"But he was—"

"No, my dear. I may be a fool, but I know a woman in love when I see one. I see the way you look at him. I've known it, I think, since I saw you at the station. You're in love with your rescuer and there's nothing I can do about it. It's not your fault. We can't always choose whom we love. Were I a woman and rescued by such as he, who's to say how I might feel? No, I don't blame you. But I care enough about you to want you to be happy. And as much as I should like you as my wife, I'd like to think I'm not selfish enough to stand in your way."

"Well said," Katharine stated from the top of the stairs, clearly struggling to control her wrath and remember that the guilty parties were still guests in her home. She turned to Johnny. "Well, Lord Whitney, you've caused quite a scandal. Are your intentions as honorable as my son's?"

Johnny, standing beside her on the landing, bowed. "I assure you, my lady, I have every intention—"

"Very well," Katharine stated in the tone of a judge. "I can't pretend to be pleased by this distressing turn of events. But as hosts, we have an obligation to salvage as much of this week's end for our guests as we possibly can. I shall put on a good face, and Roger, I expect you and your father to do the same. We shall handle this disgrace with as much dignity as we can muster. Now, if you'll all compose yourselves, we shall go down to dinner and announce the engagement of Mylene to Lord Whitney. That is, I presume, what you intend, Lord Whitney?"

"Yes, Lady Helmsley," Johnny said seriously, looking at Mylene. "That's what I intended all along."

It was a nightmare.

The news was received with a startled silence that seemed to suspend time in a panorama of horrified faces. Eyes darted from the newly betrothed couple to Roger to measure his reaction, before the breeding of centuries began to penetrate their shock. One by one, they cleared throats or wriggled in their seats as they strove to squelch the cry of "Poor Roger! Whatever will you do?" and replace it with polite, if dismayed, offerings of congratulations. It was an English mania never to reveal true feelings, so they shook Johnny's hand and wished Mylene well, saving their appalled gossip for a time when they wouldn't be overheard.

Even the prince added his blessing, surprising Johnny when he took their hands in his and wished them well. "If ever I can help you in any way," he offered to Johnny, "you will let me know, won't you? We think highly of Mylene. And you, sir, must now be added to our affections."

Dinner was a decidedly awkward affair. By all appearances, Roger seemed to take it in stride, showing a brave front to his friends and professing to be resigned, even offering a toast to the couple that caused Katharine to nod in satisfaction at having raised a gentleman for a son. But Mylene detected the flush of shame in his cheeks as he endeavored to carry his end of the conversation. Poor man, she thought, he must want nothing more than to hide his face.

If the assembled guests were taken aback by the news, Mylene was furious. That Johnny would toy with something that should be precious—that under other circumstances she might have relished—hurt and angered her. She knew why he'd forced the engagement. Not from any romantic notions of having her for his wife. But because it was the best way to serve his plan while keeping her from proceeding with her own. A clever way of shackling her to him, where he could keep an eye on her activities and control her actions. She had no doubt that he'd go through with the wedding. What better way to ensure that she didn't betray the Great Plan?

She felt trapped and used. She'd been given no opportunity to protest. Everyone assumed that what Johnny said was true. In fact, he made such a convincing case, telling them all how he'd loved Mylene upon his return from India but had despaired of her affections, and had made a valiant effort to tamp down his feelings. They remembered the scene he'd made at Mylene's engagement ball, when he'd sought her out at once, only to storm off beneath—they now assumed—the weight of her choice of another man.

"But how," he asked the stunned throng, "could I sit back and allow those ruffians to carry off my beloved? Even to return her to another man was better than the torture of what might happen were I to sit idly home. I knew I had to rescue her, if only so she could marry another. At least then, I felt, she'd be happy and safe. To see her happy is my only desire."

Then, in a master stroke, he turned to Lord Stanley with a humble bow. "My lord, I know the wishes of my beloved's heart, but I would be remiss were I not to ask you formally for her hand. If you object, I swear I'll bear it as well as such news can be borne. But if you'll have me as a son-in-law, I shall do all in my power to make your charming daughter as happy as you'll have made me."

It was bad form to put the man on the spot with so public an audience. Lord Stanley, mystified and uncomfortable as he was, took a sip of wine to stall. Finally, with all eyes turned his way, he said, "Mylene's happiness is all that I require, my lord. If she loves you, who am I to contravene?"

Mylene had to bite her lip to keep from crying out. What a hypocrite Johnny was! Treating her as if she had no feelings, and no say. Swearing his love like some milksop who considers himself beneath notice. Mylene could tell them all a thing or two about that love. But how could she, without giving herself away?

So she endured the unpleasant display in silence. If she wasn't exactly the picture of the blushing bride-to-be, everyone credited her with sensitivity to Roger's feelings, never guessing the fury that kept her teeth clenched and her eyes downcast.

That night, she couldn't sleep. She was so angry with Johnny, she paced the room for hours, succeeding only in gathering more steam. She was right about him, she decided. He didn't care whom he hurt if it accomplished his designs. Never mind that Roger was devastated, or that William and Katharine had just lost someone they'd come to think of as a daughter. Never mind that he'd shattered everything *she* wanted in the process. Finally, she could take it no longer. Pulling on a robe, careful that no one saw her along the way, she crept down the hall to duck into Johnny's room.

It took a moment for her eyes to adjust to the dark. She heard his steady breathing and knew he was asleep. Resolutely, she crossed the room, her bare feet sinking into the thick carpet, and saw him silhouetted in the poster bed. The sheet was curled about his legs, and when she peered closely she could see that his chest was naked, the dark furrowed hair giving him a rugged appearance, trailing the muscled planes and thinning to a V above the sheet. He seemed so peaceful in the shadows. No doubt he'd drifted easily to sleep, satisfied with the shambles he'd made of her life. While she had paced the floor, fuming over his duplicity.

Enraged, she shook his shoulder roughly. He shot up in the dark, reaching for the pistol he kept by his bed. But when he saw her he dropped it and, lunging from the mattress, grabbed her.

"What do you think you're doing?" he growled.

"How dare you play God with my life, you arrogant wretch!" she spat out. "If you think I'll marry you for all your conniving, you're a bigger fool than I'd hoped."

He stared at her, breathing hard. "Fool, am I? Maybe I am, to spare a feeling for an ungrateful chit like you."

"Ungrateful, you call me, because I don't thank you for chaining me to you like a hound?"

"Ungrateful because you're too wrapped up in your delusions to realize I just saved your sorry neck. I've told you Shamus Flynn won't let you marry Helmsley. Or have you forgotten your oath of obedience completely?"

"That's not why you did it. You forced this on me to keep me under watch. To keep me from divulging what I know to Lord Stanley."

"To give you a way to stick with the plan."

"Making a mockery of it all the while, professing your *noble* love before those unsuspecting souls. Love! You don't even know what it means."

His hand tightened on her arm. He was quiet for some time, digesting her words. Finally he said in a ragged voice, "I'll tell you one thing. If any man did to me what I just did to your precious Roger, I'd fight him to the death. I love you enough to fight for you, Mylene. I'd lie for you. I'd cheat for you. I'd *kill* for you. And I certainly wouldn't stand back and let another man take you from me."

She suddenly realized that he was completely naked. It made her painfully aware of his hand gripping her arm, of how she stood just a meager breath away. Diverting her eyes from his body, she gave him a rebellious stare.

"You lie with every breath you take. You said it yourself. The Fenians trained you so well you don't know where Johnny begins or ends. I can't even find the man I loved anymore. You're like a machine. You live and die by your sacred plan, and to perdition with us all. Well, I won't have it. I wouldn't marry you if—"

"Oh, but you will. You're going to be my wife, Mylene. There was never any other choice. And someday, when you're thinking clearly, you'll see that I'm doing this to protect you. From the Fenians. And from yourself."

"And who's going to protect me from *you?*" she snarled, before she wrenched her arm away and stormed out of the room.

Chapter 11

The day of the planned hunt dawned cloudy with the tang of rain in the air. Early that morning, because she'd slept little, Mylene went down for tea and overheard William and Katharine speaking in hushed tones, wondering if, under the circumstances, they should proceed as planned.

"I'm no happier with this turn of events than you, my dear," she heard William say. "But as you so aptly reminded us, we have an obligation to our other guests. We must set the tone for their sakes, as well as our own. If we cancel now, we shall be viewed as the most unseemly of hosts."

Mylene crept away, feeling the way a leper must feel when hearing her condition discussed in the form of charity.

Later, when she came down again, she found the hunt already in the works. The horses were saddled, the caged dogs barked and jumped and scrambled over one another in anticipation. Bedlam was the order of the morning, distracting the guests from the scandal of the night before, as the men dressed and sought out whips and spurs, while the women bustled about serving mugs of ale to fortify the adventurers. A hunt was normally a day of celebration, and the still reeling guests were doing their best to rally for the sake of their hosts. Many of the country folk from the village and farmers under the Helmsleys' patronage had shown up to cheer the hunters on. Some brought carts to follow in their wake. Others trudged out beneath the heavy clouds to place themselves along the acreage, to wait and applaud when the hunters galloped by. Those who could joined in, accepting the timeworn hospitality of their squire on this, the final hunt before the London season, when the Helmsleys and those country gentry who could afford it would abandon the provinces and troop into town. And before Lord Stanley made his much anticipated excursion to Dublin the following week to view the Irish situation firsthand.

"I feel a storm in the air," someone remarked over the din, causing Mylene to wonder if he meant the weather or Roger's sullen mood.

William did his best to carry the day. "What's a little storm? Only adds to the challenge, what, lads?"

The men added cheery comments, but the gaiety seemed forced to Mylene's sensitive ears.

For the most part, the women would stay behind. A few of the daughters, young and hardy enough to withstand the rigors, like Mylene, would ride with the pack, although the hunt itself was considered masculine domain. Despite the pall of Johnny's announcement, the group began to pick up the excitement of the anticipated sport. Old men strutted like youths, calling to one another with a boisterous pitch to their voices. They began to look crazed, caught up in the blood lust that seized them at thoughts of besting the fox and proving that they were good Englishmen, all. It never ceased to astonish Mylene that these men, so refined in normal circumstances that their conversation teetered on the brink of boredom, could be so dramatically transformed at the thought of chasing down and killing a defenseless creature.

But today, Mylene had other things on her mind. Her enforced engagement had made her desperate. She had to act at once, or the wheels of providence would spin out of control. She hadn't seen Johnny yet. Perhaps he'd decided to hide out after the discomfort he'd caused the night before. She almost wished he would. It would leave her free to corner Lord Stanley and have the talk she now knew couldn't wait another day. Once Lord Stanley heard the truth, once she'd made him understand her position, he'd help her figure a way out of this predicament. Yes, she must speak with him immediately.

As if reading her thoughts, Lord Stanley came up to her and took her hand. "Are you certain you've made the right choice, child?"

She had to blink to figure out what he meant.

"I'm fond of Roger, I've made no secret of that. And I'd had high hopes for the two of you. But if you truly love Lord Whitney and are assured you'll be happy, that's all I desire. I don't know him as well as I might wish. But he's from an old and venerable family. And he did, after all, return you to me. If you love him, I'm certain he's worthy of your affections."

"Lord Stanley, I wish to speak with you about that."

But, true to form, Johnny made his entrance, as if

he'd planned the moment. A hush fell over the crowd as they stared at him, not certain what to say.

"Ah, here he is now," said Lord Stanley.

Johnny looked handsome in his hunting gear, but he seemed quiet, preoccupied. He barely noticed the mistrustful glares angled his way.

William moved through the quiet crowd and assumed his role as the welcoming host. "There you are, my good fellow. Now, we've discussed this at great length. We assume you didn't have much cause to hunt fox in India. More likely chasing tigers, I daresay."

A stilted laugh followed his words. Johnny smiled but said nothing.

"We do things a little differently here at Greenwood. We'll let the fox go and give it a sporting head start. Then we'll loose the hounds and you, as our leader, will start us on the chase. The dogs will tree the fox. That's as usual. But we like to reward our guest of honor by allowing him to shoot the fox. And to further honor him by having him cut off the tail and keep it as a badge of distinction, so to speak. So once the fox is cut off completely, we'll join you to witness it, before coming back to toast the victory. Is that all clear, then?"

"And if the fox should escape?"

William looked genuinely shocked. "But my dear fellow, the fox never escapes. We continue the hunt till he's caught and killed."

"I see." Johnny cast a quick glance to Mylene, then quickly flicked his eyes away. But she caught a flash of vulnerability in his eyes. She could almost feel pity for his position, if she weren't so furious.

"Then let's off, shall we? I do believe I felt a drop of rain just now."

By the time they'd all mounted, the rain was beginning to fall in earnest. The fox was let loose with great ceremony to run for the woods as the hounds bayed and howled. When the time was deemed right, the servants let the dogs go. They shot through the riders, running in circles until they picked up the scent, then charged across the fields in clamorous pursuit.

The hornsman sounded his horn and, with Johnny at the lead, the riders took off at a gallop. Mylene kept close to Lord Stanley, awaiting her opportunity. But she soon began to despair. The pace was hard and frantic, the horses pounding across the terrain. As the rain increased, the ground became slippery. Two of the horses slid and fell. The rest galloped by as the horn kept blasting from somewhere in the pack.

It all went by in a haze. Galloping across the fields, jumping hedges, leaping over streams. They raced through the woods, the group scattering behind the running dogs. Riding was hazardous at best. They whipped and spurred their steeds to greater speed, fearlessly risking their necks as the villagers cheered them on. The rain was coming hard now, nearly blinding Mylene as the wind whipped at her hair. Thunder rumbled in the distance and lightning split the blackening sky.

It was madness. But the Englishmen seemed not to notice. Dotting the countryside, they rode up and down hills, following Johnny's lead, the hammering of the hooves drowning out all but the thunder, the horn, and the barking dogs.

They lost more riders on the treacherous terrain. Some took spills while jumping hedges higher than their heads, their horses tumbling beneath them. Some slipped and fell in the ever increasing mud. A few of the women slowed their paces, some turning back for the comfort of a warm fire as cold rain lashed and soaked them. But the men pounded on. It was all Mylene could do to stay by Lord Stanley's side.

They rode for what seemed hours, trailing the fox over hill and dale, woods and open country, as it scrambled on frantic legs to be free.

Finally, on a high hill, Lord Stanley pulled rein and Mylene did the same. He sat panting and gave her a sheepish grin. "I fear I'm not as young as I used to be."

"It's just as well," said Mylene, out of breath herself. "It will give us a chance to discuss something of great importance."

"I'm all ears, my dear. Just give me a few moments to catch my breath."

From their vantage point, they could see the countryside below, see the fox running for the woods, see the dogs in fast pursuit. Mylene spotted Johnny at the head of the group, the others following like a meandering stream behind. She was struggling to find the right words to begin the most difficult talk of her life when suddenly they heard a fearsome squeal. Looking down, Mylene saw at once that the fox had been caught in a trap at the entrance to the woods. It struggled desperately, but its leg was held fast. The dogs were barreling down on it, howling triumph.

Mylene watched in horror, realizing the dogs would likely tear the poor creature apart. She couldn't imagine a more awful death, even for one so doomed.

But then she saw Johnny increase his horse's pace, going like the wind, running down the dogs, then leaping from the galloping horse. As the dogs descended on the fox, Johnny fought his way through, pushing them aside. But the hounds, with the smell of blood in their nostrils, turned on him, savagely tearing at him as he sought to beat them off. Mylene held her breath as

Lord Stanley cried, "Good God, what's the fellow doing? He'll be killed!"

Mylene's gloved hands gripped the reins as she watched the fierce battle, the rain pouring down on Johnny as he valiantly fought his way through the marauding dogs, mindless of them biting at his arms and legs.

"We have to help him," Lord Stanley said, and took off at a gallop down the hill. Mylene followed, racing through the rain at breakneck speed.

By the time they'd reached him with the others, Johnny was holding the bleeding fox high above his head, out of reach of the dogs, who leaped and growled and tore at him in an effort to get to their prey. Johnny's clothes were ripped to ribbons, his lacerated flesh flowing blood.

Someone called the dogs to heel. They sat, whimpering, as Johnny cradled the fox in his arms, speaking to it in soft tones. He didn't even seem to notice that he'd been mauled by the dogs and his white shirt was red with his own blood.

"But my lord, you've saved the fox," someone said.

Slowly, Johnny looked up to find them sitting their horses in a semicircle, staring at him as if he'd lost his mind.

"It's the only decent thing I could do. It was caught in a trap."

"Demmed poachers," cursed William. "They're the bane of our existence, always sneaking on the land and setting their traps. Nothing we do seems to discourage them. Ruddy nuisance, is what it is. But my good fellow, you've been torn to bits—"

When Johnny looked at him, his anger turned his eyes to green sparks. But Mylene could see his efforts to calm himself and remember his role. "I call it bad sport to kill a trapped animal. It's—downright un-English. I'm certain you agree, gentlemen?"

It was brilliant, Mylene thought. To turn their own ridiculous English values back on them and make it a point of honor to save the fox.

After a momentary hush, Lord Stanley said, "Jolly bad sport, I'd say."

And the others took up the call.

"Good show, my lord!"

"What a sportsman!"

"Give the fox a sporting chance. We're not butchers, after all."

"It's hurt," Johnny said. "I'd call it equally unsporting of us to give it another go."

"Right you are, my lord."

"But what shall we do with it? Set it free?"

"Take it to the house," William suggested. "We'll nurse the poor beast back to health."

"Why, yes! We'll make a mascot of it. Give it a name. Old Red Beard. How will that do?"

"We'll be the talk of London!"

As they took up the cheer, Johnny held the fox in his arms, doing his best to shield it from the rain. His dark hair was soaked, plastered to his head, and he looked as vulnerable as a boy. The boy Mylene had known in Dublin. The protector of the persecuted. A man who would risk his life to give a fox a chance.

In that moment, she saw again the Johnny she'd known, the man who would risk everything to protect the innocent, the oppressed, those who couldn't—or wouldn't—fight for themselves. And she remembered what their mission was truly about. The higher goal that had led them to sacrifice their identities, and years of their lives, so those who suffered might be set free.

And she knew she couldn't talk to Lord Stanley. Not yet. Not like this.

But Johnny was faltering. He'd been brutally attacked by the dogs, and bore the bites and scratches to prove it. He was ever so slightly weaving on his feet. Mylene slid off her horse and went to gently take the fox from his arms. As she did, Johnny saw the tears streaming down her face.

The saving of the fox might as well have been William's idea, the way he fussed over it, cleaning its wounded leg and rubbing in the salve before bandaging it in the way he'd learned as a youth in the army. All the guests gathered round, chattering and cooing over the production, calling the fox Old Red Beard and making plans to cart it off to London and display it in the opening session of Parliament. They seemed to welcome the new focus that took their minds off the scandal that had erupted in their midst.

When at last they turned their attentions to Johnny—having put Old Red Beard in a dog's cage with a feast fit for a king—he declined their offers to bathe and bandage his wounds. Changing his clothes, he accepted their whiskey but nothing else. He was fine, he assured them wearily. He needed nothing.

But Mylene wasn't fooled. She saw the whiteness about his mouth. She saw him wince as he sat down to dinner. He hardly ate, but drank copiously of the wine. His movements were stiff, and she knew, despite his brave front, that he was in pain. He seemed preoccupied, hardly listening to the constant conversation about the fox, glancing at his pocket watch throughout the evening as if eager to be done with the entire farce.

Mylene was worried about him. He'd never been

one to care for himself. In Dublin, after a brutal street fight, it was she who'd had to nurse his wounds. Given a choice, he'd ignore his own suffering, preferring to heal in his own way.

But she knew dog bites could be dangerous. He risked infection if they weren't cleaned. Her insistence that they be attended to was ignored, so she silently determined to see to it herself when all the others were abed.

It seemed the evening would never end. But it had been a long day, and the men were tired, for all their bluster. Over port in the parlor, before a roaring fire, they began to yawn and head for bed.

As they were trooping upstairs, Lord Stanley held Mylene back. "I'd forgotten, my dear, in all the excitement, that you wished to speak with me."

Mylene watched as Johnny headed for the stairs, slightly favoring his right leg. He was all she could think of—how he'd so bravely risked himself to save that fox. She wanted to see him alone, to care for him, to tell him all the things she was bursting to say.

So she squeezed Lord Stanley's hand and said, "You're tired, my lord. It can wait for another time."

When she was alone, she went to the kitchen, where the servants were cleaning up after the feast. She asked the butler for salve for Lord Whitney's wounds. When the tin was brought forth, she headed upstairs with it.

The hall was empty. She quietly went to Johnny's door, but as she prepared to knock, she thought better of it. It wouldn't do to be seen going into Johnny's room, and a knock might alert Katharine, who was just across the hall. So instead, she turned the knob softly and stepped inside.

Just in time to see Johnny creep out the window.

He'd shed his dinner jacket and wore only pants and a white shirt, which he'd untucked and allowed to hang loose. She would have called to him, but he disappeared, the sound of his feet landing below following a moment later. Curious, she tucked the tin of salve into her dress pocket and went to the window to look out.

The rain had stopped, but the night was chill. In the filtered moonlight, she could see Johnny heading around the house in a stealthy manner. What could he be up to? She knew she had to follow, but to go out through the front door might arouse suspicions. So she stepped onto the windowsill and reached for the branch of the birch tree.

Climbing down was cumbersome in her satin skirts, but she finally made it, landing on her feet with a soft thud. She rounded the side of the house and saw Johnny heading across the drive toward the cage where the fox was kept. Then she understood. Once again, he was going to set the fox free.

This small act touched her even more than his heroism of the afternoon. That he couldn't bear to see the fox caged spoke of a caring heart she'd thought hardened beyond repair. Clinging to the shadows, she watched with tears in her eyes as he found a smaller cage, put the wounded fox inside, then headed on foot for the fields beyond.

She would have called to him, but she sensed this was something he had to do alone. So instead she followed at a distance, careful to keep her footfalls too soft for him to hear. He walked with a determined gait in spite of the limp that favored his right leg. He walked and walked, heading for the closest woods. He walked until the grand house and its manicured lawns were but a speck on the horizon, indistinct in the surrounding night.

And when he reached the woods, he bent and put the cage on the ground. Opening it, he took the fox in his hands, removed the hindering bandage, and set the creature free. She saw a flash of moonlight on its tail as it ran into the woods and safety.

When he turned back, the empty cage in hand, she stood where she was by the winding stream and let him come to her. He'd never looked more heroic as he limped through the open country, a man alone under a cloudy, moon-trickled sky.

He saw her and stopped. Then, resuming his stride, he headed for her, taking pains to disguise his limp.

"That was a fine thing you did," she told him as he came within hearing.

"I had to do it," he said. "I couldn't stand by and let those pompous curs parade him through all of London like some trophy. He'd die as surely as if I'd shot him. He's free now, and can fend for himself."

"It was grand of you. The way you risked your life to save him. I was that proud of you, Johnny."

He stopped in front of her, looking searchingly into her eyes. "I didn't do it so you'd be proud," he said softly.

"That's *why* I'm proud."

He stood still for a moment, gazing at her, then raked a hand through his tousled hair. As if her kindness baffled him. As if, having faced down her temper, he didn't quite know how to deal with her praise. But she saw him sway slightly, and she reached out to steady him. Then she remembered her mission, and the tin of salve in her pocket.

"Come back to the house with me, Johnny. I've brought salve for your wounds."

"I've no need of it," he said, but his voice betrayed his pain.

"I'll not have you die of infection for the life of one fox."

He glanced at her, then back at the house, which seemed miles away. "I'd not return yet," he told her. "It's only here, out in the open, that I can feel myself. That I can be free of Lord Whitney. I'd have that, even for a small spell."

She understood. Who knew better than she the strain of living a role, of carefully planning every word that was uttered, of watching every move, every thought, every deed? She, too, had sought solitude away from the hordes, where she could remember who she was. Sometimes it was easy to become lost in the role. Sometimes, she couldn't remember the Mylene she'd been.

She wanted to be herself now as much as he. To speak freely. Just to be, without thought or planning, or caution. Just to feel.

It scared her a little, how connected she felt to him in that moment. They were so alike, both thrust into identities so different from their own. Both needing the solace of silence to erase the echoes of senseless chatter from their minds. She felt more bonded to him than she ever had. She wanted to fight it. But more, she wanted to give in to it, freely and with an open heart.

To disguise her confusion, she hardened her voice. "If you'll not come back and let me tend you in the warmth of your room, I'll do it here, in the night air."

"And would you care, then, after all you've said, were I to perish from my wounds?"

They stared at each other, silent in the night.

Mylene knew that she cared more than she ever had. And he knew it, too.

Annoyed, she sharpened her tone. "I'll not have your death on me hands. There, you see now, you're bleeding again."

His white shirt was slowly staining red. He looked down at it as if he didn't recognize what it was.

"Don't be a fool," she snapped, to hide her concern. "If you won't be sensible for once, I'll force you, even if I have to stuff you into that cage."

He glanced at the small cage in his hand and grinned, his teeth showing white and ghostly in the dark. " 'Twould be a grand feat."

She took the cage and dropped it, then swiftly unbuttoned his shirt. She could smell his breath, sweetened by wine. It caused a tiny flutter of her heart. But when she eased the shirt from his torso, she caught her breath. His arms and chest were slashed and raw where the dogs had torn at him. Some of the wounds were bleeding, some caked with dried blood.

"Get those pants off and into the stream with you, to wash yourself clean."

He didn't protest as she unbuttoned his trousers and slid them down. But as he stepped into the stream, he gave a yelp. "It's fecking freezing."

"Your own bloody fault, it is, turning down a warm bath in your room. Now in with you, and no arguing. The cold will help stop the bleeding and close your wounds." She gave his back a nudge and he dowsed himself, cursing foully as the icy water stung his injured skin.

"You're after killing me, for all your talk," he complained as he rose and stepped out, water streaming down his naked body so he gleamed like silver. He was shivering violently, so she gathered her skirts and dried him off, careful of his injuries. Up close, she could see the cuts and scrapes along his legs.

"You're that lucky to be alive. Now hold still while I rub in the salve."

She worked as quickly as she could, rubbing the salve on each cut and scrape. But she found her fingers lingering, caressing the lean arms, the bulk of his chest, the sleek muscles of his hairy legs. He stopped shivering and took her hand in his.

" 'Tis like old times," he whispered.

"Not quite," she said, avoiding his gaze.

"Nay. We didn't know in Dublin what we know now." She looked up and caught his eyes glowing fiercely on her face. "You were always the softhearted one, nursing us back to health."

"I just can't stand to see you in pain."

He took the salve from her hand and dropped it to the ground. "Then take away my pain, girl," he said softly.

She knew what he meant. Before she could respond, he'd picked her up and was carrying her toward the woods. "Johnny, your wounds," she cried.

He ignored her. He took her into the trees, to a shelter cut off from the spring breeze, where it seemed warmer, protected, a cozy haven of oaks spreading their new leaves to the sky. And there he laid her in the soft, damp grass, to slip away her clothes until she was as naked as he.

She felt her blood quicken in her veins. She knew she wanted him. All her soft, secret places cried out for the feel of him. But as he moved toward her, she put a tender hand to his chest. "I don't want to hurt you, Johnny."

"Then stop hurting me, Mylene. Give me the

comfort I need, without restraint. Kiss me and tell me you love me."

"Ah, Johnny, how could I *not* love you?"

He kissed her then, tenderly, possessively, grateful for the soft parting of her lips beneath his own. She held him to her, careful not to hurt him, feeling his warmth against the chill of the night. She wanted nothing more than to make him feel cared for as he never had before. To give of herself, as he'd given of himself that day.

He kissed her for what seemed an eternity, as if all he wanted was the sweet compliance of her mouth. His lips moved against hers, sending lazy curls of pleasure and desire spiraling through her loins. She felt flushed and hot as he nudged her legs apart and brushed her, hard and warm, turning her breath to fire. And as he kissed her with devastating passion, he cradled her protectively in his arms, as if it were she, not he, who needed safekeeping against the scratch and scrape of the newly sprung earth. And when she was all but purring beneath his mouth, she rolled him onto his back and slowly, lovingly, kissed each and every one of the battle scars that had won her heart.

They were surrounded by the smell of earth, of damp leaves, of grass and moss, of slumbering bluebells and the bark of trees. The only sounds were the gentle lapping of the stream and the soft noises her lips made as she nursed his wounds with a woman's tender care. And as she took him in her mouth—the powerful column of manhood that surged with strength—a nightingale sang into the night.

He moved to possess her, but she stayed him with a gentle hand. "I'm supposed to be caring for *you*, remember? Tonight, let me love you. Let me do you honor, like a warrior back from battle. For it was a warrior's deed you performed today."

She straddled him with her slim, strong legs, careful not to hurt him, then put the tip of his shaft to the cove between her widely parted thighs and slid down onto his erection. He filled her so completely that she threw her head back with a cry of rapture, her long copper hair streaming down her back, brushing her bare skin in sensual waves. She began to pant, moving up and down on him as she controlled the rhythm.

"Ah, lass, you know just what a wounded warrior needs."

But they'd forgotten his wounds in the pleasure of the moment. This was more than comfort. It was love and lust unleashed and meshed into one. Mylene found that she relished the feeling of control. By leaning forward, she could position him so he grazed her core with every thrust, sparking new longings, new whorls of desire that seemed unquenchable, they were so intense.

Grabbing hold of her swaying breasts, he forgot his weakened state and began to shove himself up and into her as she bounced on him now, baring her lips and whistling her breath through gritted teeth, opening her mouth wide and gasping her bliss. She moaned, she panted, she laughed aloud, reveling in the frolic of riding him as he slammed into her, sending her racing heart into her throat. He wet his fingers and put them to her clit, rubbing in slick, moist circles, bringing a new rush of heat that caused her to buck and bob on him with wilder and more unrestrained ferocity. She looked down to find him gazing up at her with savage admiration in his eyes. She laughed again, joyfully, openly, more fully than she'd ever laughed before, as if the exultation of their union was too much to bear in silence.

He grabbed her head and yanked her close, kissing her. She gloried in the feel of his lips on hers, of his tongue twining with her own, of him hard and pulsing inside her.

Against his lips, she whispered, "Johnny, I love you. I've never loved any other man. No man has ever made me feel the way you do."

He heard in the sincerity of her words more than she'd intended to tell. He divined the loneliness of the last seven years, the frustration of a young woman not allowed to be herself except in snatches of borrowed time. He heard the plea to grab what they could, while they could, with no thought to tomorrow. With those words, his mood of passive pleasure dissolved and a new determination took its place: the intensity of an experienced lover firmly in control, seeking to please and thrill the woman he loved as she'd never been pleased or thrilled before.

With his hands on her back, gripping her close so they didn't lose contact for a second, he tumbled her onto her back. He took her hands and pinned them down, palms up. Then he ravaged her with all of his might, using the whole of his body to send her soaring, to elicit from her a cry of helpless surrender.

She forgot to talk, forgot to laugh, forgot the steps necessary to draw unshaken breath. She forgot everything but what he was doing to her, the way her body felt, as if it had never been alive until this moment, beneath the sweet torture of his thrusts. He began to speak to her with the agony and glory of potent lust pounding in his veins. He breathed hot, intimate, scandalous words, a fevered litany that blistered her ears, that fired her senses, that drove her insane with mindless, demanding, unrelenting need. She gasped and cried aloud and lost all sense of herself as he showed her how very much it was possible to revel in the mastery of his body as it moved like a brushfire, mowing her down even as it ignited her own fire and sent her bursting into flames.

They lay in each other's arms until they began to shiver. They'd forgotten the cold, their surroundings, the circumstances—forgotten everything but the feelings that had taken them over like a runaway train. But now, as the cold seeped into her body, Mylene remembered how she'd sought to soothe him and had instead been carried over the threshold of passion and surrender. "I fear I've done you more harm than good," she said, raising herself up to peer down at him in concern.

He ran a finger along her cheek with a loving smile. "You've healed me," he said simply.

"We'd best go back. You'll catch a chill."

He shook his head. "You go. I'll stay a bit."

"But, Johnny—"

The finger moved to her mouth. "I'd savor this night, while I can."

She understood. She, too, would relive every moment of this night, uncertain as she was how many such nights there might be. Reluctantly, she retrieved their clothes and they dressed in silence. But as she was leaving him, she found she couldn't tear herself away.

"Tell me things will be all right, Johnny. Tell me we can find a way."

He pulled her to him and held her in his arms. "Aye, love. Somehow. I'll see to it."

She turned to leave. But when she'd taken no more than three steps, his voice stopped her again.

"Mylene."

She looked at him, wondering at the catch in his voice.

"Will you marry me, Mylene? Be my wife? I need you, girl, to make me whole."

His wounds forgotten, she ran and threw herself into his arms. "Yes, Johnny. Oh, yes, I'll marry you. And somehow . . ."

"Somehow . . ."

His lips met hers in a searing kiss. Somehow, some way, they'd make it work.

Chapter 12

*S*he awoke the next morning to find a bouquet of bluebells on her pillow. How he'd placed them there without her knowledge was a mystery. But she held them to her nose, breathing in the scent that had filled the night, smiling dreamily and feeling light and happy for the first time in ages. As she washed and dressed, she hummed a happy tune, recalling the way he'd kissed her and pledged his faith. She felt full of hope and promise. Somehow, he'd find a way to overcome their differences. A promise was sacred between them. He'd said it himself.

She dressed carefully in a deep blue frock and pinned the bluebells in her copper hair. Then she all but skipped down the stairs, so eager to see him again that she had to pause outside the dining room door to compose herself. She knew she was glowing with the aftermath of love. She couldn't hide it if she wanted to. Well, let them see. For once, they'd see what a blushing bride-to-be really looked like.

She stepped inside and found Johnny seated with the others. When he looked up, his eyes met hers and he greeted her with a smile. It was Johnny's grin, open and unguarded, devastatingly seductive—not the polite and careful smile of Lord Whitney. He looked fresh and handsome, and it was all she could do to keep from running to him and smothering him with delighted kisses.

But as she was cautioning herself, the butler joined them and gave a discreet bow. "Lord Whitney, your valet has just arrived from India."

Johnny's face went blank. "My . . . valet?"

"Yes, my lord. He says you were expecting him."

Johnny's eyes flashed to Mylene's face, and she read in them the same startled panic she felt inside. If Lord Whitney's valet was there, Johnny's deception would be brought to an abrupt end. The fellow would know at once that a substitution had been made. What would they do to him when they found out? How could he possibly escape?

Johnny rose uneasily. "If you'll all excuse me for a moment . . ."

As he moved to quickly handle this unexpected threat in private, the voice of the prince resounded through the room. "Dash it all, see the man here. Let's hear the news from India."

Johnny was trapped. Such an order from the prince was not to be contradicted. As the butler left, Mylene saw Johnny scan the room with practiced eyes. There was only one way out—the windows at the front. He stepped toward them with studied nonchalance, holding the curtain back as if looking out at the drive. But

Mylene knew he was making ready should a fast getaway be required.

"My lord, your valet," the butler announced. He stepped aside.

And into the room stepped a man in the conservative clothes of a gentleman's valet, exact in every detail. Except that the man wearing the clothes bore the mark of the devil's thumbprint in his chin.

It was Daggett.

Mylene's happy mood dissolved like ice on a stove. Daggett's presence, unsought, served as a cruel reminder of the realities she'd shut from her mind the night before. Johnny's promise, which had offered her such hope, such a sense of vibrant joy, now seemed to wilt under the weight of impending doom even as the bluebells were wilting in her hair. For she could no longer see Daggett as the rapscallion boy she'd known and cared for. He came to her now as a symbol of all she feared. The symbol of Shamus Flynn's hammer poised to crush her fledgling optimism. Where only moments before she'd felt at the threshold of a new beginning, she now saw Daggett as the end.

She shook herself, wondering what possessed her. Daggett was her friend. Her only real friend save Johnny. And he loved her, she was sure of that now. Secretly and despairingly, perhaps, but he couldn't love her and wish her harm. Yet some sense warned her that Daggett posed a threat to all she wanted, all she held dear. Johnny might call her a fairy, but she'd learned to trust her instincts. So she shivered at the sight of Daggett standing in the doorway.

But Johnny, always at the ready, covered the awkward moment easily, striding forth to clasp Daggett's shoulder in jovial welcome. "You've arrived just in time. We're headed back to town today and you can help me prepare my things. Oh, forgive me." Turning to the curious group seated at the table, he said, with a slight edge of challenge, "My friends here are eager to be briefed on the situation in the subcontinent."

The *Times* was filled with reports of a budding rebellion in the Punjab. Johnny had no idea whether or not Daggett had read them. Fortunately he had. In precise English, he said, "My lords and ladies can be assured the Union Jack flies high as ever. There will be no repeat of the mutiny of fifty-seven."

The guests began to fire questions at him, all of which he fielded deftly as Johnny and Mylene watched. Finally, in a jovial mood, the prince said, "All those wogs needed was a taste of good English steel, eh?"

Daggett looked at the prince with a strange glow in his eyes, which the guests interpreted as awe and admiration, but which Johnny knew was a glare of barely controlled hatred. He feared that Dagget might suddenly leap across the room to tear out the prince's throat. But the situation was mercifully diffused by the reappearance of the butler.

"So sorry to bother you, Lord Helmsley, but I've just been informed of some distressing news."

"Distressing, you say? What is it, man?"

"It seems, my lord, that the mascot has escaped."

"Escaped?" cried William, darting to his feet. "What do you mean, escaped?"

"When Russell went out to feed the fox, he found the gate open. It seems Old Red Beard has taken to the woods."

"But that's monstrous! How could such a thing happen?"

He went charging out of the room, cursing his lax servants, and Katharine said, "Do excuse us. We'd taken rather a liking to the poor beast."

With that, the guests tossed their napkins to the table and followed her through the house and out the front door, where William was inspecting the empty cage. Along the way, the guests offered conjectures on what might have gone amiss.

It was just the opportunity Johnny needed. As the assemblage stormed out in a dither, he held up a cautionary hand. "We can't talk here," he whispered. Then, looking about, added, "Follow me."

He led them through the parlor and out the terrace doors, onto a shaded courtyard overlooking the sprawling gardens of rosebushes and a maze beyond. Looking back to make sure they weren't observed, he spoke in low tones.

"You gave us a fright," he told Daggett. "I was about to run for it, in case—"

Daggett had no patience with formalities. He'd been with Keenan O'Flaherty, suffering the whipsaw of his wrath. Himself in a temper, he cut in with a curt tone.

"Yer in big trouble, Johnny. We're all in trouble. They think we've turned on them. I don't have to remind you, O'Flaherty spares no love fer ye. Ye've played into his hands, so ye have. Given him the excuse he needs to rail at Shamus Flynn about how dangerous—"

"Do you think I care what O'Flaherty thinks?" Johnny hissed. "He's jealous of my position, and Shamus knows it. He'll not be fooled by the likes of him."

"He's hopping mad, Johnny. Ye've got a heap of explainin' to do to me. And I've got a heapload of explainin' to do to them. Shamus Flynn himself is hanging on every detail. Did ye not think for a minute the position ye put me in, running off from us like that?"

"What would you have me do? Turn Mylene over to them—"

"He saved my life," Mylene reminded.

Daggett wheeled on her as if he'd just noticed her presence. "I'd talked them into giving ye an ear. Did ye think I'd sit back and let them harm ye? Any more than Johnny would?"

She heard again the hurt tone of a jealous man. Touching his hand, she said, "Of course not, Daggett. Forgive me."

He jerked away. "Ye've ruined all me work, the two of you. O'Flaherty is sure Mylene will marry Helmsley, and he's after stopping it at all costs. He doesn't trust ye, Johnny. He says ye've proved ye can't take orders."

Johnny looked at Mylene and smiled. "He need worry no more about Roger Helmsley. She's not after marrying him, after all."

Daggett dropped his shoulders. " 'Tis glad I am to hear it. At least now yer talking sense."

"She's not marrying Helmsley. Because she's going to marry me."

He held out his arm and Mylene went into it, snuggling her cheek against his coat. She felt his love warm her inside, until she looked up and saw Daggett's face.

He was staring at them as if they'd just kicked him in the gut. His eyes were so horrified, she felt again the warning that Daggett had the weapon to end her happiness in his hands.

"Are ye daft, then?" he cried.

"Lower your voice," Johnny ordered sharply. "I'll not have you destroy my position here."

Daggett calmed himself with difficulty. Mylene could see him struggle to formulate his words. But when they came out, he faltered, speaking as if he were in shock. "Ye—ye can't do that without permission."

"Why can't we?" Mylene challenged.

"It's perfect," Johnny added. "If anything, it helps our cover."

"But yer mad! The both of ye. We're in this mess because Mylene acted in the first place without Shamus Flynn's say-so. What do ye think he'll say when he finds out yer going over his head and—"

"He'll see the sense of it," Johnny said. "They all will. All but you, it seems."

Daggett was silent, staring into Johnny's eyes. "I'll not let ye do it. It's not fair to me."

"What isn't?" Johnny asked softly. "That we haven't asked permission? Or that I'm marrying Mylene?"

Daggett's pause was awkward for them all. He was acting out of jealousy—he could read the accusation in their eyes. He looked away, turned his back, giving himself a moment to compose his thoughts.

"Of all the people on this earth," Johnny said softly, "I thought you'd understand. I thought you brother enough to wish us well."

Daggett stood rigid, clasping his hands in tight fists as if he couldn't trust himself to speak.

"I'm sorry," he said at last. "We have to think what this will do to our mission. For you as Lord Whitney to marry Mylene as Lord Stanley's daughter . . ." He whirled around. "Don't ye see, man? It will increase yer tie to that man. It doubles our problem."

"What problem is that?" Mylene challenged, knowing full well what he meant, but hurt and angry by her friend's rejection of their happiness.

"Ye know damn well what our problem is, girl. Our *problem*—though we didn't choose it—is that yer emotionally hog-tied to that monster and won't do what ye've been ordered. Surely I don't have to tell ye, Shamus Flynn is beside himself, worrying about what yer sainted Lord Stanley might do. He wants him stopped, and stopped now. With Parliament's opening session, and himself set to visit Ireland in a week's time—"

"You don't have to tell me that," Mylene snapped. "I'm not stupid, for all that you treat me like a child."

"And have ye thought that by marrying Johnny here, ye make him Lord Stanley's son-in-law? At least in Stanley's mind. Or are ye binding Johnny to the man in hopes that he'll care fer him as well? Is it another ploy to—"

Mylene lunged for him, but Johnny held her back. Still, she saw his gaze on her, questioning, wondering if there might be something to Daggett's accusation.

"A curse on you, Daggett," she cried, "for turning something beautiful foul. I'd intended to tell Lord Stanley the truth. To convince him to see things our way. If we can turn him around, the rest may follow in time. He's an influential man."

She'd expected Daggett to dismiss the idea as Johnny had, but his eyes lit thoughtfully on her face.

"And how do ye plan to do that?"

"He cares for me. Once he's over the shock, he'll listen. I'll tell him—"

"I've told her it's not a good idea," Johnny said dismissively.

But Daggett held up a hand. "Maybe she has something, after all. If he loves ye both, maybe ye *can* convince him."

Johnny was glaring at him. "Now who's going behind Shamus Flynn's back?"

"Maybe not. Could be Stanley's more use to Flynn if he sees the right of things. But ye can't convince a man of his opposition overnight. Maybe ye can accompany him to Ireland. Show him the world we grew up in. Maybe if he could see it from our point of view, it will change the man."

"Why, that's a grand idea!" Mylene said.

Johnny was studying Daggett. "This isn't like you."

Daggett glanced at Johnny and shrugged. "Ye said he's a fair man, didn't ye now?"

Relieved, Mylene realized she'd been wrong about Daggett. She was no doubt overly sensitive with all that was at stake.

"He *is* a fair man. I know I can convince him. Especially if he sees Dublin through our eyes. I'll take him to the orphanage to meet Father Q. If he sees the children—"

"I don't like it," Johnny said, still staring at Daggett. "It's a risky, renegade plan. To do this unsanctioned would be madness."

"And if I can get Flynn's go-ahead?"

Johnny considered with a frown, still not convinced.

"Promise me but one thing. Promise ye'll not wed before we know where Stanley stands."

Mylene exchanged a glance with Johnny. Perhaps, if they waited, it would give Daggett a chance to adjust to the idea. Perhaps he'd even be happy for them, in time. "Very well," she agreed.

"How much of the truth would he be told?" Johnny asked. "It's dangerous for him to know too much."

"I'll only tell him about my part," Mylene promised, excited now, thinking how much more joyous her wedding would be with Lord Stanley on their side.

"Nothing about you, none of the larger scheme. I'll tell him in stages. Once he's brought round, we can give him more information. I swear to you, Johnny, I won't endanger you *or* Shamus Flynn."

"He could turn on you at any point."

"We'll take that chance," said Daggett. "If Mylene thinks she can convince him, she has good reason. In three weeks, Parliament votes on a preliminary Home Rule bill. It hasn't got a chance. Lord Stanley will be expected to lead the opposition, especially after the English dogs in Dublin make their case. If ye can convince him before the vote, then all the better. Tell him part of the story. We'll take it from there."

"Daggett's right," said Mylene, turning to Johnny. "It's the only way we can come out of this. Remember your promise, Johnny? This could settle things between us. It will clear the path. With Lord Stanley on our side, we can be happy, the three of us working together. We have to take the chance."

Johnny took her hands in both of his. Looking down at her, he spoke seriously, with the air of a lover stating a difficult fact, but one that must be said.

"Listen to me, Mylene, and listen well. If you tell him part of the plan and he doesn't go along, you know what's going to happen. I'm going to have to kill him. I wouldn't want to, but I'd do it to keep you safe. Are you willing to take that chance?"

Mylene understood the meaning behind the words. As Daggett had predicted, Johnny was softening to Lord Stanley for Mylene's sake. She felt again a surge of hope. "Trust me," she told him. "It's the one thing we could always count on, the three of us. That we could trust each other with our lives."

She reached over and took Daggett's hand. He

stared at it, awkward, embarrassed. Then he looked at Johnny and in a wooden tone, said, "Trust."

When Johnny offered his free hand to his friend, Daggett took it and squeezed hard. And the three of them stood as they had as children, shoulder to shoulder, hand in hand.

Chapter 13

Mylene stood in her room in the Hotel Clarence with her face and hands pressed to the cool windowpane. She was dressed for a reception in a copper gown of ruched silk and netting that perfectly matched her hair. When the light hit the fabric, it shimmered with undertones of gold, just as Mylene's hair gleamed like rose gold in the sun. The gown had been a gift from Lord Stanley. If she was to accompany him to Dublin, he vowed, she would do so in high style.

But standing like a princess in that matchless gown, with her face pressed against the window, Mylene felt more of a fraud than she ever had before. Below her stretched the river Liffey, the only mother she'd ever known, gleaming dark and mysterious in the twilight—the dark pool for which Dublin had been named. And beyond her, the city itself, grey, forbidding, as lovely in the rosy glow of sunset as it was terrifying to her heart. Propelled toward her goal, she hadn't counted on how she'd feel when she stepped from the boat onto the shores of this loved and hated city in the guise of an English lady.

But it wasn't the city she saw now, nor the winding river that cut that city in half. She saw none of the bridges, nor the Georgian buildings, nor the confusion and clamor of the streets below. What she saw, looking out as from an ivory tower, was the picture of herself at seven years of age, bracketed on either side by a boy of nine. They stood on the street before this hotel, their faces flattened against the glass, peering in at the British dignitaries who stayed at the hotel when they came to town. She saw the three children as she hadn't then—saw how rough and dirty and slovenly they looked, how thin and ragged they were in their torn, ill-fitting clothes. She saw the hollows of their cheeks and the glitter of their eyes that could only come from slow starvation. She saw their awed faces as they stared at the lords and ladies sashaying through the lobby, as if staring at a vision that couldn't possibly be real.

And she saw herself, dressed as the enemy, looking out with a stranger's eyes over a city that had once been home.

She knew, as her heart cracked and bled, that she belonged on the other side of that window. She could remember begging along this very street, before Father Q had found her, her small hand extended to the charity of strangers. She recalled the terror of seeing her palm empty at the end of a long day, of feeling her stomach rumble and contract with a hunger that was beyond pain. And she knew she'd never forget the moment when she'd made the decision to hold her hand out in supplication of another kind—to a man, any man, who might use her frail body for the price of a crust of bread.

That foundling lived inside her even now. The fear was still there, and so was the rage. Yet that same urchin—the one who'd railed against the inequity of tyrants who would allow such monstrosities—had come to love an English earl as her father. She'd been tempered, modified, by the only truly selfless love she'd ever known. Outside, the pull of Ireland beckoned with all its memories of poverty, filth, loneliness, despair. The people who trudged the streets, going home after a punishing day of work, were her people, blood of her blood. But she knew, as she hadn't known before her return, that she'd never truly be one of them again.

Never had she been so torn. Never had she felt so cast adrift, as if she belonged nowhere, to no one. She'd have done anything in that moment to state categorically, "*This* is what I am." Yet questions tugged at her mind until she felt numb with exhaustion. Who *was* she? Where *did* she belong? Was Dublin home, or London? And why, dear God, was it so complicated, when it was once so simple and defined?

A knock sounded on her door and she turned from the window with a fearfully skipping heart. At her call, Lord Stanley entered, looking distinguished and worldly with his brushed-back grey hair and black evening attire. "Are you ready, my dear? If we don't leave soon, we shall be late."

He saw her standing with her back to the window, her hands behind her, clutching the sill as if afraid she might fall if she let go. He stopped, an elegant room away, and looked at her with compassion lighting his eyes.

"What is it, my dear? You look frightened. Is it memories of your parents, and what happened to them here?"

"I *am* frightened, I confess. But not of . . . memories."

"Of what, then?"

"Of what you'll think when I've told you what I have to say."

He considered her a moment, then draped his cloak over the nearest chair. "I don't know that I've ever seen you quite so serious."

"This is difficult for me," Mylene said, lowering her eyes. "It's probably the most difficult thing I shall ever have to tell anyone. What I say to you will shock you. You may very well hate me when I'm finished."

"Mylene, child, you know I could never hate you. Come now, what is this nonsense?"

She took a breath, feeling her hands tremble, and pressed them together. There was nothing to do but say it. As nervous as she was, she couldn't turn back now.

She looked up and met his eyes. "Lord Stanley—"

"Couldn't you please call me Father?"

This brought a rush of tears to her eyes. She fought them back and said, "Not now. Not yet. You'll decide if you still want me to after what I'm about to say. You've taken me into your home and loved me like a daughter. I can never tell you how grateful I am. It makes this all the harder. You see, I never expected it of you. I never thought you'd come to care for me as you do—or I for you."

He sat in the chair, crossing his leg. "I shall always love you, Mylene. Whatever you tell me."

Too nervous to stand still, Mylene began to pace.

"What you don't know is that all the time you were being so kind to me, I was like a knife poised at your heart."

"Isn't that a bit dramatic?" he asked with a gentle smile.

She wheeled about, looking at him. "I came to you under false pretenses. I can't tell you everything, not yet. But what you must know is that I was planted in your house."

He sat upright with a jerk. "Planted?"

"It was arranged for you to adopt me. By people I didn't know. I was just an orphan to them, someone they knew they could use."

"My dear girl, what sort of nonsense is this?"

"I'm not who you think I am. You were told that I was from an English family who'd been killed by Irish renegades. It isn't true. I'm Irish. I was brought up in an orphanage here in Dublin. There were no English parents. No parents at all."

He'd gone very still.

"I was brought up by a priest—a good man who has spent his life working for Irish liberation. It was well known that you had lost your daughter and wished a girl to take her place. I was chosen to be that girl. To play a role."

"For money?" he asked woodenly.

"No, not money. So I might use my influence to sway you."

"But this is preposterous! You expect me to believe—"

"It's true."

He looked away, shaken to his core. After a long pause, he asked, "You're part of a plot?"

"A plot, yes. They hoped to use me to sway your emotions. And your vote."

"Who are these men?" he asked between gritted teeth.

"I can't tell you that. Not yet. But I've betrayed them, and they know it."

"Betrayed them? How?"

"Because I grew to love you as a father. How could I help it? If I could choose one man in all the world to be my father, it would be you. Your kindness disarmed me. And when they wanted me to hurt you, I couldn't do it."

She continued to speak. Once started, the words flowed like running water. He listened, his hands clasped so tightly the knuckles showed white, but he said nothing until she'd finished. Then he sat still, silent, staring out the window beyond her head.

"And the kidnapping. Was it—"

"There *is* more to the story, but I have to ask your patience. I'll reveal it all to you eventually, but in stages as we go along."

He subsided into silence once again.

"Say something, please," Mylene pleaded at last.

Slowly, he looked back at her. He looked at her as if he'd never seen her before, looked deeply into her eyes as if trying to understand. Then, as if movement pained him, he stood deliberately and reached out to take her hand. There were tears in his eyes as he spoke in a quiet voice.

"You *are* my daughter. You've proved it by telling me this. When I think of the outrage, to use someone as young as you for their foul designs—"

She snatched her hand away. "You don't understand. I'm no unwilling victim. I knew what I was doing, and I willingly took the risk. But that's not important now. I've crossed them. And I've put us both in grave danger. These are desperate men. They'll kill us both."

"Don't you worry about that. We have the power of England behind us."

"They're more powerful than you think. And they're armed with a just cause."

His eyes flashed angrily on her face. "Just! You call men just who would use orphaned children for their cause?"

"I believe in that cause. That's why I agreed to help them. It's their methods I question, which is why they think I've betrayed them. By trying to protect you, I've put your life at risk."

"If they think to cow me with threats, they've another think coming. I shall face them down and keep you safe in the bargain. I have power they've never even dreamed of."

"Don't you see? That's part of the problem. I've come to you because I'm in trouble and I need your help. But not the kind of help you want to give me. That will solve nothing, except to get us both killed."

"You were right to tell me. But I need time to digest this. To plan what to do."

"There is no time. Time is running out for both of us. We have to act now."

He stared at her, weighing her words.

She rushed on. "Lord Stanley, let me show you the world of my childhood—the world that made these desperate men."

He hesitated. "You still wish to convince me to change my views?"

"I do."

"And if I agree to this and it doesn't convince me . . . what then?"

"It *will* convince you. If I'm wrong about that, I'm wrong about everything."

He turned away with an exasperated sigh. "You don't know what you're asking."

"I know exactly what I'm asking."

"Everything I stand for, all I believe in, all I've devoted my life to. You're asking me to change all that to pacify a gang of lawless thugs."

"Not for them. For me. Because I ask you to. I know I don't deserve any consideration after the way I've lied to you in the past. But I want you to know the truth. I want you to know *me*, Lord Stanley, the real me. The one who came to love you in spite of myself." She moved toward him, speaking in earnest. "I know what you believe. How could you not, living in England? You're so removed from us, from our way of life. What you know about us was told to you by other Englishmen with your same views. We're not people to you. We're policy."

"I'd like to think I—"

"I'm not blaming you. All I'm saying is maybe if you come to know the country and the people I love, if you look in our faces, talk to us, see our suffering first-hand. . . . Have you any idea what it's like to be an orphan on the streets of Dublin, dying by the day, with no one to help or care? How could you? You only know what you've been told. You hear rhetoric, but you don't hear the cries of a proud but wounded people. I feel in my heart that if you can see that suffering for yourself, you'll begin to understand. Just come listen with an open mind. That's all I ask. Let me show you where I came from and what we're fighting for. I'm trusting in your fairness because that's the one thing I've come to believe in."

He glanced toward the door as if looking about for an escape. "We have this reception . . ."

"Don't worry. We'll go afterward, when it's safe. Just say you'll come. You won't regret it . . . Father. I promise you."

Johnny, in the guise of Lord Whitney, had insisted on accompanying Lord Stanley on his state visit to Dublin. He didn't care to be parted from his fiancée, he said. Too, as a new member of the House of Lords, he could use a bit of brushing up on the subject of Irish Home Rule. He brought along no one but his valet, a quiet fellow with a pronounced cleft in his chin.

Accustomed as they were to subterfuge, it seemed odd to the trio to return to their home city under such conspicuous display. To be treated with such fawning respect by the same authorities who'd have gladly hanged them for pilfering at one time was as horrifying as it was laughable. They'd holed up in the Clarence, feted like royalty, attending back-to-back functions as the ruling statesmen endeavored to show their honored guests the necessity of keeping the Irish peasants under their well-meaning thumbs.

While Mylene had prepared to tell Lord Stanley her story, Johnny and Daggett made plans to sneak him away—a tough challenge, at best. Acutely aware of the embarrassment they'd suffer should any harm come to the esteemed peer, the government had placed a detachment of guards about the hotel to ensure Lord Stanley's safekeeping—in the street, in the lobby, before the doors of their rooms. They couldn't take so much as a step without being watched at all times.

Secrecy was of the utmost importance. They faced danger on all sides. With Lord Stanley so publicly welcomed by the authorities—with the transplanted English gentry falling over one another to be seen at his side—there was always the chance that some hotheaded Irishman might attempt assassination should Lord Stanley be spotted on the streets without his guards. On the other hand, if the authorities discovered that their illustrious guest was being transported about the city in disguise—there was no telling what conclusions they might jump to. No, it was essential that the earl remain anonymous at all cost.

The reception that night was being held in Dublin Castle, the official seat of government. Built in 1204 by King John on the sight of an Old Viking fort, it served as a menacing symbol of England's domination in Ireland. Aside from hosting state visits, it had also served as a prison for some of the more notorious Irish rebels. Upon hearing of the invitation, Johnny had winked at Mylene and said, "I never thought to set foot inside that keep, lest it be at the end of a bayonet."

On the ride over, Daggett, who Johnny had insisted on bringing along as an armed bodyguard, sat outside, next to the driver. Inside the carriage, the conversation was stilted. Lord Stanley, believing Johnny innocent of their plot, could hardly speak openly in his presence. So he stared out the window at the passing city, clearly attempting to digest all he'd been told.

When the earl wasn't looking, Johnny raised a questioning brow. Mylene nodded that she'd done the deed, signaling him to proceed.

They entered the grand salon to a burst of lights and color and music. Lord Stanley's arrival caused a stir, and they were surrounded at once by those wishing to gain favor. It took half an hour to navigate the reception line, shake each of the proffered hands and chat pleasantly before moving on.

Mylene began to feel better as she steeped herself in her role. It seemed these days that she was only comfortable when playing that role, like an actress who was lost without a script. She smiled and nodded and listened intently as Lord Stanley was asked the same questions down along the line.

"And how do you find Dublin, my lord?"

"More impressive than I'd imagined," he answered again and again. "For all that it's so much smaller than London. But how you get around is quite beyond me. Every street changes its name every third block or so. The quays along the river seem to change names every block. Each bridge has its own name, and all the streets change names yet again on the other side of the river. I've never been so confused in all my life."

In spite of his shock, he was playing his part brilliantly, covering his agitation with the gracious manners of a diplomat, distracting them with small talk so they wouldn't guess that he'd just been given the shock of his life.

They moved along the line and stopped before a man in uniform who presented himself as Major Phoebes. As Mylene extended her hand, she froze midway. She recognized him as the same captain who, seven years before, had tried to prevent them from stealing the food intended for the governor's ball.

She remembered, too, that she'd been veiled and he hadn't seen her face. So she extended her hand confidently, smiling and saying nothing. But when the major took Johnny's hand, he peered at him with an intent, thoughtful gaze. "I say, my lord, have we not met before?"

Mylene held her breath. But Johnny bowed elegantly and said, "Not unless you've been in India these last twenty years."

"India? Gracious, no. Bad enough being garrisoned in *this* Godforsaken country."

That seemed to satisfy him, for he turned to the next guest.

When at last they were free to explore on their own, Mylene glanced at Johnny and caught the glimmer of amusement in his eyes. Suddenly she felt like laughing aloud. For the first time since returning to Ireland, she felt as if she might enjoy herself yet.

"And what would you have done," she whispered to him playfully, "should the good major have recognized the young lieutenant who gave him such a thrashing once upon a time?"

His eyes on hers were warm and loving, aglow with old memories. "I never cross bridges until I get to them," he said. Then, lowering his voice, he added, "My, but it's grand, the three of us working together again. I didn't know how I'd missed it, before coming back."

"I didn't know a lot of things before coming back."

His eyes narrowed, and he looked at her as if reading her mind. "It's not the same, being here, is it?"

She lowered her lashes. "No."

"I feel that, too. Somehow being here, with all the memories, seems to point out the folly of looking back. I never felt such an orphan until I came back and saw how things have changed, yet remained eerily the same. Life goes on without me, without any of us. The river flows as it always did, and no one remembers our names. We've made no mark on this city. Our footsteps are washed clean. It's as if I never belonged here—I only thought I did. Do you feel that?"

"Aye," she whispered. "Is it all for naught?"

"We can't believe that. We mustn't let Dublin distract us from our goal. But 'tis more than that. What I'm trying to say is being here has made me see the need to look ahead. I ask myself where do I belong? And the only word that comes to my mind is 'Mylene.' You're the only home I've ever known. You're the only future I see. If we don't belong here or there, at least we can belong to each other. It's something to cling to, that."

She didn't care what people thought. She was in a public place, but to hell with them all and what they might think. She was so touched that she went into Johnny's arms and hugged him close.

And the guests paused in what they were doing and smiled, saying wasn't young love sweet?

Standing subserviently at the entrance, Daggett saw his old friends embracing like lovers for all to see. He saw Johnny's dark head bend over hers, saw his lips graze her hair tenderly. He saw the longing in their eyes to be alone. And it was more than he could bear.

He crossed the room with a determined stride. When he reached them, they kept their arms about each other and smiled at him, blinding smiles that spoke so eloquently of their love, their closeness, their wordless understanding of each other's needs. The pain of it wrenched through him like a bullet. He had a mad impulse to pull Mylene from Johnny's arms and shake her . . . and shake her . . . and . . .

Mylene saw the stark look of an outsider glaring in Daggett's eyes. His chin jutted out in the way it did when his pride was wounded. He looked like a warrior on the verge of seizing the lady of his choice, no matter the consequences. He looked like someone who knew he didn't belong, but who wanted to so desperately that he'd risk his very life.

Mylene's heart melted in empathy. One way or another, the three of them—the three friends who'd spent most of their lives together—were feeling the same thing upon returning home. They were feeling more acutely than ever before that there was nowhere they belonged. Nowhere but with one another.

"Daggett," she said, reaching a hand to him.

But he just stared at it with a contemptuous flick of his eyes. "Would ye be playin' patty-fingers with a valet, then?" he snapped, reminding her of their roles.

She lowered her hand, feeling hurt and rebuffed.

"Daggett's right," Johnny said gently. "We've a job to do. A job that's wanting attention."

"It's tonight, then," Daggett said, looking at Johnny. "We've not much time left. He's got to see Father Q at once."

"I agree," Johnny said. "But you've seen the guards about the hotel."

"We'll have to smuggle him out, then."

"And how will we do that?" Mylene asked, still stinging from Daggett's snub.

"Leave it to me," Daggett said. "Whilst the two of you have been takin' tea with the gents, I've been makin' friends with the rear guards. I'll give them a couple of bottles. I aim to get them drunk by ten o'clock. By midnight, they'll be on their arses."

Johnny looked about the room, taking in the exits, calculating in his mind the steps they'd have to take to get the earl out of there and safely to the orphanage at midnight. "What if they won't drink on duty?"

"I'll get 'em to drink, fear not about that. I'll challenge their manhood. If there's one thing these vain Brits can't refuse, it's a sportin' challenge."

"Hush now," warned Mylene. "Here comes Lord Stanley."

"You're sure, then?" Johnny asked again.

"I said leave it to me, didn't I?"

Lord Stanley joined them then with a mildly perplexed look in his eyes. "You three look to be having the most engrossing conversation," he commented. "I've decided it must be more interesting than what I've been offered up so far."

Mylene and Johnny exchanged glances. If Lord Stanley was going to the orphanage tonight, it was time he knew another piece of the puzzle. Mylene nodded. When Johnny looked at Daggett, he shrugged.

Johnny turned. Looking Lord Stanley straight in the eyes, he dropped his aristocratic accent and assumed his natural brogue, exaggerating it to emphasize his point. "We're takin' ye out at midnight, sir. If yer still willin'."

He couldn't have broken the news more succinctly. The shock of it propelled the peer back a step, before he realized what he was doing. "You, too?" he whispered. "You're *all* in this?"

"Aye," said Johnny calmly.

"But your impersonation is remarkable! I'd never have guessed." He looked at Mylene as if running memories through his mind, reliving them with this new awareness. They could see the hesitation on his face, as if he was wondering who else he might not suspect. "The plot is this big, then?"

"That it is, sir," Johnny said, in the same gentle, subservient tone. " 'Tis a grand thing you're going to be doing tonight—for Ireland *and* for England. You won't regret it. I guarantee you, sir, it will change yer life."

Or end it, Mylene thought, as a chill swept her spine.

Chapter 14

The child leaped up in bed, clutching the covers
and trembling in fear, her tear-filled eyes wide.
All she could see was the glare of the candle, blinding
her in the dark. She whimpered softly, crying beneath
her breath, "Please don't touch me. . . ."

Father Quentin lifted the candle so she could
see his face. Whispering, he soothed her. " 'Tis all
right, darlin'. There's nothing to fear. I only want a
word."

Slowly, the child remembered where she was. As
her eyes focused, she could make out the silhouette of
a row of beds on either side of her own. Behind the
priest, four shadows loomed in the darkness, hovering
close.

"What have I done?" she cried.

"Not a thing, dear. Not a thing. If you'd be good
enough to come to me office . . ."

Slowly, still shivering in fright, the girl pushed back her meager covers and rose. As Father Q moved the candle to light her way, she saw two faces come into view. One was the face of a beautiful woman with glossy copper hair. The other, an older man, looked elegant and distinguished in expensive evening clothes. They were staring at her with the same look of horror in their eyes.

She could be me, Mylene thought, looking at the ten-year-old girl with the ratted red hair. She was dreadfully thin, a ghostlike waif in a shabby nightgown that once might have been white but was now a dingy grey. It was so threadbare, Mylene could see her bony shoulders through the fabric.

Father Q put an arm about the child, but she cringed away in fear. His shoulders slumping, he instead used his voice to offer comfort, bidding her to follow them and not to fret.

They followed the beacon of the candle through the barracks and out into the hall. As they walked, Mylene and Johnny glanced about them in shock. The orphanage had been old in their days there, but now it was crumbling in disrepair. What paint had graced the walls was peeling. The rug that had warmed the hall was gone. As the child walked on bare feet, she had to pause to pull a splinter from her foot. They stepped into Father Q's office, where they could see more signs of poverty and despair. The stove was gone—no doubt pawned for food. The books the priest had treasured so were missing, the shelves looking desolate and empty. His chair was torn, and one leg was propped up with an old brick. Mylene was shivering beneath her velvet cloak. It was so cold she had to grit her teeth to keep them from chattering out loud.

Father Q had changed as much as his abode. He'd seemed to Mylene, as a young girl, to be a robust man of unconquerable energy. Now he looked gaunt and pale. He walked with a limp, and he coughed every so often with the same rattling cough she'd heard in the beggars of the slums. His white hair was thin, his cheeks hollow, his skin flaxen with age. She wondered when he'd eaten last. She knew well enough that he fed the children first, taking something for himself only when there was food to spare.

Looking at Johnny, she saw the same alarm reflected in his eyes.

"What's happened then, Father?" he asked.

"She'll be all right in a minute," the priest assured them, thinking Johnny had meant the girl.

"No, Father. The orphanage. When we left—"

"Ah. Well, it's been hard going, so it has, since the three of you left. Those you knew are all gone now. None of the new ones have the talent nor the inclination to fend fer us the way you did. I'm not complaining, mind. 'Tis proud of you three, I am. Yer serving a higher cause and helping more than a few. But you can see what's become of us. We're little more than a hospital now, where children come to—"

He stopped, looking sharply at the quivering child. But his words, unspoken, hung in the air. *Where children come to die.*

The girl had found a corner and stood with her arms clutched about her, staring brightly at the strangers who, past midnight, had so abruptly roused her from her bed. Her eyes told the tale. It could only mean trouble. She was waiting for the ax to fall.

"Sit down, dear girl, in my chair," Father Q offered. When she hesitated, suspicious, he held out his hand

and coaxed her near. She walked past him, swerving to avoid contact, then perched herself on the edge of the seat, her spindly legs hanging inches above the floor.

"I only want to talk to ye now," Father Q told her. Then he turned to Lord Stanley, who couldn't seem to take his eyes off the child. "Yer lordship, I could walk you through the dockside. I could show you the hungry who are lining up for a crust of bread outside Trinity College. But you must know that already. Yer an intelligent and educated man. You must have a million justifications for this. You've heard dinner conversations that absolve you of all blame. So I won't waste me time or yours. Instead, I wanted you to see the look in this child's eyes."

Crushed, Lord Stanley croaked, "It's an abomination. I can't believe it."

"Believe it, my lord. This is one child in many."

"But why is she so afraid? Why does she . . . cringe from you the way she does?"

The priest sighed and turned to the child. "I know yer tired, Maureen. But if you'd tell the good people a bit of what ye've told me. They're friends of mine. You can trust them as you trust meself."

"She doesn't appear to trust anyone," Lord Stanley observed.

"Ah, but there's a reason fer all things, my lord. Tell us, Maureen, where did you come from, girl?"

The child's voice sounded like the squeak of a mouse. "From the west."

"A farm in the west, wasn't it, now?"

"Aye. We had no food. Me brothers left for America. To send us money, so they said. But we never heard from them again. Me ma said they were killed by red Indians, most likely."

"And did you go to school, then?"

"No school. I begged in the village fer food."

"Then ye can't read nor write?"

She gave him a blank look, as if she couldn't even fathom the question. "There was no food," she said simply.

"What happened then, Maureen?"

"Me ma died." She said it dryly, without a tear. Her lack of emotion was more compelling than any tears she might have shed.

"And yer da?"

Again, the blank look. "I had no da."

"Was there no one to care for you?" asked Lord Stanley.

"No sir."

"But the authorities certainly—"

"Did nothing, of course," Father Q cut in. "What's another starving orphan here?" He turned back to Maureen. "What then, child?"

"I came to the city. Ma always said the city was where we could work."

"And did you find work?"

A flash of fear brightened the dead eyes. "No work. I tried to beg, but there were so many . . ."

Mylene felt tears choking her. It was as if she were reliving her own childhood, hearing the tale.

The priest continued his gentle questioning, coaxing answers the girl was more and more reluctant to give. At last it came out. How she'd given up and, at the age of eight, walked the Dublin streets. How a soldier had introduced her to the life of a child doxy. How there had been many soldiers after that, English soldiers who took her to the back of an alley and paid her a ha'penny when they were through, leaving her whimpering in a heap with the coin clutched in her palm.

"That's enough," Lord Stanley barked. "Must you put the child through this ordeal?"

Father Q turned and looked at the earl with quiet dignity. "What's such an ordeal as this, then, after the ordeal she's been through?"

Ashamed, Lord Stanley looked at the floor.

Softly, gently, Father Q said, "This could be Mylene. It would have been her a day or two later, had I not found her when I did. This child was not so fortunate."

Lord Stanley looked in horror from the face of the child to Mylene. He saw that his daughter was crying, the tears silently streaming down her face. She didn't seem to know it. She didn't so much as raise a hand to wipe them away. But he could see her reflected in the ragged red-haired child who'd so tonelessly uttered her tragic tale.

In a stupor, he went to Mylene and took her in his arms. "My child," he whispered through the tears in his eyes. "My child, forgive me. Forgive us all."

" 'Tis not that yer awful people," the priest told him calmly. " 'Tis just that we're not yer people. We Irish are cut from a different breed than you English. You don't understand us. How could you? You don't understand what becomes of people who've been occupied fer seven hundred years. You can see what yer well-planned policies have done, how they've ravaged us and left us bleedin' and beaten like dogs. And when we ask fer help, you turn a deaf ear. The only way we can take care of our people, my lord, is to rule ourselves. Surely you can see that now?"

Lord Stanley lifted his head from Mylene's to stare vacantly into space. "I didn't expect this. I thought you'd give me all the usual arguments, and there would be answers to all of them. There's no answer for this."

"Ah, but there *is* an answer, my lord."

The earl dropped his arm from Mylene's shoulders and stood upright. "Bombing buildings? Kidnapping people? Plots for blackmail?"

"Talk," said the priest. "Negotiation. The meeting of honest men."

"What exactly are you suggesting?"

"I'm suggesting a meeting between you and Shamus Flynn."

At the mention of the name, Lord Stanley's face drained white. His gaze jerked to Mylene, then to Johnny. "Shamus Flynn? Is that who's behind this?"

Mylene had never seen him so caught off guard.

"But Shamus Flynn's an outlaw. He's the most wanted Irish outlaw in— I risk my very position as peer of the realm even by speaking with the man!"

"You think Shamus Flynn's a villain, an animal. And so you've been told. But I'm telling you, he's a human being. And human beings are capable of great things and great personal change. Our shame is that we continually misjudge people. We underestimate their potential. Shamus Flynn is an honorable man, just like yerself, who's put his life behind his beliefs. He's also a shrewd man. And a shrewd man will realize that a partnership with you is the best way—the *only* way—to free Ireland."

Lord Stanley pondered the priest's words. "And you, Father. I know little of your religion, I'll admit.

But does the pope not say it's a sin for a Catholic to mix with the godless Fenians?"

Father Q shrugged. "Which is the greater sin? To sit back and let this child be desecrated by a system that doesn't care? Or to try to change that system so others like her might be spared?"

After a moment of silence, Lord Stanley said, "I'd like to fund your orphanage, Father. I'll see to it your children are decently clothed and fed. They'll want for nothing, this I swear to you."

"I'll take yer money, my lord. But what I'm after is yer help. Will you meet with Shamus Flynn, then?"

The earl looked around him at all the hopeful faces pointed his way. "I'll do it," he said at last. "It seems the least I can do."

Mylene looked at Johnny and saw the same hope and joy reflected in his eyes. No one had ever thought of such a meeting. Was it possible? To bring these two great forces together to talk out their differences? Good God, if it worked . . .

They looked at Daggett, who'd stood by in silence. He, too, seemed excited, as if this was the perfect plan. "I'll make the arrangements," he said. "Tomorrow night."

"And after ye've had this historic conference," said Father Q, "I'll claim some time with the three of you. We've a great deal to catch up on, so we have."

Outside, in the dark night, Mylene hugged Lord Stanley with all her strength. "I'm so proud of you," she told him with an appreciative kiss.

"Aye," said Johnny. "Mylene spoke rightly. Yer a man of honor, indeed."

But Lord Stanley shook off the praise. "Mylene,

I've been thinking. How would you feel if we ... adopted that poor child? Give her a decent home where she'll be loved and cared for? It won't make up for what's happened to her, but maybe—"

He couldn't finish. She'd thrown her arms about him and crushed him so tightly he couldn't breathe.

Chapter 15

D aggett had done his job well. When they arrived back at the hotel, the guards outside Lord Stanley's door were still drunk, dozing at their posts.

It had been a quiet ride back. Lord Stanley, deeply moved by what he'd seen, sat in the carriage in silence. The three friends left him to his thoughts. But they were filled with a sense of triumph and excitement that wasn't easily contained. After settling the earl in his room, they stood in the hall all but vibrating with anticipation. They looked at one another and read the same thought as if it were printed on a sign. There would be no sleep after such a marvelous feat.

"Let's go to Smuggler's Hill," Johnny suggested, his voice low so the guards wouldn't hear.

Mylene, catching his gaze, felt the brilliance of his eyes warm her loins.

"I don't know," said Daggett. " 'Tis late."

Johnny gave Mylene a cheeky wink. "If yer tired, lad, off to bed with you. We'll go on our own."

Mylene caught her breath. But Daggett knew them well and could read the unspoken longing in their locked gaze. "Bed be damned," he said. "Let's go."

They crept down the hall, but by the time they'd reached the stairs they were giggling like children. The audacity of sneaking off into the night caught them in its grip. Halfway down the stairs they began to run as one, scooting out the door of the hotel before anyone could spot them.

They laughed aloud as they left the imposing edifice behind. But soon they'd slowed their pace, wandering through the back streets of town with instincts that hadn't died in their absence. They knew these streets as no one did. As they strolled, they began to toss off memories of the past.

"Remember when we dressed as servants and sneaked into Lord Tottingham's kitchens to steal the desserts meant for his guests?"

"And the time we knocked the driver on the head and took the peat meant to warm Sir Rodney's hearth?"

A thousand memories of jobs they'd pulled, in various disguises, to keep the orphanage alive.

"Those were grand times," Daggett cried, absorbing the merry mood. "The three of us besting the Brits. There never was the like of us. Remember, Johnny, when you and meself pilfered the salmon from that jackanapes's stream? And when those shytes from down the way tried to take them from us. We showed 'em who ruled the streets that fine day."

"But look," said Mylene, "there's Old Angus the lamplighter. I thought he'd be dead and gone by now."

They saw an old man dousing lamps along the

street. Johnny called to him. He turned and blinked, then cringed, thinking he might be in trouble. But on closer inspection of the trio, his eyes lit in recognition. "Saints preserve us. I can't believe me eyes. 'Tis the three terrors. Where've ye been, then? My, but aren't ye grand."

They exchanged good-natured pleasantries, then moved on. The streets before dawn were filled with workers preparing for the bustle of the coming morning. Up the way, they saw Maeve, the lettuce lady, hauling vegetables to the Henry Street market. When they hailed her, she set down her cart and rubbed her smudged brow with the back of a meaty arm. "Jesus, Mary, and Joseph. 'Tis like I'm seein' three ghosts. Ah, but look at you now. 'Tis a fine form of a woman ye've turned into, little My."

Dooley, the manure man, was sweeping manure into a wagon to sell for fertilizer. They kept well back from the stench, but called to him just the same. "Well now," he said, leaning on his shovel as if it were a cane. "I'm not surprised at the clothes yer wearin'. I always said the three of you would own Dublin one fine day. If anyone could get things done in the old days, 'twas the three of you. Or did you steal the clothes, now? I wouldn't be puttin' it past you, so I wouldn't."

When they'd left him behind, Johnny said, "It's good to see old friends. To know we're not forgotten."

The others nodded, feeling the comfort of it warm them.

They followed the Liffey to the outskirts of town, then made their way through the dark countryside to one of the nearby raths. These were prehistoric hill forts, abandoned now. They trudged up the hill they hadn't seen for many years, instinct leading the way.

"It's likely someone's found it and destroyed it,"

Mylene said as they searched the spare brush for their secret cave. It was little more than a hollowed-out hole in the landscape, but their romantic imaginations had turned it into a smuggler's den.

"I doubt it," Daggett said. "We took pains to hide it well enough."

The hill was unkempt and overgrown. Johnny lit a match to help them see as Daggett dug through the shrubs. Finally, as the match singed Johnny's fingers and he shook it out with a curse, Daggett gave a howl of triumph.

" 'Tis here, right enough."

He cleared a path and, one by one, they crawled inside. There was barely enough room for the three of them to sit comfortably.

"I remember it being bigger," Mylene said.

"We were smaller then, no doubt."

"Do you think it's still here?" Mylene asked.

"What?" questioned Daggett.

"The trunk. Remember our trunk?"

"I'd all but forgotten."

Johnny lit another match. In the center of the small burrow were the remnants of an ancient fire. "Look. No one's built a fire here in years. We were the last, so it looks."

Daggett reached out and grabbed some of the discarded brush, and they set about making a small blaze. Then Johnny patted the ground, searching for the spot, and he and Daggett began to dig. Soon their efforts were rewarded. They reached into the hole they'd made and lifted out a small trunk. It was badly rusted, but the sight of it brought back a rush of memories.

"Open it," said Mylene in hushed reverence.

Johnny lifted the lid and removed the contents of

the trunk one by one. There was an old box of grease-paint they'd stolen from a theater and had used in their various disguises. Along with the makeup kit was a vast assortment of mustaches, beards, and wigs in various colors. Mylene reached in and pulled out a costume, mildewed with age.

"Oh, remember when I wore this?" She held it up to her. "I doubt I could fit into it now."

" 'Tis all yer rich English food," Daggett teased.

She looked at him and stuck out her tongue. It was good to feel close again, to feel the years drop away in the sweet memories that colored the small cavern.

"Oh, look," Johnny said, reaching inside. "We found this ring outside a dance hall. Remember?" He held up a tarnished tin ring with a glass stone.

Mylene reached for it. "I remember! We thought it was a diamond. I used to hide it, remember? And make the two of you find it. The one who brought it back first won the maiden's hand. My, but we were young and innocent then."

A sudden hush lingered in the cave. She looked up at Johnny. He was gazing at her sadly. When she glanced at Daggett, she saw that he was looking at Johnny with the same sadness in his eyes.

"Young, perhaps," Daggett said. "But innocent?"

Mylene put the ring back in the trunk. "Do you think it's possible? Can this really happen? Lord Stanley, meeting with Shamus Flynn?"

Johnny leaned back against the earth wall, attempting to stretch out his leg. "It almost seems too easy."

"The best things are often easy," Daggett reminded him. But the memories of happier times had changed his tone. He sounded stilted now.

"Lord Stanley will meet with Shamus Flynn,"

Mylene said. "But will Shamus Flynn sit down with Lord Stanley?"

"Aye, he will," Daggett said simply.

They were quiet for a moment, digesting the enormity of it in a way they hadn't before. Johnny reached into the trunk and withdrew the ring. Looking at it, he gave a rueful smile. "Frightening to think what a beauty this seemed to us at one time." Then his eyes lifted to Mylene's face. "I never gave you an engagement ring, did I?"

"You did *not*, come to think of it!" she cried in a mockingly scolding tone.

"A sorry oversight, indeed. Will you be accepting this as a substitute, then, till I remedy the situation?"

He held forth the discolored ring. She remembered a time when he'd run up the hill, out of breath, triumphantly holding the same ring in his hand, claiming the fair maiden for his own. Now he was claiming her for all time. "I'd be that proud," she told him sincerely.

He took her left hand and placed the ring on her finger with proper reverence. Then he lifted her hand and pressed it to his lips in a devoted kiss. His mouth lingered on the backs of her fingers, but his gaze lifted to her face. She started, as if a flash of lightning had shot from his eyes straight to her heart.

She couldn't look away. The blaze of his eyes told her all she needed to know. Her fingers trembled beneath his lips. She felt herself flush with warmth and longing. And she felt an unbearable bursting inside, an unquenchable need to feel him in her arms, to celebrate their triumph, their closeness, their new hope with the taste of him against her tongue.

She could see in his eyes that Johnny felt the same. The passion, the longing, was a palpable force in the cave. The air was suddenly singed with heat and desire.

It crackled with an electricity that couldn't be denied or ignored. Daggett saw it in their eyes, the look of lovers exploding with a need that knew no bounds and no limitations.

Keeping her hand in his, Johnny turned to Daggett, who was watching as if he'd been scorched where he sat. "Daggett, why don't you go on ahead of us? Cover for us, just in case we're missed."

For all his usual finesse, he sounded clumsy and awkward. He hadn't even bothered to think of a subtle excuse.

"And who do ye think will miss ye, then, at this hour?" Daggett demanded.

But Johnny's tone softened deceptively. "Be a good valet and go."

It wasn't a request. Daggett's chin jutted out for a moment as if he might refuse. But just as instantly, he dropped his shoulders, then gave a shrug. "Tomorrow, then. 'Twill all come right tomorrow."

"Tomorrow . . . aye . . ."

He and Johnny exchanged a look that was like an unspoken promise before Johnny turned again to Mylene.

"I thought he'd never leave," said Johnny, rubbing his lips against hers. "There are times when, indeed, three's a crowd."

She smiled against his lips. "I think he's accepting us at last. Just think of it, Johnny, if he could celebrate our love. If he could come to the wedding and stand up for us and share our joy. It would mean the world to me."

"And me. He'll come around. I know better than any man alive what the thought of losing you can do to a man's soul. But he's not the man for you. He knows it now, I think. He loves us both and will be happy in time."

"Oh, Johnny. We're so lucky. How many people come to know a love such as ours? I never thought I'd see the day. But I feel it now, that our hearts beat as one. I never thought to feel so close to anyone. I love you as I've never thought it possible to love."

He put his hand to her heart. Then he took her hand in his and put it to his chest. They sat for a moment, feeling the beating of each other's pulse beneath their fingers.

"You mean more to me than my life," he said.

He kissed her then, a consummate kiss that seemed to melt her bones until she felt herself soften and her body meld with his. He took his time, exploring with his tongue her taste and texture, rubbing his lips against hers, marking the inside of her mouth as his own. Then he drew back and darted the tip of his tongue along the tip of her own, denying her his mouth until she could stand it no longer and reached for him, drawing him into her arms as she drew his mouth to hers.

She loved his kisses, so penetratingly stirring, that spoke of his devotion in a tender yet thoroughly possessive way. She felt him shudder and coil in exquisite need, felt the meeting of their very essences with the investigation of his tongue. They met in a way that was beyond any conflict they'd ever known. They met in a place that transcended all the worries, a place of peace and calm, of needing nothing but the other's lips for solace to the soul. Her senses spun so she could no longer think, reeling beneath the onslaught of an emotion so strong it consumed them both. And as the promise of the night fused with physical longing, she felt her body come alive and respond with trembling demand. It was as if, in this one heartrending kiss, their souls had merged and become one—indistinguishable from the other, with neither beginning nor ending, a swirling mist of consciousness that was not hers, not his, but theirs.

But then she became aware of the smell of smoke. She pulled away and coughed, annoyed by the intrusion. The small cave was filling with the smoke of the fire, covering his form in a misty veil.

"Let's go outside," she suggested.

He shook his head. "I'd love you here, in our most sacred spot, the secret cove of our youth." He grabbed one of the discarded costumes and, with swift efficiency, doused the fire.

Suddenly, it was pitch black in the cave. The darkness was total, surrounded by countryside as they were, so far from the city lights. She felt disoriented. The silence, this far out, was deafening. Their gasping breath filled the small space.

And in the darkness, she felt again the presence of spirits, of all the Irishmen who'd passed this ancient hillside for centuries on end. She felt a part of them, felt she could hear the ageless melodies of the bards who'd sat on this very hill to weave the history of their land into the intricate tapestries of their songs. The countryside seemed to resound with the echoes of the harps that had carried the celebrated legends down through the ages.

As the smoke began to clear, she sat, captivated, the energy of the place seeping through her as it had when she was a child. They'd gone there in the first place because they'd been able to feel the souls of those who'd marched before them in a glorious cause. Because there, on that hillside, overlooking the city on one side and the whole of Eire on the other, they felt a part of all they hoped to achieve.

And there they were, years later, on the eve of making that dream come true.

Her voice, when she spoke, was but a whisper in the dark. "I feel myself again, Johnny. I feel that I've recovered something I lost. Something I didn't know I'd missed."

She couldn't see him. She could only feel his hands, reaching for her in the black void, feel him pull her to him and kiss her as he never had before, as if all his love and appreciation and fierce pride had called him forth to worship at her shrine.

His hands were on her then, slipping the buttons of her bodice free from their restraints, one at a time, slowly, his fingers brushing the lush swell of her breasts, savoring the feel of every stroking caress. Working in the dark from some primal instinct as timeless as his arousal, he slipped the dress from her shoulders, touching the silky skin, following the trail of his fingers with the warm, moist urgency of his mouth. He kissed her shoulders, tasted of her neck, ran the tip of his tongue over the delicate underflesh of her chin. He tracked his lips in appreciative splendor over the outthrust flesh as his mouth moved like a magnet to the beckoning soft enticement of her breasts. She clutched his head to her, clinging to the crisp strands of his hair, as she clung to all it meant to have him feasting on her nipple—to all he was, all she had in her hands, all she was destined to know.

She heard a moan of submission coming from the mottled burning of her throat. Deep inside, some sweet yielding part of her was quivering with want. She arched her back, rounding her breasts to his mouth, feeling her nipples tighten and tingle and send crazed signals of lustful abandon through her like a flood—hungry now, beyond retreat, for the drowning mercy of possession. He licked at her breasts with a wide, flat tongue, quick, fierce laps that spoke of his possession. How delicious it was to feel his mouth penetrating her core, to feel the rush of blood pounding in her head, to hear the gentle slurping sounds of his mouth devouring her as if this alone would save him from sinking into some dark and dense abyss. She felt a longing she'd never known deep within her loins, felt profoundly shaken by its indigence, by the ravaging hunger to have him inside, to fuse as one and make them whole.

His lips searched her body as if looking for answers he couldn't find. His tongue trailed a heated path down her ribs, exploring her navel as he'd plumbed the depths of her sweetly willing mouth. She felt her stomach curl and quicken, the skin pulsing and skipping in hedonistic delight. This was what she wanted! Only to feel. The sharp stab of defiant lust seized her, piercing the dark cavern like a shaft of burning sun, making her hot and slick even before he eased aside the silk of her dress to bury his hand in the slippery heat of her desire. His mouth, scorching and wet, roving her skin with luscious fervor, made her feel reckless and rash, as if she had nothing to lose and could therefore surrender herself completely to the demanding charge of his hands. She wanted him so hopelessly, she felt the shudder of it rack her body, felt the helpless, uncontrollable trembling of her limbs, as if shivering with some priceless pleasure that was beyond pain, beyond desire, beyond any force of feeling she'd ever known.

She couldn't see. And because she couldn't, she felt everything as if she were feeling it for the first time. When he leaned to kiss her, she felt the blunt ends of his hair brush her bare shoulder. It was oddly thrilling, as if she wore a blindfold and was at his mercy. His heaving breath, the increasing insistence of his hands and mouth, were all that connected them, all that told her she wasn't alone in the hollow blackness of the cave. The sound of his ragged breath aroused her extravagantly—the proof that he felt as she did, that he wanted her as much as she wanted him, that all the conflicts of the past were eased in the primal longing of his body for hers. His hand was tugging at her dress now, compulsively, as if he couldn't wait to feel her naked beneath him, to feel the soft mounds of her breasts flatten beneath his chest, to feel her velvety thighs parted against his muscular legs, the triangle of wet curls brushing the hard insistence of his arousal. To cast away the final barrier that kept them apart. But the voluminous skirts tangled in her legs, refusing to be set free.

Chafing against the delay, she sat up, moving away with a reluctant moan as she struggled to aid his efforts. She was quivering so badly she couldn't make her hands move as swiftly as her impulse wanted. Her cry was one of agony, the cry of a lover too long denied. She rose in the cramped quarters on shaking legs and hastily kicked the cumbersome skirts aside.

As she did, Johnny grabbed her legs from behind in an impetuous lunge, pulling her to him in a fierce embrace, bringing his mouth in the same motion to the softly rounded buttocks, as if he couldn't bear to lose a taste. At the touch of his warm lips nuzzling her flesh, she felt a surge of longing so intense, so over-powering, that she lost her balance and fell forward, throwing out her arms to break her fall. As her hands hit the hard floor, she felt the crush of slick satin, charred and burnt atop the lattice of smoldering sticks.

But it didn't matter now. He clutched her buttocks, yanking her back to him so she was thrust onto her knees, shoving her forward so she was open to him as her elbows grazed the packed dirt floor. He raised her hips, making her more accessible to his mouth, and spreading her wide with impatient hands, brought his mouth to the steaming portal of her desire.

His tongue found her clit, lapping at the juicy folds around it, flicking over it with a demanding pressure that was both gentle and persistent, that refused to be denied. He feasted of her as if drinking from the fountain of life, as if the juices of her body were all he needed to replenish his lost soul. She cried out in passion, hearing her cry echo off the chamber wall, feeling herself discharge inside, spreading her knees wider and wider still to his rapacious tongue, moving back against him with a restless propulsion of her hips as he plunged his tongue inside. Her fingers snarled in the discarded costume, crushing it madly, the sensations of his mouth on her too splendid to bear without some form of mainstay to her swirling, pulsing need. His hands, squeezing her buttocks open, sent shivers of carnal lust shooting through her, sparking flaming blood like a path of lighted gunpowder, extinguishing itself in its own flame. He made her feel open and exposed even in the smothering darkness that stole the sight of her deliverance from his eyes. She shivered against his mouth, opening herself further still, spreading herself before him like a feast for his taking.

Then she felt his fingers slip inside, his hand filling her as it moved with a rhythm that shattered her defenses against the stream of unbelievable rapture. His fingers moved and shimmied on their own, even as his hand pumped like an erection, fluttering fleetly, exploring her so that she felt them everywhere, caressing her fleshy walls, teasing and tantalizing her and hurtling her to some mindless state of sensual sensation. His hand twisted within her as his tongue lapped with arduous abandon, sending her spiraling higher and higher until she felt herself bursting like an exploding star. She came violently in his mouth, gasping and sobbing as her grasping hands brought the costume to her teeth and she bit down hard.

When he moved away, she cried, "No! Oh, no!" She wrenched herself around, fumbling in the dark to find the warmth of his body, her fingers coming at last upon the muscled planes of his hairy chest. As he shed his breeches with swift tugs, she found his nipples, sucking with a hunger made more potent by her climax.

"What, love? What do you want?" he asked.

"I'm wanting you inside me. Now. This minute. Hurry, Johnny, or I'll be losing my mind!"

He shoved her back into the crumpled costume so her shoulders hit the earth with a thud. Then he was on her, his body warm and heavy, damp and hot. He took her knees in his hands and thrust them wide. She could feel him, huge and pulsing, smearing her wetness with the head of his rigid shaft, teasing her beyond mercy, so she cried out in supplication for release.

Just when she thought she could stand it no more, he plunged inside with a single savage thrust that forced the breath from her lungs in a startled, happy cry. As he moved inside her, filling her completely, pounding her into breathless oblivion, he held her down, his hands on her breasts, gripping, squeezing, pinching the nipples so the pain turned to pleasure in his hands.

"I love you, Johnny," she cried. "I love you so."

He leaned over and captured her mouth with his

own. Then, his tongue in her mouth, he took her hands in his, twining the fingers so they were joined at every juncture. Kissing her fiercely, devouring her breath, he thrust into her with a commanding force that spoke of his renewal at her hands. She felt the man in him roar his supremacy. She felt tears of rejoicing slip down her cheeks. She felt the beauty of their union deeply, profoundly, stirring more than her body, bringing with it a satisfaction and fulfillment that seemed unfathomable in its enormity. In that moment she understood that there was nothing more sacred, no bond more replete, than the moment when a woman gives herself to the man she loves—and he to her—body and soul. She felt all the souls of the wandering bards hovering, encouraging, reveling in the benefaction of this sacred rite: the most sanctified of rituals between a woman and a man. And as she felt them becoming one, with no limits, no restraints, she sobbed her joy into his plundering mouth.

"Let this absolve me," he whispered. But it was so softly uttered, she wondered later if she'd imagined it.

Chapter 16

When Johnny knocked on the door of Lord Stanley's room to pick them up as they'd agreed, Mylene was already dressed in an inconspicuous black frock that would enable her to disappear into the night. As the guard outside the door allowed him in, she began to pull on the black gloves and cover her copper hair with a dark, veiled hat. But as the door closed behind him, Johnny, with his hand still on the knob, said, "No, I'll be wanting you to stay here."

Mylene paused in the act of buttoning a glove. "Stay here? You can't be serious."

"I'm that serious. You're to tell anyone who comes that Lord Stanley is indisposed."

"It isn't necessary," she argued. "All we have to do is tell the guard at the door. He'll—"

"If you want to help, distract the guard while the

two of us slip away. Then come back here and keep watch."

She stared at him, barely able to believe what she was hearing. The devoted lover of the night before was gone, replaced once again by a man with nothing but his mission on his mind. Her intellect told her it was right and proper to put the assignment first. But her woman's heart felt wounded by his unexpected rejection.

"Why are you excluding me?" she asked, the glove forgotten.

"I'm not excluding you. I'm—"

"Yes, you are. You've never left me out of a mission before. You know how important this meeting is to me. Every bit as important as it is to you and Daggett. Tell me, Johnny. What's afoot?"

He went to a nearby chair, taking Lord Stanley's cloak in his hands and wrapping it about the earl's shoulders. It seemed to Mylene that he did so to keep from looking her in the eyes.

"We can't go into battle with our rear unprotected," he snapped, a shade too sharply. "Someone has to stay here to ward off any suspicion. If you know how important this meeting is, you know how vital it is that nothing go wrong."

That was true. She couldn't fault his logic. It was just that he seemed evasive, as if he was keeping something from her. She peered at him closely, but he didn't look her way.

"What are you not telling me?" she demanded.

He whirled on her then. "Saints alive, girl, are you here to hound or help?"

She stood staring at him. She didn't move. "What's got into you?" she whispered.

Reluctantly, Johnny heaved a sigh and came to her,

taking her gloved hand in his. He lifted it and turned it over, glancing down at the sliver of exposed flesh on the underside of her wrist. Kissing it, he asked gently, "And if I want to protect you?"

"You never have before."

When he met her eyes, she caught a glint she couldn't understand. "I was never bound to marry you before. Trust me, then. I've a mission and I need to know you're—"

He stopped.

"I'm what?" she persisted.

He stood up and brusquely dropped her hand. "I need to know that fer once in yer life you can take orders and leave it at that. I need to know I can do what I must without worrying that you'll take it into yer hot head to—"

"All right. All right. I'll stay. But I don't like it one bit."

Lord Stanley gave a rueful smile. "I may have a great deal to learn about my daughter. But there's one thing I'm sure of. She never could stand to be left out of the main event."

He'd expected a smile in return. But his attempt to ease the tension fell on deaf ears. Johnny glanced at him—grimly, Mylene thought—then away. "Come then. Make ready to distract the guard. Daggett's taken care of the guard at the back door. We're to meet in but a few minutes' time."

Mylene wrapped her cloak around her and headed for the door. But once there, she turned and looked up at Johnny's taut face. "If there was anything to worry about, you'd tell me, wouldn't you?"

He didn't answer. Instead, he leaned over and gave her lips the slightest brush of a kiss. "Wish me luck," he said, then opened the door.

Mylene slipped out into the hall. The guard snapped to attention. "May I help you, mum?"

"My father's ill. We need to go get some medicine."

"I shall fetch a doctor, miss."

"No need. It's a recurring malady. I know just what's needed. We must go to the apothecary. I'd go myself, only Lord Stanley insists you come—he fears for my safety, you see. I tell him it's ridiculous, but you know how fathers—"

"I wouldn't hear of it, mum. We'll go at once."

When they were at the end of the long hall and the guard was heading down the stairs, Mylene glanced over her shoulder to see Johnny sneak Lord Stanley down the hall and out the back door.

The meeting was scheduled for eleven that night, but Daggett had asked them to arrive early. Johnny steered Lord Stanley through the back streets, surfacing a few blocks away, at an abandoned warehouse along the river. They'd rejected the orphanage as a meeting point because of the danger to the children—and because they'd wanted someplace different in case they'd been followed the night before. According to Daggett, Flynn had insisted on neutral ground. They'd settled on an empty warehouse close to the hotel, an area that was deserted at night.

As they walked, Lord Stanley said, "I say, Mylene seemed awfully worried. She isn't one to fret needlessly. I can understand your not wanting to alarm her, but if there's something amiss, I should think I deserve to know."

Johnny glanced at him. "You think I'm keeping things from you?"

"I don't jolly well know *what* to think. A sudden

change in plans. I'm in a strange city, on the verge of doing something I never imagined doing in my wildest dreams. If I'm a bit off center, I shouldn't think it odd, would you?"

Just then they heard a distinctive whistle, which Johnny answered in kind. A figure stepped from behind the warehouse. It was dark, but when the man spoke, Johnny recognized Daggett's voice.

"Did ye get rid of her as we planned?" he asked without preamble.

"Aye. You've no need to fret."

Lord Stanley stopped cold, his instincts flaring. "See here, what do you mean, *get rid of her?* What's going on here?"

Johnny answered in a low, even tone, the tone of a man who thrived in dangerous situations. "We decided it was best she didn't come."

Lord Stanley looked about the alley, anxious now. It was dark as pitch. He was out there, alone, with men he barely knew, having taken their word that he was safe. And he was about to meet with one of the most notorious and secretive outlaws this seditious country had ever spawned. He could feel the hair on the back of his neck tingle with apprehension. He wished he'd thought to insist that Father Q, at least, be present. He wasn't normally so ill prepared. He hadn't thought he'd needed the preparation, but now, on the verge of meeting his fate, he began to think again.

"You're sure Mr. Flynn will be here?" he asked.

"He'll be here," Daggett said. "It took some doin' on me part, but he'll be here with an open mind."

A chill swept through Lord Stanley, even though the night was far from cold. "What do we do now?" he asked, glancing nervously up the alley.

"Now we go inside and wait for eleven o'clock."

• • •

Mylene paced Lord Stanley's room in agitation. She'd done her part, getting the guard away, and had returned under the guise that she was caring for her father. But she couldn't sit still. Something inside her, some instinct, told her something wasn't right. As she paced, she tried to pinpoint the stimulus. It wasn't anything Johnny had said. He'd certainly played dictator with her before. But it was the *way* he'd said it, avoiding her eyes, going out of his way to be evasive. And that last look he'd given her when he'd said "Wish me luck." Not wish *us* luck. Wish *me* luck. What had he meant?

But what bothered her most was that never had she been excluded from any job they'd ever pulled. She'd made certain they couldn't claim she'd slow them down by keeping one step ahead of them every chance she had. Why now, all of a sudden, had they decided she must stay behind? On this most historic occasion, of all times! They knew what this meant to her. This was what she'd been working toward. This was why she'd bucked Shamus Flynn's authority and risked everything, that they might come to some peaceable resolution. This should be her night of triumph. Yet they'd asked her to sit it out while they played the scene off stage.

Why? she asked herself over and over as she wore a path in the carpet. Why? Why? *Why?*

She had to know. She couldn't just stay there, wondering. Something was wrong. She had an ominous feeling about this mission, as if Johnny knew something he wasn't telling her. Did he, too, feel danger lurking? She couldn't sit back and wonder. She had to go to him, in case he needed help. What if the Fenians couldn't be trusted? What if Shamus Flynn broke his word?

What if Johnny was in danger? And Lord Stanley . . .

Gathering up her cloak, she opened the door with a jerk. The guard jumped, then stood at attention as before.

"My father's asleep. I'm going to the kitchens to get him some pudding. He loves pudding. No, no, don't send for anyone. The change of scene will do me good. But I'm trusting you not to let anyone in here. Do you understand? If he's awakened, you'll answer with a demotion in rank, if not a court-martial."

She didn't wait to see his response. Instead, she went out the back door to find the guard drunkenly asleep. It was a black, cloudy night with no stars or moon to light the way. Mylene peered around the corner of the building to make certain the guards out front didn't catch sight of her. But there were no guards. They'd vanished from their post.

Something stilled inside her. Cautiously, hardly breathing, she crept forth and spied into the front windows, as she'd done years ago as a child. The lobby was empty. The guards normally stationed there were nowhere to be seen.

She felt so chilled, she couldn't move for a moment. Something was definitely wrong. Those guards had been placed there for Lord Stanley's protection. They wouldn't have left unless . . . unless . . .

She started running. She ran along the river, past one quay and another, heading for the dark alley where the warehouse stood. Just as she was approaching the alley, two explosions shattered the stillness of the night. Gunshots! Horrified, she jerked to a halt. Then she saw a detachment of uniformed guards running swiftly into the alley, their rifles in hand. The sound of their booted running feet drowned out the echoes of gunshots in her head and spurred her to action. She ran now as she'd never run in her life, up the dark alley, to yank back the warehouse door.

And inside she saw a sight of unimaginable horror. Lord Stanley lay sprawled on the cold floor, a pool of blood seeping from his head. Johnny, kneeling beside him, blood on his hands, was being wrestled to his feet by two of the soldiers. As he rose, a pistol dropped and clattered to the floor.

Without thinking, Mylene ran and knelt by Lord Stanley. She couldn't tell if the screams she heard were coming from her throat or someone else's. She only knew the man she'd come to love with all her heart was staring at her with glassy blue eyes. And when she felt for a pulse, there was none to be found.

She looked up in a daze. The soldiers were beating Johnny with the butts of their rifles, cracking his head and knocking him to his knees. His dark hair reddened with the flow of fresh blood. Mylene ran for him, crying out to him, desperate to get to him, to demand an explanation—anything to explain this horror. And all the while, her mind cried out, *It can't be true. It can't!*

But just as she'd fallen beside him and lifted Johnny's head with her hands, just as she'd caught sight of the agony in his eyes as they beat him with mindless repetition, she felt hands pulling her away. She was lifted and hauled off by the major like a troublesome cat.

And even as she was crying out for Johnny, she heard the major say, "Get her back to the hotel and lock her up. We have information this man is a Fenian spy. Who knows how deep this plot goes? We have to get you to safety, miss. Get you back to England before it's too late."

Two guards came to take her arms, but she broke away. She ran to Daggett, who was standing over the body of Lord Stanley, looking desolately down. When she grabbed his arm, he glanced at her, a look of pain and confusion glittering in his eyes. "Why did he do it, Mylene? Why?"

She glanced back at Johnny. They were beating him brutally; he was doubled over on the floor. But before she could move, before the horror of it all could settle in her heart, she felt the hands of the soldiers on her. She began to struggle, fighting them off with all her might. But they overpowered her, and she was dragged, kicking and screaming, from the scene of the awful crime.

The funeral procession stretched for miles through the streets of London on the way to Westminster Abbey. Lord Stanley had been honored with a state funeral and all the accompanying regalia. The Queen's elite regiment marched at attention, behind which Lord Stanley's old regiment followed, wearing black arm-bands to mark their mourning. Behind a riderless horse, a glass carriage containing his casket moved slowly through the lane, allowing the throngs of people lined on either side to catch a glimpse of the tragically fallen man. Behind the casket, Lord Stanley's closest associates in Parliament walked with bowed heads and folded hands. And behind them, Mylene sat in a coach with Roger and the Helmsleys, dressed in mourning, overburdened by grief.

She'd have preferred to be alone, but the Helmsleys had insisted that she needed friends at such a time.

Katharine had been invaluable, all but moving into Lord Stanley's house, making the arrangements Mylene had no stomach for with a quiet efficiency that spared her the ordeal. But while Mylene was grateful for the assistance, the constant company left her feeling vulnerable and exposed. There was no time to grieve properly. No opportunity for the feelings warring inside to be looked at and sorted into some bearable order. No chance to scream to the heavens the one word lurking at the corners of her mind: Why? Why? *Why?*

"It's a lovely funeral," Katharine remarked, looking out the window at the thousands who lined the streets. "So fitting for our poor, dear friend."

Fitting for the country, as well. The government had turned Lord Stanley's funeral into a circus as a means of reinforcing its hard line in Ireland. No one could look at the procession with its slain hero without thinking of what those murdering Irish animals had done. This single deed had proved to the world everything the English had been saying about the Irish stupidity, shortsightedness, and violent intentions. So they turned this sacred rite into an open display of propaganda.

But how could Mylene protest? In fact, she'd barely said a word since she'd been forced back to London under armed guard. All attempts to remain in Dublin failed. The authorities feared for her safety. Dublin was placed under marshal law, with troops sent in from London to squelch any rebellious impulses the Fenians might have. The prisoner, she'd heard, had been incarcerated in Kilmainham Jail, where rebels had been executed in the past. But beyond that, she'd learned nothing.

She was still reeling from the shock. She didn't

want to believe it. To believe the man who'd held her in his arms and sworn to make things right would gun down Lord Stanley . . . How could she believe it? Yet how could she not? She felt battered, pulled by swells of hurt and anger, confusion and betrayal. They'd been so close! Lord Stanley had been willing to negotiate. How in God's name could Johnny have committed such a cold-blooded crime? How could he have betrayed her so monstrously after all they'd shared? All the promises they'd made. *A promise between us is sacred.* . . . She wanted to throw those damnable words back in Johnny's face.

The mood in the coach was one of sympathy, but underlying their polite concern, Mylene felt the Helmsleys' repressed anger. They, too, had been made to look like fools, allowing Roger's engagement to be smashed to bits by an Irish thug. Celebrating his heroism in rescuing her, when all the time he'd been manipulating them like marionettes. Mylene could feel their silent stewing beneath the refined and solicitous facade. It made her conscious of her own confused emotions, and of the same anger that permeated her feelings of grief and guilt.

"He duped us all," said Roger now, as if reading her thoughts, as if unable to contain the volcano of rage threatening to erupt. "We've all been made victims of his infernal trickery. To masquerade as Lord Whitney—and then to— Mylene, my poor dear. If you'd have me . . . I'd do my best to make it all up to you."

Mylene saw the hope in his eyes and looked away. She hadn't the energy to face the thought of her future, a future that now seemed hopeless, meaningless, as much a sham as Johnny's love had been.

"Roger, really," Katharine scolded, although Mylene

caught the keen look she gave her, as if wondering if such a remedy might not clean up the entire mess. "Mylene is in no condition to make plans just yet."

"You're right, of course. Forgive me." But after a pause, he looked up sharply and cried, "But for God's sake! Couldn't you have guessed? Did he give you no clue?"

Mylene stared at him, aghast. She knew the frustration that must have caused the outburst. But she knew, too, the danger of her position. She could easily be exposed. With the scandal so public, how long would it be before others asked such questions and perhaps began to piece together the puzzle? Still, she was so wounded, so stricken by grief and betrayal, she couldn't bring herself to speak.

"We none of us had any idea, more's the pity," said Katharine, coming once again to her rescue. "Really, Roger, to badger the poor girl at such a time."

"I should have known he was an impostor," William huffed. "The way he handled himself at that fox hunt, he was certainly no Englishman."

"I will have no more of this," Katharine proclaimed in a testy tone. "True enough, that man has made a mockery of us all. Not to mention, robbed us of one of our dearest friends. But think, if we feel so betrayed, what poor Mylene must feel. She was deceived every bit as much as we. She needs our compassion, not our accusations. My dear," she added, taking Mylene's hand. "Let me assure you that, in spite of everything, we love you and shall stand by you. You have been dear to our hearts, despite our disappointment, and we shan't desert you now in your hour of need."

Mylene knew Katharine meant to be kind. But the censure was clear in her tone. If Mylene hadn't left

Roger for that scoundrel, she might have saved them all this pain. She wished for the relief of tears, but even that was denied her.

She was saved a response, though, when the procession pulled up in front of the cathedral. As they stepped down, they could see the Prince of Wales join the pallbearers to carry the casket into the church. They followed to the swells of the pipe organ accompanying them down the long aisle. Still in mourning for Prince Albert, Queen Victoria had nonetheless broken her seclusion to attend the service. She sat with her ministers off to the side of the altar, a heavy black veil covering her face and the bulk of her regal frame.

Mylene sat through the prolonged service with a heavy heart. The Archbishop of Canterbury read the eulogy, followed by a succession of outraged speeches best left for the Parliament floor. She sat through it all in a haze, keeping her back erect, feeling the sting of tears she couldn't bring herself to shed.

This is as much my fault as Johnny's, she thought, absently fingering the ring Johnny had placed on her left hand. She'd forgotten she wore it, but now it seemed to burn her finger like a curse. The thought haunted her as it had in the days leading up to the funeral. *I destroyed Lord Stanley after all.*

They entombed his body in the abbey, leaving the lowering of the stone floor until later, in the silent aftermath of the ceremony. Then, one by one, the hundreds of mourners came to Mylene to express their sympathy and their abomination. "You may rest assured, my dear, that your father's death will be avenged." She lost track of how many times she heard the same pledge.

She stood with the Helmsleys, barely able to look the mourners in the eyes. But when the last of them had gone, Inspector Worthington of Scotland Yard came to her, looking grave but strangely self-satisfied.

"My condolences," he began. "But I'm afraid we've uncovered some rather shocking news."

Mylene braced herself, so raw with emotion that she felt she could take no more.

"It appears the real Lord Whitney was murdered by his impostor."

This jolted Mylene out of her daze. "Murdered!" she cried, truly shocked.

"So it would seem. The night Lord Whitney was known to arrive from India, we found a body washed up in the Thames. He appeared by his features to be an aristocrat, but as no one claimed him, it was rather a puzzlement. He was eventually buried without fanfare. But the mystery hounded me, wondering who the chap could be. Later, when you were returned by the false Lord Whitney, I suspected his story. It seemed to me a bit too pat to be entirely trustworthy. So I wired the viceroy himself in India and asked him to tell me what he could about Lord Whitney. It seems the real Lord Whitney suffered a fall from a horse as a lad, breaking his collarbone. The break never healed properly and was said to cause him discomfort. Upon hearing of the falsity perpetuated by the false lord, I naturally thought of the mysterious chap we'd buried. I had his body exhumed. He did, indeed, have a broken collarbone. In short, this impostor—whoever he might be— murdered not only Lord Stanley but young Lord Whitney as well."

Mylene swayed on her feet so Roger had to grab her to hold her up. "It can't be true," she whispered.

Johnny had assured her Lord Whitney had been kidnapped, to be kept safe and released when their mission was accomplished. Was it possible that he'd really murdered him instead? And if that was true, had he been lying to her all along?

She recalled the strangeness of his behavior that last night. How he'd insisted she not go to the meeting. How it had seemed that he was keeping something from her.

"Have you any idea who the impostor might be? You were engaged to him. He might have slipped something out in a vulnerable mood. The authorities in Dublin have been trying to get it out of him, but the blasted fellow won't talk."

Mylene turned in Roger's arms, wishing only that she could run from the scene. How could Johnny have done this? How?

"Really, Inspector," Katharine chided, "you go too far. The poor girl's had enough for one day."

Mylene was barely conscious of being helped into the coach. Outside, the crowds saluted her, but she stared at the window unseeing. She felt as if she were spinning out of control. If only she had someone she could talk to, someone who would help her figure out what to do. She was completely alone, cast adrift in an appalling mess, with no one to blame but herself.

But she did blame someone. She blamed Johnny. Curse his soul for what he'd done!

"You must rest," Katharine told her as they at last pulled up in front of Lord Stanley's house. Her house now, she reminded herself bleakly. "I'll stay with you and see to it—"

"No," Mylene interrupted, too upset to bother with the pretense of courtesy. "I want to be alone."

It took some convincing, but finally the Helmsleys left her in peace. Exhausted, she turned the key in the lock, staring at the black wreath on the door. She went into the empty parlor where she and Lord Stanley had spent their evenings. It was dark and silent, the servants having been dismissed for the day so they could mourn in their own way. The room seemed so empty, the silence seemed to echo like a hum. Yet she could feel Lord Stanley's presence everywhere, in the chair where he'd sat, in the book he'd been reading, lying with his bookmark keeping his place, in the brandy glasses that stood at the ready for a man who would never drink from them again. With a wrenching heart, she dropped the key and sank into his chair, wishing she could take it all back, undo what had been done, feeling all of her life, her hopes, her very meaning, coming to an end.

Putting her head in her hands, she moaned aloud, "Saints forgive me, what have I done?"

She heard a footstep and jerked up. Half hidden by the drape, Daggett stood in the gloom, dressed in dusty traveling clothes.

He looked to her like the first friendly face she'd seen for days. With a cry of despair, she was on her feet in an instant, rushing into his arms, holding him tight, and finally crying the tears she'd been unable to shed.

At first it was sweet relief to have a shoulder to cry on. But as Daggett whispered "My fair lady"—the name he'd called her as a child—and as his arms came around her, holding her in an increasingly hurtful grip, so that she felt imprisoned against the wall of his soldier's chest, her fury boiled to the surface of her grief. She began to beat him with her fists, fighting to be free.

"He killed him!" she cried. "After all that work, he shot him down like a dog! He killed Lord Whitney, too, and never told me. Two innocent men who didn't deserve what he did to them."

Daggett let her go, looking at her with an inscrutable gaze.

"Daggett, why? Why did he do it? Didn't he know it would kill me?"

He crossed the room and poured a brandy from the crystal carafe. He held it up in invitation, but she shook her head, so he drained the contents himself. "He had to kill him," he said at last.

"He didn't have to," she cried heatedly. "We were on the verge—"

"He had to, I tell ye. Yer sainted Lord Stanley was after turnin' the tables on us."

Mylene stared at him, deflated. "What do you mean?"

"He had no intention of goin' through with the meetin'. He'd alerted the troops to capture Shamus Flynn."

"That's a lie!"

"Do ye think I'd make me way back to this cursed town, knowin' there are folks who've seen me face . . . do ye think I'd risk all that to tell ye somethin' I wasn't dead certain of?"

"He'd have told me."

"He betrayed ye. He knew ye'd warn us if he let on what he was about. Don't ye get it, girl? He told ye what he wanted ye to believe."

"But he trusted me."

His eyes narrowed scornfully on her face. "After ye confessed to lyin' to the man fer seven long years?"

His assertion hung in the still air as Mylene tried to digest the horror of what he was saying. "How do you know this?"

"We found out from one of the guards. Did ye not

wonder why the troops jest happened to be on the spot? Lord Stanley warned them in advance, so he did. Johnny discovered the perfidy jest in time."

"That's why he didn't want me there."

"Aye, now yer gettin' it, girl. He knew part of the betrayal would be to have ye and Father Q arrested, along with us. That's why he didn't tell ye. Lord Stanley was after turnin' ye in. Johnny couldn't let it happen. It was kill the man or take the consequences. What would ye have done?"

Stunned, Mylene sank into the closest leather chair. She heard Daggett's boots thump against the floor as he charged toward her and took her shoulders in his hands, shaking her hard. "He had to do it, I tell ye. Do ye see that now?"

"I don't care. I curse his foul deed. He could have done something else. He could have found a way—"

Daggett squatted down in front of her, his elbows resting on his knees, his cleft chin jutting up at her.

"What's done is done. They've got him holed in Kilmainham. Ye know what that means. We've tried, but we can't get in. They've got him locked up tighter than the Queen's bloody jewels. And they're torturin' him. They're doin' every bleedin' thing they can to get him to talk. To tell who's behind the scheme."

Her heart frozen with horror, Mylene lifted her gaze to Daggett's face. He looked intense, and there were shadows beneath his eyes as if he hadn't slept any more than she in the days since the murder. Still, she said nothing.

"They're *killin'* him, Mylene. You know Johnny. You know he'll never talk. They'll kill him as sure as I'm here before ye."

Her heart gave a lurch at the thought of Johnny's

pain. But anger and betrayal hardened her. Surely Johnny could have found another way.

"Dublin's become nothin' more than an arsenal. The troops are that thick, so ye can't spit without bein' hauled off and asked what yer about. But the people—ah, the people, Mylene. They've rallied behind Johnny, one and all. He's become a symbol to them. A great martyr bein' sacrificed fer the cause. It's roused them like never before. There's life in them, and the thirst fer vengeance. They'd sell their own mothers now, if he asked 'em."

He was talking as if he'd lost his mind. His eyes were sparkling with a glow she'd rarely seen in them. He looked alive, animated, the energy surging through him like a current.

"What are you saying?"

"We can use this. With the people behind Johnny, there's no tellin' how far we can go."

She stood abruptly, knocking him back. "Are you saying it was a good thing Johnny killed my father?"

He straightened, glowering down at her. "I'm sayin' we need Johnny alive. Dead he's nothin' more than one more martyr for Ireland. Alive, he can lead the people to victory. Now they know who he is—"

"You're talking crazy. Didn't you just tell me—"

"That they're after killin' the man. Aye. But not if we can get to him. Not if we get him out in time."

It seemed that an eternity passed before she drew breath. "Get him out? Of Kilmainham?"

"Aye." He grabbed her arms and shook her again, hurting her in his efforts to persuade her. "We've got to get him out of that hellhole, Mylene. That's why I'm here. We need yer help."

"My help?"

"We can't get near him. But ye've a name and

position we can use. Ye've jest inherited everything Lord Stanley had, except his Parliament seat. If ye come to Dublin, ye can get us in to see him. And once inside, we'll break him out. Think what that will mean. Johnny will be a hero the likes of which we've never seen!"

"Have you gone mad?"

His eyes narrowed and he glared at her. "Mad, perhaps. But I'll get Johnny out of that foul cage if it's the last thing I do."

She turned away, sick inside with a rash of confused emotions. "You don't know what you're asking me."

"I know if we don't get Johnny out of there in the next few days, he'll be dead. Is that what ye want?"

Dead. Did she want Johnny dead?

"Come with me, Mylene," he urged. "We need yer position, and we need yer skills. Save the life of the man you claim to love."

His words brought a rush of fresh pain. Because she knew, in spite of all he'd done, that she loved Johnny still. She'd loved him so long, so deeply, that she didn't know if she could ever stop. All she knew was that she never wanted to see his face again. She couldn't bear to hear his justifications for a crime he never should have been capable of committing. But she knew, too, that she couldn't let him die.

She wanted to cry out to the fates against their cruel crime. But instead she squared her shoulders and said, "I'll get him out. But then I'm done. Do you hear me, Daggett? I'm finished. I want no more of your bloody schemes."

He was silent for a moment, looking at her. She could feel some deep emotion he was struggling to control. When he spoke at last, it was in a cautious tone, as if biting back words he didn't dare speak aloud. "If that's yer will. The mission's finished. Johnny's been unmasked. Very well, then. Get him out and I give ye me word. I'll see to it meself that ye never have to set eyes on either of us—ever again."

Chapter 17

The city of Dublin was under siege. Johnny's audacious move had stunned the Irish residents, igniting their passions, rousing them from their decay of apathy. As rumblings of revolt shook the city, and men began to gather in pubs to "talk a little treason," armed troops continued to pour in from London daily, determined to put down the uprising they feared on the horizon.

In the entire twisted history of Anglo-Irish relations, the situation had never seemed so explosive. The Fenians, working behind the scenes, were busy building the prisoner up to be the greatest symbol of Irish Nationalism the troubled country had ever known. Slowly the word spread that he'd been an Irish orphan trained by the elite and mysterious faction of the Fenians led by Shamus Flynn himself. The people knew him only as Johnny, but that one name spread like wildfire until the whisper of it resounded through the streets.

English authorities found themselves in a peculiar and perplexing quandary. They needed to hang the prisoner and hang him quickly. Pressure from London was increasing daily. Yet the ministers with years of Irish experience were afraid of making a martyr of the man. Too, they needed time to discover the extent of the plot behind Lord Stanley's murder. Meanwhile, demonstrations were taking place outside the prison, the crowds loudly, if irrationally, demanding that the prisoner be set free. Stories of the now infamous Johnny's torture were leaking out, enflaming the mob to bolder measures. Prison officials feared for their lives as they passed through the virulent assemblage. Worse, they trembled at the thought of a jailbreak, one that would prove fools of Britain's might.

The situation had reached crisis proportions at Deerfield, the residence of the British Chief Secretary for Ireland. Lights in the mansion burned later every night. Ministers came and went. Emissaries from London arrived on the hour with the latest suggestions from Whitehall on how best to handle such a combustible predicament.

Then, on a bright morning early in June, a carriage pulled into the gated drive of the estate in Phoenix Park. A woman, dressed impeccably in black mourning, was handed down by the driver. As the guards came forth, she announced herself as Lady Mylene, daughter of the slain Lord Stanley.

After the initial hush and reclamations, she was ushered into the salon of the grand mansion. The guards couldn't help but note the bravery with which she held her head high in the face of such disaster. It was only moments after the announcement of her visit that Lord Pickney, the chief secretary, himself came rushing in to see her. He was a man in his late forties, still winning the battle with approaching age, distinguishable only by the lack of distinction of his features. He wore wire-rimmed glasses, which had slipped, in his hurry, to the bridge of his nose, but which he didn't seem to notice.

"My dear lady," he cried, taking the offering of her gloved hand, "what words are there to describe my despair over the misfortunes brought upon you? But we'd thought you in London long since."

"I must speak with you, Lord Secretary. I've made this perilous journey to speak on a most vital matter. I don't mind telling you, I fear for my safety, just being once again in this wretched city of yours."

"But my dear, surely you don't travel the streets alone!"

"My servant awaits in my carriage. He's become my protector now, more's the pity. But on to business, my lord. Might you spare a moment of your time?"

"Perhaps another time." He cast an anxious glance over his shoulder in the direction of his office upstairs, where even now a heated conference was transpiring. "You must understand what kind of crisis we have going on here," he said distractedly. Clearly, this was the last thing he needed.

"My Lord Secretary, who should understand the proportions of this crisis better than I? The fiend you hold prisoner, the man we thought to be an English nobleman, made dupes of us all by his ghastly impersonation. He convinced me to marry him, then gunned down my father coldly and brutally. In the name of my slain father, I feel I've earned the right to be heard."

She saw his hesitancy in his pale brown eyes, could almost read the thoughts flitting through his head. It would be most ungentlemanly to refuse a lady who'd been through such a harrowing ordeal. Her use of the word *slain* had hammered home his guilt that her father had been murdered while visiting his domain.

"Of course. Do have a seat. Shall I ring for tea?"

"Nothing, thank you." Mylene sat in a gold brocade chair and he perched himself on the edge of the seat opposite her, clasping his hands together to cloak his impatience.

"Now, my lady, how might I be of assistance?"

"I understand, Lord Secretary, that the trial of my father's murderer has been postponed yet again."

The secretary squirmed and belatedly pushed his glasses up the bridge of his nose. "I confess, we don't really know how to handle this matter. There have been threats of riots, should the trial begin."

"I've heard stories that the mob may storm the prison."

He straightened beneath the accusation. "We have an entire regiment surrounding the prison, mum."

"Need I say, sir, that such an occurrence must not be allowed?" She took a handkerchief from her sleeve and dabbed at her eyes. "I can't tell you the pain and suffering this indecision has caused me. Why, just the other day, I was speaking of it to Lord Helmsley."

Pickney paled in the manner of a man who knows he might be in trouble.

"Lord Helmsley said he can't understand what our people are doing over here. Nothing is being done. He asked me specifically to inquire why you haven't hanged the scoundrel yet."

"The complication, my dear, is that we risk making a martyr of the scoundrel. There have already been riots in the streets. If we allow the felon to be seen as a victim, if you will, there's no telling what sort of chaos might ensue. Looting, murder—even, as you mentioned, breaking the wretch out of prison. We dare not even take him into the streets to transport him to trial lest we chance an abduction."

"Then your movements, or lack of them, are rooted in fear, my Lord Secretary?"

He sighed, utterly exasperated by the same sort of questions he was forced to field the day long. "You don't understand how the Irish mind works, my lady. We have to be very careful with this. We could do ourselves great damage. Not just at present, but for the foreseeable future. These matters of diplomacy are most delicate and are best left, I daresay, to trained diplomats."

"You fear to take him to trial. And you fear making a martyr of the man. So you simply do nothing. In that case, my lord, the solution is obvious, is it not?"

He lifted his gaze to stare blankly into her eyes.

"Bring the scoundrel to England to stand trial."

Pickney shifted in his chair, clearing his throat. "Irish prisoners are not normally taken to England for trial."

But his body language said what he didn't dare. Her solution would absolve him of his current troubles, yet might effectively shatter his reputation. If he exported his misfortunes, allowing the authorities in England to deal with the mess, his society friends would surely frown upon him, thinking him lacking the courage and skill to solve his dilemma. Particularly with Lord Stanley having been so important a man.

Mylene leaned forward. "I assure you, my lord, that

my father's friends in Parliament would look upon this as an inspired idea on your part. Lord Helmsley himself confessed that very fact to me the day I left."

At this, Pickney brightened, straightening his back. "Actually, I *have* been toying with the idea. Your assurance has most definitely reinforced it."

"Then it's settled." Mylene tucked the kerchief back into her sleeve and rose. "When do you think you might export the prisoner? I'd like to know, for my own peace of mind, that the deed has been accomplished before I leave the country."

"Why . . . if you'll leave the name of your hotel, I'd be more than happy to get that information to you. We'll have to sneak the wretch out, naturally. I imagine we'll opt for a night sailing. In the early morning hours, when the rabble-rousers are abed. Yes, that should suffice nicely, I should think."

Mylene extended her hand. "Thank you for your kind solicitation, my lord. And I pledge to you Lord Helmsley will hear how well you took to his idea."

She left, taking the time to nod to the guards on her way out. In the carriage, Mylene looked over at Daggett as the driver lurched forward.

"So much for the first step," she said.

Mylene squirmed beneath the stiff woolen restriction of her regimental garb. Her breasts were tightly bound, her hair tucked beneath her hat. But there was a breeze, and she feared the wind might snatch the head-gear from her head, allowing her luminous hair to fall free. She stood at the dock with the other soldiers, carrying a rifle and keeping her back erect in military fashion.

The night was dark and moonless beneath the

perpetually cloudy sky. The man-of-war that would take Johnny to England stood at the ready, lanterns blazing against the gloom. In the distance, she could see the beacons of the twin lighthouses, warning an approaching clipper of the juts of land on either side of the river's mouth.

"What's that, then?" asked one of the soldiers, peering out at the ship sailing into the harbor. "We had no word of an expected clipper."

Others turned to look. The ship was sailing steadily into the harbor, its sails flapping ghostlike in the breeze.

"Likely some delayed merchant, eager for home fires," answered a man dressed in a captain's uniform.

Mylene watched the ship, wondering if it was the diversion Daggett had promised. He hadn't told her how he'd planned to distract the guards, but he'd hinted that it would be spectacular, something that would cause the needed chaos at the proper time.

"Step lively, now," added the captain. "Here they come."

They turned to see a wagon, heavily fortified with militia in uniforms similar to Mylene's, lumbering up the street. She took a breath, trying to still her erratic heart. She knew Daggett's men were mixed among the soldiers, but she didn't know who or where they were. She stepped back, hoping to keep a low profile, as the wagon pulled up to the dock.

But when she saw them help the prisoner down, it was all she could do not to gasp her horror. Johnny was manacled, with heavy chains connecting his wrists and ankles, so they rattled when he moved. Even from afar, she could see he was a beaten man. His legs collapsed beneath him, so the closest guards were forced to hold him up by his arms. His stilted movements gave the impression of great pain. As he was brought closer, into the lanterns' glow, she saw that his once fine face was swollen and discolored, red and raw, with bruises shadowing the lines of his cheeks and his darkly stubbled jaw. His arms hung limply across the soldiers' shoulders, as if the act of being alive was an agony. He looked only half conscious, but she could see his weary struggle not to disclose his pain.

They'd beaten him to a pulp. She was seized by a mad urge to run to them, to knock them off him, to scream vile recriminations. All the coldness she'd felt melted at the sight of her valiantly struggling lover being rousted forth like a mongrel beast. And she knew, as they shoved him and his head rose sharply in anguish, that nothing mattered now, except that she succeed in freeing him from this vile torture.

She didn't realize she was moving toward him. The soldiers brought him closer, mouthing warnings to be on the lookout for anyone happening by. As he stumbled past, Johnny raised his eyes and caught the look of agony on her face. He turned, lunging toward her reflexively in warning. But the nearest soldier mistook his action for an attempt at escape. Running, he raised his rifle and slammed the butt of it hard onto Johnny's head. He fell back, dazed, blood running in a trickle down his face.

Mylene cried out. The soldier turned her way. But before her voice could register in his mind, a cry was heard from the dock.

"God Almighty, the clipper's going to ram the ship!"

Bedlam broke loose as the soldiers ran forth to look. Only those struggling to hold Johnny upright stayed behind. Mylene, having mastered her horror, followed the others, cautioning herself to stay as far from Johnny as she could until the time was right.

From the dock, she could see that the clipper had raised sail and was barreling full speed toward the mighty man-of-war. Men were calling out to warn the captain of the vessel, but as the clipper descended on the ship, they began to scatter. Only then did Mylene realize what Daggett had done. With swift instinct, she began to run, away from the dock and the man-of-war.

She headed toward Johnny, knowing nothing could stop her now. As she did, other soldiers followed. Desperately, she threw herself on top of Johnny just as the clipper, loaded with explosives, collided into the man-of-war, blowing away half the larger ship. The eruption blasted the night, lighting it into violent flame as chunks of the ship were hurled into the air. Mylene felt the blow of it at her back as her body flung Johnny to the ground and covered him, protecting him.

The expected chaos erupted. Men were hurled dead from the ship. The soldiers scattered, shrieking curses. Some were flung into the air by the gust of the explosion, killed before their bodies hit the ground. Mylene was hit on the back by flying shrapnel, but she pushed away the pain. When she lifted her head to glance back, she saw the man-of-war topple and begin to sink.

Johnny moved beneath her. She heard his faint moan, and remembered belatedly the agony she must be causing him. But as the explosions continued, one after another, she lay where she was, hiding her face in his shoulder, sheltering him from harm.

"You'll be all right now, Johnny," she whispered.

She heard the pounding of booted feet. "Get the prisoner back to the prison," one of the soldiers cried.

Mylene recognized Daggett's voice. She felt herself lifted, and looked up to see Daggett's face. Johnny saw him, too. He glanced in a panic from Daggett to Mylene. "No," he said; he was so weak, it came out as a whisper.

Daggett shoved her aside and lifted Johnny, tossing him over his shoulder. Then, surrounded by a detachment of armed guards, he ran for the horses waiting down the street. As the rest of the soldiers continued to rush from the scene of the catastrophe, Mylene ran after Daggett. She saw him fling Johnny over the front of his horse, saw him mount behind and ride off into the night.

A soldier grabbed her arm. She started, staring at him with all her fear shining in her eyes. Belatedly, she realized her hat had fallen, her hair had blown free. She'd been caught. She'd given herself away.

But he merely dragged her to the nearest horse and hoisted her up. "Follow close," he warned, his voice thick with a Dublin brogue. Without thinking, she kicked her horse and followed, galloping off into the night.

They rode through the streets of town, knocking aside sleepy dwellers who'd heard the explosion and had come, dressed in bed clothes, out into the night. They rode west through the back alleys until at last they'd left the city behind. They rode like lightning through the dark countryside for hours on end. When she was certain of escape, Mylene began to fear for what this frantic ride might do to Johnny, already battered as he was. But Daggett, in the lead, never slowed his pace. He rode with the precision of one who knew exactly where he was headed.

By the time he slowed, Mylene was stiff and sore. They came to a silhouette of crumbled buildings far in the country, with nothing else around. As they drew closer, Mylene could see the ruins of an old castle. Most of the fortress was toppled along with the walls. Daggett barked orders, calling to the men to bring Johnny, as he hurried across the overgrown yard.

Mylene followed down flights of tumbling stone steps. The only light was the lantern Daggett carried. She rushed ahead, warning the men to be careful with Johnny. Finally, after many twists and turns, they came into a dark, cavernous room. As Daggett placed the lantern high, she could see that it was an old dungeon. There were chains embedded in solid rock, and cells once used to hold prisoners of war. It was damp and moldy, but safe from the night wind.

"Put him in there," Daggett ordered, pointing.

The men took Johnny into a cell and lowered him onto an ancient wooden cot, unlocking his chains with narrow files. Mylene rushed past them to kneel at Johnny's side. "Bring me some water," she told them as she wrenched off her woolen jacket and balled it into a pillow for Johnny's head.

The men stood by, looking at Daggett.

"Bring me some water, so I can clean his wounds," she repeated.

Still, they stood rooted.

"What are you waiting for, you fools?" she cried.

"You men keep look outside," Daggett told them. "Warn me of any approaching riders. You two, get some mead and water from the supplies and bring them in."

Johnny lay unconscious, but as Mylene gently lifted his head to slip her jacket underneath, he moaned and slowly opened his eyes.

She ripped a piece of fabric from her sleeve and used it to tenderly wipe the blood from his face. He was having trouble focusing. His eyes blinked, struggling to see.

"Mylene," he croaked, like a man who hadn't spoken in weeks.

She leaned and carefully kissed his swollen lips. "I'm here, love. You're going to be all right. We'll make you better now, Johnny, you'll see. Oh, my darling, how could they do this to you?"

He raised a hand, but it dropped to his side. "Daggett—"

"Hush," she said, putting a finger to his lips. "Daggett's here. He's explained everything to me. I know why you killed Lord Stanley. I know you had to. You just rest, my sweet. Don't worry about a thing."

She heard Daggett's men returning down the stairs.

With Herculean effort, Johnny reached up and grabbed a handful of her dangling hair. He pulled her close and whispered, through cracked, parched lips, "I didn't kill Lord Stanley. Daggett did."

For a moment, it was as if time stopped. She stared at Johnny, at the fierce warning of his eyes. Then she whirled to find Daggett standing behind her, close enough to have heard Johnny's words. He was staring down at her with a cruel sneer.

"Grab her," he told his men.

Before the shock could register, the men seized her arms and hauled her out of the cell.

"*You* killed him," Mylene cried, struggling against the hold of the men.

Daggett eyed her with scorn. "I did."

"But why?"

"I did it fer Ireland. And fer us." He looked at Johnny when he said the last.

"But you told me Johnny—"

"I told ye what ye needed to know to help me get Johnny out of that foul place."

"And the meeting with Shamus Flynn?"

"Shamus knew nothin' about the meetin'. I arranged it meself."

"So you could murder my father."

"Yer father me arse," Daggett spat out.

"You didn't even tell Shamus, did you?" she cried heatedly.

"Shamus Flynn is nothin'," Daggett snarled. "One more shanty Irish dreamer chasin' the English-sanctioned Home Rule that will never come. A man who hides his face, a man who hasn't the guts to take Ireland back where she belongs."

"But you let everyone believe Johnny killed him. Look at him!"

"Aye, look at him." Daggett picked up the bottle of mead his men had brought and carried it into the cell. Looking down at Johnny, he shrugged off his military jacket, then took off his shirt and soaked it with mead. "Look at the man. He's a grand Irish hero. The greatest hero in two hundred years."

"And did you kill Lord Whitney, too?" she demanded.

Daggett paused, as if uncertain whether to confess. "Sure I did. I couldn't take the chance that he might escape and expose our Johnny boy here."

Mylene saw the surprised anger that flashed in Johnny's eyes, only then realizing the injustice she'd done him by believing Daggett's tales. In a stunned voice, Johnny asked, "You . . . flat out murdered an innocent lad? A lad who did you no harm?"

Daggett shrugged, as if the matter was beneath

importance. "There's no sech thing as an innocent English dog."

He sat down on the edge of the cot and began to unbutton Johnny's prison shirt as Johnny glared at him. Underneath, Johnny's chest was marred by raw welts left by the whip. Mylene let out a cry and struggled again, trying to break the men's grip on her arms, but they held fast.

As Daggett brought the alcohol-soaked shirt to dab at Johnny's chest, Johnny reached up and took Daggett's wrist in his hand. "If you wanted a hero, Dag," he croaked, "why me? Why not you?"

"Ah, Johnny. I'll be answerin' yer questions in good time. But will ye not let me tend yer wounds? 'Tis the least I can do."

"They might have killed Johnny, thanks to you," Mylene accused.

Daggett ignored her. He sat looking into Johnny's eyes. When at last Johnny's hand fell back to the cot, Daggett pressed the shirt gently on the first of the criss-crossed wounds, holding it there as Johnny sucked in air through gritted teeth. "I know it hurts, lad. But 'twill help ye heal all the faster. These are badges of honor ye wear, Johnny."

"Why me?" Johnny ground out through the pain.

"Because I'm not as good a man as ye are, Johnny. Nobody is. Yer exactly what Ireland needs—a natural leader. Why, look at the people, riotin' in the streets, callin' yer name. Ye've roused them, Johnny. Ye've made them fightin' mad. Yer the one man with the magic of Eire in ye, with the gifts of the bards and the warriors, all in one. The one man who can make Eire rise up with him."

"To what end?" Johnny demanded as Daggett applied more of the mead.

"Why, to make ye king of Ireland, of course."

A stunned silence followed his words. Johnny looked at Mylene and she read in his eyes what she was feeling. Suddenly it began to make sense.

As one, they turned wary gazes back to Daggett, who was speaking now with the joyful relief of a man finally revealing his soul. "Think of it, Johnny. Think of the glory days, of the kings of Tara. There hasn't been a man more fit fer the crown in a thousand years. I've known ye were special fer as long as I can remember. If ever there was a man with a pure regal nature, 'tis ye, Johnny. Yer the one true eagle in a flock of pigeons. Yer the O'Neills and Brian Boru all in one. I've paved the way. I've made a symbol of ye, Johnny. The people love nothin' better than a man willin' to bleed and suffer fer their cause. Why look at ye, man. Ye even look like a king."

Mylene's struggles were forgotten. She felt her blood run cold as she realized she was listening to the ravings of a madman.

"My God, Daggett," Johnny cried, "how could you be so misguided? Why did you not tell me you were even dreaming of such a thing?"

" 'Cause the one thing ye don't have, Johnny, is the vision to see what ye are. *I've* got that."

"But don't you see? You're talking nonsense."

"Believe me, this can work. We don't need anyone else. Ye remember those two scruffs on the streets of Dublin who could do anythin'? We're grown up now, Johnny, and we can still do anythin'. But on a larger scale. Here, take a sip. 'Twill help the pain."

Daggett lifted Johnny's head and watched him as he slowly drank the mead. But even as he swallowed, Johnny's eyes never left Daggett's.

When Daggett took the bottle away, Johnny weakly wiped his mouth on his sleeve. He spoke with effort as Daggett went back to soaking his wounds. "I understand what you're saying, but it's daft. If we try to declare me, or anyone else, king of Ireland, the English will come down on us with everything they've got. Their army, their navy . . . why, they could kill every man, woman, and child in Ireland in a week!"

"I'm tellin' ye, Johnny, we have weapons we haven't even used. Lord Stanley was jest the beginnin', jest to show what we're capable of. For every Irish life they take, we'll take five. And they won't be common folk, neither. We're targetin' the whole of the royal family and half the members of Parliament. Their wives, their kids . . . It's all arranged, me lad. What do ye think I've been doin' fer the past seven years, while Shamus Flynn was makin' a topper outta ye?"

At this, Johnny assumed a cautious air, careful not to antagonize his old friend. "When did you first get this idea?"

Daggett leaned forward and took Johnny's face in his hands, looking fiercely into his eyes. "I've had it as long as I can remember. I've dreamed of it at night. When we were no bigger than leprechauns. . . . I've got three people planted in Buckingham Palace, in *trusted* positions. One of the queen's own chambermaids. Why, she could slice the throat of that old banshee and be out in a lick. I've got men inside the Parliament buildings, men I trained meself. I've got men in half the great households in England!"

"How many men?"

"Fifty, a hundred. Maybe more. So many I've lost count. I'm tellin' ye, Johnny, this is a thing of beauty."

"But . . . how can you possibly coordinate such a grand plan?"

Daggett smiled in self-congratulation. "I've arranged a signal, I have. One week from today, at the stroke of noon. I'll be in Londontown. I'll blow up one of their precious monuments, somethin' they can't fail to see. When that happens, my men will do their killin' and scatter. Two hundred, maybe three hundred of the high-and-mighty of the bleedin' British Empire. Why, 'twill paralyze the whole island. Ah, but 'tis a darlin' of a plan, Johnny. We'll wipe them out in one fell swoop and make ye what ye were born to be."

"What monument?" Johnny asked, as if taking the measure of the plan.

But Daggett only laughed. "See if ye can guess, Johnny."

Johnny looked blank. "I have no idea."

"Then let it be a surprise. Ye'll see when ye help me set off the explosives. And what a moment 'twill be, the two of us together again, doin' what we do best."

Johnny turned his head so Daggett's hands fell from him. "What is Shamus going to say when he gets wind of this?"

Daggett was silent for just a second longer than was necessary. "Shamus will be taken care of, as well."

For the first time, Mylene saw a flash of fury in Johnny's eyes. "And Father Q? Is *he* on your list, too?"

Dismissively, Daggett spat, "Of *course* not. But he'd approve of this if he knew. What man wouldn't be proud to be the Merlin to the new king of Eire?"

Mylene stared at Daggett, flabbergasted. She suddenly saw that this man, this third part of her childhood triangle, was a stranger. All those years, all those blank expressions—had he been hatching this plan all those times? Even as a wee tyke? She could see now that the twig had been bent long ago, and she hadn't noticed it. But it was astonishing to think he'd been silent for so long. To never say a word!

In an even voice, Johnny said, "But can't you see, Dag, that this will result in the deaths of hundreds— thousands—of our countrymen? What about them?"

Daggett shrugged. "Our countrymen have been dyin' fer hundreds of years. Two million in the famine, while that fat sow of a queen sent her corn to America. And what did we do? Begged with our hats in our hands for the Home Rule we knew would never come. This sham has gone on long enough. 'Tis time we take what's rightfully ours now, by whatever means we can."

"You're talking suicide. You can't win."

"Ye think that now. But when ye get used to the idea, ye'll see it's the only way."

"I won't do it," Johnny said flatly.

"I'll convince ye of the merit of it, so I will."

"You'll convince me of nothing, Daggett. I won't go through with this mad plan."

Daggett paused, then let the shirt drop to the stone floor with a sigh. "I suspected ye might feel that way. So I've thought of . . . what shall we call it, then? A contingency plan? I hate to do it, Johnny, with ye in no shape to put up a struggle. But if yer after bein' stubborn, ye leave me no choice."

He stood, then crossed the cell. Outside, he reached for the heavy iron key that hung on a hook in the wall. Jerking his head at one of the men holding Mylene, he said, "Get the whip."

The man went to the bundle he'd dropped earlier and brought forth a long, black leather whip. Daggett stood, wrapping it expertly around his hand.

"Now, bare the back," Daggett ordered. "And bring the salt."

Mylene gasped. Surely Daggett couldn't be so cruel, so crazed, that he would torture Johnny further in his battered state!

But as the men moved toward the cell and Johnny's cot, Daggett sneered sharply. "Not *him*, y'fools! *Her!*"

Chapter 18

Daggett slammed the cell door shut and turned the key, locking Johnny inside. "Tie her to the bars of his cell, so he can see her face," he ordered.

Instantly, the men grabbed her arms and roughly stretched them wide to secure her wrists to the bars above her head. As the horror of it hit her, Mylene's mouth went dry and her knees threatened to buckle beneath her. Only her desire not to fail Johnny kept her on her feet.

Johnny had pushed himself up on the cot, leaning weakly on one elbow. He was staring at her with the same mixture of horror and disbelief she felt inside.

"You can't be serious," he said.

Daggett's only answer was to step forward, grab the back of Mylene's shirt, and rip it to her waist, exposing her back. Then he yanked the knot of the cloth that bound her breasts and tugged it free. She could feel her bare breasts fall loose against the cold cell bars. Johnny's gasp caught in his throat.

She couldn't recall if she'd ever seen Johnny genuinely afraid. But as she met his gaze she saw a flash of fear in his. Fear for her. Fear of what Daggett, in his ruthless determination, might do. It terrified her. But she couldn't show him. Willing herself to be strong for his sake, she said, "Johnny, listen to me. Don't let me be your weakness. I can take whatever Daggett hands out. Do what you must without regard to me."

But Johnny wasn't listening. He said, in a tightly controlled voice, "Don't do this, Daggett. I beg you . . . don't do this."

It tore her heart to hear him beg for her sake. Glancing behind, she caught the smooth smile that deepened the cleft in Daggett's chin. He stood, feet planted apart, slapping the coiled whip into his palm as he gave her a cool, assessing stare. He possessed all the sympathy of a Roman warrior, his bare chest expanding the heavy muscles with his breath, his eyes glittering with a cruel, hard glow. Where, she asked, was the boy she'd known? She couldn't find him in the bleak, soulless eyes. Though he'd dropped the smile, his mouth quirked compulsively, as if unable to control the grin of anticipation. This wasn't pain, it was pleasure—some perverse, sadistic retribution for her sin of choosing Johnny over him.

"You son of Satan!" Johnny growled.

Daggett stepped back and uncoiled the whip, giving it a little shake. "Do ye remember, Johnny, when we were twelve years old? That time we'd just fought off ten ruffians twice our age and size along the Dublin docks? We cut our fingers and mixed our blood like the Indians of America do. We said we'd always be true to each other, above anyone else on earth . . ."

He suddenly hauled his arm back and sent the black snake of a whip hurling through the air. Mylene heard the hiss of it before it landed on her back with a might crack. She'd steeled herself, gritting her teeth, but nothing could have prepared her for the pain of it. Despite her resolve, she cried out, but she managed to choke it off by biting into her lip.

Johnny fell from the cot, dragging his broken body across the stone floor. Painfully, he reached up and gripped the bars, shaking them with all his might, so they rattled in desperate protest. "Daggett, for the love of God . . ."

"I'm doin' this fer yer own good, Johnny. I've done everything I've ever done fer ye. Whether ye know it or not."

Vying for time, Johnny asked, "How do you know I won't give my word, then run away?"

Daggett stepped closer to him, letting the whip dangle from his hand. "Because yer word is sacred, Johnny. I've never found much to believe in or count on in this miserable life, except the bond we share. The one thing I know, above all else, is that if ye give yer word to me, ye'll keep it. I believe that the same way other men believe in God, or country, or king."

He stepped back again, raised the whip into the air, and sent it crashing once again into Mylene's back, this time drawing blood. She was ready for it and didn't scream, but she was biting into her lip so hard she feared she might tear it in two.

With all his strength, Johnny pulled himself upright, swaying desperately on his feet. When he'd steadied himself, he fell against the bars and reached up with a shaking hand to cup Mylene's cheek.

"Daggett, I beg you, man. If you must torture someone, make it me."

In answer, Daggett came up behind Mylene and grabbed a fistful of hair, yanking her head back. Her lip was bleeding, her back raw with pain. But she'd be damned if she'd show him. She stared him down, her defiant eyes shooting fire into his.

"Oh, I'm thinkin' she can take a bit more—before we get to the salt," Daggett cooed. He let her go and she fell against the bars. Then he stepped into position, hauled back the whip, and put all his bodily force into the blow. As the whip lashed her, Mylene fought the cry that threatened to escape, but she felt her consciousness begin to slip. She had to hold on. She must use every weapon at her disposal to give Johnny strength. For she knew, in this moment, if she collapsed, he would too.

Daggett moved once again to Johnny's side. "All ye need do, Johnny, to stop this, is give me yer word. Tell me yer with me. Tell me ye'll come back with me. Tell me yer ready to renew our bond and do what's necessary to free Ireland."

With no warning, he let the whip fly. It hit its mark, forming a red cross on Mylene's bare back. She felt herself losing consciousness and clawed her way back with a steely resolution. In a daze, she felt Johnny's hands grip her head on either side, his thumbs grazing her cheeks, to steady her, to give her courage.

"Daggett, listen to me," he said in desperation, speaking fast through his ragged breath. "I was all for harsher measures. But you've gone too far. This is treason to Ireland herself. That meeting between Lord Stanley and Shamus was the way. When you killed

Stanley, you stabbed Ireland in the back. Don't you see?"

Daggett's voice hardened. "I see only that what Keenan O'Flaherty predicted has come true. Yer love fer Mylene has made ye soft. That's not love, Johnny, 'tis weakness. Love is strength."

Again, Mylene felt the lash on her lacerated back. She was losing track of what they were saying. Their voices began to hum in her ears like the distant buzz of bees.

"Daggett, be sensible, man. If we slaughter the royal family, all of Europe—the whole world—would perceive us as mad dogs. Why, they'd band together to exterminate the Irish race."

Daggett stepped closer, bringing his face close to Johnny's. "Then the only choice the Irish race will have is to join together behind a great king."

As he raised the whip again, Johnny's hand lunged out, grabbing Daggett's hand. "What's happened to you? Has your love of Ireland completely twisted your mind? Don't you know who this is you're beating? This is *Mylene!* Our fair lady. Our friend, our sister—"

"Our *lover?*" Daggett sneered. And raising the whip, he brought it down on Mylene's flesh again, harder than before.

She was barely holding on. But she knew Johnny. She knew he wouldn't stand by and watch her suffer. Once his attempts at reason failed, he'd buckle and sell his soul for her sake. "It doesn't hurt, Johnny," she cried through a rasping throat. "Don't listen to him."

"So it doesn't hurt, does it? Maybe it's time yer wounds tasted a wee bit o' salt."

All at once, Johnny let loose the primal growl of a wolf in pain. He reached through the bars and snatched Daggett's hand as it grasped the bag of salt. Locking eyes, he said, "Very well, Daggett. You win."

For a moment, the two men stood paralyzed, Johnny's hand still clenched round Daggett's wrist. Daggett stared at him doubtfully. "Yer word?"

Johnny glanced at the bag of salt in Daggett's hand. "My word."

Hanging limply from the bars, Mylene whispered, with her last ounce of strength, "No, Johnny."

He ignored her completely, keeping his eyes on the bag of salt.

"Yer solemn word, now?"

"Johnny," Mylene pleaded, "don't betray yourself. I can stand this."

As if she no longer existed, he said, "I'll do whatever you ask, if you let Mylene go."

Daggett smiled. "I'll let her go when our mission's accomplished."

"Why not now? Didn't you just say the one thing you trust in this life is my word?"

" 'Tis not that I don't trust ye. But I'd find it hard to trust any woman who's felt the lash of me whip across her back."

"Just kill me and be done with it, you fiend," Mylene croaked. "Better dead than to see Johnny bow to your insane folly."

Her words reverberated in the still dungeon.

It was a moment before Johnny spoke. Finally, he said softly, "Just untie her, Daggett. Let me bathe her wounds. I'll do whatever you ask."

At this, Mylene collapsed completely, wishing for the peace of oblivion, praying to be struck dead in this, their darkest hour.

Oblivious to her, Daggett stared into Johnny's eyes for what seemed an eternity, searching for any glint of deception. Then, satisfied, he said to his men, "Release him."

"But, sir—"

"Release him, I say!" His voice resounded off the walls of the room like the boom of thunder.

Reluctantly, the younger man unlocked the cell door and opened it. Johnny stepped out and stood, swaying, in front of Daggett as the door was closed behind. It was as if they were the only two people in the room. Daggett stood in front of his old friend, giving look for look, measure for measure. Then, in a rush that startled his audience, he took Johnny's arms in his hands and hauled him to his chest in a fierce embrace.

Johnny accepted the embrace with his arms hanging at his sides. As he released Johnny, Daggett was smiling without guile or anger, like the boy they'd known.

"I knew ye'd come round to reason. And now we've a whole new beginning. The world will be no match for us. Together, there's no limit to what we can do, how far we can go."

He seemed a different person, overflowing with joy and the prospect of infinite possibility. Mylene felt she couldn't bear it and leaned her head against the bars, closing her eyes.

Daggett put his arm about Johnny's shoulders with the air of a comrade. Uncomfortable, thrown off guard by this sudden intimacy, his men gripped their rifles. Taking note of their discontent, Daggett laughed.

"They don't think I should trust ye, Johnny. But they don't know, do they? They're little people. People who have no concept of how strong the bond of brotherhood can be between the likes of such men as we."

Putting the bag of salt on the table next to him, Daggett reached over and snatched one of his men's rifles, causing the man to jerk back in surprise. Then, taking the barrel in his hand, he offered it to Johnny. "These men don't understand trust!"

"But can you trust these men?" Johnny asked, ignoring the offered weapon. "Have you no doubt of their loyalty to you?"

Daggett's eyes flicked to the two men. "Aye, they're loyal. They'd die fer me and our cause."

"Is that true?" Johnny asked. "Would you risk your lives for Daggett?"

The men snapped to indignant attention.

Satisfied, Johnny took the rifle and with no hesitation, leveled it at Daggett's head. "And what would you do to save his life?"

The room was so quiet Mylene could hear the guards' caught breath.

"Drop your weapons," Johnny barked, "or Daggett dies."

As the weapons clattered to the floor, Daggett stared at Johnny with open eyes. "Yer . . . breakin' . . . yer . . . word?"

Johnny's voice was a low growl in his throat, as if fighting for control. "You lost any right to my trust when you took that whip in hand."

Keeping the rifle pointed at Daggett's head, he backed away and with one hand untied Mylene.

Daggett never took his eyes off Johnny's face. Standing rigidly before the rifle, he showed his devastation in the tightening of his jaw. But as Johnny helped Mylene to her feet, she could see the faintest trace of tears of hurt in Daggett's eyes.

"I never would've believed this of ye, Johnny. To betray our bond—"

"You broke that bond, Daggett," Johnny snarled. "Did you think I could forgive what you've done this night? What was once between us is finished. You vile monster! I should shoot you down like a rabid dog and put you out of your misery."

Weak and dizzy from her ordeal, Mylene clung to the bars and watched hatred flicker across Johnny's beaten face.

"But I won't. I'm going to take you to Shamus Flynn and let him deal with you."

Daggett raised his jaw. "Ye'd best kill me, Johnny," he said evenly.

"Killing you is not my responsibility."

"Kill me, Johnny," Daggett coaxed, stepping in front of the table. "Do it, man. Because if ye don't, I'll have to kill ye."

"Then I won't give you the chance. I'll tie you up and take you back to Dublin."

"Ye've just made the biggest mistake of yer life, Johnny," Daggett warned in a steely tone.

Ignoring the boast, Johnny reached down to pick up the ropes that had bound Mylene. But as he did, Daggett's hand swung round with the open bag of salt, dousing them both, blinding Johnny and attacking her exposed wounds. The pain was like hot irons imbedded in her flesh. Uncontrollably, she began to scream. She screamed as if she were being consumed by the flames of Hades.

In the confusion, Daggett bolted from the room, calling for his men.

Brushing the salt from his eyes, still half blinded, Johnny could make out the form of one of the two guards reaching for his discarded rifle. Leveling his own rifle at the man, Johnny fired, killing him instantly. As the second man rushed for him, Johnny crushed the rifle butt against his face, knocking him unconscious.

Then, in a flash, he reached down and pulled the still screaming Mylene to her feet. "We've got to run," he called to her. "Can you make it? Or should I carry you?"

Biting her lip to stop the compulsive screaming, she gasped, "I can make it."

Together, the two battered lovers hurried up the stairs into the night. In the distance, they could see that Daggett had run down to alert his men. Fortunately, their impromptu corral was in the other direction, the horses still saddled in case they were needed for a quick getaway.

Daggett and the men started to race back toward the castle ruin. Johnny lifted Mylene onto the nearest horse, then quickly leaped onto a second mount. Daggett's men fired, the shots blasting the stillness of the night. As the bullets whizzed past their heads, Johnny and Mylene galloped down the hill and off into the night.

But as they reached the top of the nearest rise, Johnny suddenly pulled rein. Looking back, he said, "They're not coming after us."

Mylene followed his gaze. The men they'd left behind had mounted their horses, but they were riding off in the opposite direction. "What can it mean?" she asked.

"Off to the coast, no doubt, and from there to London."

"We have to stop him," she cried.

But Johnny heard the pain seething through her voice. "That can wait. Look at you. You can barely sit that horse."

"I'm fine," she said, trying to remain brave.

"You're not fine. You need attention. Come, love. I'll take you home. I'll take you to Father Q."

He nudged his horse next to hers and eased her onto the saddle in front of him. The tears she'd been fighting began to flow. "Johnny, forgive me. I thought you'd killed Lord Stanley. How could I have thought it of you? I'm so sorry. I should have known."

His hand came up to cup her head, careful not to touch her back. "Hush, now. It doesn't matter. All that matters is getting you well. You just hang on to me."

She looked up and saw a man badly beaten, a man himself at the end of his rope. But his concern was for her. "I'll never doubt you again, Johnny," she whispered, as she laid her head against his shoulder and felt the last traces of consciousness slip away.

She awoke as he was pulling up outside of town. Johnny whispered, "We'll have to take the back alleys. There are English soldiers everywhere."

Johnny spurred the horse and they plunged into a maze of warrens that Johnny knew like the back of his hand. Thirty minutes later, they emerged at the rear of the orphanage, and ducked inside.

Hearing the noise, Father Q came out of his office. He was rumpled and looked tired, but despite the late hour, he was dressed in his priest's robes.

"Mother of God," he cried when he saw them. "What's happened?"

"We've had a little trouble," Johnny told him. "We need your help."

Johnny gently turned Mylene so Father Q could see her back through the shredded shirt. When the priest saw the welts and caked blood, he cried, "Saints preserve us! Who did this?"

"Daggett."

Father Q's eyes flashed to Johnny's face. "Daggett?"

"He's out of his mind. He's off to London with some crazy scheme to slaughter the royal family and half of Parliament."

"Oh my God." Recovering, the priest glanced about the hall, as if expecting soldiers any minute. "We can't talk here. Everyone knows about your escape. They're combin' the streets fer you, sure enough, rousin' folks from their beds. They're bound to come here sooner or later. We've got to get you to some safer place, and quick."

Mylene and Johnny followed the priest into his office and watched as he rummaged through his desk drawer and withdrew a set of keys. He gathered together some bandages and salve, then rushed to the kitchen and shoved these items, along with some staples, into a burlap bag. "Come along, then."

They left through the back door and stole down the alley for several blocks, coming to a boarded-up dry goods store along the river. Glancing about to make sure they hadn't been seen, the priest opened the door, then ushered them inside. "This place hasn't been used in many a year," he explained. "The landlord died, and his son's in America and can't be bothered. We've used it as a safe house on occasion. Shamus Flynn himself has hidden here a time or two."

He led them through the dark, empty store to a room at the back. It was small and narrow, with brick walls and no windows. Father Q lit the gaslamp after first closing the door. As light flooded the room, they could see a bed and a chest with a water pitcher and basin atop it.

"You can light the lamp in here, because it can't be seen from the street. But nowhere else, do you hear? Come, then, you're both a frightful sight. Let me tend yer wounds."

Johnny shrugged him off. "Mylene needs it more than I. But I'll tend to her myself. You've got to get to Shamus Flynn at once."

The priest studied him a moment in silence. Finally, he said, "I'll see to it. But tell me, then, what's happened? Why did you kill Lord Stanley, when the meeting was all arranged?"

Urging Mylene onto the bed, Johnny told the story quickly.

When he was finished, the priest went to Mylene and took her face in his hands. "My poor children. I always knew Daggett was a soldier at heart. Given a choice between usin' words or fists, he'd choose his fists every time. There's been somethin' driving him since the time he was a youth. But I never thought he'd go this far. To turn on those he loves . . ."

"He has to be stopped," Johnny said grimly.

"But how?"

"I know him. I know his mind. I can follow him and somehow figure out where he's planted the explosives. But first we have to warn Shamus. Daggett intends to kill him as well. I have no way of knowing if Daggett's sent someone to kill him yet or not. Also, I'll need his help if we're to get out of Dublin in one piece."

"I'll bring him round in the morn, as early as it's heavenly possible. But for now, you need rest and care.

I've brought food, and the water's fresh. There's medicine in the bag. Don't stray from this room until I return. And if anyone knocks, dowse the lights and keep still. If that fails . . ."

He lifted the shabby carpet from the floor to reveal a trapdoor. "Hide yerselves in here till they've gone. There's a candle by the bed to light yer way."

"Don't tarry, Father. We'll need every moment."

"Aye. God rest you well, then, till I see you in the morn."

When Father Q had left, Johnny leaned back against the door. His face was white, and his hands shook from exhaustion. But when he caught her looking at him, he motioned toward the bed. "Get that shirt off and lie down with your back up."

"Johnny, no—"

"Don't argue," he snapped, as if he didn't have the energy. "Let me care for you while I have the strength."

Her back was throbbing, and she knew it needed care. Just peeling the shredded linen shirt off was excruciating, as it stuck to the dried blood and reopened the cuts. But she did as he said, easing down, finding it difficult to lie flat.

Johnny poured the medicine into the bowl and sat beside her, tenderly cleaning each laceration. She winced and held her breath, wanting desperately to be brave. But he told her fiercely, "You've been brave enough, darlin'. Put up no fronts for me." And as he rubbed in the salve and the tears slipped silently down her cheek, he said, "The irony is the salt he threw on these wounds, painful as it was, will help them heal properly. I doubt you'll have so much as a scar." But when she gave an involuntary cry as he touched a tender spot, he dropped his detached manner and swore, "Christ! I should have killed him for doing this to you."

She pushed him aside and sat up to take his face in her hands. "And what has he done to you? Oh, my Johnny, to think of all you've suffered because of him."

She leaned forward and kissed his bruised lips. When even that slight pressure caused him pain, she said, "We're a sorry pair. We can't even hold each other properly."

"I can hold you well enough."

He lit the candle, then doused the gaslamp and shed his clothes. Mylene bit her lip when she saw the extent of his injuries. His chest and back were red with welts, turning black and yellow as they bruised. "It looks worse than it is," he told her, catching her horrified gaze.

"Let me tend you now—"

"Never mind that. All I need is to have you in me arms."

They settled beneath the clean sheets, kept at the ready in case they should be needed. At his instigation, she nestled into the crook of his arm. Each was careful not to hurt the other. But the feel of the other's warm flesh soothed each of them as no medicine could.

The candle created a warm golden glow that made them feel cozy and snug. Johnny idly toyed with her hair. She smiled at him, but her heart was too full of despair to smile for long. In the silence, she finally asked, "Why did he do it, Johnny? I thought he loved us."

Johnny's sigh was all that broke the silence for many moments. Finally, he said, "That I can't tell you. But I *can* say he won't get away with it. That I vow."

Soon their exhaustion got the better of them. The last thing Mylene remembered was the touch of Johnny's lips against her hair. Then they fell asleep, wrapped in each other's arms. And they stayed that way, clinging to each other, through the remaining hours of the night.

Chapter 19

Mylene awoke suddenly when she felt Johnny lunge up in bed. She shot up, clutching the covers to her, thinking desperately that they'd been caught. But standing before them was Shamus Flynn.

"I brought you some clothes," he said without preamble. "Put them on and let me know when yer through."

He tossed the bundle onto the bed, then went out and closed the door. Sensing Johnny's urgency, Mylene quickly donned the peasant dress Shamus had brought, careful not to rub her dully throbbing back.

When he returned, Shamus gave Johnny a long, searching look. There was some grey in his hair now, but he still possessed the intense, hooded eyes of a haunted man.

"Dublin's in an uproar," he told Johnny, barely glancing at Mylene. "They're turnin' the town upside down lookin' for you. 'Tis like the world's comin' to an end. Some of my men have tried to kill me. Others attacked my other men. I myself narrowly missed an ambush. These are dark days, Johnny. But tell me, then, what happened with Lord Stanley? That wasn't planned."

He sounded like an instructor lecturing his star pupil and baffled at the need.

"Daggett set us up," Johnny explained quickly. "Did you know about the meeting?"

"What meetin'?"

Mylene spoke. "We convinced Lord Stanley to meet with you, to talk over your differences. Daggett was supposed to arrange for you to be there. But he never meant for it to take place. He used it as an opportunity to get Lord Stanley alone so he could murder him instead."

Shamus's eyes narrowed sharply. "Why would he do that, then?"

"Because he doesn't want peace," Johnny said. "He has some crazy scheme to make me king of Ireland—after first killing off half the aristocrats in London. I don't have to tell you what that would mean."

"Catastrophe fer Ireland," said Shamus simply.

"Aye. He feels we've been too patient. He's after taking matters into his own hands. He's broken with us, with you, with all our plans. I told him I wanted no part of it, but that won't stop him. You'll have to hide out someplace Daggett doesn't know."

"Where is he now?"

"I think he's off to London even as we speak. He has men well placed to carry out the assassinations. He'll give the signal by blowing up some famous monument—he wouldn't tell me which one. But when that's done, his men know to commit the murders and get out. There's no way we can find out what men he has where. All we can do is stop Daggett before he can fire off the signal. *I've* got to stop him. I know his habits, and I should be able to outthink him."

"Don't forget," warned Shamus, "that ye've been apart from the man these many years."

"True enough. My memory could be dim. Still, it's all we have. But I have to get there first."

"If they catch you," Mylene said, "they'll hang you. Even if you prevent this, what's to make the English authorities believe you?"

Shamus was staring at Johnny intensely, carefully mulling over all he'd said. It was a minute before he spoke. When he did, it was in a sober, thoughtful tone.

"I'm not certain, because everything is coming apart. I may have a minor civil war on me hands. But I think I can get you to England. If not in time to head Daggett off, at least shortly thereafter. But first . . ." He dropped his gaze to the floor, then raised it again, almost defiantly, as if coming to some conclusion in that moment. "There's somethin' you need to know. You've done me a service this day, and may well have saved me life. 'Tis time you knew."

Mylene, feeling a wash of weakness sweep over her, sat on the bed and watched as Shamus stuck his hands in his pockets and began to pace the narrow room.

"This sad tale began many long years past. There was a woman—the loveliest woman ye've ever seen. Mary was her name. A fiery lass, with laughing eyes. Ah, but she had the glow of angels in her smile. I loved her with all me heart and soul. The only woman I ever loved." He paused, averting his head so they couldn't see the look in his eyes. After a pause, he added, "She was the daughter of Liam O'Dooley."

"O'Dooley, the Spear?"

"Aye. One of the original Fenians, and a fierce patriot at that. Mary loved him devotedly and helped our cause. He was my mentor, as I've been yours, Johnny. You understand what that means."

"Aye," said Johnny quietly.

"O'Dooley was imprisoned about the time this tale began. Awaitin' hanging, so he was. Mary, naturally, was desperate to get him free. One day, she was walkin' along the road when a carriage passed by. It stopped jest ahead, and a man stuck his head out the window, starin' as at a vision. He was struck by the thunderbolt that black day."

"Who was the man?" Mylene asked, wondering where this was going.

"Lord Whitney. His father had not yet died, so he hadn't inherited his Parliament seat. He had a penchant for foreign places, that one. He was first assistant to the viceroy in Dublin at the time. Mary knew who he was and wanted nothin' to do with him. Although we'd been chaste, it was understood that—well, we had an agreement, the two of us. But Lord Whitney wooed her with all the weapons at his disposal. He charmed her. He bought her gifts. He flattered her. Still, she rebuffed him. But as the day of her father's hanging approached, she thought he could help. So she married the man."

"She married Lord Whitney? But I never heard of his marrying an Irish girl—"

"There's a reason for that, which I'll get to in due course. She married him, and broke me own heart. But I understood. She'd sold herself for her father's life. The day after the weddin', she told him who she was, thinkin' he'd jump to get his new father-in-law out of prison. I don't have to tell you, the man flew into a fury. He realized if word got out that he'd married

O'Dooley's daughter—to his way of thinkin' the greatest villain in Irish history—this would ruin his career and make him a laughingstock in England. He threw her out. Just like that. She came to me that day, in tears, sobbin' her confession, askin' me to hide her and give her sanctuary. I hadn't known she was set on marryin' him—she knew what I'd say if she told me. But I knew the likes of the Whitneys, and I knew I had to act fast."

"What did you do, then?" Johnny asked.

Shamus paced the floor. "The first thing Whitney did was try to get the records of the marriage. But I'd already pilfered them, you see. I knew a day would come when I might need them to blackmail the man. Having failed in that, he decided to leave Ireland and cover his tracks. He didn't want it known what he'd done, you see. He went back to London and prompt as you please married an English girl from one of the best families."

"But that was bigamy!" Mylene cried.

"Bigamy only if word got out. He was determined not to let that happen. And what if Mary came forth? It was her word against his. He thought the records had been misplaced. Who would they believe? So he transferred to India, as far as he could get from England, and took his bride with him. No doubt to escape any scandal or close scrutiny of his marriage. What he didn't know, and I did, is that Mary was pregnant with his child. I stayed with her the awful night of his birth. She died bearin' Lord Whitney's son."

The room was deathly silent as the words resounded off the walls. Neither Johnny nor Mylene said anything, loath to break the spell.

"After she died, I read that Whitney was on his way to India. So I went to London. As he was boardin' the ship, I pulled him aside. I told him, 'She died. But she had a son. Don't try to find him, you never will. But I promise you, one day your son will use your name to get his revenge.' "

Still, the room was silent.

"When his wife got pregnant, he felt the threat of his firstborn and tried to find out where he was. But he never did. Because I had the midwife take him to an orphanage, where I could keep secret watch over him down the years. I had her take him to Father Q."

Mylene felt dizzy. She had to hold on to the bedpost to keep from swaying forward.

Shamus reached into his pocket and handed forth some folded papers, yellowed with age. "The proof."

There was a long silence as Johnny stared at the papers in his hand. Finally, his voice throbbing with trepidation, he asked, "Who was the child?"

Shamus looked him in the eye. "Who do you think?"

Later that night Shamus returned, accompanied by four men, two of them carting trunks on their backs. As they put them down in the main store, Shamus said, gesturing toward them, "Yer cover. You'll each get in a trunk and be carried aboard the ship as baggage. When the ship—the *Galway*—is well at sea, a man will go to the baggage hold and let you out. You'll follow him to an old munitions room that's no longer in use. The *Galway* is a converted man-o'-war that saw her best days twenty years past and was sold as surplus. They've no need of the munitions room now. You'll stay there until the man comes to fetch you and lock you back in the trunks. Once yer unloaded, you'll be taken to a safe house in Earl's Court. There, you'll give this letter to Keenan O'Flaherty."

"O'Flaherty hates Johnny," Mylene argued. "Who's to say he won't shoot first and ask questions later? He can't be happy about Johnny's new-gained status as Ireland's greatest symbol. Likely he'll welcome the chance to be rid of his competition."

"Tell him you've a letter from meself," Shamus said in his concentrated way. "That'll keep his finger from itchin' on the trigger. Now, in you go."

Mylene eyed the trunks distastefully. To be crouched inside for hours on end in their condition . . . but she realized there was no other safe way, with every ship being searched.

"We've gouged airholes in the side, down along the bottom, where they likely won't be seen," one of the other men explained. "If yer suffocatin' put yer nose to the holes and breathe deep. Ye should do well enough."

The men lifted the lids. The interiors measured little more than four by three feet. Mylene raised her gaze to Johnny, who was looking at her with a worried frown. "I still don't like the idea of you going. I don't think you're up to it."

She went to him and took his hands in hers. "I'm up to it," she assured him. "If we're going to outsmart Daggett, it may take the two of us. Don't forget, I know him as well as you do. Besides, love, now that I've got you back, I never intend to leave you again."

He kissed her, still favoring his cut lip. Then she ran her fingers through his wild black hair, the only part of him that looked like the handsome Johnny she'd always known. Renewed, she stepped into the trunk and hunkered down, allowing the lid to close behind her.

She heard the lock when they clicked it in place. Suddenly, a feeling of panic seized her, as she realized the black, silent reality of being confined in such a meager space. She forced herself to breathe deeply, rhythmically. One breath in, one breath out. The trunk was hoisted up, tipping her to fall against the side, crashing her throbbing back against the wood. She bit her lip so hard to keep from crying out that she tasted blood.

"God spare ye and those ye meet until yer journey is done," she heard Shamus say in parting.

The trunk was lifted, and she was carried out into the night and through the streets. At first she was jostled to and fro, until she learned to plant her hands against the sides and steady herself. She wondered how Johnny, so much larger than she, was faring.

After some time, she felt a thud as the trunk was lowered to the ground. Then she waited, hearing the bustle of loading outside. Soon she was hoisted up by rougher hands, carried up the gangplank and down a series of steps, trying desperately to keep herself still. Another thud. Grumbling voices. The closing of a door and silence.

She didn't know how much time passed. She felt the rolling of the ship and spent the time quelling her stomach as she adjusted to the sea and the lack of fresh air. But finally she heard a door open, then the click of a key in the lock. The lid was lifted and she saw the dim light of the cargo hold, with baggage all around. A slight man with red hair opened Johnny's trunk and he rose stiffly, shaking out his arms.

With a finger to his lips, the man led them through a succession of dark passageways to a far door. He opened it and ushered them inside, motioning for silence once again. Mylene knew that if he was caught there would be hell to pay.

The munitions room was cramped, with empty racks that had once held rifles behind bars. Johnny settled himself on the floor, stretching out his long legs, then held out his arms and beckoned her. She eased down next to him, into the crook of his protective arms.

They rested quietly, knowing they'd need their strength. Mylene, still weak, laid her head against his broad shoulder and closed her eyes, feeling the sweet comfort of his body. But then she froze. Outside, footsteps sounded in the hall. They held their breaths, waiting in suspended silence. Only when the footsteps passed did they relax once again.

But Mylene couldn't find true repose. She knew too well the price they'd pay if they were caught. Johnny would be seized and hanged, this time without delay.

"You're trembling," he said, his voice but a gentle whisper. "Is it the danger?"

"No. I'm used to danger. But it was only my neck on the line before this. I'm not accustomed to knowing one small slip might end the life of the man I love. I'm more afraid for you, Johnny, than ever I was for myself."

"Think of the end, when we've accomplished our task," he coaxed.

"And what end is that?"

"Why, we'll be married, you and I. We'll live together the rest of our lives. We'll wake up to the sight of each other's face till the end of our days. You can be sure I'll stay alive, just for the sight of you on the pillow beside me."

She felt warmed by his words, as if she'd just drunk

a cupful of sweet wine. "Aye, Johnny. Tell me what it will be like when we're husband and wife."

And with his lips at her ear, his breath warm and sweet, he spun a tale so pretty, she nearly forgot her dread of entering the smothering trunk once again.

Two days later, the *Galway* docked at Portsmouth. Late that night, they were taken out of their trunks and sneaked off the ship by the same man who'd helped them aboard. A carriage was waiting to take them to London. They reached Earl's Court as dawn was breaking. After some initial resistance, Keenan O'Flaherty agreed to help them. "Disloyalty must be revenged," he agreed at last.

They spent the remainder of the week trying to discover Daggett's whereabouts, with no success. As they combed the streets, searching out all the Fenian contacts they knew, they could find no one who'd heard of Daggett's plan. He'd hidden his designs so craftily that those loyal to Shamus Flynn hadn't heard so much as a whisper. They sought out James, Mylene's old comrade in his guise as Lord Stanley's driver, thinking he would surely have heard something. But he was as much in the dark as everyone else.

It proved a frustrating week for Johnny and Mylene as the days passed. They couldn't show their faces. Cooped up in the safe house, they spent their time trying to think where Daggett might have planted his explosives. What monument could he have chosen? The Bank of England? Parliament itself? They came up with a hundred possibilities, but when they'd sent men out to search, they'd uncovered nothing.

The night before Daggett's signal was to be set off, Johnny paced their room in agitation. He'd healed so the bruises were little more than darker patches of skin. His face had lost the swollen look left by his beatings, and his lacerations were red scars. Mylene, too, no longer winced every time her clothing touched her back. But they'd slept little, desperately trying to discover a clue to Daggett's scheme.

"I feel it's right before me, but I can't see it," Johnny grumbled as he paced. "Perhaps we're trying too hard. It could be something so obvious we've overlooked it."

"Or maybe we didn't know him as well as we thought," Mylene countered. "To think he was planning this for years and never dropped a hint. I'm thinking, Johnny, that there are many secrets Daggett never told us. Maybe he only let us see what he wanted us to know."

He thought a moment, rubbing a distracted thumb along the lines of his strong, stubbled jaw. "I don't believe that. I knew Daggett before you did, even. We were lads together. He trusted me. He loved me. If something happened along the way to twist his mind, I'll admit I don't know what it was. But there was a time when I knew Daggett better than any brother I could have. He wanted me to guess which monument it was. Why? Why would he think I'd know? If only I could come up with a clue."

"This is getting us nowhere. That explosion, wherever it will be, is set to go off at noon tomorrow. We have to do something. We can't just keep racking our brains over the same stale territory."

"And what do you suggest?"

She was quiet for a moment longer than necessary. Alerted, he turned to look at her. "What is it, then?"

"I think we should go to Queen Victoria herself."

Johnny glared at her. "You're not serious?"

"I am. We'll go to the woman and warn her of Daggett's plot. She can alert the other families. If we err by scaring too many, better than the massacre that will come of our silence."

"Do you know what you're saying? Those men Daggett planted are patriotic Irishmen, like you and me. Daggett will have told them they're acting under the orders of Shamus Flynn. If we alert the Queen, she likely won't be able to stop the inevitable, but even so a lot of these men will be killed because of what we've done. We can't betray them."

"We have to. Think of how many more will die if this plot isn't stopped. Shamus said it himself. If Daggett succeeds, it will mean an apocalypse for Ireland. It will mean senseless slaughter on a scale no one's ever dreamed of."

He gave her a hard glare. "I'm thinking the slaughter you're most worried about is that of your friend the Queen."

She raised her chin defiantly. "And what of it? She's a person, isn't she? She has a face, a heart, a soul. Does she suffer less than you or I?"

He was staring at her in silence.

She rushed forth and took his hands, squeezing tight. "Johnny, you have to think on a grander scale. We're not children anymore. We have the fate of two countries resting on our shoulders, if only until tomorrow. Victoria knows and likes me. If we can get to her without being caught first, I think she'll listen to what we have to say. We'll use the weapon Shamus Flynn handed us."

"What weapon is that?"

"We'll tell her you're Lord Whitney's son."

He said nothing, but she saw a spark of light leap into his eyes.

"You know what Daggett is trying to do is wrong," she urged. "For Ireland, for England, for all of us. You've been so trained to protect your own that you haven't thought about the larger picture. I hope those men don't have to die. I hope, when word gets out, that they scatter before it's too late. But if they die, Johnny, Daggett killed them, not us."

He dropped her hand and ran it through his tousled hair.

"We've only a few hours left, Johnny. You have to decide."

Chapter 20

*B*y eight the next morning, they'd passed through a succession of guards at Buckingham Palace, where Queen Victoria was in temporary residence holding meetings with her ministers regarding the Irish situation. Dressed in appropriate mourning, Mylene presented herself as the daughter of Lord Stanley, there to offer the Queen a portion of her recent inheritance that would have special meaning to Her Majesty—a pocket watch Prince Albert had once given Lord Stanley. When they proposed to pass it along, she explained, "My father left instructions in his will that I must present it to Her Majesty personally. We mustn't leave to chance anything that once belonged to Her Majesty's beloved consort."

The guards, being well acquainted with Victoria's prolonged mourning for her cherished husband, understood the logic but questioned the presence of the man at her side, stiffly attired in Lord Stanley's livery of maroon and black. When they suggested he wait outside, Mylene protested that he was there to guard the gift she'd come to bestow, a measure set down in the terms of Lord Stanley's will.

The ruse proved infallible. Given the honors with which Lord Stanley had been buried and was still being mourned, no one would dare question his last wishes. After multiple explanations along the way, Mylene and Johnny were finally taken to Victoria's private parlor and warned that they would have to wait.

"Please inform Her Majesty that this is of utmost importance," Mylene requested.

The Chief of the Royal Household, the Earl of Rochester, bowed his understanding. "Her Majesty is even now in an emergency meeting with her ministers. I can't predict when they shall conclude. But I assure you, my lady, I will inform Her Majesty of your arrival the minute her ministers withdraw."

They settled in to wait. Minutes passed and tea was brought. They drank it in silence, watching the clock, feeling the minutes tick away. Almost nine, and the explosion was set to go off at noon.

"You're sure this will work?" Johnny asked, squirming in the stiff uniform.

"It's perfect. Victoria can't pass up an opportunity to have something of Prince Albert's returned to her. She lives in the past, surrounded by his things. I hear she even talks to him. Lord Stanley and Prince Albert were the best of friends, which is why the prince gave him the watch in the first place and why we've had such access to the Queen even in her seclusion. If she sees anyone at all, she prefers to see friends she knew with Albert. Once she hears, she'll come right away."

"Pray God she hears in time."

It was difficult to sit and wait after the flurry of the morning. Before dawn, they'd sneaked into Lord Stanley's house to retrieve the proper clothing and the watch Lord Stanley kept in his jewelry box. Careful not to alert the servants, they'd harnessed the coach and driven to Buckingham Palace in the hope of catching the Queen before her daily round of meetings began.

An hour passed. And yet another. Johnny gave up sitting and paced the floor of the grand room, his hands behind his back. The tension in the room mounted as the hands of the clock crept slowly toward eleven. Not much more than one hour to go. So little time . . .

"If she doesn't come soon, we'll have to break in on that meeting," Johnny said.

Mylene could hear the ticking of the clock in the silent room. She felt as if the sands of the hourglass of her life were slipping away. What would they do if she didn't come? What *could* they do?

Just then the doors opened and the Earl of Rochester stepped in. "I apologize for the delay. It's been a hectic morning all around. But I have the pleasure of presenting Her Majesty the Queen."

He stepped aside and a handful of guards came in. Behind them, walking slowly, her stiff satin mourning gown rustling with each step, was the Queen herself. She was a short, stout woman, white-haired now and stern-looking beneath her glasses, carrying the prominence of her position and the sadness of her widowhood like a cross.

Mylene shot to her feet as Johnny joined her, bowing over the hand Victoria extended.

"Your Majesty," greeted Mylene, "so good of you to see us. We know how busy you are."

"My dear, I've heard about the unpleasantness you've had to endure. I've been meaning to communicate our concern, but the last I heard, you'd returned to Dublin. Do you think that wise?"

"Under the circumstances, Your Majesty—"

"Oh, but it's a beastly business all around. You can't imagine the repercussions with which I've had to deal."

"I'm so sorry, Your Majesty, for the trouble I've caused. I assure you—"

"Heavens, I don't blame *you*, my dear. How could you know? I daresay you've suffered more than any of us. How thoughtful of you to think of me at such a time. Do show me what you've brought, won't you?"

Mylene extended the gift, carefully wrapped in silk. As Victoria opened it as she would the folds of a new-born's blanket, Mylene caught one of the guards peering at Johnny curiously. Johnny saw it and averted his face.

Victoria, when she saw the watch, gave a small gasp of pleasure. "Ah, yes, I remember this well. I recall the occasion when my beloved Albert presented this to your father. For his birthday, here in this very room. What a gay occasion that was. Such laughter and singing. All that's gone now . . . gone . . ."

She opened the watch cover and tilted her head in memory at the strains of Shubert emitted from the watch. "He admired this so. How very kind you are to return it. It's as if I have a piece of my Albert back with me."

With tears in her eyes, she turned to the guards and said, "You may leave us now."

With a last look at Johnny, the guard followed the others out.

As soon as the door closed, Mylene felt Johnny's impatient stir.

"Your Majesty, I have a confession to make. This gift was heartfelt, but it was also part of an excuse to break your seclusion. You must listen to us, for we haven't much time. England is in grave danger. You personally are in danger. Imminent danger."

"What is this?" asked Victoria, straightening herself in her most queenly manner.

"I can't explain now. We came to warn you. You must act at once. A renegade faction of the Irish Fenians is preparing to mount a devastating attack on England. They have agents infiltrated into dozens of prominent families, with instructions for a mass slaughter once the signal is given."

"Good heavens, you can't be serious, my girl!"

"I'm deadly serious, Your Majesty. The explosives are in place. Men you trust are prepared to assassinate you and the entire royal family, as well as various members of Parliament. It's going to happen today— only an hour from now. You must send men out immediately to warn as many families as possible. Get everyone out of Westminster. It doesn't matter where they—"

Just then, the door opened and the Earl of Rochester stepped in, bowing his apologies. With him was the guard who'd been staring suspiciously at Johnny. "Ma'am, we have reason to believe these two have some connection with Lord Stanley's assassination."

Victoria's horrified eyes flashed to each of their faces.

The guard stepped forth. "Your Majesty, I recognize this man as the one who impersonated Lord Whitney."

Victoria was staring at Johnny. "Is this true, young man?"

Johnny straightened his shoulders. "It's true to a certain extent. But I did not kill Lord Stanley. And I'm not an impostor."

"What's this?"

Johnny reached into his jacket and withdrew the yellowed papers Shamus had given him. These he handed to the Earl. "I have proof that I'm the legitimate son of Lord Whitney. Before he married the woman you presumed to be his wife, he took an Irish girl as bride. I'm the issue of that marriage. Since he never divorced the girl, and married before she died, his second marriage wasn't legal. The son who died was illegitimate. I'm his rightful heir. I believe this proof will stand up in any court of law."

The earl had been perusing the papers while Johnny spoke. Now, calmly, he looked at Victoria and nodded. "It's all here. Marriage certificate, birth certificate, all duly signed and witnessed. Seems to be in order, ma'am."

"But how—"

"Ma'am, forgive me, but we haven't time," Mylene said. "You know me, and you trusted my father. And I tell you in his memory that this man, this Lord Whitney, did not murder Lord Stanley. He's come at great personal risk to warn you of a treacherous plot. You must get word out as fast as you can. And you, my lord, must get the Queen to safety. Once the explosion occurs, it will be a signal for the agents to strike, and it will be too late."

"There must surely be some way to avert this," said the earl.

"When the signal goes off, it will happen. The only way to stop it is to stop that signal. But we don't know where it will be. They're going to blow up some monument. A symbol of England. It could be the Tower of London, it could be Parliament, it could be a castle, a hotel, a bridge . . . we have no idea."

Suddenly, she felt the grip of Johnny's hand on her arm. She turned to see a light glowing in his eyes. "Mylene, a bridge!"

She peered at him, not understanding. But as she strained to think, the mists in her mind parted and a dim memory surfaced with a jolt. "Oh, my God!"

"Aye. The song he sang as a lad. '*London Bridge is falling down . . .*'"

Without a word, they turned to run. But the earl stepped in front of them, blocking the door. "I'm afraid, sir, that you're not going anywhere."

"You don't understand," Mylene cried. "We just figured out where the explosion will be."

The earl looked at the Queen. "This man may well be the genuine Lord Whitney, but there still remains the matter of his escape from prison."

Mylene glanced at the clock. It was half past eleven. Only half an hour to go. *London Bridge is falling down . . . falling down . . .*

"Everything can be explained, but we haven't time," she said desperately.

"I'm sorry to have to do this," Johnny said before slamming his fist into the earl's face. The man hit the door behind him hard, and stood for a moment with his eyes wide, before slipping slowly to the floor. In seconds, Johnny had pulled him aside and was opening the door.

Mylene glanced back at the startled Queen. "Forgive us, Your Majesty. We'll explain later."

She followed Johnny into the long hall. He ran ahead, knocking two guards aside as he went so they tumbled to Mylene's feet like bowling pins. She leapt over them, racing after Johnny for the door. He grabbed her hand and ran across the courtyard to the gates, where their carriage waited beyond. Before the two guards there could turn rifles on them, Johnny grabbed one and hurled him at the other. As they fell in a heap, he threw open the gates. They rushed past, leaping onto the coach, Johnny slapping the reins and sending the horses galloping up the Mall.

They flew down the wide boulevard to Charing Cross, then along the Strand. Pedestrians stopped to stare, but Mylene was looking for clocks along the way. Fifteen minutes to go, and still a great distance to travel.

"If only we were riding," she lamented. "This coach is slowing us down."

They passed Waterloo Bridge and turned up Fleet Street, only to come across a huge hay wagon blocking the way. Cursing, Johnny yanked the horses to a halt. Looking about, he spotted a couple of approaching riders. He jumped to the street, ran to them, and yanked first one then the other from his horse. By the time he'd mounted one horse, Mylene was putting her foot in the stirrup of the other, calling apologies behind as they resumed their pace.

They clattered up Fleet Street past grand business facades and rounded the circle at St. Paul's Cathedral. They had to slow before a mass of tourists crossing the street for the pub. Mylene felt the ticking of the clock in the rushing of her blood.

Finally they reached Cannon Street and beyond it Fish Street Hill. With five minutes to spare, they saw the granite structure of London Bridge stretching out before them to cross the Thames.

Mylene had expected a great commotion. But what she found instead was a perfectly ordinary scene. No sign of Daggett, no hint of a disturbance. The river traffic flowed beneath the bridge as a stream of carriages and lorries traversed it.

"We guessed wrong," she said, panting, her disappointment bitter in her throat.

"No we haven't. How many times did we hear him sing that song when we were young? It was like a threat to England. It can't be anything else."

"Then where is he?"

Johnny was scanning the bridge with narrowed eyes. Suddenly he said, "Under the bridge."

"I don't see . . ."

"There's bound to be some sort of substructure. He'd put the explosives there, as near to the center as possible, so the whole of the bridge would collapse. Stay here," he added, then began to run across the bridge.

The driver of a lorry called out a warning, then swerved to keep from hitting Johnny. Mylene watched for a moment, but she couldn't remain where she was. Johnny might need help. If he could keep Daggett distracted, she could destroy the explosives before he had a chance to set them off. She ran after him.

In the middle of the expanse, hanging over the side, was a rope ladder leading to a parapet below. This lower level was obviously used by workmen for maintenance of the bridge. Johnny tossed his leg over the side of the bridge, grabbed the ladder, and started to climb down. But when he saw Mylene getting ready to follow, he called, "Get back. Get off the bridge completely. Warn as many people as you can to get away."

"There's no time," she called, looking over the bridge at the vast rushing river far below. "And you may need help."

Ignoring the sensation of vertigo, she carefully climbed over the granite rail and reached for the ladder. It swayed precariously, throwing her out above the water along the way.

Below, behind an iron railing, was a platform that ran the width of the bridge. Daggett was standing in front of a dozen huge kegs filled to their brims with gunpowder, a match in hand. His hair was disheveled from the blast of river wind. His shock at seeing them gradually transformed into a look of grudging admiration.

"So ye figured it out after all, Johnny me boy. I guess I'd have been disappointed if ye hadn't."

"You know I have to stop you, Dag."

"Do ye now?" Daggett's mouth broadened to a grin. "Well, then, Johnny, ye've got yer work cut out fer ye."

Mylene stood rooted, staring at the match in Daggett's hand. Johnny glanced back, calling, "Get off. Now!"

His voice stirred her to action. "You deal with Daggett. I'll pull out the fuse."

Johnny raced for Daggett, knocking him to the ground. But as Mylene ran toward the fuse, Daggett raised his legs and kicked Johnny aside. Leaping up, he lunged for Mylene, backhanding her across the side of her head, a flash of icy triumph in his eyes. The impact of the blow sent her flying backward, hard against the rail. But the rail didn't stop her. Instead, it acted as a lever, flipping her head over heels and tumbling her over the side. Grasping frantically, she was just able to grab the rail before falling to the river below. The force of her fall wrenched her arms. She looked down, saw the churning water far below as her head spun and the wind swirled round her. Desperately, she tried to reach the parapet with her foot, to climb back up, but her skirts hampered her movements, and the wind blew her back over the river every time she moved.

She saw Johnny's face before her as he leaned over the rail. But Daggett seized him, holding him back.

"Forget her, Johnny," she heard his coaxing voice. "Come with me. Forget the past. Let's run, Johnny. Once this bridge blows, Ireland will be ours for the grabbin'."

"You raving totter," Johnny cried, pushing him back.

But Daggett reached for him again. "Yer destiny lies not with her, Johnny, nor with savin' some English swells." Johnny slammed his fist into Daggett's face, but Daggett recovered at once and pushed him back against the rail. Mylene felt it tremble. "Yer destiny is Ireland, Johnny. And it's me."

"Hold on," Johnny called to her.

"The fuse," she cried. "Get the fuse."

She heard the sounds of struggle from above as the two men beat at each other, one trying to get to the fuse, the other blocking the way. She glanced at the riverbank to see that a crowd had gathered. She wanted to call to them, to warn them to flee. But it was all she could do to keep her grip.

"I'm disappointed in ye, Johnny," she heard Daggett say from above, followed by the sound of a loud whack. "Do I have to beat some sense into ye, then?"

Johnny shook off the blow and lunged for him. The two men were struggling when Johnny spotted the knife tucked into the belt of Daggett's pants, the knife he'd used to cut the fuse. Wresting his arm free, he made a grab for it, snatching it from the waistband.

He raised it high, saying, "I'll kill you, Daggett, so help me God."

Daggett made a mighty charge but Johnny parried it. Daggett charged again, and Johnny caught his arm at the wrist, holding it in his iron grip. In the same instant, he kicked Daggett's legs out from under him and the two men fell to the floor, rolling over and over, their bodies grinding into the granite. When they finally stopped, Johnny was on top. He raised his knife. But as he sought to lower it, Daggett managed to take hold of Johnny's wrist.

Locked in this deathly embrace, they stared long and hard into each other's eyes, reading the secrets of their souls.

As the knife in Johnny's hand inched closer to his throat, Daggett met his eyes. "Ah, Johnny boy, 'tis so sad. What a grand king ye would have made. How I could have served ye."

Johnny pushed harder, but Daggett held the weapon off.

"If we can't have this, 'tis better we die together. If I can't have ye, let no one have ye then."

Johnny pushed harder, but Daggett was able to hold him back.

"Ye'll never know how much I really love ye, Johnny. Ye never knew the feelin's I have fer ye. Ye never learned how a man can love another man. What I could have taught ye! What ye don't understand Johnny is, I don't jest love ye, I *desire* ye."

In shock, Johnny searched the eyes of his oldest and once dearest friend, reliving a thousand different memories in the light of this revelation. For a moment, Johnny released some of the pressure on his weapon, and Daggett responded in kind.

"What are you saying?" Johnny cried.

"I'm sayin' ye desire me, as well. I'm sayin' ye care nothin' fer this wench. 'Tis me ye care fer in that way. Ye jest don't know it, Johnny."

Johnny eased even more of his pressure on the knife. Feeling this, seeing the slowly dawning comprehension in Johnny's eyes, Daggett let up an equal amount of resistance.

"*That's* why you whipped Mylene?" Johnny said at last, his voice so strained that it might have been dragged from his throat.

"Aye, Mylene is nothin' to us. She's never been anythin' to us."

The force in Johnny's arm collapsed. As it did, Daggett dropped his hand from Johnny's wrist. "You never loved Mylene. All those times you called her 'my fair lady' . . . 'London Bridge is falling down, my fair lady . . .' You didn't mean it as endearment. You meant it as a threat!" Johnny said.

"Of course I never loved her. How could I love the woman who took ye from me? I love *ye*. I've always loved ye. I've lived me life fer ye, Johnny. And now I'm goin' to die with ye."

It was the moment of truth. Johnny looked at Mylene hanging from the bridge. He looked at the fuse. He looked at Daggett.

"You fecking bastard! None of this was for Ireland, was it? All you put us through . . . it was just for some private lust! You made them think I killed Stanley. You let them torture me. For what? So you could have me for yourself? How dare you do this to our friendship? How dare you do this to Mylene! Well, you can just die alone."

With that he lunged toward the fuse. But Daggett was right behind him, grabbing his coat, determined to stop him. Johnny gave a mighty roar. With all the strength he'd ever possessed, he grabbed Daggett and, using the force of his body, hurled him crashing toward the rail. Screaming Johnny's name, Daggett fell over the side. Mylene felt the force of his body knock her on the way down, loosening one of her hands. As she swung precariously, she saw Daggett's body fall into the water.

Mylene was struggling to hold on with one hand, growing weaker by the second. She felt her hand slip on the rail, felt her body begin to fall.

But just as her hand let go, she saw Johnny reach over the side, saw his hand, with a dreamy slowness, as it reached for her. She felt the pressure of flesh, felt his hand close on hers as her arm was racked with pain. As she swayed, she felt him hoist her up with one mighty tug. The next thing she knew, she was falling into his arms.

Chapter 21

Mylene stood at the back of the church, dressed once again as a bride. Her gown was exquisite. Fashioned from Flemish silk that shimmered with the faintest hue of pink, the bodice daringly plunged so it exposed her shoulder blades and back—which, thanks to Johnny's care, had quickly healed without scars. The silk skirt, edged with scalloped lace, draped to her slippers in soft, silky folds. But it was the train that was the crowning glory of the dress. Yards and yards of it with scalloped lace edges, draping fifteen feet behind her like something a fairy godmother had waved her wand to create. The same scalloped lace formed a series of gently sloping points up the back. The perfect gown in which to marry the true love of her heart.

She had every reason to feel wonderful. But all day long, as she'd dressed and conferred with her brides-maids, as she'd made the journey in the carriage to the church, she'd been seized by the feeling that something wasn't right. It was a feeling of uneasiness, warning her that she wasn't destined to be a real bride, that fate was going to strike her down.

It made no logical sense. Everything had turned out better than she'd had the right to hope. In the aftermath of the near catastrophe, the Earl of Rochester had raced to the scene on their heels. When he'd seen the kegs of gunpowder, he'd forgotten that Johnny had knocked him cold. He'd declared him a hero for saving one of London's oldest symbols and for averting a plot that would have had disastrous repercussions. A subsequent inquiry had exonerated him of all charges in Lord Stanley's death. The records he'd produced had been examined and, despite the ensuing scandal over the old Lord Whitney's early marriage, Johnny had been officially recognized as the current Lord Whitney, with full rights and privileges. Johnny would take Lord Whitney's old seat in the next session of Parliament.

Daggett's plot had collapsed, his men scattering and returning to seek new orders from Shamus Flynn. Shamus, risking the journey to London, had met secretly with Johnny and had agreed with Johnny's proposal that he continue more openly with their original plan; that Johnny, in his new standing as the real Lord Whitney, would use his seat to fight for Home Rule of Ireland. As soon as word got out, the leadership for Home Rule coalesced around him, offering support.

Not everyone was pleased. Although Queen Victoria awarded Johnny with a special commendation for his heroism, there were those who resented one more voice in Parliament speaking for Irish rights. The opposition made it known that they'd fight him as they'd always battled the Irish cause. But he was marrying Lord Stanley's heiress, and that afforded him a grudging respect, even among those who disapproved of his politics. And they couldn't deny the fact that he'd saved them from being massacred. No one ever knew for sure who the intended victims were, but naturally, each one assumed that he was important enough to make the list.

Suddenly the swells of the pipe organ floated through the nave. Heads turned toward Mylene. Throats cleared in anticipation. The moment was finally at hand. But Mylene was gripped by a strange fear. She remembered the last time she'd walked down the aisle, with the intention of marrying Roger. When she'd looked up to see Daggett's face in place of the priest.

As she began her long walk down the aisle, the fear numbed her. On all sides were the same faces who'd attended her first aborted wedding. Maybe they, too, were expecting theatrics. Ahead was a flight of marble stairs, leading to the altar high above. She couldn't yet see those standing there, waiting for her. She and Johnny had asked Father Quentin to come to London to perform the ceremony. She knew he waited with Johnny up ahead. But her mind was playing tricks. She kept imagining him turning toward her slowly, and instead of Father Q, it was Daggett she beheld.

It was ridiculous. A bloated body had washed up on the banks of the Thames a week after Daggett had taken his plunge. The authorities were certain it was Daggett, even though there wasn't much left of him. Why, then, couldn't she make herself believe him gone? Almost every night since his death, she'd awakened, bathed in sweat, from some horrible nightmare of him. His revelation, followed so swiftly by his death, had left her with the feeling that *nothing* had been resolved. Mylene feared Daggett's presence would haunt them for the rest of their lives, preventing them from ever truly being husband and wife.

She paused halfway up the stairs. She could feel the audience holding their breaths, wondering what was wrong. She had to stop these thoughts. This was her wedding, the wedding she'd never thought to have. She was marrying Johnny. *Johnny*. She must concentrate on him.

She stepped up to the rise and saw her beloved. He was resplendent in black tails, his black hair combed back, looking every inch the English lord, but with the twinkle of the Irish rebel in his eyes. He gave her a grin that calmed some of her fears, promising that the years ahead would be sublime.

She wanted to believe. She glanced at Father Q for confirmation. But he had his back turned. Again, she faltered. It was a vision from her nightmare. He wore the headdress, so she couldn't see his hair. She stopped again, paralyzed by fear. No, it couldn't be.

She had to move. They were waiting for her. She took up the rhythm of Bach once again and crossed the distance to take Johnny's outstretched hand. He seemed so calm, so happy. Completely unperturbed. Why, then, couldn't she feel the same? Why did she feel once again that the spirits were whispering a warning of doom?

The music stopped and a hush swept the church. The priest raised a golden cross. She had a flash of Daggett swinging the cross to knock Roger to the ground. The priest seemed frozen in place, as if time stood still. Then, slowly, ever so slowly, he began to turn. Mylene tensed. He turned and turned, with slow deliberation. She couldn't breathe.

And then she saw his face. The face of Father Q,

the man who'd raised them, taught them, nurtured them to adulthood. The man she'd loved as a father, the way she'd loved Lord Stanley.

The relief that washed over her was so intense, she swayed. Johnny put his arm around her shoulders to steady her, his hand brushing her bare back. The touch of his fingers in so public a place sent a thrill racing through her. It was all right. They *were* going to be married, just as she'd always hoped.

She was suddenly overcome with a joy like none she'd ever known. Johnny looked down at her and she beamed a smile into his face. As Father Q read the mass in his familiar lilting voice, and as they exchanged the vows that made them husband and wife, Mylene's eyes filled with tears. "I, Mylene, take you, Johnny, to be my lawfully wedded husband." She felt she'd never heard more beautiful words than those that were joining them together forevermore. As Johnny placed the ring on her finger—a perfect replica of the one he'd given her at their hideout outside Dublin, but with a diamond replacing the glass—she saw that tears welled in his eyes. She'd never felt closer to anyone in her life. Her heart overflowed with love, with happiness, with emotions so deep, so profound, she felt utterly transformed. When Father Q told Johnny he could kiss his bride, they flew into each other's arms and drowned in a kiss of such celebration, they forgot the existence of the crowd.

The music thundered through the hall, bringing them back to where they were. As she looked at her husband, a magical feeling replaced all the dread and fear. It was over. Nothing could stop them now.

They rushed down the aisle together, holding hands, glowing with exhilaration. Out into the afternoon sun. Up into the coach that waited to take them to the gala reception at the Helmsleys'.

In their joy and excitement, they didn't notice the driver of the coach, his hat lowered over his face to hide the deep cleft in his chin.

As the coach lurched away, Johnny pulled Mylene to him and nuzzled the exposed flesh of her back. "My beloved," he whispered. "Now you're really mine."

She felt so close to tears, she choked on the words. "I was always yours, Johnny. Always."

"I wish to God we didn't have to go to the Helmsleys'. All those people, and all I want is to be alone with my bride."

She pushed away and looked up at him, noting the glow of happiness in his eyes. He'd never looked so happy, so relaxed. As if he was finally right where he belonged. She felt it, too, the unaccustomed feeling of truly belonging, of being right where she'd been born to be. "Tell me, Johnny. Where are we going for our honeymoon?"

He grinned. "Can't you guess?"

"Ireland?"

"Nay, love. Not Ireland. Somewhere special. Somewhere—"

Suddenly he stopped. He sat up, pulling his arm away, and looked outside. "This isn't the way to the Helmsleys'."

She looked out the window. They were headed in the opposite direction. As they watched, the coach began to charge through the narrow streets.

They exchanged a look. "Something's wrong," Johnny said.

The icy fear that had possessed her all morning returned like a knife to her heart. "You don't think—"

Above them, they heard the crack of the coachman's whip as the horses raced even faster, more recklessly, tossing the passengers to and fro.

Struggling, Johnny opened the door and climbed out to have a look. Ahead, the four white horses were plunging onward beneath the driver's whip, scattering pedestrians and narrowly missing hitching posts along the way. When Johnny called to him, the driver turned.

He saw Johnny clinging to the side of the coach, and whacked the horses to increase their speed. Johnny was nearly bounced off, barely grabbing onto the swinging door. "Hold on tight," he yelled to Mylene before grabbing the top rail to pull himself up.

Mylene clutched his leg. "Is it Daggett?" she cried. When he didn't answer, she called again, more desperately, "*Is it, Johnny?*"

His silence told her all she needed to know.

Her hands dropped from his leg. As the coach bounced over the cobblestones, Johnny reached out to the luggage rack with first one hand and then the other, slowly pulling himself up. Then he swung his legs over and climbed on top. Fighting to keep himself from being hurled off, he inched toward the driver's box over the slippery roof of the coach.

The open door was swaying, knocking into lamp-posts along the way. On the opposite side of the coach, Mylene opened her window and thrust herself out, climbing onto the ledge to see what was happening above. Daggett was fighting with the horses, whipping them and reining with his free hand, sending them barreling through one street after the other. Johnny had almost made it to the driver's box when Daggett turned and began to lay the whip on him. He lashed Johnny's arms, his shoulders, cutting his face as he battled to beat him back.

Johnny grabbed for the whip, but Daggett yanked it free and landed another blow. Then, ignoring the fall of the lash, Johnny dove for Daggett, nearly knocking him off his seat. But Daggett righted himself. As the horses barreled around a corner, running wild, the two men struggled. Mylene tried to climb on top and give Johnny a hand, but the opposite door slammed shut, catching the train of her gown and holding her pinned.

She raced to the other side. From there, she saw Johnny fall back on her side of the coach. Reaching out, she gave him a push that enabled him to charge after Daggett and land a blow to his face. Daggett dropped the reins and furiously seized Johnny's neck, desperately trying to choke him as he called, "Ye bastard, ye bastard!"

As Mylene was struggling to free her train, the horses bolted, thundering now up onto the sidewalk and veering off again. As they did, Johnny was thrown forward from the driver's box, between the coach and horses, falling for the street. But just before he hit, his arms shot out to grip the harness that fastened the horses to the coach. He tried to climb up, but the horses whirled to avoid an oncoming wagon and he was hurled back, hanging from the harness with his arms and legs, his back inches from the street.

"Ye bleedin' bastard," Daggett yelled over the clamor of hooves and the screech of the wheels. "What a joke this is on me! I wanted to make ye king of all of Ireland. And all that time ye were English scum . . . a pasty-faced English bastard. . . . No wonder ye betrayed me. What else could I expect from Lord Whitney, high-and-mighty bastard of the realm!"

Johnny was struggling to hold on. But he looked up at Daggett and called in a panting voice, "I'm not Lord Whitney, Daggett."

Daggett raised the whip and gave Johnny a tremendous lash. "Ye'll not save yerself now, ye lyin' bastard."

"I'm *not* Lord Whitney. I only pretended to be. It's a ruse, Dag, the way it was before."

"Do ye dare go to heaven with a lie on yer lips?"

"I'm not Lord Whitney, Daggett. *You* are!"

Daggett had raised the whip, but he stopped short. His eyes widened. "What!"

"As God is my witness, Daggett, *you're* Lord Whitney."

For a moment, Daggett was paralyzed. Clearly, this was the last thing he'd expected. "Liar," he whispered. Then, raising the whip high, he laid it on Johnny's body with all his might, crying out, "Liar! Liar! Liar!"

Johnny felt his hands losing their grip. But he steadied his voice and called back, "That was *your* birth certificate, not mine."

"Liar!"

"Shamus thought me better suited to play the role. Ask him, Daggett. He'll tell you. You're Lord Whitney's son."

Daggett suddenly stopped cold. The fight drained from him. He could see Johnny was telling the truth.

"Help me up," Johnny called. "I'll show you the proof."

Daggett sat transfixed, reeling from the revelation. But after a slight pause, he reached down like a man in a trance, extending his hand.

Just then the coach hit a huge bump in the road. Off balance, Daggett was thrown forward, high into the air, so he fell onto the street in the horses' path. As Mylene screamed, the four horses plowed over Daggett's body, the coach wheels crushing it moments later, dragging the twisted form along the cobblestones before finally setting it free.

Mylene opened the door and pulled her train loose. Just as she was climbing up, Johnny found the reins. He jerked back on them, finally slowing the horses, until at last they came to a halt.

Johnny lowered himself to the street, then jumped up to help her. "Are you all right?"

She nodded, but already she was looking back at the prone figure of Daggett lying a hundred yards or so down the street.

Without another word, they ran to him. Johnny knelt and carefully rolled Daggett onto his back. He convulsed in pain. As Mylene drew up, she could see that his body was shattered. He was bleeding, his clothes torn away to expose raw flesh where the cobblestones had scraped away the skin. She put her hand to her mouth. She'd never seen such an awful sight.

Daggett was dying. The knowledge of it dimmed his eyes. In his agony, he searched Johnny's face.

"Johnny, please," he rasped in a voice nearly gone. "Tell me it isn't true."

Johnny looked into the eyes of his childhood friend. "It's true," he said in a steady tone.

Daggett let out a wail. "Mother of God, the son of an English dog. I want to die, Johnny. I can't bear the shame of it."

Johnny looked up to see the tears in Mylene's eyes. They stared at each other and felt compassion stir their hearts. The horrid spectacle of this man who'd shared so much of their lives was heartbreaking. They could see only the proud boy, the dear friend, the loving brother he'd once been. And they knew, in spite of all he'd done, that they couldn't let him die this way. Mylene nodded her answer to Johnny's unspoken question, then looked at Daggett once again.

In a gentle voice, Johnny said, "Maybe so. But your mother was the daughter of Liam O'Dooley."

"O'Dooley, the Spear?"

"Aye."

Hope brought a renewed spark to the dying light in Daggett's eyes. "Ye don't mean it, Johnny? I'm the grandson of the great O'Dooley?"

"Aye, lad. One of the greatest Irish patriots that ever lived."

"The first of the Fenians . . ." Daggett's eyes glowed with wonder. But then pain ripped through him and his eyes shuddered closed. He struggled for breath, the air rasping through his lungs. He swallowed hard. Then, in a faint voice, he said, "Thank ye, Johnny. Thank ye fer that."

"Don't talk, Daggett. Save your—"

"My strength, Johnny? I'm dyin' and don't we know it."

"Hang on. We'll get help."

" 'Tis too late. If I'd only known . . . what a difference it might have made. To know who ye are . . . that's everythin', isn't it, Johnny?" Again, he closed his eyes in pain. "Forgive me, Johnny. I did it 'cause I love ye so."

Mylene and Johnny exchanged a long look. Then, as one, they reached out and each took one of Daggett's hands in their own. They sat so, united in a circle, as they had been as children.

When Daggett opened his eyes, he glanced from Johnny to Mylene. His manner seemed to plead forgiveness. Mylene squeezed his hand, granting it.

"I'd have your blessing, Daggett," Johnny said.

Daggett's eyes searched once again for Johnny's face. He looked at him for several moments, his face full of the love he'd hidden all through the long years. "Then take it, Johnny," he said at last. "Take Lord Whitney's fortune and use it to help our beloved Eire . . . and take—yer bride. I'd die knowin' I gave ye that, at least."

Johnny leaned over and, with his mouth at Daggett's ear, whispered the act of contrition. As he did, Daggett's tortured face settled into peaceful lines, his gratitude showing in the dim windows of his eyes. Moments later, his breath slowed. He clutched their hands until the last breath escaped like a sigh through his lips.

Chapter 22

*I*t was late when they arrived. Hours had passed before they were free to leave. They had to send to Scotland Yard for Inspector Worthington and explain what had happened. Father Quentin was fetched from the reception at the Helmsleys' to read the last rights. And the inspector had to be convinced to allow the priest to return Daggett's body to Ireland and bury him in his beloved homeland, the land he'd fought for and died to free. Then came the endless questions of their guests and rushing to make the train to Salisbury.

But all that was past. They rode now on horses they'd hired from the inn. Rode through the dark chalky plains that stretched before them, around them, so vast and empty they might have been traveling through another world. They rode in silence, in mounting anticipation, their eyes straining the

Cimmerian landscape for the first, long-awaited, sight of the shrine.

As they rode through the wild grassland, Mylene could feel the pressures of the day slip away. She'd felt haunted by tragedy—a bride in danger of never knowing the fruits of wedded bliss. Daggett's reappearance and pitiable death had thrown a pall on what she'd hoped to be the happiest day of her life. Even when she'd discovered their destination, even when she'd been touched by the perfection of Johnny's honeymoon choice, she'd still felt the heavy hex of Daggett's sad, misguided love. She felt chained to the past, haunted by the apprehension that she could never be truly happy in her husband's arms.

But as she sank into the saddle, the savage, ghost-like plains seemed to call her name. She felt again the presence of those who'd come before, beckoning to her, leading the way through the sloping terrain, as if whispering with the breath of the wind that she was home. The spirits she felt held no danger, no sense of menace. She felt their smiles, felt the warm, open welcome of their arms in the tremendous scope of this ancient land.

She peered through the darkness at Johnny, silhouetted against the starry sky. He'd been quiet, thoughtful, since leaving London and Daggett behind. As if he, too, needed time to sort out his thoughts, to find some way to put it all behind. But it was a comfortable silence, the hush of two people who knew each other so well they didn't feel the need of useless chatter. The rhythm of the horses, the clean crisp air, the endless panorama that held an eerie mixture of tranquil quietude and vibrant, unseen forces, allowed them to share their feelings in wordless communion. They'd ridden with their eyes ahead, drinking in the stillness of the night that wrapped around them as if protecting them from harm.

But now, Mylene began to feel there were things that must be said. Now, before they reached their destination, she had to try to make her peace.

She called to him then, her voice carrying softly in the breeze. "Do you feel the spirits?"

He gave her a quick glance. "Aye."

"Do you think Daggett's spirit is here? Do you think he'll haunt us?"

He looked at her then, really looked, as if hearing the dread that lurked behind the words. Then he reined his horse so they were side by side, reached over and took her horse's bridle, easing him to a halt. Facing her, he brushed a tender knuckle across her cheek. "Nay, love. I think he's a ghost who's haunted us all our lives, whether we knew it or not. As crazed as he became, he had a decent heart. He loved me the only way he knew how. I think he found his peace in the end."

"I hope so. I can't blame him for loving you, when I love you so much myself. Only for trying to come between us. For channeling his frustrated love into something evil, however good his intentions."

Johnny took her chin and lifted her head to look her in the eyes. "Until Ireland is free, there will be other ghosts, Mylene. Other Daggetts, who look to violence as the only way. I'm one of the fortunate. Through your love and your patience, you've taught me there are other, better ways. That soft heart I once cursed you for has worked a miracle on this doleful soul."

"Will we be happy, Johnny?"

He gave a wistful smile. "Aye. We have each other, and we've a purpose we both love. We'll do what we can. I'll take Lord Whitney's seat and fight with words instead of guns. I know not what we can accomplish. But together we'll put up an admirable fight. If not in our lifetime, then in our children's . . . or our grand-children's . . . but someday, Ireland will be free. What matters is that we work together. My hopes, my dreams, all that I desire . . . I see them all in you."

She felt soothed by his words, but still something was nagging at the corners of her mind. "I keep thinking of something Daggett said. 'To know who you are . . . that's everything . . .' "

His hand dropped from her chin. "Aye," he said.

"We'll never know who we really are, will we, Johnny?"

Just then, the moon began to rise over the plains. The light it cast gleamed with a silver glow, illuminating the gloom and shadows of the night. Johnny glanced aside, and she saw a look of satisfaction slowly transform his face.

"There," he said, gesturing beyond.

She turned to look. Ahead, on the tor, rose the mighty sentinels of Stonehenge, looming in all their mystery, as if they'd just risen from the earth and the lost mists of time. The stones glistened like sterling in the dawning light, like a land of promise.

"That's who we are," Johnny said softly, his voice as awed as Mylene felt. "Do you see us, darlin'? Standing in the moonlight in the circle of the stones? Knowing we were born to be together in this sacred place?"

Her eyes must be playing tricks on her. Because as his voice lulled her, she did, indeed, see the image of them as they'd been months before, she in her wedding gown, standing pinned against the great pillar like a prisoner, he the savage young abductor bent on having her for himself. She heard the echo of the words he'd spoken on that fateful night.

You're mine, Mylene. You'll be mine until the day you die.

She looked at Johnny, startled by the intensity of her vision, wondering if he'd spoken the words aloud. But he was looking off in the distance, off toward the shrine where the spirits of their earlier selves still lived. "That's who we are, Mylene," he repeated. "Two people beyond space and time, who were brought together because that's where we belong."

His eyes shifted and found her face. And she saw in them the same comprehension, the same flush of joy she felt inside. The same knowledge that all had been revealed in those simple words.

"It doesn't matter who our families were," he said, "or why they gave us up. We're family now. No one can take that away. You know why? Because it was ordained."

She knew that he was right. Nothing could destroy that which had been ordained since the dawn of time. It had taken this enchanted place to help her see.

She glanced back at the great stones. They were empty now. "They're gone," she said.

"We're meant to take their place."

Their eyes met. Suddenly, as if all the wistful melancholy had been burned away, Johnny grinned. "Let's not keep them waiting," he advised.

But it was she who couldn't wait. Couldn't wait to enter the sacred circle, to cast off her qualms and begin her life anew. She read the same impatience in his laughing eyes.

Together, they kicked their slumbering horses, startling them. They took off at a gallop, pounding across the rises and hollows, the long grasses parting beneath their hooves. In the light of the moon, they rode and rode, swirling round the mammoth pillars, exhilarated, blissful, their spirits breaking free.

And then, as suddenly, Johnny cut her off. Her horse jarred to a halt as Johnny leapt out of the saddle, coming round to lift her down. She fell into his arms and he hoisted her up, his arms cradling her back and the hollow of her knees. And then he was carrying her, with swift, powerful strides, across the flowing grass, under the threshold of the timeless stones.

With her in his arms, he crossed the tor to the middle of the circle. There they stopped, bathed in moonlight, dwarfed by their mystical surroundings, yet strangely significant, conscious of the full nobility and grandeur of their souls. As the moon rose higher in the sky, illuminating them like a spotlight from the heavens, they clung to each other in the luminous, healing rays.

"Oh, Johnny," she breathed. "It's perfect."

Finding her mouth with his, he gave her a drowning kiss. She sank into him, relishing the feel of him. Nothing had ever felt so good as his warm, protective arms, holding her close, where she belonged.

"It's our wedding day," she said wondrously, recalling that she'd said something similar the last time they were here. But then she hadn't known all she knew now—that the thought of marriage to any other man was a travesty to her fate.

"I'm so happy," she murmured, as Johnny set her down so that she lay in the grass. "But, Johnny?"

"Aye, love?" he asked, nestling beside her and holding her in his arms.

"I can't help but think of Father Q and the state of St. Columba. If he'd only told us, Johnny, we could have helped. I'd like to use Lord Stanley's money to do what he promised, to help build the orphanage into a grand place. And add a hospital where we can really help the children."

"And I suppose you'll be wanting to adopt them all, and raise them under our roof?" he teased.

"Would you object, then?"

"Nay, love. We'll fill five houses with needy children, if that's your wish."

She smiled. "Tell me, Johnny," she said, her voice but a tender sigh. "Why was it I didn't want to marry you? I must have been out of my mind."

He lifted his head and looked down lovingly into her eyes. "Something, I think, about the lack of a last name."

She felt the bathing light of the moon on her face. "We're both still spies," she reminded him. "Neither one of us is what England thinks we are. You're going to have to pretend to be Lord Whitney for the rest of your life. Can you do it, then?"

He gave a thoughtful smile. "We've done this all our lives. I wouldn't know how to do anything else. 'Tis not a curse, I'm thinking, but a blessing in disguise. If I really was Lord Whitney, I couldn't stand it. I wouldn't know how to be him. I only know how to *pretend* to be him."

"Then we'll pretend together, you and I. But at home . . ."

His brow arched, his smile deepened to a grin. "Aye? At home?"

"At home, you won't be Lord Whitney. You'll just be my Johnny, the spy I adore."

And in the filtered rays of the moon, in the shadows of the great stone pillars where they'd made their peace at last, Mylene pulled her spy's mouth to hers and pledged their vows with a kiss.

Acknowledgments

Special thanks go to

Beth de Guzman, a true champion in the face of adversity, for her tremendous faith, support and encouragement.

Meg Ruley for her valued friendship and ever-willing assistance.

Kathe Robin of *Romantic Times* and the kind reviewers of *Affaire de Coeur* and *Rendezvous* magazines for their continued enthusiasm for my books.

My two Johnnys for their inspiration.

And the most special One of all: the one to whom I dedicate all that I do and all that I am. The one who inspires, supports, guides and encourages every action I take. My devotion to you is unquestioned, my faith in you unending, and my delight with our divinely fated connection and our unprecedented voyage of discovery is the greatest thrill of my life.

About the Author

Katherine O'Neal is the daughter of a U.S. Air Force pilot and a fiercely British artist who met in India in the fifties. The family traveled extensively and lived for many years in Asia. Katherine is married to William Arnold, a noted film critic and author of the bestselling books *Shawdowland* and *China Gate*—a man she feels makes her heroes pale in comparison. They make their home in Seattle, but continue the tradition of travel whenever possible. Their daughter, Janie, spent a year in France as an exchange student. They've recently returned from an exotic trip to the eastern Mediterranean, where Katherine did research for her fifth book, a treasure-hunting romantic adventure.

Katherine loves to hear from readers. Please write to her at:

P.O. Box 2452
Seattle, WA 98111-2452

Encose a SASE for a response and news of upcoming books.

DON'T MISS THESE FABULOUS
BANTAM WOMEN'S FICTION TITLES

On Sale in August

DARK PARADISE

by TAMI HOAG,
The New York Times *bestselling author of* GUILTY AS SIN

A breathtakingly sensual novel filled with heart-stopping suspense and shocking passion . . . a story of a woman drawn to a man as hard and untamable as the land he loves, and to a town steeped in secrets—where a killer lurks. ___ 56161-8 $6.50/$8.99

THE MERMAID

by New York Times *bestseller* BETINA KRAHN,
author of THE UNLIKELY ANGEL

An enchanting new romance about a woman who works with dolphins in Victorian England and an academic who must decide if he will risk his career, credibility—and his heart—to side with the Lady Mermaid. ___ 57617-8 $5.99/$7.99

BRIDE OF DANGER

by KATHERINE O'NEAL,
winner of the Romantic Times *Award
for Best Sensual Historical Romance*

A spellbinding adventure about a beautiful spy who graces London's most elegant soirees and a devastatingly handsome rebel who asks her to betray everything she has come to believe in. ___ 57379-9 $5.99/$7.99